Magic & Manners

Also by C. E. Murphy

The Walker Papers

Urban Shaman • Winter Moon
Thunderbird Falls • Coyote Dreams
Walking Dead • Demon Hunts
Spirit Dances • Raven Calls
No Dominion • Mountain Echoes
Shaman Rises

& with Faith Hunter

Easy Pickings
a Joanne Walker/Jane Yellowrock crossover

The Old Races Universe

Heart of Stone
House of Cards
Hands of Flame

Baba Yaga's Daughter

The Inheritors' Cycle

The Queen's Bastard
The Pretender's Crown

The Worldwalker Duology

Truthseeker
Wayfinder

Stone's Throe
A Spirit of the Century Novel

Magic & Manners

An Austen Chronicle

C. E. Murphy

a miz kit production

MAGIC & MANNERS

ISBN-13: 978-1-61317-105-9

Book design: The Barbarienne's Den
Cover art & design: Tara O'Shea / fringe-element.net
Copy editing: Richard Shealy / sffcopyediting.com
Editing services: Mary-Theresa Hussey / goodstorieswelltold.com

For Chrysoula

(1)

That each and every one of Mrs Dover's five daughters was afflicted with an inconvenient magic inherited from their father was no barrier to their impending nuptials: on this, Mrs Dover was determined.

"It has not," she said to her long-suffering husband for perhaps the six hundredth time in their marriage, "been the most desirable situation, but one must make do."

"One must," he agreed most amiably, and into that agreement a silence fell, for one had, in fact, made do, both in Mrs Dover's case and in Mr Dover's. She, unmarried at the age of twenty-three, had been obliged to accept the suitor who offered, and he, veritably in the grave at thirty-two and in want of heirs, had been minded to offer. There was no scandal attached, much to the dismay of the neighbouring gossips: Mrs Dover did not do in seven months what took a cow or countess nine, but instead gave birth to the first of many girls a stately and sedate fourteen months after marriage to Mr Dover.

Mr Dover had been, by all intelligence, an entirely suitable match: he had one thousand pounds a year and a quick humour which his wife had never fully learnt to appreciate. He was laconic in spirit and gentle with horses, and had a handsome leg and a fine nose. All in all, he ought to have been married long before Mrs Dover was obliged to accept him. It was the unspeakable question of magic that had forced (or permitted) him to remain unwed for so long.

Mrs Dover's mother, Mrs Hampshire, had wilfully seen nor heard anything of such rumours: no one in good society would. Certainly if Mr Dover was of that sort he had kept it quiet enough, with little more than his long-standing bachelorhood to hint at a family taint. Magic was the kind of thing that happened to someone else, to lesser persons or to those who had fallen from a higher station; it certainly did not appear unexplained in a family of good standing. Mr Dover had no mysterious deaths attached to him: he had not previously been married to a woman who then wasted away in a high tower, nor had his parents, siblings or other relatives disappeared under inexplicable circumstances. Certainly Mrs Dover the Elder was of exceedingly good breeding and, indeed, still alive when Mrs Hampshire oversaw the engagement of two (relatively) young persons to one another, while Mr Dover the Elder had died most respectably, at sea. Nor had Mr Dover the Younger any unexplained wards to care for, no suggestion of impropriety hanging over him in such a way. He was an eminently suitable young man for Mrs Hampshire's rapidly ageing daughter. The match was made, and Mrs Hampshire breathed a sigh of relief.

It ought not have taken three years and twenty to marry Miss Hampshire off; she was very pretty, with blushing apple cheeks and wide light eyes beneath lemon-yellow hair that was indeed washed with lemon juice as often as possible to retain that soft bright colour. Mr Hampshire, her father, was a man of reasonable means, though much of his money had gone to buying the new Mrs Dover's brother a Captaincy, and little had been left over for the dowries of the two Hampshire girls. The elder Miss Hampshire had some few years earlier settled well, if not remarkably, with a merchant called Moore, and it was imagined that the younger Miss Hampshire, with her prettiness, would marry a little above herself.

By all lights it should have been an easy task, but Miss Hampshire, Mrs-Dover-to-be, possessed what an aunt charitably called a tongue tied in the middle and loose at both ends. She meant no harm at all, but it proved very difficult for Mrs Hampshire to seclude any potential bridegrooms from her daughter long enough for them to fall in love with her mien and fail to notice her chatter. Mr Dover was a blessing, and so if the church walkway was lined with freshly blooming spring flowers, or the trees were budding new green leaves under a gloriously warm sun on his wedding day, it certainly was no more than auspicious, and no one dared comment too loudly that it was the third of January, or that two nights earlier snow had fallen deeply enough to swallow horses' ankles as they trod down frozen winter roads.

Mrs Hampshire had never been certain whether the new Mrs Dover had fully understood the unlikelihood of the blooming weather that graced her wedding; she appeared simply to take it as her due, and Mrs Hampshire had returned home triumphant that her silly younger daughter was safely married.

The new Mrs Dover marked no complaints about a home where the tea remained mysteriously hot even after standing unattended for hours, or where a warm breeze seemed to waft from the kitchen's roaring fires into all the coldest places in the halls. The laundry dried remarkably quickly, and stains never set in tablecloths; these were the unrealised advantages to marrying a man rumoured to have magic of his own. Mr Dover had more money than Mr Hampshire; perhaps it was the greater income which allowed grass to grow more greenly or the dogs to be particularly well mannered and disinclined to shedding.

This was a fantasy upon which Mrs Dover was permitted to dwell until her second daughter's third birthday, when an explosive sneeze from the child lit the tablecloth on fire, and only the quick calm hands of the oldest daughter kept the entire house from burning down. Even that might have been dismissible—the sneeze might have knocked a candle aside, the tablecloth might have been saved by doubling it and patting the fire out—but for the servants who were in the room at the time, and who most clearly saw what Mrs Dover denied. Rosamund, the eldest, patted the flames out with her bare hands, and left ice drippings on the wood beneath, and Elsabeth, the birthday girl, sneezed a second time for fun and dripped fire as if she were a little dragon, and not a girl at all.

Two of the servants gave notice and a third left in screams. Those who remained did so with forbearance, but the damage was done. By teatime, the story had been put around that the Dovers were infested with barbarous magic, when all good Englishmen had rejected such superstition and rot with the arrival of the Tudors upon the throne; by supper, each of Mrs Dover's appointments for the next week had returned her calling cards.

By morning, it could not be said a crowd had gathered outside the Dover's' London home, but there were more men, and with an uglier look to them, than would usually loiter in a finer part of town. The stories they told one another drifted through the Dover house windows, stories of plagues and desolation wrought by magicians, and stories of how those magic-users screamed when they were burned at the stake.

It was hardly three full days from Elsa's birthday that the Dovers retired to Mr Dover's modest country estate, where they could be forgotten about for a while. They left behind enough coin for the servants—even the one who had run from the house screaming—to reconsider the tales they might tell.

Mr Dover found it no burden at all to be well removed from Town, and Mrs Dover bore it with good humour, which was to say she spoke of the difficulties of country living with every breath, most particularly the difficulties of finding suitable husbands for five—five!—daughters whose dowries were modest at best, though certainly they all had lovely faces to make up for such moderate means.

"But," Mrs Dover burst out, as though they had not fallen into a brief and companionable silence, "but certainly there is no doubt that a single man of good fortune must be in want of a wife, and what can you imagine, Mr Dover, but that Newsbury Manor has been let at last!"

"I am sure I can hardly imagine such a thing," Mr Dover replied with usual good nature. He had his paper and his tea;

nothing much could disturb him from these, and he had long since learnt to bend when the wind blew in, as it so often did in the form of Mrs Dover. She, for her part, had barely come through the door before making impetuous statements regarding the desirability or lack thereof of their daughters' situation, and only now wrested her hat from its perch atop her head to a spot on the table, where later she would scold a servant for having left it.

"Are you not the slightest bit curious about who might have let it?"

"Indeed, I am not, as Newsbury Manor is much too large for my liking. I could never wish to visit it myself, so am of no mind to know who has the poor taste to admire it."

"Oh! How cruel you are. But I will tell you, as I know that the welfare of your daughters is close to your heart despite your pretences to the contrary. It is indeed a young man of good fortune, as I have just had it from Mrs Langfield, a young man known to have at least three thousand pounds a year! At least, Mr Dover! Perhaps more!"

"Has this fortunate young man with poor taste in homes a name?"

Were she a bird settled against a cold north wind, Mrs Dover could not be more fluffed of feather. "His name is Mr Webber, and he is single! It is a great relief for our girls! You must go visit him at once, Mr Dover; I insist upon it. The very happiness of your daughters depends on it."

"My dear Mrs Dover, how can the happiness of five girls depend on a single man— other than their beloved papa, of course—"

"Oh!" Mrs Dover picked up her hat for the sole purpose of flinging it down again. "Surely you must understand I mean Mr Webber to marry one of them!"

"And has Mr Webber any awareness of these designs?"

Mrs Dover's feathers settled, and though the uncharitable might call her expression shrewish, it was in truth more measured, all silliness temporarily dismissed. This chance change in manner was perhaps what made the Dovers' marriage a happy one: beneath her frothy exterior, Mrs Dover was possessed of a fine enough mind when she was of the rare inclination to use it. Dry wit was a permissible weapon in a lady's armoury, and it was drily enough indeed that she spoke. "Does any man?"

The very corner of Mr Dover's mouth twitched. He applied himself to his tea and papers, and Mrs Dover, quite satisfied that she had made her mark, returned to her dithering ways. "Certainly he can have no mind of it at all if you do not visit him, Mr Dover! You must go at once."

Mr Dover folded his paper. "I shall go at this very moment."

"Not now!" said his lady in desperate exasperation. "For Heaven's sake, Mr Dover, Mr Webber has not yet even taken up residence at Newsbury Manor!"

"Then you are entirely too hasty, my dear, and I must insist that you sit down and take some tea. It is wonderfully warm and there is just enough honey to sweeten it. I am certain that when this young Mr Webber arrives, he will be most pleased to have you and our daughters visit him yourselves, and leave all such nonsense out of my incapable hands, as it seems I can hardly be trusted to know when I should or should not go." Mr Dover shook his papers out again and made no secret of watching Mrs Dover over their tops, none too secretly amused at the flush of colour in her cheeks, or at the way she struggled not to stamp an impatient foot.

"Certainly, we cannot visit until you have done so, Mr Dover!"

"Then none of us shall, and your tea is getting cold." That it would never get cold was not a point to be considered; in principle, tea grew cooler, and one made such comments because they were appropriate, not because they were necessarily truthful. "I shall write your eminent Mr Webber a note," Mr Dover conceded, "and indicate to him that he may marry whichever of my daughters he wishes. Certainly that should suffice for your needs, Mrs Dover. I shall," he concluded magnanimously, "put in a particularly good word for Elsabeth, who I dare say is the cleverest of the lot."

"You will do no such thing," Mrs Dover said, very nearly in despair. "Your fondness for Elsa is inexcusable. She is not half so pretty as Rosamund nor half so charming as Leopoldina, and she is certainly no better than the others. You cannot continue this way, Mr Dover; you have no consideration for my nerves."

"My dear lady, your nerves are my constant consideration, entangled as I have been with them for the past twenty years and some. You must have your tea now: I insist upon it, that your nerves might be settled and you might live to see a dozen more young men with three thousand a year or more come to the neighbourhood."

"There is no use at all in living to see it if you will not take it upon yourself to visit them. We shall have five daughters, old maids all, all for want of an introduction." Mrs Dover settled herself for tea at last, skirts sinking as if fluffed feathers finally gave way to dejection.

"I believe you see it all in the most unfavourable light possible. Rather, think of it as having five daughters to warm our hearts and home as we age," Mr Dover disagreed pleasantly. "You shall not be obliged to attend to my feeble and tiresome needs all on your own. Indeed, if we are very fortunate, Mrs Dover, not one of our girls will marry, and we shall live together in peace and comfort until the end of our days."

(2)

"We shall do what?" asked the youngest Miss Dover in perfect horror. "Live with you and Papa *forever?* Mamma, you cannot mean it. Oh, Mamma, I should rather die. I shall die! I shall die instantly! Matilda! Tildy, would you not rather die?"

Tildy, the second-youngest Miss Dover, flung down her embroidery with a sob. "I would! I would rather die too, Mamma! However could Papa be so cruel? Should we become the laughingstock of all the county, unable to even show our faces at a ball?"

"A ball!" wailed the youngest Miss Dover. The youngest Miss Dover, who suffered the given name of Leopoldina, had embraced a flighty nature for the whole of her fifteen years. She enjoyed not only hysterics, but the most unexpected lifting of skirts and hair by errant breezes, looking with innocent eyes at her mother each time the scandalous wind exposed more of a calf or shoulder than it should. Thus far it seemed Mrs Dover had not thought to blame anything other than the breeze for her youngest daughter's impetuosity. "Should we not even be allowed to attend the ball to be held in a fortnight? Mamma, it cannot be tolerated!"

"It can and it must be tolerated," opined the middle-most Miss Dover, a slight and serious girl called Ruth. Of all the Miss Dovers, Ruth was considered the most obviously eligible by her mother, as she either had little natural knack for her father's unfortunate gift or such a personality to thoroughly quench whatever magic might seep through. Sadly for Miss Dover the Third, such a personality was in every other way unpleasant as well. At nineteen years of age, Ruth Dover was generally agreed to be pedantic, humourless, dull and without talent.

One could almost feel sorry for her, were she not so painfully stiff and priggish. Due to those traits, though, even Rosamund, the eldest, gentlest and most temperate of the sisters, had been known to roll her eyes at Ruth's stiffness, though only when she was quite certain Ruth herself could not see. Indeed, she would not permit herself such an activity where anyone except perhaps Elsabeth, her closest confidante of the sisters, might notice; such was Rosamund's kind heart, that she would not risk hurting even the most rigid of the sisters.

For the nonce, however, Rosamund had no exasperation to offer Ruth, only a fond smile and a nod of agreement. "If Papa is quite serious, then there is nothing to be done, I fear."

"Papa," that worthy said, entering the room only in time to hear Rosamund's remark, "is always quite serious, and indeed, there is nothing to be done about it. Elsa, what is that thing you are bedecking?"

"A saddle, Papa," Miss Elsabeth said with perfect equanimity. "I think it shall look very fine with white ribbon, do you not?"

"It is a *hat*, Elsa," Ruth said in the most severe tone at her disposal. "You must not mock our father. It shows an ugliness of spirit."

"I cannot believe our Elsa has any ugliness in her at all," Mr Dover replied. He sat, collected a newspaper and shook it into fullness before peering over its topmost edge. "I am, however, pleased to hear it is a hat and not a saddle, for while I believe its structure would not stand up to being ridden upon, it seems to me it would sit nicely upon a young woman's head. I hope Mr Webber will like it."

"We shall never know *what* Mr Webber likes," Mrs Dover said resentfully, "for we shall never meet him."

"You are too bothered, Mamma," said Miss Elsabeth. "I am sure we will meet Mr Webber at church, and Sophia's mamma, Mrs Enton, has promised to introduce us."

"Mrs Enton has Sophia's future to attend to," Mrs Dover said with a sniff, "and I do not believe she shall do any such thing. Sophia may be old and plain—"

"Mamma!" Elsabeth put down both ribbon and hat in dismay. "That is an unkind thing to say."

"Unkind," Leopoldina sang out, "but true."

"Even if it is"—and it was, although Miss Elsabeth would never venture to think, much less say, such a heartless thing about her dearest friend—"even Mrs Enton cannot refuse to make the introduction should we be together with this Mr Webber in public. Surely he is gentleman enough to ask after our names, and she would be obliged to offer them."

"Except Mrs Enton is away." Mrs Dover spoke with the formidable certainty of one who knows that her next words are inarguable. "She will not be back until a fortnight today, and the next ball to be held is a fortnight tomorrow. She will not be introduced to him herself by the ball, and so not one of you shall marry Mr Webber."

"Certainly I cannot speak to the impending nuptials," Mr Dover proclaimed from behind his newspapers, "but surely if such a tremendous amount of time is to pass between now and the ball, at least one of my dear girls will be able to make this Mr Webber's acquaintance and therefore introduce poor Sophia Enton to *him*."

"Do not be absurd." Mrs Dover drew herself up, looking like nothing so much as a kestrel whose hunting skills have been offended. "It is simply impossible, when we are not ourselves acquainted with the gentleman in question. Do not tease us so, Mr Dover."

"I should never dismiss your convictions," Mr Dover said to his papers, then folded them down in a flash to reveal a most serious gaze. "It is true that a fortnight is no time at all in which to know a man, and it is not beyond reason that his character should be shown to be quite dreadful. Even so, I fear that if you do not introduce the Entons to Mr Webber, someone else shall, and your friendships will be marred by it. I will take it upon myself to make the introductions, if you will not."

"Nonsense," declared his wife stoutly. "You are speaking utter nonsense, Mr Dover, and I will not have it."

It would be a falsehood to say that Mr Dover did not enjoy the consternation of the six women returning his gaze. Chief among them in pleasing him was Elsabeth, whose fine dark eyes narrowed ever so slightly as she sought to break through the perfect solemnity of his expression. He could not let that happen, so averted his gaze from hers, and in so doing, saw delighted comprehension flash across her pretty features. Daring not to look at her, he addressed Mrs Dover. "Nonsense? What, then, is nonsense? The art of introduction? Perhaps, and yet we hold it in the highest esteem. What do you think, Ruth? You are, of all of us, well-studied and thoughtful."

Ruth, never in the least anticipating to be called upon, nonethe-less straightened and drew breath for a discourse on the practicalities and impracticalities of the necessity of public introduction. Mr Dover, seeing that he had nearly unleashed a lecture, spoke quickly. "While Ruth considers her topic, let us return to Mr Webber."

"Mr Webber," said Mrs Dover bitterly. "I am sick of Mr Webber!"

At long last, the papers were folded in their entirety, coming to rest in Mr Dover's lap. "How I wish I had known that, Mrs Dover! Had I known that, I should never have taken myself to Newsbury Manor this morning to call upon him! But I did not know it, and now I fear we are obliged to pursue the acquaintance. I am sure, though, that we will find him an unseemly young fellow with callow views and an unsightly leg, and that we shall soon be able to rid ourselves of his undesirable presence."

A tremendous and wonderful silence met this declaration, only to be shattered by Leopoldina's girlish shriek of joy. With Tildy in her wake, she fell upon Mr Dover to shower him with kisses and hugs, while Rosamund folded her hands in her lap and smiled shyly at them. Poor Ruth sat stiff with disapproval, though whether it was born from a dislike of teasing or disappointment at being unable to speak in a scholarly fashion about the practise of introductions could not be said.

Elsabeth, who had suspected Mr Dover in these last minutes, only clapped her hands together in delight, and pressed her fingertips to her lips. Of all the astonishment and raptures shown by wife and daughters, this by far pleased Mr Dover the most. He smiled and smiled again, and only when Mrs Dover proclaimed, "I knew that you only teased us all along," did he allow his humour to drop a wink at his second eldest and most beloved girl. Elsa smiled from behind the steeple of her fingertips.

"You could not have done so ill by all of us," Mrs Dover went on, as though she had never once trusted her husband's chicanery. "I knew I would persuade you at the last, and I am sure you have always had your girls' best interests in mind. And how clever you are to make a joke of it, and not tell us at all until you have been to see him already! Oh, what an excellent father you have, girls! What an excellent man he is!"

"It is true," agreed Mr Dover, and upon those accolades, sailed from the room.

(3)

Indeed, for three full days Mr Dover found it expedient to confine himself to his library at all costs, for on those occasions that he departed its safe walls, he was beset by women demanding that he reveal each and every detail of Mr Webber's face, form and personality. To his daughters' unending dismay, and his wife's exasperation, Mr Dover had taken no notice whatso-ever of any of these things, save a confidence that Mr Webber was indeed a young man, and that he had not been adorned in any startling garb. From this Mrs Dover deduced that Mr Webber dressed well, though Elsa and Rosamund exchanged a glance that confided their lack of certainty in Mr Dover's sartorial awareness.

But no other trifling bit of knowledge was forthcoming from the husband and father of the house; the ladies Dover were obliged to go elsewhere for their gossip. And such gossip was to be had! Mr Webber was handsome, fair, exceedingly gentle of spirit ("A fine match for our Rosamund!" thought Mrs Dover), with a ready smile and a gallant bow, and most delightfully, was known to attend balls and galas at the slightest provocation. This, above all, set Mrs Dover's heart alight, for any young man happy to dance was a young man sure to quickly fall in love.

This sentiment was broadly shared by other hopeful mothers, though it was also widely agreed—out of Mrs Dover's hearing—

that their own daughters, being untainted by the speculation of magic—speculation only, of course, for no one had ever actually *seen* any of the Dover girls display obviously untoward talents—their own daughters would surely be more appealing to the handsome young Mr Webber than even the admittedly lovely Rosamund Dover. Indeed, they were determined of it, and most particularly of all, one Mrs Enton, upon her return from holiday, was determined of it.

It was not that Mrs Enton disliked Mrs Dover, although she did; they had been bosom friends since girlhood, until Mrs Enton's triumph in marrying well had been usurped by Mrs Dover's own somewhat scandalous marriage to a suspected magician. Even that would have been forgivable, had Mrs Dover not produced several lovely girls to Mrs Enton's singular daughter of uninspiring looks. Certainly Sophia Enton was no less attractive than Ruth Dover, and of much gentler and appealing personality, which ought to have had her married long since. However, to Mrs Enton's grim horror, Sophia's *twenty-eighth* birthday was approaching. Should she not snare Mr Webber, it was certain that Sophia would spend her life being cared for, and finally caring for, her parents.

Mrs Enton had wished for a middling age of no responsibilities; she had had quite enough of those, and to have a daughter still at home a full decade after she had expected to divest herself of that burden was nigh unto unbearable. Mr Webber was Mrs Enton's very last chance.

It was therefore with this thought in mind that she put forth the idea that Mr Webber had brought with him a full dozen young ladies from town, sisters and cousins and second-cousins-once-removed, who might in their great numbers dissuade the sisters Dover from bothering to attend the forthcoming ball at Newsbury Manor.

This news, while met with dismay, was no more likely to discourage Mrs Dover than it was to send the Thames swimming backwards in its banks. It was with all sisters flying that the Dovers arrived at Newsbury Manor, and at once that all sisters learned that indeed, Mr Webber's personal party consisted of no more than five: himself, the Gibbses, who consisted of Mr Webber's married sister and her husband, an unmarried sister who was of course Miss Webber, and another gentleman, perhaps a few years Mr Webber's senior, called Archer.

It was generally and instantly agreed that Mr Webber was a handsome young man. His eyes were a brilliant blue, his hair the colour of a midsummer sunrise, and his smile quick and ready. Half of the attending ladies were in love with him before he spoke a word.

The other half were given entirely to palpitations over Mr Archer, who had not Mr Webber's easily pleasing mien, but whose colouring and height were singularly arresting. He was black-haired, with curiously grey-green eyes that gave some hint of English blood in his African heritage. His bearing was regal, his aristocratic features not given to smiling, and his suit of impeccable quality. Upon the approach of the family Dover, he turned away to the precise degree necessary that it became positively impossible to broach an introduction, whereas the charming Mr Webber put both hands out and grasped Mr Dover's with enthusiasm. "Sir! It is to my great regret that I was unable to accept your dinner invitation, most particularly now that I have seen the ladies of your house! Would you be so good as to introduce me, Mr Dover, that I might have their acquaintance?"

Mr Dover gave the tall Mr Archer's rudely turned shoulders a brief and thoughtful examination without ever seeming to ignore Mr Webber's request. Indeed, he brought Mrs Dover forward even as he gave that unfavourable look to Mr Archer, and said with full attention to Mr Webber, "My wife, Mrs Dover. My daughters, Miss Dover, Miss Elsabeth, Miss Ruth, Miss Matilda—"

"Tildy," burst that child before anyone could stop her. Mr Dover's eyelids pressed closed at more length and with greater force than an ordinary blink might require, but Mr Webber only smiled genially at the fourth Miss Dover and said, "Miss Tildy," with perfect respect and charm.

"And Miss Leopoldina," said Mr Dover with an unusual note of steel in his voice, and Leopoldina swallowed her protest with such vigour that her eyes bulged.

Mr Webber, though, lowered his voice and said, as if begging a boon, "Miss Leopoldina. Might I make so bold as to call you Miss Dina? It seems a more favourable name for such a delightful young lady."

Joy swept Dina's countenance, and to the great relief of her two eldest sisters and father, she flounced and curtseyed but was for once too overwhelmed to speak. Mr Webber, smiling as though he had personally averted a disaster, made introductions all around: "My sister, Mrs Gibbs; her husband, Mr Gibbs. My sister, Miss Webber, and, good God, Archer, turn and be seen. Have you no manners at all?"

So entreated, Mr Archer could hardly refuse, though his greetings were brusque and he made no effort to ingratiate himself to the family Dover. His distasteful gaze lingered on the three youngest sisters; Elsabeth he could hardly seem to look at, and Rosamund he only barely tolerated. That was as well: Mr Webber in turn had eyes only for Rosamund, and though she was not given to outward displays of emotion, she blushed with pleasure when Mr Webber offered a hand toward the dance floor with more youthful hope and admiration than polite gallantry.

Mrs Dover clutched Elsabeth's arm so hard as the lovely young pair stepped onto the floor that Elsabeth was obliged to disengage her before a mark was imprinted on her flesh. Miss Webber, who had very much the look of her brother about her, save that her hair was sandier in colour than his, observed this and allowed the corners of her mouth to turn up, although in no wise could Elsabeth regard her expression as a smile. With this aspect firmly in place, and somewhat to the collected Dovers' astonishment, Miss Webber departed their little group without further conversation. Mr Archer retreated with her, and Mr Gibbs obligingly requested a dance of Mrs Gibbs, leaving the Dovers abandoned.

"What a lovely young woman," said Mrs Dover brightly.

"She would certainly make a most suitable sister-in-law for our Rosamund."

'As would a viper,' thought Elsabeth, but was wise enough to keep that opinion unspoken. "Look, Mamma, there is Sophia. I must introduce her to Mr Webber when Rosamund's dance is done."

"If we are fortunate," Mrs Dover said with asperity, "it will never be done. I do not understand why you must put Sophia forward, Elsa, when you have four unmarried sisters and are yourself unwe—"

The rest of her familiar scold was lost to the noise and cheer of the ball, and to the pleasure of friends meeting again. Sophia, who had been obliged to travel with her mother, was gladder of nothing than to see Elsabeth, and Elsa, in her turn, was pleased to introduce her dear friend to Mr Webber as he exited the dance floor with Rosamund, whose face shone with happiness. Obliging and polite, Mr Webber pressed Sophia, then Elsabeth, for the next dances, but it was Rosamund he begged the promise of at least one more dance from, and no one, not even Sophia, begrudged the eldest Dover girl that grace. Upon completion of their turns with Mr Webber, Elsa and Sophia stood to the side, heads bowed close so they might speak to one another rather than dance, as there were too few gentlemen for the ladies to always be on the floor.

"Though," Sophia remarked, "that does not seem to distress your sisters."

Elsa looked to them with perhaps too much indulgence: Leopoldina and Matilda danced together when they had no other partner, though Ruth stood stiff and straight against a wall, ready to lecture on the impropriety of too much exercise gained through dance if anyone should give her the opportunity. "Nor should it distress them," Elsa proclaimed. "It does not distress me, although I am astonished to see that certain gentlemen choose not to dance at all, when there are so many ladies wanting a partner."

As one, they looked to Mr Archer, who had danced and spoken with only those ladies in his own party. "I hear he has ten thousand a year," Sophia said, and Elsa's smile lit with mischief.

"He would need at least that for a lady to overlook his distasteful pride. Oh, look, he disdains poor Rosamund; that will not do." Elsa's humour fled as both lips and eyes narrowed, but Sophia, who knew her friend well, put a gentling hand on Elsa's elbow.

"Do nothing that Rosamund might have cause to regret, Elsa."

Elsabeth quirked her head, then let go the thin and insulted line of her lips. "You are too good, Sophia. Your mother would have me do something entirely unsuitable, that you might come to Mr Webber's eye in an appealing light."

"My mamma," Sophia said with great and precise restraint, "sometimes mistakes the pursuit of my welfare for kindness, when to someone else it might be a terrible cruelty."

"You are too good." Elsa embraced Sophia, then, smiling again, returned to the joy of dancing and, she was not too proud to admit, the embarrassment of sometimes standing aside as others danced. She could not, though, be sad when it was her sisters who danced, or even Sophia: her heart was a merry thing, and she took as much joy in the happiness of others as in her own.

It was in this merry state that Mr Dover looked up from nearby conversation to see her cross behind Masters Webber and Archer, the one speaking to the other in a scolding tone: "You must dance, Archer; I insist upon it. You look a perfect fool, standing upon imagined dignity when the room is full of lovely girls and too many of them lacking a partner."

Upon hearing this, Elsabeth paused, a smile curving her lips and curiosity cocking her head. She was quite unseen by the men, who stood shoulder to shoulder and gazed outward, overlooking the ballroom and its denizens as Archer spoke. The depth and smoothness of his voice could have been considered beautiful, had it not been so clearly marked with distaste. "I certainly shall not dance. I detest the exercise unless I am particularly acquainted with my partner; you saw me dance with your sisters, and Julia is the only unmarried female here worth bestirring myself for. There is not another woman in this room with whom I could possibly stand up."

"I would not have your standards for a kingdom, Archer. I have never seen half so many pleasant girls in my life, and a fair portion of them are very pretty besides."

"You have danced twice with the only lovely girl in the room."

"Oh!" cried Mr Webber, "is she not the most beautiful creature you have ever seen? But you cannot imagine that she is the only fair woman here. Why, her next sister, Miss Elsabeth, to whom I introduced you, is very agreeable as well. You must find her, Archer, and ask her to dance."

Archer did not so much as look around, else he might have seen Elsabeth's eyebrows rise and the interested gaze she settled on his black-clad shoulders. "I recall," he said instead, and with such stiffness that his entire person might have been laden with starch. "She was, I suppose, tolerable, but not nearly handsome enough to tempt *me*, nor, it seems, many of the other gentlemen here tonight. I certainly have no interest in young ladies who are slighted by other men. Go, Webber. Return to your partner, and waste no more effort conspiring to waste my time."

Mr Webber replied, "You are confoundingly stubborn, Archer," but did as he was bid, never looking behind himself to see Elsabeth Dover unmoving, a strained smile fixed beneath highly coloured cheeks.

Archer *did* turn, and for the sharpest and most breathless of instants, was transfixed by the very same sort of strain that held Elsabeth in place. For a measure, it seemed he might speak, or give in to some small impulse of regret or apology, but the moment passed and he drew himself more stiffly upright. Elsabeth procured a smile no warmer than the one offered by Miss Webber earlier, then, dropping her gaze to the floor, indulged in a small curtsey as Archer strode past.

A floorboard that surely had been flush with its brethren only seconds before caught the toe of his beautiful boot. Elsabeth took a cunning half-step backward, removing herself from harm's way, and the full length of Master Fitzgerald Archer's tall body was laid out on the floor with a crash that silenced every sound in the hall.

Mr Dover, careful to hide any hint of pride in his smile, appeared to offer Elsa his arm, and together they fetched their party and their coats.

(4)

"I HAVE NEVER SEEN SUCH A THING," DECLARED MRS DOVER THE following morning at breakfast, as if she had not also declared it innumerable times the night before as the family Dover left Newsbury Manor, "never in my life. Not one person could find the flaw in the floor, Mr Dover, not one. I cannot imagine how a gentleman of Mr Archer's stature could trip and fall so ignominiously in such company. I can hardly imagine his embarrassment, although Mr Dover tells me"—and this was said with great ferocity—"Mr Dover tells me that he was perfectly dreadful with regards to our darling Elsa, and so I cannot find it in myself to sympathise with such a fellow, even if he has been served up with a great dash of humility. I have never seen such a thing!"

"A gentleman should be known for his grace," Ruth volunteered so sternly into the stream of her mamma's repetitious astonishment that for a moment even Mrs Dover was silenced. All eyes turned to the middle-most sister, who, not expecting the pleasure of attention, was obliged to clear her throat to gain a moment in which to find something else to say. But find it she did, and with conviction. "If he is not graceful, perhaps he is not a gentleman,"

"That," Mrs Dover said with some irascibility, "is clearly the case, given his dreadful behaviour toward our Elsabeth, although I cannot quite comprehend how a man of his means can also be not a gentleman—"

"*And*," said Ruth, who, having gained an opportunity to speak, did not wish to lose it, "if *he* is not a gentleman, then I fear that perhaps those who have the poor taste to associate with him cannot themselves be considered gentlemen, either. We must all," she concluded with triumph, "for the sake of our reputations, divorce ourselves from any proceedings with the party at Newbury Manor!"

It was very nearly impossible to say whose wail of protest rose the most fervently: Dina's, Tildy's or Mrs Dover's, but it was Rosamund's cold hand clutching Elsabeth's beneath the table that bespoke the truest dismay at the prospect. Elsabeth turned her palm up to press a reassurance into Rosa's fingers, and the sweetest of the Dover sisters smiled in tremulous thanks at the most stubborn of them.

Mr Dover, interested only in returning the breakfast table, at which he was obliged to sit despite his preference to take the morning meal in the privacy of his library, to quiet, spoke clearly and without lifting his gaze from his papers: "Having gone to such trouble as to acquaint not only myself but my many daughters with Mr Webber, I assure you that unless he is actually seen partaking in abominable behaviour, we shall not be shut of him. Besides, he is invited to dinner a week hence and I cannot renege on that invitation; it would be"—and here he lifted his gaze from the papers to fix Ruth with a droll, yet gimlet, eye, before finishing—"ungentlemanly."

Ruth shut her mouth with a sound that could only be defined as unladylike, had anyone been able to hear it beneath the renewed histrionics of the two youngest Dover daughters and their mother. Although their cries were now joyful, they were no quieter than before; poor Mr Dover sank into his chair and brought his papers up, shielding himself from the noise. Elsabeth, already hand in hand with her beloved eldest sister, hastily excused them both from the table and darted into the garden with a flush-cheeked Rosamund in tow. No sooner were they able to speak and be heard than Rosamund did, her hands folded to her bosom with Elsabeth's still held between them.

"Oh, he is to come to dinner, Elsa! I confess I like him very much; is that wrong of me, on so little acquaintance? He is everything a young man ought to be, full of sensibility and good humour, happily mannered and of impeccable breeding!"

"And very handsome," replied Elsa, "which a young man also ought to be, if he can possibly arrange it. He comes to dinner for you, Rosa, I am certain of it."

"He comes because Papa invited him," Rosamund answered, though hope lit her eyes. "Though I did not expect him to ask me to dance a second time; that was a very great compliment from such a gentleman."

"Well." Elsabeth made the most of a stern and ferocious face, though it was not easy with Rosa's muffled laughter to break the performance. "I have it on the best authority that you were the handsomest woman in the room, Rosa, so it does not surprise me at all that Mr Webber should pay you such a compliment."

"Oh, but Mr Archer should not have been so cruel." All of Rosa's burgeoning fondness for Webber was forgotten in sympathy for Elsabeth, who pressed her hand to Rosa's again and clucked her tongue like a mother hen calling for her chicks.

"Even if Archer—I shall not grace him with an honourific!—even if he had not insulted me, I could very well have seen by myself that you were easily the prettiest girl in the room, Rosa. If Archer had been wiser, he would have asked you to dance first, and your charms would have made his evening—and my own!—a more pleasant one. I do wish Papa had not been quite so candid with Mamma about the reason for our hasty departure last night; I feel I am quite able to master my own battles, without Mamma's fluttering outrage on my behalf."

"I am very afraid you are entirely able to do so," Rosa agreed cautiously. "Indeed, I worry about the fall Mr Archer took."

Elsa quite wilfully chose to misunderstand, and patted Rosa's hand in gentle reassurance. "I am sure the only injury was to his pride, Rosa, and he has so very much of it that a little damage cannot do any lasting harm."

Rosa, who was sweet, not senseless, nudged Elsabeth and offered a shy smile. "I think you might forgive him his pride, had he not injured yours. He *is* very handsome."

"You are right," Elsa agreed, "on both counts. But his handsomeness is marred by his aloofness, and as I have no expectation of ever speaking to the man again, I think we should speak no more of him."

(5)

"Confound it, Archer," said Webber, not for the first—not for the fourth, should he be so pedantic as to point it out to his friend—time, "there is nothing there to find. Even the best of us trip over the toe of our shoe from time to time."

The man to whom he spoke, Master Fitzgerald Archer, of whom Elsabeth and Rosamund Dover were at that very moment sworn to discuss no more, might yet have become a topic of their conversation had they been able to see the curious activity in which he was currently engaged. He lay in a most undignified manner, belly-down on the Newbury Manor ballroom floor, with one cheek pressed directly against the highly polished wood, from which all rugs, chairs and tables had been removed so he might examine its uninterrupted surface. From this position he snapped, "I have never tripped on my shoe in my life, Webber, nor have I ever seen you move gracelessly. And that woman moved—"

"Miss Elsabeth," Webber interrupted with a weight of disapproval entirely outside his usual purview. He was a generous man, both kind and gentle of spirit, and, not unlike the eldest Dover sister, both inclined to see the very best in people and deeply concerned when others did not. "Her name is Miss Elsabeth, not That Woman, which is unconscionably rude, Archer. Indeed, I cannot help but think that your very rudeness, both last night and in your refusal to acknowledge her name, might suggest that you were more taken with her beauty than you are willing to admit to."

Archer was too dark to blush, but his glower indicated a powerful disapproval of Webber's fancy. "Don't be absurd, Webber."

"Is it absurd? Certainly, I have seen ladies play at that game, pretending to vehemently dislike what they most admire, all the better to present a challenge to the desired gentleman." Webber, pleased with his deduction even if Archer would not confirm it, all but waggled a finger in admonition. "Perhaps if you had been less rude last night—"

"What then?" Archer bounded to his feet with the athletic vigour of a young man accustomed to hunting, riding and walking the lands that he owned. "Had I been less rude—not, Webber, that I concede rudeness, as I was surrounded by persons not nearly of my class and therefore unworthy of my attention. I could not possibly *be* rude to such creatures. But go on. I dare say you were about to say that had I been less forthright in my honest opinions, I might not have fallen."

"Well, yes," replied a discomfited Webber, who had meant that to be his argument before he was taken with the more delightful idea that politeness might have forced Archer to admit he would like to dance with Miss Elsabeth. Amenable soul that he was, Webber tucked that thought away and embraced the argument Archer appeared more interested in pursuing. "Truthfully, Archer, it seemed only swiftly meted justice, that you should insult Miss Elsabeth and then be made prostrate before her."

"And do you believe in a God who metes such justice so quickly?"

Webber drew his finely clad shoulders back stiffly. "I doubt God has the inclination to look in on our lesser moments, Archer, but perhaps one of his angels."

All his discomfiture fell away into a blinding smile; Webber smiled easily and genuinely, a trait which Archer verbally disdained and secretly—so secretly, perhaps, that he had no notion of it himself—admired. This and other aspects of Webber's usual pleasantry were what drew Archer to him; they were unalike in all but circumstance of birth, which fortunate status was enough for an acquaintance, but that the men held between them a close and personal friendship spoke deeply to the unspoken admiration Archer had for Webber's amiable nature.

In turn, it was Archer's reserve and ferocity that Webber most appreciated, for he knew himself to be passing gentle at times when a little boldness might have stood him in good stead. Archer felt things unequivocally where Webber was of a mind to be swayed by the tide, and it was this resoluteness which Webber most admired about his friend. But it was not of these aspects that either man thought now: Archer retained his affront at the very idea he could have been in the wrong whilst Webber dreamed now of angels, and with a sighing sincerity said, "Perhaps Miss Dover is one of those angels, and through her eyes God watched us yesterday evening."

"You cannot possibly be suggesting that God, acting through Miss Dover, who was dancing and entirely unaware of the unfortunate exchange overheard by her sister, caused me to trip on a perfectly flush floor," Archer said so dourly that Webber was returned from his flights of fancy to blink with astonished rapidity at his friend.

"No. No, of course not, Archer; don't be absurd. I'm only saying everyone has a moment of awkwardness from time to time, and that if Miss Elsabeth saw some hint of that clumsiness in your step and removed herself from harm's way, you can hardly blame her for that. What was she to do, try to catch you and instead be borne to the floor herself by your weight? Dear God, Archer, *that* would have put you in a compromising position. You'd have had to marry the girl immediately."

"What an appalling idea," drawled Miss Webber from the ballroom doorway, whence she had, unbeknownst to the men, been listening for some time. She minced into the room, skirt lifted enough to show the cunningly worked soft leather of new shoes, and upon reaching the gentlemen put forth a hand so that

Archer was obliged by politeness to offer his arm. Miss Webber, who regarded Archer as her personal property out of a necessity to marry suitably rather than any especially deep affection, took his elbow with the casual possessiveness of a woman who could not imagine she might ever be denied. "Robby is right, of course; you might have found yourself obliged to Miss Elsabeth in an utterly inappropriate way. In fact, I could quite forgive her for stepping out of your path had she not stood above you without a trace of distress on her features once you fell. At the very least, she might have been concerned for your welfare."

Webber, whose gentle spirit perhaps offered him greater insight to the behaviours of one to whom insult has been given, did not suppose that Miss Elsabeth Dover had any comprehensible reason for showing concern over Archer's welfare at the time of his fall, but also did not suppose either his sister or Archer would appreciate that observation. He held his tongue while Julia simpered over Archer, and while Archer assumed a look of noble, distant suffering which would no doubt set certain ladies' hearts aflutter.

Julia Webber was not among those ladies, and soon lost interest in assuaging Archer's wounded pride in preference to addressing her brother in a forthright and unqualified manner. "It seems to me that while Miss Elsabeth may suffer the folly of pride, her sister is a charming, sweet creature with whom I should like to have greater acquaintance."

"Very good!" Webber cried, having with Julia's words instantly put out of his mind all thoughts of unpleasantry. "Mr Dover has invited me to dinner a week tomorrow; we shall all attend!"

"Lord, no," Miss Webber said with perfectly genuine horror. "That simpering mother, those dreadful younger daughters? It is bad enough that after the ball, they will come calling and my sister and I will be obliged in turn to call upon them. You cannot expect me to spend an entire evening with them. I cannot imagine what that mother might consider an acceptable table, but I am sure that I will not sit for it. Rosamund Dover must come to Newsbury Manor instead. It will be far more suitable for all involved."

Webber blinked at his sister in slow and owlish astonishment. "But I have given my word, Julia."

"Then you may go," Julia said with a delicate shudder, "but certainly Archer and myself will not be joining you."

"In this, Julia speaks for me," Archer agreed in such dour tones that Webber was inclined to blush about it.

"Very well. You shall all regret it, I am sure, but I will go by myself to Oakden House and enjoy myself very much."

(6)

The Dover household was for days in a futher; Mrs Dover could have nothing less than the best for the arrival of a man she already thought fondly of as her son. To this end, she harried the cook, berated the maids, bullied the gardener and, above all, related each instance of their imagined failures in minute detail to Mr Dover, whose closed library door did not prove the barrier he might have hoped it to. The only respites from these activities were the Dover ladies' necessary visit to the ladies of Newsbury Manor, and the visit paid in return, which in themselves were new fodder for breathless discussion and hope, for it was clear that the sisters Webber found Rosamund in particular and Elsabeth to a lesser degree to be entirely charming companions. Further invitations were not as of yet issued to the two eldest Dover daughters, but, as Mrs Dover related to Mr Dover at great length and considerable repetition, it was all very promising.

Driven away by feminine palpitations, Mr Dover had taken to passing his time in the gardens, at as great a distance from the house as he could achieve without taking a horse and leaving for Bodton, the nearby village that gave itself airs of being a town.

Nor was he the only member of his family so inclined to escape the walls of their loved and crumbling family home. Rosamund weathered her mother's fits with equanimity, and Ruth enjoyed helping with the preparations because it allowed her to feel as if she did penance with each shrill exclamation that flowed from Mrs Dover's lips. Tildy and Dina were of no especial use, but ran after Mrs Dover, echoing her admonitions and clinging to one another, full of giggles, whenever they thought of Mr Webber's visit. But Elsabeth, though not unwilling to help, could not long bear their mother's prattling, and so Mr Dover often saw her in the gardens as well, examining apple trees for their burgeoning fruit or simply treading soft grass pathways in endless repetitions, as if a pacing lioness had been bound into the body of a young woman. When they saw each other, they smiled and nodded, but otherwise left well enough alone, recognising that neither required company save the solidarity of knowing they were understood by at least one other member of the household.

On the morning of the day upon which Mr Webber was expected for dinner, Elsabeth's solitary wanderings were interrupted by a glad visitor: her dear friend Sophia Enton, who had danced first with Mr Webber at the ball and who had allowed herself an entire week to savour that before visiting the Dovers, whose oldest, prettiest daughter was clearly the more favoured by Mr Webber. Sophia was not envious; she was too pragmatic for that, and knew herself to be stronger of feature than was the current fashion, but it did no harm to hold the illusion in place a little while longer than necessary.

Elsabeth, upon seeing her, seized Sophia's hands and proclaimed with all sincerity—for though she was not as generous of spirit as Rosamund, she loved Sophia dearly and wanted nothing more than her happiness—"Oh, Sophia, I wish that you were coming to dinner tonight. I would trade my three younger sisters to your mother, that we could have pleasant and sensible conversation throughout the evening."

"But not your eldest," Sophia said with true amusement that became quiet laughter as sisterly loyalty came to odds with friendship's fondness on Elsa's expressive features. "It is no matter, Elsa; I know that he seemed very fond of Rosamund from the outset, and I have heard that he made some effort to be in attendance when you called upon Miss Webber and Mrs Gibbs; that, indeed, he remained most attentive for the entire duration of your visit."

"It is true," Elsabeth confessed with a happy sigh. "He seemed to quite dote upon her, and insisted upon driving Miss Webber and Mrs Gibbs to our dear Oakden House himself when they paid us a return visit."

Sophia, without evident humour, said, "Do you not mean when they paid you the honour of a return visit, Elsabeth?"

"Hah! Oh, I should not have let that sound escape," Elsa said through fingers interlaced over her mouth. "I know I am dismissive of society's prescribed manners, but for Rosa's happiness I must curtail my tongue. That said, I do not believe their visits to be an honour, Sophia, but rather a burden; I do not care for the way they look down their noses at all of us, yes, all of us, even Rosamund, as if they are certain they are our superiors, even though their family money came from trade only a generation ago. Your own father's success in trade has made him very rich and yet not an unbearable snob, so it cannot be merely that they are defensive."

"I believe Mamma would be happily snobbish if she were not burdened with an unmarriageable daughter. No, stop, Elsa; it is true. I am nearly twenty-eight and have no prospects. I would remove myself from their worries by taking the gentle arts they have educated me in and becoming a governess, but you know that I do not like children. The prospect of spending a lifetime educating them is worse than growing old in Papa's house and caring for Mamma and Papa in their dotage."

"We shall grow old together, then." Elsa tucked her arm through Sophia's with cheery confidence. "For I see little hope for myself either, unless I am to go to London for a Season, and we are all quite certain that will not happen. At least Rosamund will marry for love while we two spinsters smile and watch."

"You are only twenty," Sophia pointed out, but did not choose to argue the rest, save to say, "A Season might not be so *very* bad,

Elsa, but I wonder if Mr Archer's...difficulty...at the Newsbury ball might be repeated in London if someone should set your temper alight."

Elsa, blithe as a sprite, sang, "Master Archer sat on a wall, Master Archer had a great fall," and turned innocently sparkling eyes upon her friend. "Whatever can you mean, Sophia?"

Shocked and delighted, Sophia gasped, "Elsabeth! You did not!" as one who did not so much scold as hoped dearly to be told more.

"I did nothing that anyone could ever be certain of, my dearest Sophia." Elsa glanced around the garden, making certain they were quite alone before releasing Sophia's arm and reaching upward to touch her fingertips to a small green apple. It swelled beneath her touch, reddening until it fell, perfectly ripe, into her palm. She presented this morsel to Sophia, who clutched it against her bosom in both hands and watched in wordless joy as Elsa quickened a second apple for herself. "There," said Miss Dover with a certain satisfaction. "*This* is worthy of scandal in London, and all the more delicious for being our secret."

"If an unseasonable apple is all that is required to scandalise London, I believe you ought to have a Season there, for it is very dull indeed and you would liven it up. And when your Season is over and you are married to a dull but rich man, you may bring me into your home as your companion so that you do not go mad from boredom. I shall tend to your garden, and eat apples out of season all year long." Sophia defied propriety and took a large, wet bite of her apple before sighing in contentment.

"If London is that easily scandalised, I should far rather stay in Bodton, where I can ripen apples without notice. Rosamund will marry Webber and we will be saved from both the pox of primogeniture and of dubious sorcer—"

Sophia put a hand over Elsa's mouth, silencing the word. "Do not speak it aloud, Elsa. You are discreet enough, but even the whisper of the word could set everything awry for Rosamund. If she is to ensnare Webber, he must know nothing of your heritage, nothing at all."

"Even before my parents married, Papa was looked upon suspiciously. If we are to meet ruin, there are many here who might whisper rumours into Mr Webber's ear, even if I should speak and behave with perfect decorum."

"You are mistaken. If Bodton were inclined to believe the tales, they would have sprung up again, loudly, after Archer's fall at Newsbury Manor. I worried for you, and have been listening, Elsa. The rumours are so old and so unproven as to be dismissed: even my own mother, who sees Mr Webber as her last chance to be rid of me, sniffed in disdain at the idea his fall might have been orchestrated through occultish means. Do *nothing* to lend credence to them, and all anyone will remember as an impediment to Rosa's marriage is that your mother is—"

"Silly," Elsa finished, gently, when Sophia's kindness would not allow her to, "and my younger sisters absurd. Surely that is not enough to distract from old stories taking root, if the Webbers cared to pursue them."

"Your father removed you to Bodton nearly eighteen years since, Elsa, and in that time, no one save myself has ever seen any truly remarkable activities from your family, and even then, it has only ever been you, in secret. Your mother and sisters are enough to rise above. Do not offer any other hint of difficulty." Sophia paused as though finished, then spoke again, more quietly and more swiftly. "You know what you would be reduced to, Elsa, if your talents were confirmed. You are women, unable to join the army. More, there are five of you. Some madman would see you as a coven, and you would all be burned for the sin of being gentlewomen with magic."

Elsabeth turned her face away as if the words were a blow, though they were not: Sophia spoke nothing more than a common truth. "There is no evil in magic, Sophia."

"No." Her friend's voice was touched with dry laughter that faded slowly into something near to anger. "No, it is only gauche. It is only just bearable that the most wretched Englishman might have a touch of magic, and only then because those poor folk can be pressed into taking the King's shilling and made to fight with whatever talent they command. It is for savages, such as the poor, or for hedonists, such as the French. It is simply unthinkable that a well-bred English family should be afflicted with it, and to ensure it remains that way, they will destroy you if they find out."

Elsabeth could not help but smile. "You speak so well, Sophia. Why are you so good? Why protect us so fiercely?"

Sophia balanced her half-eaten apple on her fingertips and smiled. "Because I love apples, Elsa, and I love you."

"You ought to have been my sister, too." Elsa embraced Sophia, kissed her cheek, and together they went away into the gardens.

(7)

That Mr Webber would attend dinner was inevitable; that Mr Archer should find himself in accompaniment was not, and yet that worthy stood stiff and uncomfortable at Webber's side when Webber knocked briskly on the Oakden door. It was not necessary to knock; a servant awaited them on the other side, but so did a flustered Mrs Dover, who had observed not one but two rich and handsome young men approaching on her drive, and was now so discombobulated that nothing could be done but that she greet them herself.

The servant, a young woman named Margaret whose unlimited patience for Mrs Dover was born of an acute awareness that an elderly mother, three younger brothers and two small sisters depended on the wages Margaret sent home each week, had heard rumour enough of the two gentlemen at the door to know that one would be forgiving and delighted should the lady of the house meet them at the door, and that the other, whose fortune was at least twice that of the genial man's, would be sufficiently horrified as to never again darken the Oakden door, and indeed to go to some effort to make certain the breach of protocol was well known so that no other gentlemen of means would be so foolish as to approach any of the sisters Dover.

It was to this end that Margaret stood flapping her skirts at Mrs Dover as if the latter were a chicken to be rousted from her roost, and hissing, "I can't open the door, ma'am, until you're well out of the way, else there'll be no room for the gentlemen in the hall!" In that same contained tone of panic, she attempted to summon Mr Dover to fetch his wife, but her pleas, calculated not to carry through the front door, could also not carry into the sitting room, nor the library beyond.

Unaware of the performance within, on the doorstep, Archer's already-dark countenance grew darker. "I did not agree to come with you only to be left on the stoop, Webber."

"No," said the other, placidly, "you came because I rightfully impressed upon you not only the boorishness of your behaviour a week since but also the dreadful imbalance at the Oakden table, with six women to only two men. With your presence it shall be three to six, and I trust any one of us is doughty enough to manage two ladies at once."

"I do not believe Mr Dover manages any at all, and you will be attending on Miss Dover, which will leave me five when I had no wish to encounter even one. I should not have come." Archer made as if to withdraw immediately, and had Rosamund not come to the hall and taken Mrs Dover away at that very moment, thus freeing beleaguered Margaret to fling open the door, he might well have succeeded. As it was, he was presented with a picture that failed to hearten him: a red-cheeked serving girl, from her dress not even so much as a housemaid, much less a lady's maid, gasped a breathless greeting, dipped into a curtsey of depth appropriate to royalty rather than young gentlemen, and stepped back into a granite-floored hall to afford them entrance.

Webber strode in gladly, instantly and genuinely admiring the floors—"Local stone? The very best, nothing could be better than a home built of the very land it rests upon"—the windows—"Fine and large, with good light, and facing south, too, I see; Newsbury Manor has the ill fortune to face east, although it makes for excellent evenings in the back gardens"—and the scent of food wafting through the house—"I believe I have not smelled something so delicious in the weeks I have been at Newsbury. I am eager to commend the cook."

All of this was directed in a genial fashion at Margaret, who was entirely smitten by the young gentleman by the time she had received their coats and directed them with shy happiness to the sitting room, where six ladies and one master of the house all awaited their entrance with highly piqued curiosity. Webber seized Mr Dover's hand in both of his, pumping away enthusiastically. "A delight to be here, sir, and what a charming home it is. You recall my friend Archer, do you not? He has agreed to accompany me so that our table might be more evenly matched; I hope, Mrs Dover," he said, turning to the lady of the house with all due embarrassed apology, "that I have not upset your cook by being so bold, but Archer only relented this very afternoon, so I had not the time to warn you."

"Oh, no, we are well prepared for another appetite," promised Mrs Dover, who did not know where to look. She would swear she had never encountered such fine manners as Webber presented, but neither could she forget the dreadful slight Archer had impressed upon Elsabeth. Yet the matter of three other daughters besides Rosa and Elsa was also to be considered, and Archer was wealthy, handsome and within the walls of her home.

To this end, and with a somewhat wild look in her eyes as a decision was made, she edged forward the three youngest daughters, murmuring, "You will recall Misses Dina, Tildy and...Ruth." She finished with a degree of thoughtfulness, for if Archer was to prove an unbearable prig, it might well be that the middle Dover daughter's humourless ways might be more appealing than not. If only Ruth were prettier; but she was not, and all Mrs Dover could say in the end was, "I am sure we are all most pleased to further our acquaintance, Mr Archer."

"Indeed," said Mr Dover, whose favouritism toward Elsa was less inclined to forgive Archer for the benefit of his other daughters, but he did not cause a scene. Mrs Dover squeezed his hand in approval and gratitude when, upon the announcement that dinner was ready, Webber offered Rosamund his arm and escorted her to the dining room, where it soon proved that young

Mr Webber was quite able to attend to six women and one gentleman all on his own, as Archer sat stiffly, ate little, spoke not at all unless directly addressed, and then only answered as briefly as possible. Was the lamb tender enough? It was. Had he been bothered by the spot of rain that fell earlier? He had not. Were the vegetables to his liking? They were. Did he enjoy the previous Season in London? No.

This last was spoken with such resounding finality that even Mrs Dover was silenced by it, though Elsabeth spoke as if he had done nothing untoward, all of her attention directed at Mr Webber, whose besotment with Rosa was not enough to leave him unaware of Archer's rudeness. "I can only imagine, Mr Webber, that if a young gentleman could so violently dislike the Season, he must have some close-held and secret reason for doing so. Do you suppose that Mr Archer's heart is already given away, and that he therefore cannot bear the lighthearted foolishness of courtship?"

She may have been looking at Mr Webber, but Elsa observed Archer sideways, and saw that his eyes darkened considerably at this speculation. All the green fled from his eyes, leaving them such a stony grey as to be nearly black. She had never seen such eyes, fathomless and intriguing, and, despite herself, turned her regard on him fully.

He was shockingly handsome, in truth; she had already forgotten that, in her distaste at his manners. His attraction was a brooding challenge at perfect odds with Mr Webber's open friendliness. But he was dreadful: Elsabeth reminded herself of that, and lifted her chin fractionally to stop a blush of interest from rising at the idea of such a challenge.

Archer saw only the cool regard and the brief lift of her chin, disdainful and dismissive of her social superior. She appeared to expect an answer her supposition, to the arch accusation of romance he could barely recall the content of any longer.

"I have suddenly remembered pressing business elsewhere. I must take my leave of you at once." With this announcement, he did, leaving a flustered Webber to make apologies and then retreat after his friend, with two courses of dinner still to come. Elsabeth half rose from her own seat, of a mind to follow, then could think of nothing to say that would not worsen the moment, and sank back down in astonishment to simply stare in their wake.

Rosamund, eyes bright with tears, pressed her fingertips to her lips, turned to Mr Dover as he spoke with as much anger as he was known to be capable of. "You may marry that Webber lad if you wish, Rosamund, but I will not have his companion under this roof again. I hope that your young man is not of a mind to forever choose his ill-mannered friends over his wife's family."

"Oh, Papa," Rosa replied, but even she was unable to explain Archer's behaviour, only finally venturing "Perhaps he is very shy, and cannot bear to be teased," as an excuse so tremulous that not even she believed it.

"I, for one, am glad of his departure," Elsa confessed with as much mischievousness as she could muster, which was little indeed, for she had had no intention of driving away her sister's best marriage prospect, nor even the irritable Mr Archer, with her arch words, and was horrified at what she had wrought, "for the pudding tonight is almond, a particular favourite of mine, and now we have two fewer with whom I must share. Why, Rosamund, I think your Mr Webber has done me a deliberate favour!"

"That is very kind of you, Elsa," Rosa answered softly. "I shall try to think of it that way, and not imagine that to follow Mr Archer in such a hurry means that Mr Webber has no real fondness for me at all."

(8)

Rosamund's fears were laid to rest the very next morning when, at the earliest possible hour deemed polite by society, an invitation for Miss Dover to dine with the Webber sisters was delivered to her by a footman in a suit so beautifully cut that even Mr Dover felt a momentary pang of envy regarding the status of his own servants' clothing. Not that he would be moved to amend their garb, for while he was by no means bereft of a viable income, the bulk of it was bound up in irrevocable promise to the male heir of the Dover estate. This was one part common practise and one part the grim-fisted determination of Mr Dover's grandfather, who believed, rightly or wrongly, that the questionable gift for magic passed through the female line, and who had been quite determined that no sorcery-ridden female would ever become undisputed mistress of the Dover fortune.

It had not, of course, occurred to that gentleman, nor to the subsequent generations, that a time might come when the Dover name would have no son to be passed to, not until the current Mrs Dover, having borne five girls in eleven years, put her foot down on the matter and proclaimed there would be no more attempts at a son unless Mr Dover himself wished to work a miracle and carry, birth and nurse the next five children himself.

Mr Dover was quite content to have tea that did not cool and a garden that grew unusually green even in the coldest months;

to presume more profoundly upon Nature's acts was beyond his capability and his proclivities. Had he been acquainted with more than the name of the young man to whom the Dover estate was to be bequeathed, he might well have gone about trying to persuade Nature of the delights of trying something new, but he did not, and so the family Dover lived on a modest sum with enough to draw equally modest dowries for each of the five daughters, even if it was Mr Dover's private opinion that Ruth would not find a man dour enough to suit her, much less be suited by her, and that any man fool enough to marry Leopoldina or Matilda was not a man he wished to pay a dowry to. It would, however, be beneath him to actively assume the worst of his three youngest and make use of those funds to improve the wardrobe of his servants, and so envy would prick, and that would be that.

But if envy pricked at Mr Dover's heart, hope and confidence blossomed in Mrs Dover's. "You will wear your prettiest dress," she announced to Rosamund, "and you will walk. It intends on raining tonight; you will be obliged to stay, and in a day, Mr Webber will be entirely yours. I have planned it perfectly."

"Oh, Mamma," the eldest Miss Dover replied in dismay, "these are fine people, gentlemen and ladies. Surely they will expect me to arrive in a carriage. May I have the carriage, Papa?"

"Of course—"

"*Not,*" Mrs Dover interrupted firmly. "They are in the country now and must not expect everyone to sally to and fro in carriages, as if they were in the finest of London Society. Besides, the walk will bring a healthy glow to your cheeks, Rosa; it will make you all the more appealing."

"I dare say Rosa is appealing enough," Elsa protested. "Mamma, it is already damp, with a heavy mist in the air. Rosa's dress will be wet through and through before she arrives."

"Miss Webber is of a size with Rosa," Mrs Dover said with triumph, and in the momentary pause that followed, she examined Rosa's bosom with a pleasantly critical eye. "Nearly of a size, but that will do no harm either. If she is wet, they will have to clothe her, and surely Miss Webber's gowns will show our Rosa to her very best advantage."

"Miss Webber is of yellower hue," Elsa tried once more, "where Rosa is entirely fair. Surely Rosamund's own dresses would suit her better. Papa, you must insist that Rosa take the carriage."

"It would be such a pity," Mrs Dover said in clarion tones, "if the wind should blow open the library windows and the coming rain lay ruin to all of Mr Dover's books, don't you think, Dina?"

Leopoldina, who had waited through all of the discussion for an opportunity to finagle her way into visiting Newsbury Manor with Rosa, sat up so straightly as to nearly spill her tea, and blurted, "Yes, of course, Mamma," before realising that without the carriage, she would certainly never be permitted to join Rosamund at dinner. Gloomy with understanding, she took two biscuits from the nearest plate, then, defiantly, stole one of Ruth's as well.

Mr Dover lowered his papers, which he had not been reading anyway, and exchanged a merciless look with Mrs Dover, at the end of which he said, grimly, "I must use the carriage this afternoon myself, Rosa; I am sorry."

"Then I shall walk with you," Elsa proclaimed, "to carry a parasol and keep the worst of the damp off you, Rosa."

"Absolutely not," said Mrs Dover. "They would feel obliged to invite you to dinner as well."

Elsabeth smiled. "Not if Mr Archer is on hand. He will cut Webber to shreds with a glance, and Miss Webber will not gainsay her brother. I suspect her of having her own intentions toward Archer, and think they are very well suited to one another."

"Oh, no," Rosa said in dismay. "Miss Webber is very kind, and Mr Archer so..." Her own kind heart could not allow her to choose the words that Elsabeth would, and so she ended with "reserved" in a soft and gentle voice.

"Then perhaps Miss Webber's brand of kindness is just what a reserved gentleman requires. Come, let me go with you, Rosamund, and I shall abandon you at the gate to satisfy our Mamma; the Newsbury party will never know I am near."

Mrs Dover, mollified by this prospect, replied, "Very well," and it was only a short time later that the two eldest Dover sisters set out to Newsbury Manor. Both wore oilskins, for it was damp; both wore bonnets tied close to their heads, though Rosamund's was not as snug as Elsabeth would have liked, for Mrs Dover had feared damaging Rosa's fetchingly-arranged curls.

"As if a three-mile walk in the rain will not do them harm enough," an exasperated Elsa had snapped, but the wounded concern in Rosamund's large eyes had held Elsabeth's tongue from there on out. Elsa *did* carry an oiled parasol, protecting Rosa from the worst of the drifting mist while peering around its edge to watch their path. When Rosa protested that she, Elsa, would be wet to the bone, the second Miss Dover only laughed. "The wind and mist have no use for me, Rosa; I have no suitor to concern myself with, and so the elements have no reason to distress me. If only they would not look askance should you arrive on foot and yet entirely dry and warm—!"

"Shh," Rosamund said gently, and then, because it was true, "besides, Dina has more skill at the wind than you or I. If I were to be delivered dry to their door, she would have been the best to accompany me."

"And to your arm she would have clung like a leech, until they were obliged to invite her to dinner too, and then all your chances of a happy life with Mr Webber would be dashed."

"Dina is impetuous, but her heart is good."

"You have never met a bad-hearted soul in your life, Rosamund, which is why everyone loves you so."

Within a very little time, for the walk was not insurmountably far, Elsa kissed Rosa on the cheek and left her to wend her way up the drive alone, both of them trusting that no one within Newsbury Manor would be the wiser. Indeed, it might have been so, had one of the Newsbury party not left the premises himself some hours earlier, only to be making his way back just as Elsa and Rosamund parted ways.

Master Fitzgerald Archer, loath to pass a day without some form of exercise, had taken his horse, a big, talkative creature inclined to fill Archer's habitual silences with his own conversation, out for a gallop as much to stretch the horse's legs as clear Archer's own mind; he had been discomfited the night before by Elsabeth Dover's arch commentary, and had since been unable to shake thoughts of the woman from his head.

She ought not have been able to discomfit him to begin with; she was of lesser station, her family rudimentary in their manners and their table barely presentable. Only the eldest sister, with whom Webber was so smitten, showed the grace and sensibility one would expect from a young lady; *she* would not be the sort to invent a relationship as the reason a gentleman might not enjoy a Season.

She was also not the one who preyed upon his mind, and a long ride to acquaint himself with the countryside was the very best way Archer knew to shake unpleasantries away. It had succeeded: his thoughts were filled with plans for hunting, with admiration for a pretty stretch of country—nothing compared to his own acreage at Streyfield, of course, but for parceled lands held by small land-owners, they were suitable enough—and with a pleasant anticipation for dinner, where Miss Dover would be removed from her unfortunate family and Archer could at last determine whether *he* felt she was suitable for his good friend Webber.

It was in this happy frame of mind, then, that he saw, from a distant hill, Rosamund and Elsabeth Dover parting ways from one another at the foot of Newbury Manor's long drive, the latter having first pressed a parasol into the former's hands. He reined in his horse, patting its shoulder in promise of another run soon, and watched in what he was obliged to name astonishment as Miss Elsabeth stood in the mist, watching until her sister was well up the drive; indeed, until she was out of Elsabeth's sight, upon which time Elsabeth flung her arms wide and spun circles in the fog until it whirled with her. Though he could not hear her, he saw how she threw her head back and knew that she laughed like a madwoman or a child, and then, unselfconscious with joy, embarked on the road she had come on, having, it seemed, delivered her sister to safety with no further ambitions of her own.

With an again-unsettled mind, Archer returned to the manor and the meal, and if he was often silent as they ate, that was to his friends no more than the usual mark of the man, and no sign of deep musings.

(9)

THE OILSKINS HAD NOT DONE THEIR JOB: BEFORE THE EVENING'S meal was concluded, Rosamund Dover's pretty nose was swollen and reddened to a degree that would please her mother immensely, if only that good woman could see it. Less pleasing to Mrs Dover would be the worrying wheeze that settled in Rosamund's chest almost immediately, and the feverish brightness of her lovely eyes. A servant was dispatched at once to inform the Dover household that Miss Dover would be a guest at Newsbury Manor until morning. Mrs Dover, upon receiving this news, was restrained from performing a jig only by Elsa's expression, the severity of which would more commonly be found upon Ruth's countenance.

"Pshaw," said Mrs Dover, in tones that could only be regarded as defensive, "a summer cold will do her no harm and may do us all a great deal of good." Come morning, however, another servant was sent from Newsbury Manor with the knowledge that Miss Dover had worsened considerably in the night. Elsa, flushed with anger, no sooner finished her breakfast than put on her shoes and struck out, for the second time inside a day, toward Newsbury Manor. She did not ask permission, nor did she feel it necessary to tell her family where she intended to go; it was obvious to all, even flighty Leopoldina, who sat and held Matilda's hand in concern as a fretful Mrs Dover paced the parlour, watching her second daughter go to support the eldest.

Of all the party at Newsbury Manor, it was Archer who was least surprised to see Elsabeth Dover striding up the drive. He was not first to see her; that distinction belonged to Miss Webber, who drifted from her morning rooms to the sitting room with the air of one tragically condemned to a lifestyle which did not suit her. It was her hope that she would elicit sympathy from Archer with this pose, although he had been retired for some time to the sitting room himself and was unaware of her posturing until the moment her voice cracked through the halls, carrying such a distance that the servants whispered of it among themselves: "Good *God*," proclaimed Miss Webber from the height and vantage of a first floor window, "could that be Elsabeth Dover? She is all over mud, and her hat has come off!"

"If her hat has come off," Archer murmured to no one but himself, though Mr Gibbs was close enough to hear and did, "then can there be any question that it is Miss Elsabeth? No," he answered himself, "I thought not," and upon this satisfactory reply, rose to attend not the shrill Miss Webber and the astonishing view upon which she exclaimed, but rather the entrance hall, as a dark and sobering shadow to the butler.

The butler, whose name was Peters, had come from London with Webber out of fondness, not obligation; the house in town might have been his to command while his master was away, and the difficulties presented by Mrs Gibbs and her husband, or Miss Webber, not his to contend with at all for weeks or even months, dependent on how long the country manor was to remain let. But his preference was to tend to the good-hearted youth's staff wherever Webber might be, and as he waited for the precise moment before sweeping the manor door open to greet Miss Elsabeth Dover, Peters was quietly pleased that he had chosen as he did. London did not condone well-bred young ladies taking matters into their own hands, as Miss Elsabeth clearly intended to do. It was not proper, Peters conceded, but it was interesting, whereas London Society was too often predictable, even for those below-stairs.

It was a rain-lashed, pink-cheeked and highly muddy young woman to whom he opened the door, though she showed not a whit of discomfiture at her disheveled state. "I am Elsabeth Dover," she announced. "I have come to look after my sister. Pray tell me where she is."

"Of course, Miss." Peters bowed as he stepped back, then took a second, prudent step out of the way as he captured a glimpse of Master Archer from the corner of his eye. Archer, as though it was natural he should be there, moved more fully into the light cast by the open door, but before Elsabeth could appreciate that he alone had come to greet her, a flurry of activity and footsteps echoed through the hall and it was suddenly no longer he, but he and Webber and Miss Webber, who stood as one before the wind-swept Miss Elsabeth.

"Miss Elsabeth," Miss Webber said with an astonished titter poorly hidden in her voice. "You did not walk all this way in such weather, surely?"

Elsabeth performed a polite smile. "I did, Miss Webber. It is a mere three miles or so. Too far, perhaps, for a London lady like yourself, but I am accustomed to taking my exercise. I should like to take it the remaining distance to my sister, if you please; Mr Webber, where is Rosamund?"

Webber, his usually cheerful face now muddled with worry, said, "This way, Miss Elsabeth. I'm glad you've come. Miss Dover is not well. A doctor has been sent for." He whisked her away, their footsteps fading quickly down the long halls.

Miss Webber's gaze followed them in stiff offense, and her tone begged that she should be corrected: "I believe she cut me there, Archer."

"I believe she did, Miss Webber." Archer bowed and retreated to the sitting room, where he studiously bent his hand to the letters he had earlier abandoned.

Elsabeth Dover had not even looked at him.

(10)

"ELSA!" WAS ROSA'S GLAD CRY WHEN THAT LADY ENTERED HER room, though much to Elsabeth's dismay, it seemed that all of her sister's strength was spent by that single ejaculation. At once, Rosa faded back into the bedclothes; Elsa rushed to her side to feel her brow and hold her hand comfortingly. Mr Webber, who surely could not remain in the room with any degree of propriety, did so regardless, hovering at the door like a nervous manservant.

"I am so very glad you have come," Rosa whispered once she had recovered herself a little. "I had not wanted to ask, but I am sure that already I am better because you are with me, Elsa. Mr Webber and his sisters have been so kind. You must entertain them, Elsa, for to my embarrassment, I cannot."

"I must do nothing of the sort. I am here for you alone, Rosa. I shall read to you"—and upon hearing these words from Elsa, Mr Webber fled the room—"and I shall tell you fanciful tales of home until you are well enough to return to them yourself. That is my duty here, Rosa, not to fall in with the sisters. They think highly of you already, and I have no need to parade myself before them. Oh," Elsa said with a certain pleasure as Mr Webber returned with a small stack of books, which he presented to the sisters Dover as if they were paged with gold.

"I have only a small library," he said apologetically. "Better you should have fallen ill at Streyfield, Miss Dover, for the library there goes on for miles."

"Streyfield?" Elsa was obliged to ask, and was rewarded by an exclamation of surprise.

"Surely you know of Archer's holdings? They are to the north, to be sure, but they are known throughout the *ton* for their beauty, their spaciousness and their hunting. Streyfield itself must be five times the size of Newsbury Manor, with galleries of art that even the Prince Regent is known to envy. Oh, you must see it, Miss Elsabeth! Your heart would swell!"

Elsa directed a smile at her lap, then lifted that smile to meet Rosa's eyes with laughter dancing in her own. "I am afraid, Mr Webber, that we are less versed with London's high society than we might be, so you will forgive us our ignorance of Mr Archer's lands. But I think it in every way unlikely that we should ever find ourselves in a position as to fall ill at Streyfield, so it is better by far to find ourselves here, at Newsbury Manor, with such fine companionship as yourself and your sisters." This last Elsa was obliged to look away from Rosa in order to speak, for fear that Rosa's pleased and grateful relief would send Elsa into undignified laughter. "These books will do splendidly, and I thank you for your thoughtfulness. Mr Webber, I wonder if I could trouble your household for tea and perhaps some dry bread or crackers with salt; I am certain Rosa needs to eat a little, but it must be something that will not upset her stomach."

"It is my very wish," Webber proclaimed, and with a gentle smile for Rosa, went, it seemed, to fetch these things himself. Betwixt his comings and goings, and the visits of Mrs Gibbs and Miss Webber, and Elsa's reading, the day went swiftly. So swiftly, indeed, that the three o'clock bells came as an unpleasant surprise to Elsabeth, who rose and said she supposed she must excuse herself.

Rosa caught her hand immediately, her dismay so evident that Miss Webber insisted at once that Elsabeth stay at Newsbury until Rosa was well. Yet another servant was dispatched, and in short order, Rosa, relieved that her most beloved sister would remain at her side, succumbed to gentle sleep. With Rosa resting, when the call came for dinner, Elsa was of a mind to attend, though she was no less mud-stained than she had been upon her arrival that morning.

The party was gathered in the hall beside the dining room, waiting to go in, when she arrived. Their finery gave her a moment's hesitation; it was not, she believed, above Miss Webber to have chosen a delicately yellow, high-waisted gown and the jewelry to match in the awareness that Elsabeth could not possibly dress so well. Mrs Gibbs was equally well presented in light blue, though her husband, a round and dull-eyed man, looked as though he had already spilled the soup on his own evening wear.

The other gentlemen were at the height of presentability: Archer stood stiff and handsome a few steps from the door, and turned when Elsa entered. His expression became, if anything, stiffer yet, and Elsabeth's heart sank. But Webber, the more sensible of the two men by far, forewent his conversation with Miss Webber instantly and all but flew to Elsabeth's side, clasping his hands around hers. "Miss Dover is improved, I hope?"

"Not nearly so much as I would like," Elsabeth replied. "She is resting, else I could not in conscience join you for dinner."

"Then we will eat swiftly," Webber announced, "so that she will awaken to your presence and not feel herself bereft. I shall call for the doctor again before I sit down, Miss Elsabeth; I will have nothing less than the best care for your sister."

"I think—I hope—she is not so unwell as all that," Elsabeth said. "If she is not better by morning, Mr Webber, I will gladly accept your offer, but—let us not trouble him a second time. Not yet."

It was Mr Webber, then, who looked troubled, but, unwilling to disagree with a young lady, acquiesced. Mr Archer, eternally less agreeable, said, "After dinner, perhaps," to the surprise of all attending and none more than Elsabeth Dover.

She gazed at him curiously, wondering without being able to ask when he had assumed such a concern for her sister, but feeling much as Webber felt, for the peace she said, "Perhaps," to Archer's suggestion.

Miss Webber, observing the intensity with which Elsabeth and Archer regarded one another, produced a trilling laugh and tucked her arm into Elsabeth's. "Surely a family of such strong young women who are inclined to walk the many muddy miles betwixt Oakden and Newsbury cannot be ill for long. Why, Miss Elsabeth, you will not take it amiss if I confess to you that I had never seen such a sight as your appearance this morning. Oh!" she said with another of the false laughs, "I do not mean your *appearance*, of course, but your *arrival*!"

Elsabeth, whose interest in walking with Miss Webber was, in her own best estimation, limited, examined their linked elbows with the expressionless dismay of one quite unable to extract herself politely. It was with her gaze upon their entwinement that she replied, "My dear Miss Webber, I could hardly imagine that you did not say exactly what you meant. I am sure my appearance was dramatic, being wind-blown and muddy both, and I am sure it is a rare sight in London Society that a young woman of quality should be seen in such a fashion."

"What fashion?" Webber asked with evidently genuine surprise. "I only saw that you looked remarkably well upon your arrival this morning, Miss Elsabeth. It seems to me that your appearance"—and if he put a slight strain on the word, it was only to emphasize that he meant what Miss Webber claimed to—"showed nothing more than positively credible concern for your sister. Would you not agree, Archer?"

"I would say that exercise benefits even ladies of Society, regardless of how unwilling they are to take it," Archer replied rather severely, and at Elsabeth's side, Miss Webber's jaw clicked shut.

A terrible twitch made itself felt at the corner of Elsa's mouth: a twitch quite determined to turn itself to laughter. She swiftly looked away, finding Webber's earnest gaze to be a safe landing place for her attentions, and she thought, 'So, that is how it is with Miss Webber.' Well, then. Archer was perhaps odious, but he at least had the grace to wear it on his sleeve, whereas Miss Webber's inclinations were all sweet-coated poison. Perhaps, Elsabeth decided, despite his atrocious behaviour, she might find it in herself to be ever so slightly kinder to Mr Archer, for no other reason than to tweak Miss Webber.

Rosamund would cluck and *tsk* with disapproval. Pleased by the prospect of providing her sister with this modicum of entertainment in her convalescence, Elsabeth took the decision. Her smile formed first at Webber, at whom she was already looking, and then at Archer, at whom she took some effort to redirect her attention. "You're very kind to say so, Mr Archer. I have always thought it better to be healthy than to be overly concerned with Society's decorum. Of course, I have that advantage, living in the country as I do. I am sure that it is more common to be frail in Town."

Miss Webber, with a strength that belied any hint of fragility, released Elsabeth, stalked to Archer's side and took his arm so that he was obliged to escort her to dinner. "Not at all," she said sharply. "I'm sure I know many fine, strong young ladies, and would like to count myself among them. Perhaps it is only that there is less *mud* in London."

"There is a tremendous amount of mud at Streyfield," Archer said thoughtfully, and Elsabeth, trying not to laugh, welcomed Webber's escort into the dining room.

(11)

Rosamund, though, was not to be amused by Elsabeth's antics; not that night. Elsabeth returned to her side to find her newly feverish and quite wretched with sweat and shivers. There was nothing to be done: the fire was high and water was at hand; Elsabeth coddled Rosamund by the one and fed her small sips of the other, and, when Rosa was too tired anymore to sit by the fire, tucked her into the duvets and mopped her forehead. Twice, Mr Webber called in to attend to her; after the second, Elsa muttered, "If only he would stay away I might at least warm you with a little fire here at the bed, Rosa."

"Oh!" Rosamund's eyes flew open. "No, it would be too dangerous even if he did not visit. The bedclothes could burn so easily!"

"You have far too little faith in my skill," Elsa assured her, but did not light the flame she could call between her palms. Indeed, gazing hopelessly into her lightless fingers, she whispered, "What good is being magic-ridden, Rosa, if the power cannot be used for something such as this? To heal you, when you are so ill? It is bad enough to be kept from Society out of fear of discovery, but to also be useless with power! It is intolerable!"

No sooner had she spoken than she wished the words had not passed her lips: Rosamund's green eyes stood wide with distress. "*Elsa.* Elsa, you must not say—not even think!—such things.

You know the stories that are told. Do not wish yourself so low!"

"No. No, of course not, Rosa. My poor sweet Rosa, plagued with a sister who says whatever frightful flight of fancy that comes into her mind. I shall cease such nonsense and sing to you instead, perhaps one of Mamma's tunes? It will soothe you, and you will sleep."

Wan but smiling with relief, Rosamund clung to Elsabeth's fingers as she sang a sweet and pretty song composed by their mother when they had been ill as children. But the tune was simple and the words rote; they took no great part of Elsabeth's attention, leaving her to think on what Rosa had not allowed her to say.

Magic was the provenance of the low; good breeding did not sorcerers get. If Papa Dover knew whence his family had been infected with the bad blood, he never spoke of it; Elsabeth assumed he did not know. It happened from time to time, just as a bay mare might throw a white foal. Soldiers—not officers, but the common men, foot-soldiers and sailors—might have a knack for turning bullets or calling a helpful wind; magic was permitted, even grudgingly acknowledged as necessary in military matters. It was even suspected that Bonaparte himself commanded a certain amount of esoteric power. But it was certain—and Elsabeth herself was certainly not supposed to know it—that the very lowest of the low, the camp followers of the French legions, had magic. *Healing* magic, at that: they were the source, it was whispered, of Bonaparte's great successes, for he lost one man to every ten the British lost, or so it seemed to those who had fought on the battlefields.

And to know, sitting at Rosa's sickbed, to *know* that in the world, amongst those who had nothing to lose by practising the magic that was in them, that there were skills that could help Rosamund now—no. Elsa let the words to her mother's sweet and simple song fill her mind, thinking of each word as it came as if there was nothing else in the world. To do less now would ignite the fire, always the easiest and most natural of Elsa's gifts, and the fire, fuelled by rage, burned too hot to quench. It was necessary to forget, necessary to do as Rosa had instructed, and not even think of it, for though she knew herself to be naive, Elsa believed she would trade her position with any one of the French camp followers for the ability to help her sister, and that it would be well worth the trade. So, she sang, and in singing, forced herself to forget, and took some small, bitter comfort in Rosamund's slow drift toward a restless sleep.

Half an hour passed; then an hour, and Rosamund slept. The clock called out, announcing it was as yet still too early for Elsabeth to retire when her hosts might be waiting news of Rosamund's recovery. Reluctant with obligation, Elsabeth rose and joined the party below, where Webbers and Gibbses sat together, losing at cards to Archer, whose approach to the game appeared indolent and yet highly successful.

"I will only be a little while," Elsabeth assured them. "Rosamund is sleeping, but I must return to her soon, and so will entertain myself by reading rather than disrupt your game."

"You cannot possibly like to read more than a game of cards," Mr Gibbs said with the air of a man personally offended.

"I am sure Miss Elsabeth is uninterested in all things so crass as cards," Miss Webber put forth. "Indeed, I am sure I have heard tell that she is a great reader; that she prefers reading to all else, and looks down upon those who do not read for pleasure."

"Quite," Elsabeth said drily. "Tell me, Miss Webber, do you read for pleasure?"

A line drew itself instantly between Miss Webber's eyebrows, and her response of "Of course" perhaps lacked conviction.

That, however, was not Elsabeth's concern; she only smiled gently and replied, "I could never look down upon you for choosing to play cards, but rather stand in envy of one who does so with more skill than I have."

"What," Archer wondered aloud, "was the last book you read, Miss Webber? Perhaps we might discuss it over our game."

Heightened colour streaked Miss Webber's cheekbones as her brother, unable to bear the sniping any longer, leapt to his feet so that he might show Elsabeth the small offering of books available. "I have brought most of them to your sister's room already," he said in woeful apology. "I can only once more wish I had a library like Archer's. You must invite Miss Elsabeth to Streyfield someday, Archer; one as fond of reading as she is should be granted access to such an array of books as you have."

"I am not," Elsabeth said mildly, "*that* fond of reading, despite Miss Webber's protestations. There are many things in which I find enjoyment, and I promise you, Mr Webber, that your selection is quite adequate to my needs. I must thank you, sir, and insist I keep you no longer from your game."

"Shall I not invite you to Streyfield, then, Miss Elsabeth?" Archer asked.

Elsabeth lifted her gaze with slow astonishment to find Archer's attention wholly on her, and to find Miss Webber's countenance, just beyond him, tight-jawed with silence. It was, Elsabeth thought, one thing to tweak the other young woman; it was quite something else to make any motions toward encouraging Archer, whose manners were, after all, abominable. "I'm sure my family and I would be honoured by your invitation, Mr Archer. I can hardly imagine who would be more enamoured by your library, my father or myself."

Archer's face closed down as swiftly as Miss Webber's lit up. Satisfied with the one, if not the other, Elsabeth selected a book and retired to a chair, whereupon the gathered card-players took it upon themselves to resume the conversation they had been engaged in before her arrival. Or perhaps not, Elsabeth thought; Miss Webber was quite of a mind to discuss Streyfield now, and to put the invitation to Elsa in its proper light. "It has been such a long time since we have been to Streyfield ourselves, Mr Archer. I do long to see it again, and even more, to see your sweet sister Persephone."

Elsabeth, all unintending, made a noise of surprise. The entire party turned their attention to her, Archer most of all. "I beg your pardon, Miss Elsabeth?"

"Forgive me, Mr Archer. I was only surprised to hear your sister's name. It is both classic and unusual, is it not? And if I may say so, a rather dreadful thing to do to a child. I believe I should grow up with a fear of spending half my days in the sunless shadows of Hades, with a name like that."

Beyond Archer, Miss Webber's eyes assumed a roundness so profound, it could only be thought of as bulging; Elsabeth, trying not to think that, trained her gaze on Archer, whose lips were compressed in an expression made equally of dislike and approval. "You are correct. Our mother died in childbirth, and to my father, my sister's birth was therefore a source of both the brightest joy and deepest grief. Her name reflects that conflict. I do not often speak of this, Miss Elsabeth, but you are...uncommonly insightful."

"Oh, Mr Archer," Elsabeth said, faint with horror. "Forgive me. I should never have been so opinionated."

"I am beginning to believe that there is no power of this earth that could cause you to be otherwise," Archer replied, and, with this comment, returned to the game. This time, although the conversation continued about the charming Miss Archer, touching on her accomplishments and indeed the accomplishments of all young ladies, Elsabeth did not again join the discussion. Nor did she recall a single word of the book she read, though periodically she thought to turn the page, as would be naturally expected. Twice as she gazed sightlessly at the pages, she saw Mr Archer glance her way, as if he expected another interjection, and though she had many thoughts on their topic, she resolutely held her tongue until the hour had grown late enough that she could politely take her leave and return to Rosamund's side.

There, Rosamund, who was not at all better but who had wakened, was subjected to a nearly endless flurry of exclamations regarding Elsa's own lack of discretion, Miss Webber's endless litany of the traits that an accomplished woman might call her own—all of which Miss Archer displayed in spades, and which Miss Webber, by extrapolation, was presumed to command—and finally Mr Archer's opinions regarding how overused the term *accomplished* was, given what he himself regarded as necessary to deserve the word.

"I should like to see any gentleman with as many skills as an accomplished woman of Mr Archer's acquaintance must display," Elsa finally snapped in a proper fury. "I should think he knows not a single soul of accomplishment, man or woman, for his standards are impossible and he is himself odious beyond measure."

By the end of her outburst, Rosamund sat cross-legged beneath the duvet, her smiling face cupped in her hands and the beads of sweat on her brow fading. "I believe you have chased my fever away with your outrage," announced Rosa happily. "I believe I shall sleep well now, Elsa, although I will cringe a little for that remark you made about Miss Archer's name. Please, if I may have a little water, then you shall lie down with me and I will sleep in the eye of my sister's storm." And, upon receiving the asked-for water, so she did.

(12)

Rosamund was, if not well, at least past danger by morning; this, Elsa was pleased to report to her hosts, though it was the combined opinion of both the doctor, who had, after all, been called for the night before and who arrived early in the morning, and of Mrs Dover, who had not been called for at all but who arrived with her two youngest daughters in a flurry of concern only shortly after the doctor, that to move Rosamund now would be beyond the pale. The doctor's opinion was borne from a concern for relapse; Mrs Dover's, from a concern for marriage: the longer Rosa stayed under the Newsbury roof, the more time Mr Webber had to fall deeply in love with her. Once satisfied that her eldest was not in any real danger, there could be, in Mrs Dover's opinion, no more suitable situation than Rosamund remain at Newbury to convalesce.

It was therefore with great passion that, at breakfast, Mrs Dover informed Mr Webber that Rosamund was very poorly indeed and could not possibly be moved for some time yet.

"Move her!" cried Webber. "I should think not! She must remain here, under the best care the doctor can offer! I will hear nothing else! And Miss Elsabeth must stay as well, for of course Miss Dover will not recover so quickly without her sister's presence for comfort."

"It will be our delight to have them," Miss Webber said in a tone of rote necessity that Mrs Dover heard as nothing less than genuine welcome. Leopoldina, who was as selective of hearing as her mother, sought an opportunity in Miss Webber's words to invite *herself* to stay at Newsbury; Elsabeth, neither so selective of hearing nor in the least unwise in her youngest sister's ways, shifted in her chair and put a foot firmly on top of Dina's, pressing down until the younger girl glowered and thus missed the moment of opportunity.

Mrs Dover's foot, much to Elsabeth's regret, was out of reach; she had no way to prevent her mother from thanking the Webbers with too great enthusiasm, or from sitting straight and putting on what she imagined to be the airs of a great lady as she complimented the Newsbury lands, overlooks and rooms. "There is not a prettier place to be found in the country," she declared. "I hope you will not quit it any time soon, Mr Webber. It should break all of our hearts, and I dare say you could find no more agreeable young lady in all of England than our Rosamund to pass a summer day with. She is quite the prettiest girl in the county, though I am of course biased. But others have said so as well, so I think perhaps my fondness does not entirely turn my head the wrong way on this matter. And there are such charming people here, Mr Webber, more charming, I should think, than you will find in the city."

As each of their hosts was most lately from Town, and as Mr Webber himself had no country lands to claim as his own as Mr Archer did, this observation was met with a certain pointed silence that Mrs Dover did not notice at all. Indeed, she carried on blithely, full of conviction that the country was superior in every way to Town, save, she admitted, for the shops; the people, she felt, were quite the best in the country.

"It has been some time since you yourself have lived in London," Miss Webber observed in a tone meant to question.

"Oh yes," Mrs Dover replied, and then to the astonishment of Webbers, Gibbses and Archers alike, her ready, bubbling speech came to a sudden halt, a breath trapped behind sharply pursed lips. For the briefest moment, the Dover ladies did not look at one another at all, as if for fear doing so would betray the secret held close to each of their hearts. Then Mrs Dover rallied, as light and airy as she had ever been. "That is how I know the country to be more suitable: I have never had any desire to return to London myself."

"But you always say—!" Dina's outburst was silenced not by a pressing foot this time, but by Elsabeth's swift kick to her sister's shin.

Mrs Dover fixed her youngest with a gimlet stare. "That I am grateful for the peace and quiet of the country, which is a far more suitable place to raise a large family than London's bustle. I am sure you would agree, Mr Webber, would you not? Can you imagine any better place to bring up sons and daughters than this very house?"

"I cannot," Mr Webber said obligingly, "but then, I am happiest wherever I am in the very moment that I am there, Mrs Dover. It is my gift and my curse to be a simple man made happy by simple things. I have little ambition but a great deal of enjoyment in the world."

"Our Rosa is very like you," Mrs Dover said in triumph. "Though I should say she is a gentle and happy soul rather than a simple one. I should like to say that of you, too, Mr Webber, for I feel you have depths that go unplumbed."

"There is nothing to suggest that a deep and intricate soul is more worthy than a light and forthright one," Elsabeth objected, and chose not to look at Mr Archer while she spoke. "Indeed, the gift of accepting the world for what it is, without judging or disapproving, is far more worthy than seeking out reasons to be offended by it."

Mrs Dover, squinting between Elsabeth and Mr Archer, replied, "Quite," in as thoughtful a tone as she had at her disposal. The very next moment, she rose, proclaiming, "We must be going. We are in your debt, Mr Webber; I cannot thank you enough for your solicitous care of our Rosamund. I am sure she will be able to return to us in a week or so"—a phrase which Elsabeth saw caused Miss Webber's face to pale—"and until then,

I hope we may have some chance of seeing you again. Girls, we will go to the village before returning home, for I believe you have some intention of—"

"Yes!" Leopoldina cried as she stood. "I promised you a ball, Mr Webber, in return for the one you so kindly hosted here. We shall have one as soon as Rosamund is well enough, and this time, there shall be no shortage of gentlemen, our good friend Colonel White has returned and all his officers will attend. You will find yourself fighting for Rosamund's attentions, Mr Webber! You had best secure them while you can!"

Elsabeth, mortified, could do no more than hurry her family toward their waiting carriage, though it was with some relief that she glanced back once and saw consideration writ on Webber's brow, even if Archer and the others looked as appalled as Elsa herself felt. In Elsabeth's ear, though, Mrs Dover chattered, "I believe that went as well as it ever could have. So well done, Dina! You could not have done better than to press Mr Webber on the topic of both ball and Rosamund, though I dare say he is already quite taken with her. Why, if we are fortunate, he will have asked for her hand before the ball is even held! Elsabeth, perhaps you will come with us to the village—"

"I will not," Elsa said with too-emphatic horror. "I must tend to Rosa, Mamma; you know that. I will send daily missives to keep you abreast of her health, but I think it is best you stay away for the next several days. After all, we would not want to distract Mr Webber's attentions from Rosa in any way, would we?"

An approving smile blossomed across Mrs Dover's pretty face. "Indeed, you are right, Elsa. Very well, girls, let us hasten to town and then home again to tell your father all the news. I'm sure he is eager to hear all about Rosamund's prospects."

"Rosamund's prospects are quite in hand," Dina said with a sniff. "It is our own that we should be worried about now, Mamma. You would think we were quite invisible, for all the attention we are paid by the officers. Why, perhaps we *are* invisible! Elsa, can you see me?" Winking with mischief, Leopoldina raised her hands as she stepped toward the carriage, and a whisk of dust-heavy wind spun around her skirts.

Elsabeth seized her hand and propelled her bodily into the carriage, then stood upon the footstep to hiss, "Do not risk such foolishness, Dina! Never mind your own happiness: Rosa's, and perhaps the fortunes of our entire family, depend on discretion! You are not invisible!" Shaking with passion, she stood back to gaze in frustrated sympathy at her youngest sister, toward whom she felt a slow softening. She was a pretty girl, was Leopoldina. More open and fresh-faced than Rosamund's quiet and beautiful reserve, she chafed more than any of them save perhaps Elsa herself at the constraints they had to observe.

More gently this time, Elsabeth repeated, "You are not invisible, Dina. Indeed, you are quite one of the loveliest creatures I have ever seen, and you are barely fifteen. In time, you will catch the eye of a handsome officer. Try not to be impatient, my sweet."

"But I don't want to wait," Dina said in desperation. "We *always* have to wait, Elsa. We have to wait for everything!"

Unspoken went the acknowledgment that the one thing these two sisters wanted most deeply was the one thing for which they would wait forever. Elsabeth sighed and squeezed Dina's hand, then stepped back to see Tildy looking between them with a longing that said she, too, shared their frustration at what they could not do. Perhaps it was easier for Rosamund and Ruth; the one seemed happy enough without using her magic, and the other disapproved of it entirely.

"We will not always have to wait," Elsabeth said, and, knowing it to be an empty promise, sent her sisters and mother away.

(13)

We will not always have to wait WAS A PHRASE TAKEN PERHAPS TOO much to heart by the youngest Dover girl. Leopoldina clasped Tildy's hand as they drove to town with their mother, whose happy commentary about Rosamund's health and future was the stuff to which Dina would usually be most attentive. Today, though, as dust kicked up from the horses' heels and clouded the blue sky above, and Elsa's words rang in her mind, Dina could not listen to their mother. It was not that Rosamund's fate was trivial: indeed, it was critical to them all. But it was *Rosa*'s fate, not Dina's own, and her own seemed so long delayed.

Dina could not remember being unready to start her own life, being unready to have a husband instead of a father; being unready to command her own household instead of following the law of her mother's. She was no fool, despite what Papa thought. To live as she wished, she needed a husband, and moreover, needed one who did not much care about social standing or, indeed, her activities. She did not want to *flaunt* her magic; Papa did not flaunt his. It remained within the household, warming tea and drying clothes. But she wanted to *use* it, and Society be damned. Dina blushed to even think the bold words, but there it was: Society be damned! She would sail to America if she had to: surely, on the frontier, even a woman's magic would be welcomed against the known power of the native savages. But she needed a husband, or an income, and neither were to be found.

Tildy sneezed twice and fanned a hand in front of her face, miserable with dust crusting her cheeks. Dina squeezed her fingers and spread her other hand, low, where Mamma could not see what she was doing. Wind was so quick to respond; it always had been. A signal, Papa said, of Leopoldina's flighty nature. Perhaps it was true, but it was a stance which discounted both the strength of the wind and its delicacy. It took so little effort to guide it around the carriage, yellow dust sweeping past them on either side and mixing together behind them again. No one could see that magic was at work, or so Dina told herself: from above, it still appeared that heels and wheels kicked up dust, and that the swift passage of the carriage left it behind. Matilda took a sudden deep and grateful breath, her lungs clear again, and squeezed Dina's hand in return.

Mamma, rattling on as surely as did the carriage wheels, noticed not a thing. Their driver, a rather handsome fellow with sandy hair and brown eyes, did; he glanced back without expression to meet Dina's gaze, then returned his attention to the road where it belonged.

Satisfaction rose in Leopoldina's chest. It was not a secret amongst the servants, of course, that the Dovers had magic. It had not been since they had fled London two years before Dina's birth; some of the servants had come with them, and those who had joined them in the years since had been carefully chosen not by Mrs Dover but by the other staff, who had gradually sought out those who would not be afraid of or betray the Dover secret.

No one of quality could doubt that their household servants could destroy them, should they be of a mind to do so, though few on either side of the stairs ever considered it. A servant who ruined the family she worked for would never work again; a family with secrets to keep had to trust that their staff would not wish to break that trust. The unspoken choice of the Dover family was to ease their servants' way as much as possible in order to assure that trust remained in place: Elsabeth's mud-drenched skirts usually went to the laundry suspiciously clean by comparison to when she'd removed them; never once did Dover servants have to bathe in icy water. Coach drivers were protected from swirling dust on the road; on and on it went, a secret agreement to achieve a quiet life.

Leopoldina Dover did not want a quiet life. She studied the approving coachman's shoulders, thought of the scandal and held Tildy's hand so that she would not do anything ruinous for her family. It was therefore Tildy who straightened with a squeal and pointed ahead as they approached the town's edge: red-coated soldiers made bright splashes against the morning sky, standing out amongst the black-clad gentlemen and the pastel-coloured ladies. "Mamma! Mamma!" Tildy cried. "Oh, we are fortunate today! Perhaps we shall meet an officer or two!"

Mrs Dover, smiling beneficently, did not deign to turn and look, but rather admired the soldiers as they sailed past in their coach. "Oh, my," she said with a satisfied sigh. "A uniformed man always could catch my eye, and I dare say I caught the eye of a few myself, in my day. No longer, of course; I am too old now, although I find I am not too old to admire them still."

Tildy, rashly, wondered, "If you so fancied the officers, why did you marry Papa, then, Mamma?"

"I admired his shoulders, too," Mrs Dover said tartly. "Now, girls, I must find new lace for our dresses for the ball. You may stay outside, if you wish, but I expect you to behave decorously." She signaled the coachman to stop and accepted his assistance in disembarking, as did Tildy; Dina met his brown-eyed gaze for too long and with too warm a smile as he presented his hand for her own departure. A flutter of excitement made her smile even more, and when he released her hand, Dina felt its warm pressure for long moments after he returned to his seat.

He was forgotten, though, as a regiment of soldiers strode by in step, much to the admiration of not only the Dover girls but a wide assortment of other young women gathered along the edges of the street. Among them was Sophia Enton, Elsabeth's particular friend. Dina seized Tildy's hand and together they hurried to join Miss Enton, who smiled and embraced them. "I have heard Rosamund is unwell. Is it true? Does she recover?"

"She recovers at Newsbury Manor," Dina reported with a triumphant note much like her mother's, knowing that this news would not be received gladly by Mrs Enton. "Do you not think the soldiers are very fine?"

Miss Enton glanced toward the marching regiment. "They are very brightly coloured, and I suppose they are terribly warm in wool under this sun. Perhaps, if Rosa is much improved, I might call upon Miss Webber and see Elsa, who I am sure would like news of town. The regiment's arrival, and all."

"Oh, not today. Perhaps tomorrow, but you must visit Mamma first and see what letters she has had from Elsa regarding Rosa's health. Oh, Tildy, *look* at them. Officer! Oh, Officer! Welcome to Bodton! We are most pleased to have you!" Dina put herself forward with a bob and a wave, but not one officer in the lot stopped his forward gaze.

"Tsk, Dina," Miss Enton murmured. "You know they are not meant to look aside at the young ladies while they march. Do not put yourself about so."

"You sound far too much like my sisters. I mean to be noticed, and so I shall be. Will we not, Tildy?"

"What? Yes, of course we shall. We shall? How?"

"Leopoldina." Sophia Enton caught Dina's arm, arresting her forward motion before it began. "Do nothing foolish, Dina. Not with Rosamund's happiness in the balance."

"What about my own?!" Dina threw Miss Enton off with an unexpected violence, anger flushing her cheeks and raising a wildness in her breast. "Why must it always be her happiness, simply because she is the beauty of the family? Why can I not think of mine? I will *not* go unseen! I will *not!*" Released from Sophia's grip, Leopoldina dashed ahead of the regiment to mount the arching stone bridge that spanned the Bodton river. It seemed a very high point indeed, suddenly, all of Bodton town spread around with only the church's steeple rising very far above her. Like so much else, the bridge was riddled with dust, yellow threads outlining the spaces between cobbled stones and building up along the sides where no feet fell. She had felt invisible in the dust; well, then, she would wash it away.

The river did not respond as easily to her as wind did; her heart strained and beat too hard with the effort, stars dancing violet in her eyes as the soldiers approached. Waters grew choppy, burgeoning waves slapping against the bridge's stone walls. Above, the blue sky darkened to grey, winds whipping around until Dina's light walking dress felt a prison wrapped around her body. She would be noticed. She would pursue her own happiness. She would pay the cost, whatever it was. It could not be worse than the interminable *waiting*.

The soldiers came on, striding toward her as though she was not even there. Beyond them, standing as sparks of paleness beyond their red coats, stood Sophia Enton and Matilda, who leaned into the roaring wind and held her fists clenched as though she could stop Dina by will alone. The will, though, was Dina's; no one in the family imagined that Tildy did anything other than follow Leopoldina's lead.

Water roared from the river, a sudden swell that seized Dina and tore her from her stance on the bridge. A scream ripped from her throat as she flew against the bridge wall then in a dizzying tumble, over it and into water both shockingly cold and dreadfully deep. Her breath was gone with the scream; her lungs, when she tried to draw more air in, filled with water that tasted fresh and clean and frightening. A current seized her skirts, drawing her down deeply as if she were *Hamlet*'s Ophelia, and a terrible truth awakened in Dina's heart: that her desire to be noticed had brought her to her doom. She fought the current, struggling upward, only to feel her skirts catch on some murderous weight at the river's bottom. It pulled her down, unwilling to relinquish her. Sunlight glinted above, a bright glittering promise that she would never reach.

A shadow passed between her and the light: Death itself, given form by a frantic imagination. She could not sob, not this deep in the water, not with her chest already filled to aching with the river's pounding strength. *Tildy:* Tildy would be destroyed by Dina's death. And Rosamund; oh, God, they must not tell Rosamund until she had regained her strength after this illness. How could she have been so selfish, so foolish—

A hand seized her wrist, and powerful strokes dragged her upward. Even in the rushing current, Dina felt her skirt tear, releasing her from the river's greedy grasp. Moments later, she was flung upon the bank and strong hands crashed against her back, expelling the water that had gathered in her lungs. She coughed and spat, tears streaming from her eyes, and when she could draw in a trustworthy breath, she turned, searching in astonishment for her saviour.

A gasping paragon of male handsomeness lay beside her, his golden head framed by sunlight that made him seem an angel indeed. His red coat had been stripped away, leaving him in white cotton soaked through and clinging in a most becoming fashion to the strong lines of his torso. "Thank God," he said as Dina's eyes opened. "I had feared you lost. I must introduce myself. I am Captain David Hartnell, and I believe your life now belongs to me."

(14)

Whilst Leopoldina lay trembling in Captain Hartnell's embrace, Rosamund rose from her bed with a healthy colour in her cheeks for the first time in days. She was not well; that was too much to be said, but she was able, with Elsabeth's arm to lean upon, to drift gently down the stairs and to sit a little while beside the fire in the drawing room. There, Mr Webber paid her all the tender attentions she might hope for, and even as he read to her, fetched her tea and wrapped her shoulders in a stole to help keep warm, she was able to watch a curious game played out by Miss Webber, with Mr Archer and her own sister Elsabeth the other two unwilling participants.

Mr Archer sat at a writing-desk in the bay window, his posture impeccable as he sketched lines across fine white paper. Elsabeth, absorbed in a book, sat nearer the fire and Rosamund; her back was three-quarters turned to Archer and she had no evident awareness of his presence. Miss Webber, however, sat with full view of the both of them, and perhaps saw what Rosamund, in her own kind-hearted way, observed: that Archer and Elsa were a fine match in physicality, both with dark hair and straight noses; both with a line of conviction to their eyebrows and jaws, as if the one was the reflection of the other. They were, to Rosa's eyes, a study in opposites for their clothing: Archer wore black that must be very warm in the window's sunshine.

His skin absorbed that kind light until it seemed burnished gold beneath its darkness, and his cravat stood as fiercely starched and pressed as it might be for the most formal of dinners. Elsabeth, in contrast, looked a picture of softness, her white gown dotted with tiny yellow flowers that Rosamund, largely, had embroidered, as she found more joy in making things pretty than did Elsa. A shawl was thrown around her in Elsa's absent way, its fall making the most of showing one shoulder in a manner all the more artful for its genuine artlessness; where the sunlight touched her there, her skin reflected it, all the brighter for the sun's kiss.

Into this still life, Miss Webber, quite suddenly, said, "How quickly you write, Mr Archer. I am sure it is a gift to write so quickly."

The scratch of Archer's pen paused momentarily, then began again. "Not at all, Miss Webber. I believe I write somewhat slowly, for I find I must to maintain an elegant penmanship."

"But you write so attentively," Miss Webber insisted. "Such long letters to your sweet sister. How I miss her! Do tell her how I miss her, Archer. I hope to see her again very soon; you must tell her that as well. I should never be so good at writing so many letters as you do. You must write very many in the name of business, and I already know how attentive you are to your sister. I was delighted last night to hear you tell of how she has improved at the piano. She was already so very good; I am quite eager to hear her play again. You must tell her that as well."

During this monologue, Archer continued to write as if Miss Webber did not speak, and Elsabeth, to Rosa's view, stared rather fixedly at her page. At this last, however, she could no longer contain herself, and looked up with a smile so sweet that Rosa feared what would pass her lips.

"Miss Webber," Elsabeth said in tones of such admiration that even Rosa's kind-heartedness could not mistake them for anything other than pointed, "you are so wonderfully thoughtful toward Miss Archer that I am quite desperate to meet her myself. I cannot help but wonder that you do not write to her yourself, to express your raptures in your own words, rather than urge Mr Archer to take your dictation."

A faint pink blush appeared along Miss Webber's cheekbones. "I would, save that my pen is dull."

Mr Webber looked up in surprise. "Why, Julia, but you take such pride in sharpening your own pens. Surely, that cannot stop you."

Elsabeth's mouth twitched. She returned her gaze to her book, and Rosamund, dismayed, sought refuge in looking to the fire but could not long keep her attention there: Miss Webber's falsely gay laugh called it back. "You are right, Robert. The truth is that I cannot bear to sit and write knowing how much finer Mr Archer's hand and skill with words are than mine. Instead, I shall call upon Miss Elsabeth to take a turn with me about the parlour. You will, will you not, Miss Elsabeth? If you can be torn from your book. Such an obsession with words you share with Mr Archer!"

"I am sure I share very little with Mr Archer." Elsabeth obligingly put her book aside to rise as Miss Webber did. Miss Webber immediately put her arm through Elsa's, and together they paced the length and breadth of the parlour, pausing only for Miss Webber to invite Rosamund to join them and for Rosamund to decline with a smile.

"Do not be foolish, Julia," Mr Webber said. "Miss Dover is only barely recovered from her illness. She cannot expend her energy in such a manner."

"No, of course not. How silly I am. Perhaps you will join us, Mr Archer."

This was said as they passed Archer, who paused again in his writing and this time paid some slight attention to the young ladies as they paraded. "I think not," he replied after a moment's consideration. "I have seen Miss Elsabeth walk, and suspect that she may have something competitive in her nature; given one such as myself to match herself against, I fear that would not only match but outstrip me in pace and stamina, and I should be quite ashamed. It is better that I allow you to pursue your idle entertainments while I pursue mine, and no one shall be considered better than another."

"Indeed, Mr Archer," Elsa said so archly that Rosamund again feared what next she might say, and found herself in the midst of a coughing fit that slew all chance of Elsa making inopportune remarks. Elsa rushed to her side, Mr Webber fetched more tea and Miss Webber returned to her chair with an unbecoming squint toward the Dover sisters.

It was as well that Miss Dover had been taken by such a cough, Archer felt; he had very little doubt that Miss Elsabeth would have pursued his statement that not one of them should be considered better than another. He had meant, of course, in the game of walking, and yet could see that he had placed himself in a compromising position regarding their unequal stations in life. He could not, certainly, have apologised for his earlier disdain of her lower situation, nor did it feel at all comfortable to him to even imagine doing so. And yet there could be no other reason for him to broach the topic at all. It made him deeply uncomfortable, for a woman with a mother and younger sisters such as Elsabeth Dover had could not be suitable, never minding that the family as a whole was too poor to be considered. He ought not think of her at all, and yet the mud stains on her skirt—now thoroughly washed out, he noted—and the freedom with which she had spun on the road, would not leave his mind.

He watched, pen set aside, as Elsabeth begged leave to take Rosamund back to her room, for it was clear the elder sister had undergone too much excitement for the afternoon and once more needed to rest in order to be certain that her illness would not return. They were given leave, with Webber full of concern, Miss Webber narrow-eyed and Rosamund Dover departing on a too-observant glance toward Archer himself.

"I am quite well," that lady insisted privately to her sister as they navigated the broad shallow steps of Newbury Manor. "Elsabeth, what *were* you about to say to Mr Archer?"

"Only that it was certainly too late for anyone to forgive a matter of established stature," Elsabeth replied without pity.

"Miss Webber's fears that he may harbor some interest in me are so risible as to be worth playing to, but the man himself has made it quite clear that station lies above all for him. Did you see how very black his suit was, Rosa? At two in the afternoon! Whereas your Mr Webber has the exquisite taste to wear a very handsome blue, marking himself as a pleasant fellow not determined to be dour on all accounts."

"Perhaps you ought to forgive Mr Archer a little," Rosamund ventured as she was tucked back into bed. "I do believe he meant to make an apology, Elsa, and I was dreadfully afraid that you would respond in such a manner as to turn him away from you forever."

"Rosamund Dover!" Elsabeth stood, no longer straightening blankets or arranging pillows. "Do you mean to say you manufactured that cough to save me from myself? How devious of you! I believe Miss Webber is providing ill influence, and you have hardly seen her! You must be brought home at once," she said merrily, "else by the time you are well, you shall be as inclined toward machinations and matchmaking as Mamma! But never fear. If Mr Archer truly wishes to apologise for being abhorrent, I shall listen, for I confess he *is* very handsome."

"And very rich," Rosamund put in with as much slyness her sweet soul had available, which brought a laugh to Elsa's lips.

"Yes, and very rich, and possessed, according to Miss Webber, of an excellent penmanship and a fondness for books." Elsa could not help another laugh: laid out so, Archer's good aspects seemed very appealing indeed. "Very well, you may almost convince me that he is nearly perfect, save for snobbery, and it is the last that makes me unable to imagine that he might be moved to offer an apology. I am nothing to him, nor do I wish to be. You shall marry Mr Webber and I will be your happy spinster sister, living on your kindness and making certain your servants don't take advantage of your generosity, as they will no doubt be inclined to do. Now, because you were so wicked as to cough falsely so I would not say something unretractable, I shall cruelly leave you to rest for a few hours and return home to collect a dress or two more suitable for dinner than that which we have with us. You must rest," Elsa said in her best attempt at scolding, "and idle away the time until I return."

"I shall try not to relapse," Rosa promised solemnly, and nestled into a smiling sleep as Elsabeth took her leave.

(15)

Miss Webber was quite horrified at Elsabeth's stated intention of walking home for the afternoon, though not quite horrified enough to offer use of the Webber carriage. Mr Webber, who might well have done, was not within the drawing room when Elsabeth paused to announce her plans; nor was Mr Archer. This was pleasing to Elsabeth, who regarded Rosamund's opinion of Archer's apology attempts as nonsensical, and yet, having half-argued herself into acknowledging his appeal, did not wish to involve herself with the gentleman in any more conversation than absolutely necessary, in case Rosa was right. It was therefore with a light and happy heart that Elsa struck off down the drive and thence, as soon as the Newsbury walls fell away, across the fields toward her own home. It had been some days since she had taken exercise, and felt its lack keenly: to be out in the wind and air refreshed her in a way that nothing else could, even the delight of dancing at a ball.

There had been little rain since the downpour that had brought on Rosamund's illness. Now the green fields were dusted with loosening dirt, and the sky, relentlessly blue, let sun pour onto Elsa's shoulders until the heat was enough to make her breathless. She did not need the coat she wore, but neither did she want the burn that would come if she removed it, and so she hurried along, smiling into the wind and at the dusty horizon. It seemed that she could pour some of the warmth from her walk into magic and thus cool herself, and only mindfulness of Rosa's tantalisingly close future kept her from doing so. She was as alone as one could be in the countryside, but even so, there might be company over the next rise, or some idle farmer watching from a distance behind her. It would never do to risk Rosa's happiness on a moment's playfulness, even if her walk was so vigourous as to dampen her hairline and cheeks.

So intent was she upon her own walk, and so determined to do nothing unwise, that Fitzgerald Archer was quite upon her before she saw him at all. His path was at angles to hers, determined, it seemed, that they should meet: Elsa stopped where she was, standing surprised in soft dirt and grass, as the gentleman strode along the crest of a rise at such a pace as to meet her.

It had not been his intention when he left Newsbury; indeed, it could not have been, as Elsabeth had not yet made clear her own plans to leave the manor. Archer could not, though, say that Miss Elsabeth had not been his inspiration to walk; Miss Webber had called attention to Miss Elsabeth's proclivities toward the exercise in her insistence that the ladies wander the room together, and, upon Miss Elsabeth's departure with Miss Dover, Archer had felt it necessary to take some air himself. Certainly, if he had said as much to Miss Webber, she *would* have offered the carriage to Miss Elsabeth, but he had not, only excusing himself with the bare necessaries of politeness before departing.

He did not break stride, seeing her stop; after a moment, Elsabeth was obliged to carry on, as there was nowhere else for her to go. Within minutes, they met, Archer bowing shortly and Elsabeth curtseying just as briefly. "Forgive me," Archer said. "I had not meant to intrude upon your walk."

"Nor I upon yours. Now we must decide, Mr Archer, whether we are to pretend we are not acquainted and must only mumble greetings at one another, or whether we are to walk along together as companions. I understand," Elsabeth said drolly, "that I may be a competitive spirit, and as such may drive you into your grave with the pace of my walk. I should not like to be regarded as responsible for your doom, so if you prefer to pretend you do not know me, I shall continue on down this hill and you may carry on across it."

"Ah." Archer looked the length of the rise, which was unremarkable in comparison to any other around them. There were no especial landmarks to be seen; no houses save the ordinary, no lakes or rivers or copses that might mark where they stood in the countryside. "The truth is, Miss Elsabeth, that while I can return to Newsbury by retracing my footsteps, I am a man who is loath to retread territory I have already explored. But that said, I do not know these lands well enough to wander on my own and be certain of finding my way home again. If I can promise that my heart is hale and my wind unlikely to be broken by a strenuous pace, perhaps I might walk with you so far as a road, whence you might direct me home again?"

"Will the sun not tell you where you are?" Elsabeth asked, but nodded an agreement. "I'm afraid we will be very nearly at Oakden before I can set you on a road again, but you will at least know your way from there."

Archer glanced at the sun as if it had betrayed him, but fell into step with Elsabeth in a distinctly non-companionable way: his hands were held behind his back and his gaze was fixed on the uneven earth before them. As he did not feel pressed to make conversation, neither did Elsabeth, and within a few minutes, she was all but able to forget he walked a few steps behind her. The urge to bring wisps of fire to life came upon her again, and, thinking of his inevitable horror, she laughed as they came close to her father's lands. Archer hurried the handful of steps to catch up, a curious "Miss Elsabeth?" accompanying the rush.

"A frivolous thought, Mr Archer. I fear I'm plagued with them, and yet I hate to be considered silly, so I dare not speak them."

"You seem entirely too certain of yourself for anyone to think you silly, Miss Elsabeth, if you will forgive me saying so."

"I should rather be thought sure of myself than foolish," Elsabeth replied with a certain degree of satisfaction. "Now, look, here is Oakden, and—oh! Sophia comes to visit. Have you met Miss Enton, Mr Archer? I shall introduce you. Sophia! *Sophia*!" Elsabeth raised her voice in an entirely unladylike fashion and waved wildly until Sophia Enton, approaching the Oakden gates, turned to see Elsabeth Dover and Fitzgerald Archer crossing stepping stones over the stream that ran close to the Oakden house. Elsabeth outpaced Archer by some distance to reach and hug her friend, who returned the embrace with astonishment.

"Did you hear already? Is that why you've come home so quickly?"

"Hear?" Elsabeth asked in alarm. "Hear what?"

"Leopoldina—oh, dear." Sophia froze whatever she had to say on her lips and curtsied to Archer as he joined them.

Elsabeth, afire with curiosity, introduced them unnecessarily—Archer remembered Miss Enton and bowed over her hand more gallantly than Elsabeth might have expected—and seized Sophia's hand as if to squeeze news from her. "What of Dina, Sophia? What has happened?"

"Oh, Elsa. A summer storm struck Bodton this afternoon, a terrible sudden storm. Dina was nearly washed away. She *was* washed away, Elsa! Pulled into the river, and only through the good graces and swift actions of a Captain Hartnell was she saved!"

Elsa paled quite dramatically, so that Sophia was obliged to support her. More surprisingly, so too did Archer, though even as he did so, his customary stiffness returned. "A Captain *David* Hartnell, perchance?"

"Indeed!" cried Sophia. "The very same! Do you know him, sir? He is the hero of the hour, and even now has been welcomed to Oakden as Leopoldina's saviour!"

"I should leave you at once," Archer said to Elsa. "You will want to attend to your sister. I am acquainted with Captain Hartnell and am certain he will be relentlessly charming. Miss Enton, it has been a pleasure to renew our acquaintance. I am sure you too have come to view Hartnell."

"Not at all," Sophia replied in surprise. "Mamma has sent me to ask after Rosamund. If she is well enough, Mamma hopes to call upon the Webbers tomorrow afternoon. I am to look my best," she said with a faint smile. "As if at my best, I might draw any man's eye from Rosamund to myself."

Though in the midst of extracting himself for departure, Archer said, suddenly enough to surprise all of them, "Perhaps your mother would be satisfied if you were to join us for dinner tonight. If Miss Dover is well enough to join us, I'm sure she would be pleased to see you, and if she is not, you will keep the table lively with new thoughts and opinions."

Elsabeth, still leaning on Sophia, could not keep her eyebrows in place: they rose in surprise, and when Sophia met her gaze, her eyes rounded in question, Elsabeth allowed herself a tiny nod. "Please, yes, Sophia, though I am astonished that Mr Archer is so willing to surround himself with country opinions."

"Perhaps I am learning to find them refreshing," Archer replied.

"I have no time to return home to dress suitably," Sophia protested. "I fear I must decline."

Archer examined her quickly and carefully. "No, I think not. You are a little taller than Miss Webber, but I am sure with a hem let out, one of her gowns would fit you, and would be most becoming. Please, Miss Enton, we would all enjoy your company very much."

Sophia cast a second, slightly more alarmed, look toward Elsabeth, but Elsa only smiled, a startling hope blooming in her chest. Archer might be intolerable, but she could quite easily learn to tolerate him should he have the uncommonly good sense to fall in love with Miss Enton. "You must, Sophia," she said with newly blossomed enthusiasm. "Rosamund would be delighted, and you will never meet a more nicely mannered man than Mr Webber. You will be most welcome there, I am sure, and I should myself be grateful to see a friendly face for a few hours, especially if I must leave Leopoldina behind after her own frightening adventures."

"Very good," Archer said. "I will go to Newsbury and inform

them of another guest for dinner, and ask Miss Webber if one of her gowns might be borrowed. All will be ready for you when you arrive." He bowed to both young women, then strode off, leaving a bemused pair of young ladies behind.

"Are we very sure he's the same gentleman as we met at the ball?" Sophia asked when he was out of earshot, but Elsabeth cried aloud, casting the question away. "A summer storm, Sophia?"

A sigh trembled from Sophia's lips. "I could hardly say anything else in front of Mr Archer, could I? And perhaps that's all it was. Surely no one will think otherwise. How could they? Oh, you had better go see her, Elsabeth. You are the only one who might speak sense to the girl."

(16)

Elsabeth entered the Dover drawing room still supported by Sophia's strength, and, standing within the doorway, was struck with the sense of being a stranger to the chaos of the family. It was a profoundly varied group within the room's four handsomely papered walls: Leopoldina lay dramatically across the lounge, looking robust and strong despite the dampness of her hair. Tildy, always her younger sister's shadow, stood behind the lounge in a very prettily embroidered gown that Elsa was certain she had not been wearing earlier, and yet appeared to go unnoticed in the business of the room. Ruth, pinch-faced and pale, sat to one side with such rigid posture as to appear accusatory as Mrs Dover darted around like a plump butterfly, tending to her beloved youngest's swoon while maintaining a chatter swifter and more full of commentary than a squirrel's. Mr Dover also stood to one side, but unlike Ruth, he seemed the picture of health, a vigourous man of a certain age. If only Rosamund, fragile and delicate creature that she was, could be added to the room, then it would be as broad a spectrum of human condition as could possibly be seen within one family.

At the heart of all this bustle was a young gentleman whom Elsa had never before seen: clearly Captain Hartnell, whom Sophia had failed to describe as angelically handsome. He, too, was damp beneath his woolen coat, and held a cup of steaming tea as if it were all that warmed him, though his delighted smile suggested he found as much warmth in the family as the tea. Upon seeing Elsabeth, he set the tea aside and sprang to his feet, crying out, "And this must be Miss Dover, though I had not expected to see her, having heard tales of her illness."

"Not at all, sir," Elsa said in surprise. "I am only Miss Elsabeth, and cannot imagine why you thought me to be Rosamund."

"Oh," Hartnell replied, and for a moment, they were subjected to the proper method of introductions before he explained himself by saying, "Forgive me, Miss Elsabeth, but I have been told quite extensively already that Miss Dover is considered the fairest of the Dover daughters, and I could not imagine a creature more lovely than the one who graced the doorway when I spoke."

Sophia breathed, "Oh, my," in amusement and released Elsabeth to embrace Mrs Dover and show concern for Leopoldina, whose gaze fell unforgiving on Elsabeth for a moment. She, amused, did not notice, instead assuring Captain Hartnell that Rosamund was considerably fairer than she, though she thanked him for his generosity and for his gallantry. "I am given to understand that, without you, I might be in mourning for a beloved sister now. We cannot thank you enough, Captain Hartnell."

"You need not. Any man confident of his swimming might have done the same; I was only the first one on hand."

"I belong to him now," Dina murmured dreamily. "Is that not true? When a life is saved, it belongs to the one who saved it? I could not have been so lucky to have been saved by anyone else so worthy of holding my life in his hands."

"It is a curious notion," Ruth put forth. "Surely our lives belong to the Almighty, who sees fit to arrange them as they are most needed. One human being cannot hold another's life in his hands. Think of all the lives a doctor would own, then. Would that not be akin to slavery, if a saved life belongs to the saviour? If the one saved must do with her life as her saviour commands?"

"I should gladly do anything Captain Hartnell commands!" cried Dina, at which statement Mr Dover felt it necessary to engage in the conversation before it grew dangerously out of hand. "Surely, in the case of young, foolish daughters, it is not the young lady whose life is her saviour's to command, but her father's. Our gratitude knows no bounds, Captain Hartnell, and I hope I might welcome you to my home as a son."

"You are all too, too kind." Hartnell beamed around at the gathered family, including Sophia Enton in his compassion. "Truly, I have done nothing more than my duty, and am only glad to have been of service. I must return to my regiment now that I am certain all is well with Miss Leopoldina, as Colonel White will be wondering what has become of me."

"Oh! You are of the Colonel's regiment! Nothing could be better!" For a young lady so nearly drowned, Dina showed no sign of her spirits being diminished. "We shall have a ball very soon, Captain Hartnell, and all the regiment must come! *You* must come, and I must dance with you at least twice! I could do nothing less for the officer who saved my life!"

Hartnell placed a hand over his heart. "I can think of nothing I would like more. Only name the day and we shall attend. I must away now," he announced again, regretfully, and caught Elsabeth's gaze with his own. "Perhaps I might return in a day or two to attend the ladies of the house and perhaps walk in the garden if it is fine and everyone is well?"

"Tomorrow," Mrs Dover said instantly. "I am sure Dina will be entirely well by then—"

"I am well now! I can walk now!"

"But Captain Hartnell cannot," Elsabeth said gently to her sister. "He must return to his duties, Dina."

"Fie upon his duties! Am I not—" Leopoldina's eyes widened as Mr Dover turned a sharp gaze upon her. She sank into the lounge with a shiver, whispering, "Perhaps I am not so well after all," and commenced to swoon. Both Mrs Dover and Tildy shrieked while Ruth looked increasingly prim and the remaining participants in the scene, Sophia and Hartnell included, exchanged faintly embarrassed, wry smiles at the performance being put on for their sakes. Elsabeth opened the door, permitting Captain Hartnell to pass, although he objected that she should open it for him and not the other way around; Mr Dover solved the problem by putting a hand on the door himself and allowing them both to exit.

"Forgive Dina," Elsabeth implored as, with Mr Dover trailing behind, she showed Captain Hartnell to the door. "She is young and impulsive and often acts without thinking."

"I am tremendously glad she did today," Hartnell announced. "It permitted me to meet you, Miss Elsabeth, and I can think of no more delightful acquaintance to make early in my assignment to Bodton. I hope it was not forward of me to invite myself to visit again. I should like to make certain your sister is well and to renew our acquaintance."

"It is not forward at all," Elsabeth said warmly. "You may have to return once or twice to see me again, though, as I am attending my older sister in her illness at Newsbury Manor, and do not expect to be back for another day or two."

"What a dreadful thing to face, many visits with your charming family," Hartnell said so solemnly that Elsabeth laughed. "There! I shall leave with that memory, of your laughter, and nothing could make me happier. Good afternoon, Miss Elsabeth. I shall hope for your sister's swift recovery and that we shall see one another again soon."

Archer had certainly been right, Elsabeth concluded as Hartnell departed: the captain was strikingly charming, and warmed all their hearts. Archer had not seemed to approve of that, but despite Mr Webber's easy manners, it did not appear that Archer approved much at all of charm in general; it was no surprise that he seemed disinclined to like Hartnell, although it was something of a mystery that the gentleman knew the soldier at all.

Mr Dover waited for Elsa with a genial smile as she turned away from the door. "I believe you have a conquest there, my dear."

"I believe Leopoldina may be upset with me if that's true," Elsa replied.

"Yes, but she is still only a child, and you would be a far

more suitable match for a young man of his age. Now—" Mr Dover tucked his arm through Elsa's and escorted her back to the drawing room, where he lifted his voice to be heard above the furor. "Since we are already in a flutter, I may as well add a little to the pot. On Sunday, Mrs Dover, I hope that you will have an especially fine dinner for us, as we will have a guest: Mr Reginald Cox, who has lately written me a very pretty letter and will come to visit."

Silence met this remark before Mrs Dover's shrieking protest broke it: "Mr Reginald Cox, that dreadful man who will inherit Oakden when you are dead? The beast who can turn us out at any moment once the estate is his? No! I will not have it! I will not have him in this house!"

Even as she protested, Dina recovered from her swoon to gaze with at her father with interest. "Another gentleman at Oakden?"

"He is a pastor, Dina," Ruth said quickly. "You could not possibly be interested in such a dull fellow."

"There is no knowing that he is dull," protested Tildy. "Why, I have heard sermons that must allow a fiery heart in the speaker! Perhaps he will be splendid."

"He cannot possibly be splendid!" cried Mrs Dover. "He is to inherit Oakden, and can be seen only as a cruel interloper!"

"My dear Mrs Dover," said her husband, "I cannot see how you, who bemoan the presence of five daughters and a dearth of eligible men for them almost as constantly as you breathe, can regard this as anything less than an opportunity. If he is suitable, then perhaps a happy match shall be made, and if he is not—"

"If he is not, then I will spend my last days in desperation and fear of being cast out of the home I love so dearly, a widow with no hearth or husband to warm her, and the looming shadow of he who stole it all from us betwixt myself and the sun! No! Eligible or not, I shall not have him here!"

"You will." Mr Dover spoke implacably to his wife, but his regard was for the one woman in his family who had not commented on the topic of Mr Cox or his eligibility, and found in Elsabeth's eyes a soft concern, and spoke to that. "You will, for he is already invited, and though I have no reason to expect that I should be supplanted sooner rather than later, I am most curious to see what manner of man shall follow in my place."

(17)

Mrs Dover's distress at the impending arrival of one Mr Reginald Cox caused her to forget herself, which in turn permitted Elsabeth to make use of the Dover carriage for her return to Newsbury, a use for which Miss Sophia Enton was particularly grateful. It was not that Sophia lacked the strength or stamina to make the walk, but rather that she was already far too aware that she lacked beauty and did not want to compound her plainness by arriving at Newsbury Manor flushed and damp from a vigourous walk. Elsabeth, who on this one topic was very like her sister Rosamund, could never be convinced of Sophia's plainness, and *tish*ed at her friend's concerns, but neither was she dismayed to have the use of the carriage for their return. Among other things, the driver's presence made inappropriate discussing Leopoldina's wild behaviour and, as Elsabeth was not yet prepared to consider, much less face, the consequences of her youngest sister's actions, this was a great relief to her.

"We shall have to tell Rosamund," Elsabeth concluded after an unusually grim and silent journey. "I am loath to do so for fear of forcing her into relapse, but how much worse if she should hear it from someone else. Surely, Mr Archer will have had the good sense to hold his tongue"—which was a comment made more in hope than confidence.

"Mr Archer will have said no more than that he has invited

another to dinner," Sophia said with such stout conviction that Elsabeth felt inclined to believe her. "I am very nervous, Elsa," Sophia confessed more quietly and quite suddenly. "What if Miss Webber has not a dress she is willing to lend? I will be dreadfully out of place and an embarrassment to you and Rosamund. I wish that I did not tower over the rest of you so; I should have been more confident in one of your gowns, Elsabeth."

"And we should all have been scandalised at the sight of your ankles. Sophia, you could never embarrass either of us, and Mr Webber is himself the absolute soul of kindness. Even if Miss Webber has not seen fit to have a dress prepared, Mr Webber will make you feel like the finest lady at the ball; I am certain of this."

Sophia still entered Newsbury Manor with the air of a supplicant, too afeared to present herself in any other way. She was, however, greeted handsomely by both Webber and Archer, and when Miss Webber appeared, it was with a sudden stop and a long gaze for Sophia, who fought to keep her hands from twisting in her skirts. "Well," Miss Webber announced after their introduction, "I can see that I have chosen entirely the wrong colour for our guest. Miss Enton, please ignore the gown that has already been sent to Miss Dover's room. I shall have another, more suitable one sent immediately."

Elsabeth, suspecting a jape, bristled beneath but kept a smile in place while Sophia blushed uncertainly and thanked Miss Webber with a humbleness that would please even the most discerning audience. "I must see Rosamund," Elsa said after these offers and thanks were done, and together the young ladies went to the eldest Miss Dover's room.

Rosamund was awake and examining not one but two gowns sent by Miss Webber. One was softly pink and entirely appropriate for Rosa herself; the other was of strong marigold and perhaps the most dreadful choice for Sophia's skin tones that could be made without deliberately intending to present her at her worst. Elsa said, "Oh, no," in honest dismay.

Even as she spoke, a knock sounded at the door and a maid

entered bearing a satin gown of puce with expensively dyed blue lace as trim. It was as perfectly suited to Sophia as the other was badly; for a moment, all three young ladies simply gazed at it, until Sophia echoed Elsa's words: "Oh, no. No, I couldn't...I'm sure I couldn't..."

"But you must," Elsabeth said joyfully, "for you would hardly wish to insult our hostess. Oh, and you must wear the pink, Rosa; it is far more suitable than anything I have brought."

"You," Rosa opined, "should wear the marigold, Elsabeth; it is also no doubt more suitable than anything you brought, and while the colour would do Sophia no favours, I believe it would be very kind to you."

"Not at all. I shall be the wallflower, the better to compare two such fetching ladies as yourselves to." And so saying, Elsabeth chose her own gown, a simple and pretty thing of white with deftly made trim, and allowed the maid to pin up her hair in a simple fashion no doubt more suitable to a country dinner than a manor house meal. She was not an embarrassment; that was sufficient, when Rosamund glowed healthily in the pink and looked large-eyed and lovely from under a cascade of gold curls that fell beautifully around her cheeks. Sophia's hair was done more extravagantly, as suited the gown; once its stubborn straightness had been teased into curls, it was adorned with a headdress of feathers that sent her already remarkable height to a soaring presence.

Rosamund, in smiling admiration, murmured, "Sophia, I have never seen you look so well," and Elsabeth, who could never see Sophia's plainness for herself, could do no less than agree. The puce gown sank recklessly low over Sophia's shoulders, exposing an unexpectedly attractive width to them, and cupped lower than that across her bosom, until the eye could not help but be enticed by its rise and fall. The skirt had not been let out; instead, Miss Webber had provided a petticoat in the same blue as the gown's lace, and it gave length to the ensemble as well as bringing the colours together. Gloves of the same hue rose high on Sophia's arms, but were not gartered: her arms were too well-formed to deny the gloves their chance to slip a little and expose their flesh to the interested eye.

Mr Archer, Elsabeth concluded with nothing less than delight, would be entirely taken with Sophia's new presentation. Elsabeth herself might be obliged to revise her opinion of Miss Webber, whom she would not have imagined bedecking a potential rival in such a fetching fashion. "Your mother has been going about presenting you entirely wrongly, Sophia," Elsabeth announced. "It seems she has been trying to make you smaller and more like her, when she ought to have been celebrating your natural aspects to great advantage. You are positively breathtaking."

"I almost think I am," Sophia said in wonder, examining herself in a mirror. "I must thank Miss Webber again."

"We all must." Rosamund tucked her arms into Elsabeth's and Sophia's. "Let us go do that very thing, for I am sure nothing will give her more joy than seeing us looking so well in her gowns. You ought to have worn the marigold, Elsa."

"She sent it for Sophia, however mistakenly," Elsabeth replied placidly. "It would have been bold to take it for myself. I am quite satisfied as I am, and have no doubt Miss Webber will be satisfied with me as well."

Indeed, it was as well Elsabeth had not taken the marigold, for upon their arrival in the dining hall, it proved that Miss Webber herself had chosen an orange that lay too close to the marigold for comfort; Elsa would have seemed to be competing with her, and the colour suited Miss Webber more than it ever could Elsabeth. For a mean moment, Elsa wondered if Miss Webber *had* hoped Elsabeth would wear it, then remembered that it had first been meant for Sophia, and was then certain that Miss Webber had intended herself to look finer by far in a similar shade when the unexpected guest came to the table. Why, then, Miss Webber had chosen a new gown for Sophia was beyond Elsa's estimation, but to her surprise and delight, Miss Webber gave a glad cry upon seeing Sophia and came toward her with hands extended. "Oh, I was right! This is so much more suitable to you, Miss Enton! You would turn every head in London!"

Sophia, blushing with pleasure, accepted Miss Webber's happy embrace, and Elsabeth saw how well the colours they wore complemented the other: entwined together, they seemed a complex and layered bloom.

"Now," Miss Webber said, "Archer has quite unbalanced our table, Miss Enton, and so I must beg you to accept my escort to the dining room, as we simply do not have enough gentlemen to go around."

"Of course," Sophia said, still blushing, and so, to her own astonishment, Elsabeth found herself on Archer's arm, and warmed to him momentarily as he murmured, "Miss Enton cuts a striking figure, does she not? I had not imagined she would look so regal."

"I have always known Sophia was magnificent," Elsabeth replied with a certain proprietary pride. "I am pleased you have the eyes to see it, Mr. Archer."

"Indeed, I think any man should." Archer brought Elsabeth to her seat and took his own before saying, "But forgive me; I am remiss in asking after your sister's welfare. I trust she is none the worse for her adventures?"

Rosamund looked toward them, alarmed. "Sister? Adventure? What has Leopoldina done now?"

Dismay replaced Elsabeth's pleasure as she realised that in the excitement of dressing, they had forgotten entirely to tell Rosamund of Dina's misadventures. Archer, however, found her insight amusing. "Is it always Miss Leopoldina who has adventures, then?"

"Usually," Elsa said somewhat more dourly than Archer's tone called for. "She is quite well, Rosamund; there is no call for worry."

"But what has happened?" Rosamund's colour had faded, concern shaking her voice. Wishing she had spoken earlier, Elsa said, "She had a mishap with the river, nothing more. A gallant army captain saved her, and I believe Dina regards the entire escapade as nothing more than the correct amount of excitement in her life. It would not have slipped my mind if she had been in any real danger, Rosa, I promise you."

The audacity of this falsehood was such that Elsabeth did not dare look at Sophia, but Rosamund's colour slowly returned, and, after pressing Elsabeth for a detail or two, she was prepared to continue her conversation with Mr Webber. Only then did Elsabeth glance toward Sophia, but Miss Enton was as engaged with her own Webber as was Rosa. Archer, observing this, said, "It appears we shall be forced to converse with one another, Miss Elsabeth, or eat our dinner in flawless silence."

"Very little is flawless, Mr Archer," Elsabeth replied with an absent-minded asperity, "and given the inevitable clink of glass and tableware, I can hardly imagine how dinner might be conducted in such an enviable quiet."

"Perhaps we must try," Archer said, and proceeded to eat with such soundless perfection that it was only in the final course that Elsabeth, whose own idle commentary had achieved not a single response from Archer, finally realised she was being mocked. Of the three Bodton ladies, then, she was the only one to retire from the evening meal less than wholly pleased with it: Rosamund had been sweetly courted by Webber the entire time, and Sophia had never before been so animated as she was in conversation with Miss Webber. It would not trouble her, Elsabeth decided, to quit Newsbury Manor as soon as Rosamund was well enough; had she not sent the carriage home already, she might even have pressed to leave that very evening.

But it was not to be; Rosamund, though stronger, was still prepared to retire early, and Sophia, though reluctant, felt that she must return home once Rosamund had said her good-nights.

Archer, finally breaking his silence on Sophia's behalf, said, "Not at all, Miss Enton. Did you not say your mother hoped to call on Newsbury Manor tomorrow if Miss Dover was well enough? Surely, she would never demand you leave us so early, when you are within the very arms of those she most wishes to acquaint you with. Tell me, Miss Elsabeth, do you play the pianoforte?"

Elsabeth, looking longingly toward a book, replied, "Poorly, Mr Archer, but my singing voice is worse," before wishing she was not quite so prone to honesty.

"We shall look elsewhere for the evening's entertainment, then," he said with no hint of his own amusement. "Miss Enton? I know Miss Webber is most accomplished"—a phrase rolled out so drily that even Elsabeth suspected him of drollness—"but no doubt she would prefer an evening's rest herself, so often do we call on her for music of one kind or another."

As Miss Webber had neither sung nor played anything but cards in the nights Elsabeth had been at Newsbury Manor, she found this remark unlikely, but, reminding herself of her intentions for Archer and Sophia, put forth, "Sophia is too shy to confess to it, but her voice is quite beautiful. She is often singled out as the richest voice in our choir."

"Then she must sing, if she will," Archer said, and before Sophia could protest, Miss Webber sat at the pianoforte, crying out, "And I shall play! What shall we have, Miss Enton? Surely we must have a piece or two in common."

"I believe that leaves us obliged to dance," Archer said to Elsabeth, a comment she did not deign worthy of noticing, much less replying to, until he said, "Or do you not enjoy dancing, Miss Elsabeth?"

Astonished that he should pursue the topic, Elsabeth turned a gaze she knew to be cool upon him. "I believe you have made it quite plain that *you* do not, Mr Archer, and I should never wish to put out my host in such a dreadful fashion as to engage him in activities he does not care for. We will be quite sufficiently entertained by Sophia's singing and Miss Webber's playing, I am sure." She sat and gathered her book, though she had no intention of reading it, and from then on paid steadfast attention to the musicians.

She could not, therefore, be aware that Archer's gaze lingered on her rather more than on the performers; nor could she know that in the recesses of his heart, he recognised that he had quite deserved her dismissal. It was, nonetheless, an unaccustomed recognition, and beneath it began to bloom the slow realisation that he was increasingly inclined to admire Miss Elsabeth, which sentiment could lead nowhere suitable. Determined to put it out of his mind, he turned his attention to Miss Enton, who was, of course, only barely more suitable than Miss Elsabeth, and then finally to Miss Webber, whose suitability was without question.

He did not notice the gradual sinking of his enthusiasm as he looked upon Miss Webber, nor, in time, that his attention drifted back to Miss Elsabeth, upon whom he gazed, unmolested by a return of awareness, for the remainder of the evening.

(18)

"I believe Miss Dover and Miss Elsabeth ought to stay another few days," Webber proclaimed over breakfast the following morning. Neither Dover sister had joined them; Elsa had sent down a note stating that Rosamund had been taxed by the previous evening's festivities and required more rest, and that she, Elsabeth, was not hungry and would therefore remain with her sister. Moreover, Miss Webber, never an early riser, had not yet joined them, and it was therefore with impunity that Webber made his observation to Archer.

"If Miss Dover is well enough to dine with us, certainly she will be well enough to travel home in a carriage this afternoon," Archer replied thoughtlessly, then lowered his tea to examine his friend. "Or are you less concerned with her welfare and more with your own, Robert?"

"Oh, both, I'm sure," Webber replied cheerfully. He was not entirely insensible to the attention Archer had paid to Miss Elsabeth the night before, and rather thought that with a few more days in close quarters with her, Archer might be in real danger of falling in love with the second Dover sister. Nothing, from Webber's besotted viewpoint, could possibly be better: the two sisters were clearly dear to one another, and would make certain that they should all be best friends to the grave, if they married so closely.

"You're rash, Webber. You overheard my inquiries regarding the youngest Miss Dover's health yesterday evening, but you do not share the further knowledge on the topic that I possess."

"Well, out with it, man. You can hardly leave me with bated breath when this very excellent marmalade awaits."

"Miss Leopoldina was rescued by David Hartnell."

This piece of intelligence broke the journey of marmalade-laden toast to Webber's eager lips; after a moment, he went so far as to replace the bread on his breakfast plate. "You cannot possibly mean *your* Hartnell, Archer. What on earth would he be doing here?"

"I mean the very one. He has a commission in the army and his regiment is stationed in Bodton; I investigated promptly upon hearing his name."

"Blast it all. Does Persephone know?"

"How could she, when I have only learned it last night? No, and neither shall your sister be given to know, else she might be inspired to write Persephone after all, and I do not wish to distress her any further. But you can see that if Hartnell is the sort the Dovers consider appropriate, they must be looked on questionably in all matters."

"Here, now, Archer, is that fair? The man dove into a river to save a drowning girl. Her family should certainly look highly upon him, and perhaps it is a measure of the man, that he has changed for the better. Besides, if you have not shared your wisdom with *them*, how might they possibly know to be wary of him? Have you?"

"Of course not. What could I say that they would not regard as suspect?"

Webber, in the process of taking up his toast a second time, paused again and gave Archer an uncharacteristically shrewd look. "Perhaps nothing, although you might then be obliged to consider why it is that they should receive any information from you as instantly suspicious. Perhaps the parents are too much in need of marriageable husbands for so many daughters to hear you; perhaps the daughter in most danger is too silly to heed, and perhaps Miss Elsabeth is naturally unlikely to listen to a warning from your lips. But Miss Dover is not one to form biases, and would, I think, take any commentary from you most seriously."

"First, I agree that Miss Dover is *not* one to form biases, which suggests that she is no more likely to heed me than any of the others, though her refusal would be out of the goodness of her heart. Second," Archer said, ticking the numbers off on his fingers, "you share that goodwill toward people, else you should not consider the possibility that Hartnell has reformed, a sentiment I do not share. Third, I can say nothing without compromising my own dear sister, which I will not do."

"Instead, you may allow someone else's sister to be compromised," Webber replied, and bit into his toast as if in defiance. "Either speak up, man, or do not condemn Miss Dover's family for what they cannot know."

Archer's eyebrows rose. "I believe affection has made you bold, Robert."

"I should think you found it high past time." Webber finished his toast placidly, and Archer, unable to argue, frowned a long silence at his cooling tea. Once satisfied that his friend could find no answers to be read in its leaves, Webber spoke again. "So, they shall stay a few days longer. Perhaps, in that time, you will find a way to broach the topic of Hartnell. I say, Archer, did you notice how very well my sister got on with that lovely Miss Enton? I do believe I had been introduced to the lady before, but I had not noticed her in nearly such a fine light as she appeared in last night. I hope she will attend the Dovers' ball, and I will be glad to see her stand up with some of the officers, as we had far too few dancers at our own ball."

"She looked very well indeed." Archer downed the last of his cold tea and stood. "The white suited her. Good morning, Robert. I believe I shall take some exercise this morning. It will clear my head."

"Of course," Webber said obligingly, and only after Archer departed did he observe, aloud and with pleasure, "but it was

Miss Elsabeth in white last night, old chap, not Miss Enton. Not Miss Enton at all."

Archer was not insensible to this; his mistake came upon him after he had left the room. Peters, the butler, was the only one to observe how the brooding young lord of Streyfield came to an abrupt halt in the entryway, or how his single sharp, short curse echoed from the entry's high ceilings and hard floors. Discreet as his kind often were, Peters remained nestled in a shadow until the hard clip of Archer's heels clicked across the floor and out the door.

Shortly thereafter, a lady's maid suggested to Miss Elsabeth that the morning was especially fine, and that she could look after Miss Dover a little while if Miss Elsabeth should like to take some air. Rosamund, who was really much recovered, encouraged Elsabeth to go, and in a fit of gladness, Elsa excused herself from the manor with the half-formed intention of walking home and fetching the carriage for Rosa all by herself.

It was something of an unexpected encounter on the parts of both parties, then, when two persons both bent on a healthy excursion rounded opposite corners in the fine Newsbury gardens and nearly stalked headlong into one another. Both stopped with the precision of urgency; Archer put forth a hand to steady Miss Elsabeth, who snatched her own arm away as if he had offered an adder instead. "Mr Archer," she said breathlessly, when she had recovered herself a little. "Forgive me. I did not see you approach."

"Around this hedge? I should think not. Are you well? I thought I might have impacted you."

"I should be flattened on the earth if you had, and I suppose you would only wish that a ballroom full of dancers might be on hand to observe my ignominy if I was."

It seemed very likely that only a handful of days ago, that might have been true, and yet, in the moment, Archer could only say, "Do you think so little of me, Miss Elsabeth?"

"In truth, Mr Archer, when you are out of my sight, I do not think of you at all, which is perhaps a little more often than I might imagine you are inclined to think of me. We each have our pride to attend to, after all."

"I have recently considered that I may attend to mine too greatly."

"Yes," Elsabeth said with a sudden bright smile, "I have considered that you may, as well. But I cannot fault you for that, Mr Archer, for I am sure you have considered the same about me. Our faults lie too closely in alignment for comfort. It is as well that we are soon to be quitted of one another, for my sister is well and I am quite determined that we should return home rather than impose on Mr Webber's goodwill another night."

"Surely, you have only been here a little while," Archer protested. "You cannot leave so soon. Miss Webber would be distressed at the departure of her dear friend Rosamund."

"You need not be so polite, Mr Archer. Miss Webber will go on without us, though I like to think that *Mr* Webber might be bereft at Rosamund's absence, and I myself have no wish to tax you with my presence any longer. If we remain at Newsbury another night, I might be obliged to sing, and it is better for all that no one is subjected to that disturbance. I will walk home now and return with our carriage—"

"I insist that if you must leave, you will use Webber's carriage, and not wear yourself out with the journey to and fro." Determined and somewhat alarmed at his own determination, Archer offered Miss Elsabeth his arm, and felt a sudden shard of concern pierce him when she examined it in mild surprise rather than taking it immediately.

"I believe you know the strength of my constitution and my fondness for walking," she replied, but finally put her hand into the crook of his elbow. "It may be easier to convince Mr Webber for the use of his carriage, though, than to convince my mother, who—" Elsabeth cleared her throat gently, and though she spoke again without hesitation, it still seemed to Archer that she had changed the direction of her words—"who is inclined to believe that young ladies should take their exercise whenever they can, and prefers not to lend us the coach unless she herself expects to be in it as well."

Archer murmured, "Is that how it is?" and thought of what she might have said had she been less discreet. "I had wondered why Miss Dover had arrived on foot, with the weather threatening so badly."

"I believe my mother also expects the weather to behave as she wishes it to," Elsabeth said drily, and herself thought that for Rosamund's walk, the weather *had*, and also that Mrs Dover was unusually fortunate in that the sky at Oakden often *did* behave in just the manner she most wanted.

"We should all be so fortunate," Archer said. "I think, though, that it did not behave in Miss Leopoldina's favour yesterday. Did you meet Captain Hartnell, Miss Elsabeth?"

"A very charming and handsome young man," Elsa replied warmly. "Dina was very lucky that someone with such strong swimming skills was on hand in her moment of need. It is very unusual, is it not? So few people swim well, and I do not imagine a captain in the army has much call to."

"As it happens," Archer began, somewhat less warmly, but before he could continue, Webber appeared on the manor steps to wave vigourously.

"Come along! Miss Dover is convinced that Miss Elsabeth has gone home to fetch the carriage, and I must prove her wrong! Furthermore, I positively insist that they stay at least one more night, as we have not yet truly had the pleasure of Miss Dover's company for the course of a full evening, for fear of tiring her! Three nights," he proclaimed as Archer and Elsabeth climbed the steps. "Three nights would be better."

Elsabeth, thinking longingly of avoiding Miss Webber's prickly presence, and thinking equally of Rosamund's future, smiled prettily and acquiesced with "Two nights, Mr Webber. Two nights, and then we shall be away."

(19)

Two nights were not enough for Mrs Dover's tastes; she would have had her daughters at Newsbury a full two weeks if she could. A week could suffice in a pinch, but to return home after two more nights added up to only six. Hardly enough, even if Rosamund was the prettiest girl in the county; it would take a week to be positive of Mr Webber's affections.

Had Captain Hartnell not attended the Dover family every day the older girls were absent, Mrs Dover would have found the mere six nights to be entirely unbearable. But attend he did, and paid polite, gentlemanly court to all of them, even thin-lipped Ruth, whilst still giving no impression of having a special favourite. After his second visit, Mrs Dover began to harbour a certain suspicion, and if she did not welcome her oldest daughters home with absolutely open arms on the day they finally arrived, neither was she dismayed when Captain Hartnell's handsome face lit in genuine delight at Elsabeth's return.

Elsabeth, having nothing to compare it to, did not see the additional pleasure he shone with; Leopoldina, having several visits for comparison, did. "It is not fair," she said to Tildy as they climbed into bed together that night. "He saved *me*, Tildy. He ought to smile so at *me*."

"He will at the ball," Tildy promised sleepily, and, satisfied, Dina went to sleep and dreamed of dancing.

Those dreams were entirely dashed with dawn's advent, for it was not dancing but bustle that Mrs Dover had in mind. The day had come: it was Sunday at last, and the odious Mr Cox would arrive before supper. The servants had already cleaned, but nothing would do save the house should gleam: Mrs Dover was determined it should be presented in its best light, and only glowered forbiddingly at Elsabeth when she murmured, "Perhaps we ought to be spreading pig muck about, Mamma, in hopes that Mr Cox will be repulsed and give up his inheritance."

Dina laughed, and for her audacity was obliged to whisk a breeze over every surface of the house, carrying speckles of dust out wide-open windows. The servants *had*, of course, done their job: there was little left for magic to accomplish, but whatever could be done was eked out of the daughters three; Ruth, of course, got down on her knees and scrubbed the floor with soap and a brush, and looked disapproving when Tildy gently swept the water out with a word and Dina dried the flagstones with a gesture. Rosamund was not, in Mrs Dover's opinion, enough recovered to risk herself on magic. Elsabeth, pleasantly grateful for any excuse to work with magic, gathered flowers and cleaned the stoop with a whistle as she worked, until Ruth could bear it no more and stood to lecture her equally on the evils of magic and of whistling.

"You are correct," Elsabeth said cheerfully. "With each note that leaves my lips, I no doubt render myself increasingly ineligible for marriage, for which our mamma would not thank me. Unless she would, for my remaining unwed would assure her of someone to care for her in her dotage"—and she lifted her voice enough to make certain both Dover parents would hear her teasing remark.

Sour Ruth, though, already sensitive to the likelihood that she, of all the Dover sisters, was the least likely to wed, thought that Elsa was having unkind fun at her expense, and, to everyone's astonishment, fled the front garden in tears. Even Mr Dover, accustomed to and unworried by the histrionics of his many females, rose from his place at the table to gaze after his middle daughter in concern, and Elsabeth, who had intended to mock herself, gathered her skirts and ran after her sister.

The eldest two Dover girls shared a room, as did the three youngest. Their door was locked when Elsa tried it. Troubled, Elsabeth leaned her cheek and palm against the old polished wood and called, "Ruth? Please let me in."

A hard cry answered her. "As if I could stop you coming in if you wished. What is a locked door to you?"

Elsabeth trailed a fingertip to the lock, but sought no twist or fall of the tumblers. "Very little," she admitted, "but my sister's pride is a great deal. Ruthie, forgive me. I was truly thinking of myself when I spoke. I meant no hurt."

Footsteps fell inside the room, though Ruth's voice remained muffled. "But you are able to laugh about it, Elsabeth, because you know you are in no danger of remaining unmarried. We all know Captain Hartnell admires you greatly."

"Ruth." Elsabeth, struck with a genuine curiosity, murmured, "Would you care for such a man yourself?"

The door she leaned against came open with such suddenness that Elsabeth was obliged to catch herself on the frame lest she fall into Ruth's arms, and Ruth looked of no mind to catch her. Her cheeks were streaked with the evidence of tears, but her colour was high and her gaze incredulous. "Captain Hartnell gives all appearance of being a man of frippery. His greatest ambition seems to be to make you laugh, and he spends an inordinate amount of time polishing his boots. What interest could I have in such a man?"

"He is very handsome," Elsabeth offered tentatively.

"I do not care for handsomeness," Ruth replied with such grandeur that Elsabeth felt foolish for having suggested it. "I am only concerned with character. No, Elsabeth, I am not interested in the Captain Hartnells of the world, and the Mr Webbers would not have me. For one in such a position as ours, there is very little left."

"I did not know you felt so strongly," Elsabeth said quietly.

"You have never cared enough to learn." Ruth shut the door

gently in Elsabeth's face, and did not bother to lock it again.

Nor did Elsabeth try to open it; she merely stood, swaying slightly as she gazed at the painted-over grain, and recognised with dismay that her middle sister was entirely correct. Burdened by that knowledge, she returned to the sitting room, where, house-cleaning abandoned, the whole of her family sat awaiting news of Ruth's condition. Their unusual attentive silence as Elsabeth entered the room caught her tongue, and she could find nothing to say until Mrs Dover, sharply, demanded, "*Well?*"

"She is overwrought," Elsabeth said with a startle. "The excitement of the upcoming ball, no doubt, and Captain Hartnell's visits, and the knowledge of what Mr Cox's position in our lives means. She will be all right in a little while."

Comprehension swept the whole of the Dover family's faces; even Tildy and Dina looked relieved to understand Ruth's outburst. Almost at once, their chatter returned to normal, with Mrs Dover's piping tones rising and falling above them as Mr Dover retreated once more behind his newspapers. Under their prattle, Elsabeth sat beside Rosamund and murmured, "Rosa, did you know that Ruth is unhappy?"

Thoughtful surprise drew a line across Rosamund's forehead. "Yes," she said slowly, "but I have always supposed that being unhappy was what made her happiest. She works so hard at it, after all."

"Yes, but I thought that was only because it's how she is. But it's more than that. She's afraid," Elsa whispered. "As afraid as any of us are, of never marrying, of being a burden, or of being bereft. I never knew."

Nor, from the tender pain that marked Rosamund's face, had she. She made to stand at once, but Elsabeth stopped her with a hand on her arm. "She turned me away. I think perhaps she wishes to be alone now."

"Or perhaps that's what she wants us to believe, and hopes someone will come to her." Rosamund stood after all, departed the sitting room, and returned so swiftly and with such poorly hidden anxiety on her pretty features that Elsabeth knew Ruth had sent her away as well. No one else noticed her distress, and she busied herself with embroidery so that it would remain unremarked-upon.

Ruth did not emerge until Mr Cox's carriage kicked up dust on their drive, and when she did, she looked more severe than usual: her hair, often bound tightly, lay so thin against her skull that Elsabeth was certain the strands were strained to breaking. Her face was no longer flushed with anger's colour, but pinched and white, and her gown, which tended toward conservative in the best of times, had been altered so that a high collar impressed itself against her throat. She did not speak, nor was she spoken to, though Rosamund offered her a hand, and, for the first time Elsabeth could remember, Ruth obliged by coming to sit with her instead of taking a seat where she could grimace disapprovingly at all of them.

Outside, carriage wheels rattled and came to a stop on the drive as horses' hooves stamped a few times, then settled. Mr and Mrs Dover exchanged glances and stood as one, but it was the latter who spoke grimly as they all trooped toward the front doors: "Very well, girls. Let us go to meet our doom."

(20)

If anything was to give hope in Mr Cox's arrival, it was the elegance of his carriage. Painted black and gilded hither and thither, it gleamed in the afternoon light; the inner rims of the wheels, painted red, did not seem to be diminished in colour by the dust of the road. A finely postured driver sat at the front, and a set of four dappled greys spoke of both wealth and speed. Rosamund's hand crept into Elsabeth's and squeezed, and the entire Dover family held their breath with anticipation as they waited for the carriage to disgorge its occupant.

The man who emerged was by no means as elegant as his means of arrival. Tall, but given to a certain softness, he wore a vicar's suit in a size too small, and the broad black hat of his profession sat upon the top of his head as if it had lost a struggle to escape. Rosamund took a small, quiet breath; Leopoldina, at the other end of the line of sisters, was not so discreet, and squeaked with amusement.

Even Mr Dover hesitated, peering into the carriage as if he expected it to issue another, more suitable option as the choice for Reginald Cox. When no one else came forth, Mr Dover stepped forward. "Mr Cox, I am Mr Dover. It is our pleasure to receive you here at Oakden. May I introduce my wife, Mrs Dover?"

Mrs Dover curtsied nicely, then released a surprised trill of laughter as Mr Cox seized her hand and pressed a heavy kiss against it. "Mrs Dover. It is my honour. I have so long wished to visit the lands that will someday be my own."

Mrs Dover's laughter turned directly to a wheeze, almost a cough, and Mr Dover murmured, "How forthright you are, Mr Cox. Such candour is so often lacking in our society. May I introduce my daughters, Miss Dover, Miss Elsabeth, Miss Ruth, Miss Matilda, Miss Leopoldina."

Cox seized Rosamund's hand with as much vigour as he had taken Mrs Dover's, and though she was far too polite to protest, Rosamund sent a brief, wild glance toward Elsabeth, who saw cords stand out in her eldest sister's neck before Cox moved on to her.

His hands were cool but damp; his mouth, fleshy against her skin. Elsabeth had to spread her fingers widely to prevent herself from wiping them against her skirt when Cox released them. Down the line he went, breathing heavily over each girl and smacking his lips together after each sentence as if he had offered a profound proclamation. "Surely it is a danger to have so many daughters of such beauty. God is generous in his gifts but cannot like a father to hoard his women-folk himself; I am sure He intends for each of your daughters to find an honest husband to guide her through her days. Indeed, I can only believe that He has now sent such a man to one of them, through His grace and love."

By this Elsabeth correctly took him to mean he meant to marry one of them; she exchanged a look of alarm with Rosamund and found Mr Dover's eyes on them in an expression of genuine horror. Mrs Dover, with unlikely skill, murmured, "How right you are, Mr Cox, as it seems our dear Rosamund is very soon to be engaged to a gentleman who has been at Newsbury Manor for some weeks now."

"I see," replied Cox, and, wasting no time, fixed his gaze upon Elsabeth. He had not even crossed the threshold yet, she thought with distaste; he might have at least made a pretence of—of what, she did not know. Propriety, perhaps; a pretence of propriety, and not that he had come to a horse market to buy himself a broodmare. As she considered these unpleasant thoughts, Cox, without taking his eyes from Elsabeth, said, "My most beneficent felicitations to you upon the auspice of your impending engagement, Miss Dover. You will not be in my parish, of course, but I should consider myself most fortunate if you were to consider me, your dearest cousin, as the servant of God to speak the marriage vows over you and your intended."

"Oh," Rosamund said faintly, and sent a wide-eyed look toward Elsabeth. "I am sure the offer is most generous, Mr Cox, but I am hardly in a position to be making arrangements yet."

Mrs Dover could not be said to do anything so obvious or crass as wincing, and yet there was something in the shift of her shoulders and tightening of her throat that suggested that she had been struck by a blow. Mr Cox returned his attention to Rosamund so greedily that Elsabeth felt that she had been released from a heavy weight, and wondered that her feet were still firmly pressed to the ground. She might have called the sensation relief, had Mr Cox not at that moment begun a veritable speech to Rosamund. "Of course you cannot yet make such arrangements; I fear that looking too far ahead is both my gift and burden alike. Let me assure you, however, that having recently been graced with a fine parish as a gift from my patroness, the Lady Beatrice Derrington, that I am most utterly suited to perform such ceremonies, and nothing could give me, or, I dare say, the Lady Beatrice, more pleasure than to see a family member well wedded. You will be well wedded, will you not? For I, and I should dare say the Lady Beatrice, could only expect that you will marry well, even far above your station, or I am sure that otherwise you could consider a marriage of equals or"—and he glanced down as if in modesty, save for that his small eyes glittered as he spoke—"to one whose recent fortunes might be said to outstrip your own."

By this time, Mr Dover looked as though he wished very much that he had not invited Mr Cox to stay at Oakden, an expression in which he could indulge himself, for it was clear that Cox would not look away from the daughters Dover unless prodded to do so. Rosamund, whose kind heart would not permit her to be rude to Mr Cox, began a stammering reply, but her father, his face now perfectly schooled, took it upon himself to interrupt her before she might be forced into saying something damning.

"Candid indeed," Mr Dover said. "Mr Cox, we are behaving unconscionably, keeping you standing outdoors after your long journey. Let us retire to the house. There we shall dine and you can tell us more of your patroness. I do not know the Lady Beatrice."

"Oh, she is an extraordinary woman," Cox promised as he was escorted within. "Such generosity, such wisdom, such clear expectations of those in her employ. I will be happy to tell you—oh, but she would not approve of this; it has been some time since Oakden has been updated, has it not? Well, my patroness is an understanding woman, as benefits one of her station and intelligence; she could not expect country cousins to keep up to the standards of London. Still, one might do something about the flagstone here...." His further commentary was lost to the insides of the house as Elsabeth hung back with her sisters and mother, the latter of whom grew pink with indignation.

"Those stones have lain upon the floor at Oakden since it was built!" snapped Mrs Dover. "They are imbued with *history*. Five generations of Dovers or more have walked those floors! How dare he—"

Ruth, unexpectedly, replied, "They *are* worn, Mother," and, with this observation, passed into the house behind Misters Dover and Cox, leaving behind four startled females.

Mrs Dover, after a moment's silence, continued on almost as if Ruth had not spoken. "And certainly they should be a little worn, after decades of service. Why, if everything was to be replaced the moment it showed a little wear, how might we ever dress ourselves? We are not so fine as to buy new gowns when a thread loosens or a stain appears! Why—"

"Oh, but, Mamma," Dina said breathlessly, "we *will* have new gowns for the ball, will we not? We cannot be expected to host a ball and wear the same dull things that everyone has seen us in before! You know as well as I that a bit of pretty ribbon will not be enough to turn Captain Hartnell's head, nor any of his brothers in red!"

"You know that those gowns have been purchased already," Mrs Dover replied severely. "The need for new ballgowns is a different matter entirely. Come, girls. Elsabeth, you must make yourself as pretty as possible for dinner; I believe you have already caught Mr Cox's eye, and we might all be so fortunate as to be allowed to stay in our home if one of you girls should marry him." Upon this entire reversal of her earlier position regarding Mr Cox, Mrs Dover entered Oakden with Tildy and Dina on her arms, and did not look back to see if Elsa and Rosa chose to follow.

They did not: Elsabeth swayed where she stood, and finally murmured, "'One' of us girls, but not her beloved Dina, nor Tildy, Dina's shadow, and not Rosa, who has prospects, nor Ruth, who has none. Oh!" she cried as Rosamund drew a breath of dismay, "I do not mean to hurt you, Rosamund. It is only that it is Dina who wishes most to marry, and Tildy who wants it next most because it is what Dina wants, whereas I myself should rather remain unmarried and your bosom companion than wed any man I have thus far met, and yet it is I who am to make myself pretty for that odious man."

"Mr Archer no longer seems so dreadful, does he?" Rosamund received Elsabeth's sour glance with good graces. "Perhaps he is only nervous, Elsa. Perhaps he will become more... appealing...as he becomes more comfortable with us."

"If it would not mean leaving you alone with him, Rosamund, I should come down with a sharp fever at this very moment and suffer from it for the entirety of Mr Cox's visit, even if it should mean missing the ball Leopoldina has instigated."

(21)

Elsabeth did not, to her mother's chagrin, take any especial care with dressing for supper, nor, to her own chagrin—if not surprise—did Mr Cox improve as he became more comfortable with his surrounds. Indeed, while he praised everything from dinner to daughters with great excess, none of what passed his lips could be considered on its own; it must all be examined in regard to what Lady Beatrice might think, and while, for his own part, each aspect of Oakden was most suitable, it must all be made more suitable in order to live up to his patroness's standards. They were not to fear, Mr Cox assured them; Lady Beatrice would regard Oakden as charming and quaint, appropriate for a small country manor kept by a family without much income, but in due time—due time! he insisted ingratiatingly to Mr Dover—it would come to him, and, as he was a man bestowed with such honourable patronage as the Lady Beatrice's, something would have to be done.

"And yet," Ruth put in whilst the remainder of the family sat in appalled silence, searching for a response to Mr Cox's cheerful, if not instantaneous, dismissal of Mr Dover from their lives, "yet one would not want the Lady Beatrice to imagine the proprietor of a small country manor to be above himself; I am sure she has a very great understanding of place in Society. One could hardly place a hearth such as graces Her Ladyship's drawing room—"

—for Mr Cox had gone on at some length about the magnificent size and cost of that very hearth; it was, they were all informed, of Connemara marble, and wide enough to stand inside, arms outstretched, without touching either side; this he knew because he had tried, before, of course, the hearth had been lit, and now on all days save the very warmest, a fire banked within its enormous hollow, in order to warm the room for Lady Beatrice's invalid daughter Annabel, who was frail and easily chilled, but otherwise a jewel in the crown of the Empire, and no doubt sorely missed in London Society by those who had never met her—

"—in Oakden's modest halls," Ruth continued, "without overwhelming it and making a small country family look as though they had pretensions of grandeur. Surely, it is better to show that one who lives in a house such as Oakden understands her place in the world, and can show all due deference to the great ladies such as your patroness by accepting her own less grandiose station with grace."

"Beauty and intelligence both," Mr Cox said to Mr Dover. "Surely, you are blessed in your daughters."

Mr Dover, who, with the rest of his family, had observed Ruth's quiet argument with increasing astonishment, said, "Surely, I am. Ruth, perhaps, after dinner, you will select something for Mr Cox to read to us."

Matilda groaned, and Elsabeth, mindful of Ruth's pleased blush, kicked her under the table. Tildy's eyes widened in offense and Leopoldina giggled; Rosamund, who would never stoop to kicking, frowned, a rarity that quelled even Dina. Ruth, gaze fixed on the table, murmured, "I should like that very much, Papa," and, when the meal was done, selected a passage of sermons that caused Dina to sag across the drawing room chaise. Cox's soporific voice droned on as Mr Dover settled back with a sigh, his eyes closed as the women slowly took up embroidery or letter-writing; all save Ruth, who sat nearby, hands clenched in her lap as she leaned toward Cox in her intensity.

Upon the conclusion of the first sermon, Leopoldina stabbed her finger so hard with a needle that there was no more reading that night; instead, lying on the chaise with her finger wrapped and elevated, she whispered, "Mamma, will I be well enough for the ball?" with such tremulous pathos that Elsabeth coughed away laughter.

"Of course," their mother replied indignantly. "Unless it should become infected, in which case you have done it to yourself, and if you die of the fever, I shall have no pity for you."

"That cannot be allowed," Mr Cox said in horror. "For any of these lovely young women to miss the ball would be unforgivable."

"Really, Mr Cox," said Elsabeth with some surprise. "You approve of dancing?"

"It is a most suitable form of exercise for young ladies, and one of the ways society permits young men and women to meet socially. Indeed, I am very fond of dancing myself, and am told by Lady Beatrice that I have a light foot. Perhaps you would honour me with the first dance at the forthcoming ball, Miss Elsabeth."

Elsabeth, unable to refuse and cursing herself for having spoken, produced a smile that strained her cheeks. "The second, Mr Cox. I have already promised the first to another."

Rosamund looked at her sharply, but Elsabeth allowed no tell-tale blush to creep up her cheeks whilst her mother and other sisters made a game of guessing to whom she had promised that dance. "It will be Captain Hartnell, of course," Tildy finally said, whereupon Leopoldina burst into tears and ran from the room.

"How *could* you, Elsabeth," Mrs Dover said severely, and rose to follow her beloved youngest. Matilda looked from face to face, protesting, "What? What have I done?" as a faint crease appeared between Mr Cox's large eyebrows. Elsabeth smiled at him, pained, and as he recalled the promise she had made, all else was forgotten. "The second dance, then. It shall be my pleasure, and I must plead now to press my chance for a second dance."

"So bold, Mr Cox," Elsabeth murmured. "We have only just met."

"But we are cousins!" he objected. "There can be no strangeness between us."

"Indeed, I am afraid of too much familiarity," Elsabeth replied, and would not be drawn into a promise of a second dance. Only when Mr Dover, obliged by necessity to offer his guest entertainment in lieu of the interrupted reading, invited Mr Cox to join him in a game of backgammon did Rosamund finally dare lean slightly toward Elsabeth and whisper, "You have promised the first dance to someone?"

Elsabeth, aware of the grimness in her voice, replied, "I shall have by morning," and had the mitigating pleasure of watching Rosamund's eyes widen slightly in shocked admiration at her falsehood.

It was to this end that early the next day, Elsabeth proposed to her mother and sisters that they should go to town. Bodton was rich with redcoats, and, though Elsa sought one in particular, both Matilda and Leopoldina were eager to accompany her. Rosa, who was not strictly certain of her own health yet, begged off, but it was she who, watching the others bustle about with their preparations, observed what they had not: "Where is Ruth?"

"She has taken up studies with Mr Cox," Mr Dover announced from behind his papers. "They are in my library, having forbidden me from the place, and examine the sermons with such devotion that I find myself relieved that I have been expelled."

"Mr Dover!" exclaimed his wife with such shock that he lowered his papers to meet her gaze.

"Never fear, my dear; I have set Margaret to dusting in there, that they are not alone. I expect to find it no less dusty than before, though; I believe the poor lass will find herself lulled to sleep by the"—he paused and inhaled deeply before drolly selecting "*melodious* tones of Mr Cox's voice. That is just as well; our illustrious guest arose at half past four this morning to attend to his devotions, and insisted upon both hot food and a fire at that hour; apparently, his God cannot do with cold prayers and a crust of bread. Margaret will no doubt appreciate the nap."

The lady of the house cried, "Mr Dover!" a second time, and if her shock sounded somewhat less sincere than it had before, the note of disapproval was somewhat stronger, though whether she objected to the slight directed at Mr Cox or at God was not to be known.

Elsabeth placed a bonnet on her mother's head, smiled and announced, "We are prepared," before Mrs Dover could be any further distracted by her husband's questionable humour. "Rosa, I do not think we will be home for dinner before one, and perhaps not then; will you ask the servants to prepare something simple that we may eat upon our return without requiring their services?"

Rosamund replied in the affirmative, and the bulk of the Dover women exited Oakden. Mrs Dover's presence demanded the carriage, and Elsabeth was not sorry for that; it was difficult enough to connive a gentleman into asking for a dance without adding the warm glow of walking to the air. So intent was she on considering that task that they arrived in Bodton in what seemed to her a wink, and she had hardly realized they were there than Dina, in her usual impetuous way, stood in the carriage and began waving vigourously. "Captain Hartnell! Captain Hartnell! I declare, Captain, who *are* your friends?"

—for Hartnell was quite surrounded by men in scarlet dress, and not one of them looked dismayed to see Dina's enthusiastic greeting. Hartnell himself came to their carriage's side and smiled up at the ladies as he made introductions hither and thither. Long before he was finished, Dina scrambled out of the carriage and became quite the centre of attention; Elsabeth saw her stealing glances at Hartnell, clearly hoping he would be overcome with envy. He was not; his gaze was for Elsabeth, which was a great relief to her. "Would you walk with me a little, Captain Hartnell? I have a situation I most earnestly require your assistance with."

"Anything," Hartnell replied gallantly, and, within moments, they walked together along the very same riverbank that had brought the captain into the Dover family's awareness. It was there that Elsabeth realised she did not now know how to proceed; a well-bred young woman did not ask a gentleman for a dance, and despite the Dover taint, she was a gentlewoman. Fortunately, Captain Hartnell seemed in no hurry to press the subject; they spoke idly of the weather and drily of Leopoldina's sudden popularity—"I should think her dance card will be full before the ball begins," Hartnell said with a smile.

Elsabeth, sensing her opportunity, drew breath to speak, but was stayed by the captain pausing in their walk and turning to face her with a most earnest expression. "Now that I have broached the topic—Miss Elsabeth, I wondered if I might press you for the first dance at the ball? There is no lady in Bodton I would rather dance it with, if you do not think me too brash for saying so."

"Oh," Elsa said with a laugh, "no, I do not. Yes, Captain Hartnell. I would be very pleased to dance with you, and if I may confess—I was at this very moment searching for a way to ask *you* for that dance. I'm afraid I was deplorably rude and told another gentleman it had already been promised."

Hartnell, with a laugh of his own, seized her hands and pressed his lips to their backs. "I am now eager to meet this *gentleman*, as I have never seen anyone make quite such a face when they spoke that word. Is he disagreeable, this gentleman?"

Elsa said, "*Very*," and might have said more had not a rider astride a fine horse approached them along the river path. She knew at once from the breadth of his shoulders and the cut of his coat that it was Mr Archer, and a queer pang of embarrassment struck her, that he should see her with her hands in Captain

Hartnell's. Her face must have told the story again, for Hartnell, with curious eyebrows, turned to see who approached, though he did not release Elsabeth's hands as he did so.

Because he did not, she felt the heat drain from them, just as merry colour drained from his face. His smile remained in place but became fixed; it was no longer an expression of pleasure, nor did he seem to breathe easily. Astonished, Elsabeth looked to Archer, whose judgemental mien became more severe than ever. They stared at one another thusly for an extended moment, then broke suddenly with Archer's formal "Miss Elsabeth," which he followed by the very stiffest of nod at Hartnell, who returned it far more gracefully. Archer rode past, leaving Elsabeth to gaze at Hartnell in astonishment; he looked rueful and began to speak, but Leopoldina, at the bridge behind them, cried Elsabeth's name, and the moment was lost.

(22)

It was lost to good cause: Dina had happened upon Mrs Moore, sister to Mrs Dover and wife to Mr Moore, whose profession was accounts and whose passion was horse racing. He lost no more than he won, being not given to the excesses of gambling that so many lovers of the greatest sport were, but his fondness for the tracks left him bulbous of nose from too much standing in the weather, and he smelt of horses. Mrs Moore, who tended to gossip with the same assiduous study that her husband paid the races, was still her sister's favourite companion, and swiftly invited the whole of the Dover family to dinner on the morrow. The invitation was promptly accepted. Leopoldina's cry of protest, that the women should vastly outnumber the men, was swiftly sorted by an extension of the invitation to not only Captain Hartnell but several others of the regiment, until it could very nearly be considered a fine social occasion—were it not for the lingering odor of horseflesh.

Elsabeth, when visiting the Moores, could never help but think of her father's sister and husband: she who had once been a Miss Dover had wed a Mr Penney, who, the story went, had been quite mad with love for her. But his advocacy business lay in London, where even a whisper of magic would undo him; for this reason, the Dover girls saw their Aunt and Uncle Penney rarely, though they were greatly spoilt by them when they did.

Elsabeth had often, quietly, wondered if her and her sisters' talents had warned the Penney family off having children, for they had none. They were in every way markedly different from Mr and Mrs Moore, whose four children were in spirit and action all very like Leopoldina. Elsabeth always felt a little ashamed that she so much preferred her Town relatives to her Country ones.

But her Town family could not have invited Captain Hartnell to dinner with such impunity; for that, at least, Elsabeth was grateful, and did not pretend to be indifferent when he arrived. Indeed, as she had confessed to Rosamund, her curiosity was piqued: Captain Hartnell was clearly acquainted with Mr Archer in a less than desirous manner, and, upon reflection, it seemed to Elsabeth that when she had spoken of the captain's rescuing Leopoldina to Archer, there had perhaps been some glint in his eye indicating a mind to speak which she, in her concern for her youngest sister, had not fully appreciated. Mr Archer's opinion was, of course, not to be much considered—although given his admiration of Sophia Enton, Elsabeth might be slightly swayed on that regard—but Rosamund could not fathom that there could truly be anything of note between the two men, much less any ill will. Elsabeth, being of less generous nature, imagined there must somehow be a secret to be ferreted out, and was as pleased to see Captain Hartnell for curiosity's sake as for the simple pleasure of his company.

Dinner was taken with much enjoyment, though Mr Cox—who could not have been left behind at Oakden, no matter how much the Dovers might have wished it—somewhat dominated the conversation with observations of his patroness's wealth and other admirable qualities. Once, Captain Hartnell caught Elsabeth's eye and, with a quirk of his eyebrow, queried her as to the identity of the man whom she had not wished to first dance; with a widening of her own eyes, she confirmed his suspicion, and they were both obliged to fight away laughter wholly inappropriate to Cox's extemporizations. After the meal, all guests retired to the drawing room, where Ruth sat at the pianoforte.

She had always played with heavy precision, bringing joy to neither herself nor her audience, but tonight, her fingers danced more lightly over the keys and called forth a merry tune. In very little time, Leopoldina and Matilda could not bear it and began to dance; shortly thereafter, several of the young officers joined them, and under the cover of this merriment, Hartnell approached Elsabeth.

"Would it be forward of me, Miss Elsabeth, to ask if you might walk with me in the garden? I do not object to a chaperon, if we should have one; I only hope to speak with you uninterrupted, which in the current clime seems...improbable." With the suggestion of a chaperon, he glanced toward Rosa; with the implication of interruption he looked at Cox, whose own approach had been scuppered by Hartnell's.

Elsa, who had been watching Cox with alarm and Hartnell with hope, rose at once and called to Rosamund, who joined them and walked with her arm through Elsabeth's until they reached the garden, at which time she confessed a sudden interest in their aunt's wild roses, and perforce to examine them with great attention to detail. Released from her chaperonage, Hartnell escorted Elsabeth a little way down the garden, pausing beneath an arch of blooms quite within Rosamund's sight but well out of ear-shot. "I have a suspicion that there are questions you would like to ask me, Miss Elsabeth. I think you cannot have missed the tension betwixt myself and Mr Fitzgerald Archer yesterday morning."

"Oh! I did not," confessed Elizabeth, "and I have wondered at it. But I would not press you, Captain Hartnell, if it is a topic upon which you do not wish to speak."

"I think it is best if I do, although I hesitate to ask—are you much acquainted with Mr Archer?"

Elsabeth allowed herself a sniff of disdain. "More than I might wish to be, Captain Hartnell. He is only lately come to Bodton, little more than a month ago. I have recently been obliged to remain a full six nights under the same roof as he, and I confess that I found him in—" She hesitated suddenly, recalling Archer's gallantry with Sophia, and in that light gentled her commentary a little. "—in many aspects disagreeable and aloof. I dare say so only because I sense your relations with him are also strained, and that you would not repeat such a forthright opinion to others."

Hartnell captured her hand momentarily and, holding it, smiled. "I would not, Miss Elsabeth; do not fear. But you will perhaps be surprised to hear that my acquaintance with him extends back to our very births; we were, once, as close as brothers."

"No! How, then, came you to be so unfamiliar with each other?"

"It is a long tale, and reflects poorly on Archer. Perhaps it reflects poorly on me as well; I cannot tell. Miss Elsabeth, I see that there is a bench only a little farther along; do you think Miss Dover would object if we were to retire to it while I share my tale?"

"Not at all, and even less so if we should suggest that she might examine the chrysanthemums some little distance beyond it, where there is another bench she might rest comfortably upon for the duration of our conversation." With these things swiftly arranged, Elsabeth and Hartnell sat and, to the outside eye, had the look of intimacy, so closely together were their heads aligned, and so intent were their low voices as Hartnell began his tale of woe.

"My father was vicar to the old Archer's estate, and through happy alignment, my mother and his wife bore we two boy children within weeks of one another. The old Archer saw a companion for his son as a good and necessary thing, and my parents had provided one. Thanks to his generosity, I was educated along with Archer, raised beside him as if we were brothers together, looked upon his sister as my own, and was promised the parish upon my own father's inevitable passing, for he was not a young man when I was born. But calamity struck."

Hartnell fell silent until Elsabeth, intrigued, prompted, "Calamity?" and caused a start in the handsome captain, as if he had been lost to his own thoughts.

"I find I hardly know how to tell you, Miss Elsabeth. It is an uncomfortable confession, and I fear that you will judge me harshly, as so many others have done."

"Captain Hartnell, I can think of nothing you could say that would cause me to shy from you," Elsabeth said as warmly as she could. "Surely, it cannot be *that* dreadful."

"Perhaps not to the lower classes," Hartnell replied, "but you are a gentlewoman, just as the Archers are gentlemen. I am only the son of a vicar, with a bought commission in the army, and my prospects—"

"Enough. If I am a gentlewoman such as Archer is a gentleman, then I have no use for myself at all, for he has shown no part of himself as gentlemanly," save for his appreciation of Sophia, Elsabeth reminded herself again, as her hopes for her friend remained bright in her mind. But that was a consideration beyond the moment, and so she concluded, "And I should hope myself better than that. I will withhold all judgment until you have said your piece, and then I shall consider carefully before I condemn or praise at all."

Hartnell met her eyes with a gaze both curious and hopeful before it melted into a winning gentleness. "I believe you mean that, Miss Elsabeth. Very well: I shall steel myself and say that as I reached an age to begin my religious studies in earnest, I developed a—a—" Even now he hesitated, then took a breath and plunged onward: "A small gift for magic, Miss Elsabeth; a modest natural talent for coaxing water, most particularly, to do my will. Oh, I have loathed that part of me, but I can say so no longer, for without it, I might not have dared the river to save your sister, and we should never have met!"

Ungainly laughter brayed from Elsabeth's throat, and she clasped her hands over her mouth, horrified and amused at once. Rosamund looked up and Elsa hastily waved her concerns away; Rosa, with an elevated eyebrow of interest, returned to her consideration of the flowers, and Elsabeth ejaculated, "Is *that* all!" to Hartnell, whose face was a picture of consternation and confusion.

"Is that *all*? Miss Elsabeth, it has been the ruin of me. The old Archer passed and the younger would have nothing to do with a youth, even one he had considered a brother, who was tainted with talent. What manner of astonishing creature are you, that you should say *is that all* of a man plagued by magic?"

"One of great imagination!" Elsabeth burst out in reply. "A calamity, for goodness' sakes, Captain Hartnell! You might have—you might have accidentally run down a child with a carriage, or—or—" Her imagination failed her, and she carried on with passion. "*Magic*, magic is an inconvenience, an embarrassment, something, yes, that the lower classes, when beleaguered with it, are forced to hide or join the service whilst the upper classes eschew it wholly, but by your own admission, you are not of gentle blood! Good heavens, Captain, do not frighten me in such a way. What did Archer do?"

"Cast me out without a penny," Hartnell replied, but the venom had gone from his voice. Instead, he looked upon Elsabeth with delighted bemusement, and with a spark deep in his eyes that she dared not gaze into for too long, such was its heat. "He called me—well, I shall not repeat it, but he clearly no longer thought of me as a brother. I was thrown from his lands without so much as the opportunity to say my goodbyes to his sister, whom I had seen as my own. I had never expected an inheritance—that is to say, an income—but he denied me the opportunity to follow my father's profession and left me with no choice but to scrounge for a commission, which I received only because the army has some small use for magic itself. I believe I would have been happy as a vicar, Miss Elsabeth."

Elsabeth, impulsively, laid her hand upon Hartnell's. "Are you not happy now, Captain?"

Hartnell looked at her hand pressing his, then lifted a slow and warm smile to Elsabeth. "I have never been happier than I am in this very moment."

"Then fie on Mr Archer," Elsabeth said with considerable anger. "To bear magical talent is not a condemnation, nor should it be. If he is so shallow as to throw away a lifetime's brotherhood over society's trappings, then he cannot be a man of any real substance, which is only as I have suspected since the beginning. Come, Captain Hartnell. We must return to my aunt's company, but we may do so united in the intention to think no more of Mr Archer."

(23)

To think no more of Archer was a pretty proposition, but could not be acted on as easily as it was said. Although eager to share her new intelligence with Rosamund, Elsabeth remained silent on the carriage ride home after dinner. There was no lack of chatter, despite her silence: between Mr Cox and Leopoldina, the conversation did not flag, though neither of them spoke to one another as they reported upon, on one part, the admirable food, the fine company, the excellent house and the propriety of the occasion, and, upon the other part, the details of numerous of the young officers who had been in attendance, their prospects, their family obligations and the appealing breadth of their red-clad shoulders.

"I have rarely had such a pleasant evening," Mr Cox announced as they approached Oakden, "for Miss Derrington's health is so fragile that Lady Beatrice does not often entertain even the company of her beloved nephew, to whom Miss Derrington is, I believe, engaged."

"Oh!" cried Dina, "must *everyone*, even the sickly, be engaged before I am? To whom is she engaged, Mr Cox? I must know, so that I might understand what manner of man likes frail ladies. Perhaps I should not be so robust."

"To a Mr Archer, son of Lady Beatrice's sister, dead these several years. I have never had the pleasure of meeting Mr Archer, but I understand him to be exceedingly wealthy and of exceptional breeding. But of course he must be, if he is to marry my patroness's lovely daughter! No one but the very best could do for Miss Derrington, and I believe it is Lady Beatrice's intention to have the two estates become one through marriage. Nothing could be finer, I am sure, and it will be my utmost joy to perform the ceremony when that happy day arrives."

Enthralled with his own exposition, Mr Cox did not notice that the entirety of the Dover party had fallen into stunned quiet, each of them for once gazing at him as though the words falling from his lips had become pearls. Elsabeth recovered herself enough to speak, exclaiming, "Can you mean Mr *Fitzgerald* Archer, Mr Cox?"

"I can indeed. Are you acquainted with the man?"

"He is lately come to Newsbury Manor," Elsabeth replied in astonishment, and, exchanging a look with Rosamund, thought of Julia Webber's ambitions toward Archer, and then of her own for Sophia and Archer, and could not smile. Had it only been Miss Webber, she might have indulged in an unkind pleasure, but it was not in her to be cruel towards Sophia. "What an extraordinary piece of news. He had made no mention of engagement."

"Perhaps it explains his aloofness," Rosamund put forth softly and with evident happiness, for she could not bear the idea that anyone should be as unapproachable as Mr Archer. Elsabeth, with a pang, thought it might be kinder to withhold what she had learned from Hartnell, and, with a greater pang still, thought that it would be necessary to warn Sophia as soon as possible.

But the hour was far too late to presume upon the Entons; the news of Archer's engagement would have to wait until morning, and, in truth, there was so much to share with Rosamund that Elsabeth offered good-nights to her family with unseemly haste. Rosa, bemused, allowed herself to be drawn off to the bedroom, and there learned the scandal of Captain Hartnell's magic with increasing astonishment. "But this is splendid news, Elsa! He is clearly very fond of you, and would surely never find a gift you both share as a reason to dismiss his suit!"

"I should hope not," Elsabeth replied, "although it seems that what one might find forgiveable in oneself is less acceptable in a wife. But I am not thinking of marrying him, Rosa—"

At this, one of Rosamund's pretty eyebrows rose a questioning half-inch, causing Elsabeth to blush. "Very well, perhaps I am, but that was not where my thoughts lay at the moment. I am more concerned with the influence Mr Archer has on Mr Webber now. If Archer could cast away a man who had been his brother in all but blood over a question of magic, I fear how his prejudices might colour Mr Webber's behaviours. Forgive me for sounding like Mamma, Rosamund, but I believe it may be necessary to secure an engagement with Mr Webber sooner rather than later."

"You feel I should trick him?" Rosamund asked with soft but genuine horror. "Elsabeth, I could not!"

"Of course not! There is no trickery involved here, Rosamund. It would merely be entering an engagement without telling him absolutely everything about yourself, which is, I am quite sure, the natural manner of these things anyway. Once you are engaged, it will be safe to reveal the truth, for no gentleman would break an engagement. I am sure his affections for you will in the end prove greater than his concerns over the very little magic you possess, but should he learn of your magic before—if *Archer* should learn of it before—"

"No. I cannot believe any man would throw away his friend like that," Rosamund declared. "I am sure there is some deception here, some influence on this dreadful situation that neither of us—perhaps neither Mr Archer nor Captain Hartnell themselves!—are fully aware of. I cannot believe it, and I shall not believe that Mr Archer might interfere in Mr Webber's affairs so cruelly." She would not be swayed from her determination despite Elsabeth's arguments, and, finally, with the candles guttering, both young ladies took to sleep with neither of them satisfied by their discussion.

Morning was no gladder a time for Elsabeth, who not only endured Mr Cox over the course of breakfast—his second full breakfast, as he had once more risen at half past four in the morning and insisted upon a hot meal then, and then could not, as he explained, be so rude as to fail to join the family in breaking their fast—but who also had the unpleasant task of visiting Sophia Enton to tell her of Mr Archer's engagement. They were in the garden and, by design, quite alone when Elsabeth broke this news to her friend; she did not want to subject Sophia to Mrs Enton's temper when it was learned that Archer could not be relied upon as a potential husband.

Sophia, for her part, gazed at Elsabeth in pure astonishment upon the relating of this news. "What could it matter to me that Mr Archer is engaged?"

"Well, he—he spoke very highly of you! He was most taken with your form at dinner last week!"

"Was he? How kind of him." Sophia smiled, a rather polite expression that gradually grew more amused as Elsabeth's amazement became clear to her. "Forgive me, Elsa! I hadn't thought to set my cap so high. In truth, while I know that Mr Archer is a handsome man, I cannot recall exchanging two words with him over dinner. I was much engaged in conversation with Miss Webber, whom I found to be exceedingly warm and pleasant. I wonder that you and she do not get along."

"Such accolades for Miss Webber from you and Rosamund both," Elsabeth replied. "Now *I* begin to wonder that we do not get along. Perhaps there is something in her that I cannot see. Indeed, there must be, that my bosom friend and dearest sister both admire her when I do not." She did not entirely mean what she said, being quite confident of her own opinions, but she had thought Sophia would side with her on the matter of Miss Webber, and to learn otherwise startled her. "I shall have to think on this," she conceded, and Sophia, laughing, opined that to make Elsabeth Dover reconsider an opinion was an achievement indeed.

"Now," Sophia added, "I have a thought about this ball your sisters keep insisting will happen. You cannot hold it at Oakden,

Elsa; it is not large enough. Nor can you sensibly hire the Bodton Hall, which lacks grandeur. I have spoken to Mamma and have nearly convinced her that it would be the event of the season to have it at Enton Manor. I believe, in fact, that she almost believes it to be her own idea, and that it would take little more than a nudge from a certain well-placed gentleman to make it a certainty."

Elsabeth's hands flew to her mouth, hiding both a gasp and a smile. "Sophia! How cunning of you, and how kind. I do not believe Mamma has in any way considered the difficulties of hosting a ball ourselves, but Enton Manor is as grand as Newsbury, and newer. What gentleman did you have in mind?"

"I believe Mamma still harbours certain hopes for Mr Webber. A word from him...?"

"Thank goodness you asked for Mr Webber, and not Mr Archer—although I still believe he looked very kindly upon you, Sophia. Oh, I am sure that might be possible. Perhaps we might arrange to accidentally meet in Bodton Square tomorrow, perhaps at half past two? A day is surely enough time for Rosamund to prevail upon Mr Webber's kindness and to provide such a... nudge."

"I shall make certain we are shopping at half past two tomorrow," Sophia replied with an air of triumph. "Perhaps Miss Webber could be in the party, Elsa. I believe I could rely upon her fine breeding to convince Mamma that a dress selected by Miss Webber would be the most flattering thing I could wear at a ball...?"

"Sophia Enton," Elsabeth said with admiration. "You have become wily."

"I am not wily. I am tall and rather plain, but with—perhaps—just a spark of magnificence in me. If Miss Webber can bring it out, then maybe Mamma will not be burdened with me forever."

"My dear friend, you have far more than a spark of magnificence. Let me go now: I shall make all these arrangements, and you will be the talk of Bodton at your ball."

(24)

A CALLING CARD WAS SENT; AN ACCEPTABLE AGREEMENT WAS received, and, that very afternoon, the two oldest Dover girls descended once more upon Newsbury Manor, where, much to Elsabeth's surprise, not only was Mr Webber amenable to their plans, but so too was Miss Webber. The following afternoon, a seemingly chance encounter led Mr Webber to praise Mrs Enton on the remarkable descriptions he had heard of her home and to insinuate he hoped he might have the opportunity to see it himself. Her very next words were to issue a declaration that the Dovers' ball was to be the Enton ball, and to press Mr Webber into promising to attend.

Miss Webber, with all the skill of a trained actress, cried, "Oh! We must find you a new gown!" to Sophia Enton, and, without further consultation with Mrs Enton, drew Sophia into the most expensive shop in Bodton. Mrs Enton followed; some time later, they emerged with the mother looking faint and the daughter radiant with pleasure as she squired Miss Webber back to the Newsbury carriage. Elsabeth, watching from a distance, was obliged to admire Miss Webber's deftness as she turned a sweet smile upon Mrs Enton and commended her, loudly enough for the whole town square to hear, on her exquisite taste in clothing and her extremely good eye for what a daughter of Sophia's height and build should wear. "I should never have thought to choose that mulberry," Miss Webber declared, "but it will look exquisite on Miss Enton. I do so look forward to admiring her at your ball, and to seeing your magnificent home."

With this speech lingering on the air, the Newsbury contingent was driven away. Sophia, looking very much as though she struggled not to laugh with joy, caught Elsabeth's eye and satisfied herself with a bright smile. Elsabeth herself returned home on the wings of that smile, feeling like she might fly, buoyed by her friend's delight.

It was something of a horror, then, to traipse lightly up the Oakden walk and encounter Mr Reginald Cox busy at the act of gardening. Upon Elsabeth's arrival, he leapt to his feet more lightly than a man of his size might be expected to, and made much of wiping suspiciously undirtied hands cleaner on his trousers. "Miss Elsabeth! What a surprise to encounter you."

"Indeed, it cannot be much of a surprise, as this is my home. I do hope you have not disturbed Mamma's nasturtiums, Mr Cox; it would distress her greatly." As it was clear he had done little more than kneel in their vicinity, Elsabeth felt this was a safe remark; she did not expect the flow of assurances and apologies that the comment engendered. "Enough, enough, Mr Cox," she was obliged to say after some minutes of this behaviour. "I can see that you have done them no damage. Forgive me—"

"Do forgive *me*, Cousin. I am quite overtaken with emotion, as you can see. I should hate to upset you in any way. Perhaps I might beg your forgiveness by offering to escort you on a walk around the gardens; I know how you like to walk."

"I have only just returned from walking to and from town, Mr Cox. It had rather been my hope to retire to the house for a drink and perhaps some quiet reading."

"I should be delighted to read to you." The unshakable Mr Cox fell into step beside Elsabeth, deaf to her protest that *quiet* reading seemed to her by its very definition to be not done aloud. Desperate to escape, she hurried ahead and threw the door open to rush inside, and instead collided with first an enormous jug, and then Ruth, who bore the jug in both hands.

Scummy water sloshed upward and spilled down Elsabeth's front in dark streaks. It pattered on the floor, turning flagstones black. Elsabeth's shriek, more borne of startlement than anger, was followed hard upon by the sound of falling water, and Ruth, trembling, looked up with two hard spots of colour appearing on her cheeks. Elsabeth gasped, "*Ruth!*" with anger burgeoning, but even as she spoke, saw a strange combination of stubbornness and fear rising in her middle sister's gaze.

It gave her pause, if only for an instant. Ruth did not by nature blush: indeed, the colour in her cheeks was unnatural, as if unpracticed and therefore unable to be pretty. Her hair, though, which was always knotted tightly against her head, *was* rather pretty today: though still snugger than any other Dover sister would wear it, it had been loosened enough to suggest there might be some native body to it, and she appeared, of all things, to have borrowed one of Matilda's more conservative dresses: it scooped along her collarbones and had long sleeves that puffed gently at the shoulders.

Moreover, the jug she still clutched in her arms was one of the laundry jugs, filled with dirty water, and there was no sensible reason for her to be carrying it out the front door. Elsabeth, with a sudden suspicion, let go of all anger and instead completed her exclamation with, "Are you all right?"

Ruth gazed at her in evident mortification. "Oh, Elsabeth, forgive me. Let me help you into something dry—"

"No, no, I'm quite all right," Elsabeth said hastily. "I'll just go upstairs and change. But goodness, Ruth, you shouldn't be carrying something so dreadfully heavy. Mr Cox, you are such a very strong and able gentleman, perhaps you could help poor Ruth with this jug; she's far too fragile to be carrying such a weight herself." She stepped nimbly around Ruth, whose mortified expression softened just slightly into gratitude. Elsabeth allowed herself one glance backward to see Mr Cox taking on the weight of the jug with what appeared to be his best effort at gallantry, and, joyful once more, Elsa whispered, "Well done, Ruth, well done!" as she hurried to change her dress.

(25)

The sennight betwixt Mrs Enton's appropriation of the Dover ball and the event itself dragged on interminably, with Leopoldina and Matilda keeping close watch on the dressmakers upon whom all their hopes for a magnificent evening lay. It would not be past Mrs Enton, they agreed with their mother, to postpone the ball should Sophia Enton's dress not be finished in time, and it was with a great sigh of relief that the gown was passed from seamstress to maidservant as a sign that the ball would proceed as planned.

For the duration of that week, Mr Cox continued to pay especial attention to Elsabeth, who grew increasingly grateful that she had slipped his grasp for the first dance of the evening, and all too often exchanged rueful glances with Rosamund, with whom she had entered a pact to allow Ruth as much access to Mr Cox as could be socially permissible. Ruth grew prettier yet, even her gaze softening behind her round spectacles as she wore both hair and gowns more fashionably. If Mr Cox remained unaware, no one else in the Dover family missed her transformation. Nor did a scarlet-coated youth upon their arrival at the ball: Ruth, who had an empty dance card upon crossing the threshold, found herself sought after for one dance, then another, whilst Mrs Dover looked on with astonishment.

It was dismay rather than astonishment that beleaguered

Elsa, though: having been promised the first dance by Captain Hartnell, it had not crossed her mind that he might not present himself at the ball. Escaping her sisters—who were, by order of age, engaged in conversation with Mr Webber, a serious-looking young lieutenant who held in one hand a Bible and with the other pointed out the passage of which he spoke, and a bevy of handsome officers all heartily attendant on the liveliest and most pliant of the Dover girls—Elsabeth slipped through the Enton public rooms in subtle search of Hartnell.

He was not to be found, although Miss Julia Webber and Sophia Enton were ensconced together in a darkened corner, whispering secrets to one another—a sight which gave Elsabeth a strange sorrow; Sophia had long since been her special friend, and she found, to her own shame, that a thread of jealousy wound through her heart that she should have to share Sophia with another—and Mr Fitzgerald Archer was lurking about in a disagreeably handsome manner rather than participating in any sort of usual conversation. He nodded stiffly when he saw Elsabeth; she, after glancing about to see whom he might have chosen to acknowledge, realised it was herself, and offered a curtsy as formal as his greeting had been. Instruments began to be tuned, and a peculiar look came over Archer's face as Elsabeth glanced around once more in resignation, but before she could interpret it, to her consternation, Mr Cox appeared at her side.

"My dear cousin," he said with insultingly deep solicitude, "I could not help but note that you seem to be without a partner for these first dances after all. I should consider it no more than my duty, but it is also my profound pleasure to stand up with you now. Miss Dover has consented to dance the next set with me, and I have engaged your younger sisters for dances later in the evening. I should hate to fail in my familial obligations by not dancing with you as well, for it is quite proper I should attend each lady of the family throughout the course of the evening."

Elsabeth, who could not now say no, agreed with as little evident pleasure as she dared show, and suffered thoroughly the ineptitudes of Mr Cox's dancing, although, she dared say to Sophia some time later, she had not suffered them any *more* than those around them had, for his skill led him to trounce not only her own toes, but those of the gentlemen and ladies who passed him by. One of the latter had nearly lost the train to her skirt to his mis-stepping, and he had simply collided with two other gentlemen when, it seemed, he was unable to tell his left from his right in the pattern of the dance. Her regret over Captain Hartnell's failure to appear had been lessened by the time she spoke with Sophia, as she had in the interim danced with two far more agreeable young men as well, one of whom was an officer and had spoken warmly of Hartnell, though he did not know why the captain had not joined them for the evening. She was therefore quite able to laugh at the misadventure with Mr Cox, and was, indeed, doing so when Mr Archer appeared at her side and asked in dreadfully formal tones if she might agree to dance with him.

For the second time in the evening, she looked about in search of the woman Archer intended to address and once again found only herself, for Sophia, sparkling with amusement, had stepped back and—despite her height and the rich mulberry tones of her gown—had made herself inconspicuous. Too startled to make an excuse, Elsabeth replied, "I should be pleased to," and turned a look of accusation upon Sophia as Archer departed as abruptly as he had arrived.

Sophia, still merry and quite lovely with it, stepped forward again to say, "I thought you should never dance with him, Elsabeth. Fear not: I have spent some time with Miss Webber and Mr Archer over the past week, and I think you might find him agreeable after all."

Elsabeth had not revealed and could not now reveal the tale of woe betwixt Archer and Hartnell, and so could only say, "I most sincerely doubt it, but I am sure he only meant it as a jape, and will not come to collect the dance."

A steely look of practicality came into Sophia's eyes. "Perhaps, but if he does, Elsa, remember that his fortune is ten times that of Mr Webber's, and a thousand times that of an officer's."

"You have no romance in your soul," Elsabeth replied lightly.

Determination glittered in Sophia's gaze. "I am nearly twenty-eight years old. I cannot afford romance, and you ought not rely on it. Here he comes, Elsabeth. Try not to stand on your pride; both of you have too much of it."

In truth, though, without pride Elsabeth thought she could not join Archer in the dance at all. Without pride, the astonished looks of her fellow dancers as they glanced from Archer to herself might have felled her; without pride, they certainly would have seen that she shared their astonishment and perhaps felt it even more deeply than they did. She was not certain they didn't see it anyway: she felt as though her amazement at dancing with Archer was writ large on her face for all to see, and she was not above exchanging a wide-eyed glance with a young woman of her distant acquaintance who stood nearby.

For his part, Archer showed no sort of discomfort at all. Indeed, to Elsabeth's view, he seemed to gaze at some distant point above her head, no more interested in her as an individual dance partner than he might be interested in the difference between one cow and another in a field.

It might have done her some good to know that beneath his lofty visage, Mr Fitzgerald Archer was equally taken aback by his actions. He had not intended on asking Miss Elsabeth to dance; it had, after all, been made manifestly clear—on both their parts, he was loath to admit—that they found one another to be undesirable dance partners. He was even more loath to admit—did not, in fact, admit it on any recognisable level—that she had quite captured his attention with her arrival at the ball. She was prettily gowned in pale pink, which in no way made her stand out from the sea of similarly gowned young ladies; it was only the bold or very wealthy who wore stronger colours this evening. Miss Webber and her protégé Miss Enton were among them, and Miss Enton in particular looked well for it, but to Archer's eye, Miss Elsabeth had no need to adorn herself in the more dramatic shades of dress for an evening.

Nor, certainly, was it her family who caused her to so thoroughly ensnare him, save she and her eldest sister seemed demure and proper in comparison to the garish mother, loud sisters and daft father. No: she had separated from them as soon as she could, leaving Miss Dover to charm Webber on topics Archer had nothing to say about. He had not meant to follow Miss Elsabeth through the ballrooms, and he was not above admitting a small, mean gladness in his heart when he realised she searched for, and could not find, David Hartnell. It was in the midst of her disappointment that they saw one another, and, suddenly struck by the opportunity, he had thought then to ask her to dance.

He ought to have moved more swiftly: a tall, plump, oily man in an ill-fitting suit appeared to press Miss Elsabeth for a dance instead, and proceeded to escort her around the floor so badly as to embarrass even Archer, a task which most would regard as impossible. Miss Elsabeth, showing admirable forbearance, survived the sets and quit the man as soon as she could, but Archer regarded his own opportunity as quite lost.

It was therefore a shock to him when, some time later, he turned to discover Miss Elsabeth at his elbow and made the offer of a dance without a moment's thought or hesitation. She accepted with surprise evident even through her grace, and now he stood across from her in the opening positions of the dance and could not think of a word to say. So complete was his inability to speak that he dared not even meet her eyes, for fear that she would—reasonably—expect him to offer some polite inanity, or worse, that she would recognise that he was tongue-tied and—equally reasonably—laugh at him.

Curse it, but why could he not be a little more like Webber? Robert had never once been unable to speak charmingly to a young woman; Robert would never find himself staring stonily at curtains and candles rather than risk glancing at his dance partner. He commanded himself to pretend, just for a moment, that he was Robert, and finally met Miss Elsabeth's eyes, only to find her struggling to hold back laughter. "I find the quadrille to be an exceedingly diverting dance," she said as swiftly as could be, as if she had been waiting for him to break and finally look her way, "do you not?"

"I do," he replied, and, unable to find some idle pleasantry to follow this abrupt comment with, fell into dreadful silence again. It had to be a question of her position within Society; he had never been so ill suited to speaking to women of his own rank. He spoke to Julia Webber with ease, and of course it was no difficulty to discuss matters of dress or friendship with his own cousin, Miss Annabel Derrington.

Satisfied and somewhat relieved to have hit upon a reason for his reticence, Archer was prepared to complete the dance in silence when Miss Elsabeth spoke again. "It is your turn, Mr Archer. I have spoken of the dance; you might now mention the weather or how well our hosts look this evening. I believe we must talk for at least some part of our time together." She said all of this with such solemnity that Archer glanced at her again, suspecting—and finding—that humour danced in her dark eyes.

He was not a man who cared for being laughed at, and found some release in a dark glower. "Must we, Miss Elsabeth? Why is that?"

"Because if we do not, Mr Archer, then others will." Her smile no longer laughed at him: it thrust, a pin-point strike to his very heart. "What do you suppose they might say, to watch two young people—I use the word advisedly in your regard, of course—spend the whole of a half hour straight-faced and mute even as they enjoy the intimacy of a dance? I should think," she said in a murmur, "that they would imagine that the young people were trying very hard to hide something from the rest of them."

"I am only twenty-eight!"

At this outburst—and it was, Archer feared, an outburst—Elsabeth Dover threw her head back and laughed aloud, drawing the attention of every individual in the room, and some from the rooms beyond. Archer, hot with humiliation, paraded stiffly through the next segment of the dance whilst attempting to ignore the muffled, but still visible, laughter of his partner, who finally recovered herself to whisper, "I had thought intimations of secret affection would raise your ire, Mr Archer. I had not realised it would be a chide about your age that would draw blood. Oh, my, how ill suited we are to partnering one another, for I cannot help but be merry and you, sir, cannot help but be dour."

"Is that your estimation of my character, then?"

"Is it not your estimation of your own? If I am wrong, pray, set me straight, for I should dislike to hold to a bad judgment, in the event that I have made one." Her tone implied she had not made an error; her expression, all girlish curiosity, charged him to deny it.

"You are not wrong," Archer finally replied, and in Miss Elsabeth's satisfaction saw a different sort of truth: that it was her very merriment that drew him to her. He, who had always been concerned with that which was right and proper, was rarely drawn to that which was simply gay; even Robert Webber's kindness and soft heart were seated within a very suitable gentleman. "That disposition which you so correctly ascertain," Archer said then, with some caution, "causes me to have some difficulty in making friends easily, though I like to think that my friendship, once secured, is unflagging."

The joy fled from Miss Elsabeth's face and she struck as quickly as a viper. "How, then, do you explain Captain Hartnell?"

Displeasure twisted Archer's face, for he had opened himself to that strike without thinking of it. "Hartnell is not the man you think he is, Miss Elsabeth."

"Captain Hartnell has confessed his sins to me, and I could never look kindly upon a man who has denied him a vocation over such trivial matters."

"I should be very interested to hear what sins he has confessed, for I cannot believe they are the very ones I know to be his. Mark me, Miss Elsabeth: where he has the gift of making friends, he has not the knack of holding them. He is dangerous and a friendship with him is ill conceived."

"Dangerous," snapped Elsabeth Dover. "Give me but a moment's opportunity, Mr Archer, and I shall show you dangerous—"

"Why, Mr Archer," said a pleased voice from the edge of the dance floor, "how excellently you dance, and with such passion. I am most pleased to see you with our dear Miss Elsabeth, and dare say there could be no finer set of matches made than yourself and herself along with good Mr Webber and darling Miss Dover. I do believe that is a match almost made, would you not say so yourself? Entirely splendid, I say, entirely splendid. But I have interrupted the steps of your dance; let me remove myself and we shall speak again of this later. Mr Archer, Miss Elsabeth."

Sophia's father, Mr Enton, a fine and kind-hearted gentleman himself, excused himself from the midst of what had been a battlefield, and Archer, gazing after the man, could not say whether he had performed a deliberate and timely interruption or had, as it appeared, merely seen something that pleased him in the two of them and stopped to comment upon it. But he and Elsabeth had been spatting quietly; surely, Enton could not have heard them over the bustle of the ball. Moreover, his commentary—absurdly inappropriate with regards to himself and Miss Elsabeth—had sparked an awareness in Archer, who forgot his partner for a moment and looked over the ballroom until he found Webber deep in conversation with Miss Dover.

No: Archer dismissed the thought. Webber could not be genuinely serious about the oldest Dover girl; she came from too little, and had a wretched family besides. Archer was now inclined to include Miss Elsabeth in that wretchedness; if she would not listen to his warnings, then the consequences could be on her own head. They finished the dance in the silence in which it had begun, and it was with a certain mean satisfaction that Archer saw Elsabeth's first dance partner of the evening approach her again and demand her attention.

"My dear cousin," Mr Cox said upon approaching Elsabeth, "could that gentleman with whom you were dancing be Mr Archer? Mr Fitzgerald Archer?"

"Yes." Even one word was too many to speak to Cox, particularly after such a tête-à-tête with Archer, but Elsabeth could not simply turn away from her cousin, much as she might like to.

"Why, he is the very nephew of my dear patroness. I shall introduce myself; I believe it is the only appropriate thing to do."

"You cannot possibly be serious, Mr Cox. Mr Archer is extremely proper, and one does not simply introduce oneself to a man of his station. You must be introduced. Ask Papa to do so if you must, although I think it is better that you do not."

"I insist upon it." Cox edged his way through the ballroom toward Archer as Elsabeth, helpless with dismay, searched the room for a glimpse of Ruth, whose treatise on the necessity of proper introductions had been crushed by the family weeks before. If only they had not hushed her, Elsa felt, she herself might have had the words to dissuade Cox; even now, if Ruth could be found, she might yet convince him of the folly of his ways.

Too late: Cox was at Archer's elbow, plucking at his sleeve and speaking to him. Archer gazed at him with the amazement of a man who has discovered an inexplicable stain on the elbow of his jacket, and briefly—terribly—flickered a glance toward Elsabeth, thus informing her that he was entirely aware that Cox was a creature of her acquaintance. She could not allow herself to cringe externally, but within, she shrank away, embarrassed for herself and her family alike. Archer's opinion ought not bear any weight with her, and should certainly not be worthy of embarrassment, but to Elsabeth's dismay, she found it did. Certainly, it was only that he was so well placed in Society; no one would want to gain the censure of a man in his standing. Thus reassured by her own logic, Elsabeth watched in dismay as Cox persisted with Archer.

Twice, Archer attempted to disengage himself; twice, Cox failed to recognise he was being dismissed, until finally Archer simply turned away and engaged in conversation with someone else. Elsabeth, unmoving with mortification, realised too late that she had lost the opportunity to slip away into the crowd, and found herself the centre of Cox's pleased attentions again. "What an exceedingly polite gentleman," he announced. "I believe he was most pleased to make my acquaintance, and very glad to hear that his aunt retains her health and vigor, or at least had done so when last I saw her, a mere fortnight ago. I dared tell him that I presumed she should enjoy his company—"

"Mr Cox," Elsabeth said in dismay, "had you that intelligence from the Lady Derrington herself, or was it a surmising of your own?"

"Entirely my own. I believe a man of ambition should seize the initiative, Miss Elsabeth, as I should like to seize it upon a topic near and dear to both of—"

"Mr Cox, I suddenly recall Ruth mentioning that she was quite famished," Elsabeth said in a burst of terror. "Do you suppose you might procure for her some bit of meat or bread and bring it to her?"

"Miss Ruth?" Cox glanced about the room, then swelled with purpose. "For you, my dear cousin, I should be most pleased to—"

"Excellent, thank you, now please forgive me; I see someone seeking my attention—" Elsabeth veritably fled from Cox into Rosamund's arms, where, for a few glorious moments, she was surrounded by the laughter and pleasantry of the Newsbury party, save with Sophia Enton standing in the place of Mr Archer at Julia Webber's side. A more delightful gathering could not have been found, but all too soon, Rosamund and Mr Webber joined the dancers, leaving the rest of them to disperse into dances or whispered intimacies, as with Sophia and Julia. Bereft and determined not to show it, Elsabeth approached her own family, only to hear her mother in an endless discussion of how lovely it would be when Rosa and Mr Webber were settled at Newsbury together, only a three-mile walk, it did a mother's heart good, with all those who passed by or settled within earshot.

Mr Archer was amongst the latter, and the more Mrs Dover spoke on the topic of Rosamund and Mr Webber, the grimmer Archer's expression became. Thrice, Elsabeth tried to draw her mother onto another subject, but Mrs Dover would have none of it: her eldest daughter's good fortune, and the good fortune of the Dover family by extension, was the only matter upon which she had any desire to speak. When Archer turned abruptly and strode away, Elsabeth, no longer able to bear Mrs Dover's endless litany, departed that conversation only to be caught and ensnared for the remainder of the evening by Mr Cox, who, having done his cousinly duty to Ruth, was eager to regale Elsabeth with news of his good deed.

"I had hoped you and she might find a topic of conversation suitable to both of you as she ate," Elsabeth replied wearily, rather than extol his virtues. Not to be dissuaded, Cox protested that he could not sit and talk with a younger sister when an older one, and one of such intelligence and beauty, remained unaccompanied.

It could not be said aloud that, without Cox's pervading presence, Elsabeth was unlikely to have remained unaccompanied. Instead, with the least encouraging expression she could manage, Elsa sat and listened to her cousin drone on. When, some hours later, she chanced to meet Archer's eye again, she was forced to the unusual activity of wishing she had behaved differently earlier. Had she not thrown the matter of Hartnell in Archer's face, her evening might have been spent a little more with him, which might have been unpleasant, but far more interesting, than an evening in the company of Reginald Cox.

(26)

Worse still than the evening was the following morning, when, at breakfast, Mr Cox asked Mrs Dover if he might have a moment of Miss Elsabeth's time, alone. Mrs Dover alone rose with delight; every other family member startled in one degree or another; even Mr Dover emerged from behind his papers to proclaim, "I am sure there is nothing Mr Cox has to say to Elsabeth that he cannot say to all of us."

"Do not be absurd, Mr Dover," Mrs Dover said through her teeth. "Rise, and permit these young people a moment of privacy."

Elsabeth seized Rosamund and Ruth's hands; they were beside her at the table, and all the shield she could muster. Rosamund gazed at her with horrified sympathy and Ruth with heartbroken betrayal. A similar expression graced Leopoldina's face, though, Elsabeth suspected, for wholly different reasons: no one had asked for a moment alone with *her*, and it was unforgiveable that someone should choose Elsabeth first. Matilda appeared less dismayed, but followed Dina's path in this as in everything, and allowed her chin to quiver with sorrow.

"Perhaps I could stay, Mamma," Rosamund ventured. "For seemliness."

"It is not unseemly for two young persons of a certain age and expectation to spend a little time without chaperones," Mrs

Dover replied severely. "Girls. Mr Dover. We shall await them in the drawing room. *Now.*"

With a helpless glance toward Elsabeth, Rosamund and Mr Dover rose and followed the rest of the family out of the dining room. Mr Cox made much of presenting himself well: he straightened his collar, brushed his lapels, and finally turned what he no doubt fondly imagined as a winsome smile at Elsabeth, who in alarmed response proclaimed, "I feel I must go for a walk in the garden," as loudly as she dared. Without further warning, she darted through the kitchen and out the door with the desperate hope that rescue might await her outside in the form of her father, whom she trusted had been listening at the dining room door with the rest of the family.

Mr Dover was nowhere to be seen. Elsabeth, faint with dread, struck out through the garden regardless, hoping against hope that she could lose Mr Cox in the twists and turns. But Oakden's gardens were not the tangled deep things that Newsbury's were, much less some truly grand manor such as Streyfield was rumoured to be. Mr Cox, once again proving quicker on his feet than a man of his size might be expected to be, chased her hither and yon throughout the gardens, laughing merrily about the games she played, whilst Elsabeth herself grew more frantic and determined to escape. Not until she found herself backed into a corner of half-wild hedges littered with late blooms did she cease her retreat, and, standing there, trembling, she thought that the flowers' rich, sweet scents were cloying, as if a poisoned trap themselves.

Now certain she could not flee again, Mr Cox once more went through the motions of beautifying himself: his hat, removed, lent the opportunity to smooth back thick, greasy hair, and his breath, although checked, smelled of breakfast sausages. Elsabeth wilted against the flowers before catching the defeat in her own posture and defiantly straightening again.

Cox performed an ingratiating smile, but did not, to her great relief, go so far as to kneel. "Miss Elsabeth, I know my own heart and I believe that I know yours. It is incumbent upon me to marry, and—"

"Mr Cox," Elsa said desperately, but before she could go on, behind Cox, a footstep fell upon the grass nearby. Elsabeth's gaze darted that way, widened, and before wisdom could prevail, she caught Cox's hand in her own and offered him a blinding smile of her own. "Mr Cox, I can only commend you for the sensibility of spirit that moves you to beg my approval before making your proposal. I know that it is your own shyness that sends you to me to seek verification that your suit should be accepted, and it gives me all happiness to—"

Before she completed this statement to a befuddled Reginald Cox, Elsabeth looked once more beyond him, to where Ruth Dover, with her hair worn loose in ringlets and her form bedecked in one of Matilda's prettiest gowns, stood with both hands clenched in anticipation of thwarted desire. Her eyes, though, were round with hope behind their spectacles, and at Elsa's querying glance, she gave a single fierce nod of acquiescence.

"—*all* happiness," Elsabeth repeated joyfully, "to tell you that I am quite certain that my darling sister Ruth is as fond of you as you are about to profess to me that you are of her. She stands behind you now as a vision of your future, and I must away, but not too far, that I might be the very first to wish you all due felicitations. To wish it to both of you," Elsa whispered, and, as she turned the astonished Mr Cox to face Ruth, she found a great love welling up from her soul and bringing tears of joy to her eyes.

Before Cox had recovered himself, Elsabeth skipped past him to catch Ruth's hands and fold them to her bosom in a sign of greater sisterly affection than she could remember sharing with Ruth since they were children. "You are happy?" she whispered. "This is what you want?"

Ruth's smile was not so much of joy as triumph. "I have no use for the Hartnells of this world," she responded in equally soft kind, "and the Webbers have no use for me. But *this* one I can make a husband of, Elsabeth, and it shall be very well for both of us. I shall have a household of my own, children to care for, books to read and a proper lady to learn from. This is *precisely* what I want."

"Then I shall go tell Father to expect a knock on his study door and to be polite about it," Elsabeth replied happily, and tripped lightly away with only a single backward glance to see Mr Cox rearranging his expectations and desires as easily now as he had when told that Rosamund was shortly to be engaged. Indeed, gazing at the third Miss Dover, Mr Cox recalled Ruth's solemnity, her intellect, her proper manners and how often he had come gallantly to her rescue in the past two weeks; by the time Elsabeth slipped away through the garden, he was quite convinced he had been in love with Ruth all along, and that Miss Elsabeth's interpretation of his approaching *her* was the only possible one.

Mr Dover, when presented with this intelligence a few minutes later, peered at his favourite daughter so assiduously that he was obliged to remove and replace his reading glasses twice before he could speak. "Forgive me, my dear Elsabeth, but I think I could not have heard you correctly. Ruth is *what*?"

"By now, I should think she is well engaged to Mr Cox, Papa, and she is happy."

"But Mr Cox is...is...is so..." Mr Dover's imagination failed him before a certain truth set in. "Then again, Ruth is also...is very..."

"I believe they may be perfectly suited for one another, Papa. And is it not the most perfect solution to all our problems? Mr Cox shall remain in Lady Derrington's parish and Ruth's son will inherit Oakden! It shall remain in our family, close to our family, after all, and poor Mamma's nerves will finally be settled."

"On the contrary," Mr Dover said drily, "I believe Mrs Dover's nerves will be entirely alight. She shall have to keep Tildy to herself now, so that someone will be here to care for us in our dotage. Dina will suffer an apoplexy, one part over losing Tildy and two parts over Ruth—Ruth!—marrying before she does, never mind that Ruth is nineteen and certainly old enough to be wed, whereas Dina is fifteen and silly. Well. You had best go, my dear, so that the dreadful Mr Cox might come and plead, in his supercilious way, for the hand of my middle daughter."

Elsabeth, positively buoyant with her own escape, departed her father's library only to find Dina standing suspiciously close to the door, and with a dangerous glint in her eyes. "Did you *see* Ruth, Elsa? I have never seen her look so pretty. I do not believe she *can* look so pretty! Is she using magic? Has she ensnared a husband through magic? What must *I* do to be wed? I cannot bear it! I cannot bear it, Elsabeth, I simply cannot bear it!"

"I saw her," Elsa replied before the brunt of Dina's complaint broke free. Well before it had reached its peak, Elsabeth caught her youngest sister's upper arm and propelled her through the house and up the stairs to the room Dina shared with Tildy and Ruth. "Hush. Hush! No, of course she has not used magic, Leopoldina! She has only loosened her hair and begun to dress more attractively. You should know better than any of us that glamours and charms of that nature do not work!"

This unpleasant truth stole the strength from Dina's tantrum; she, of all the Dover girls, had tried time and again as a child to make herself look older or influence her parents' decisions through the use of magic. She had only given up the attempts in the past year or two, sullenly demanding what good magic was, if it couldn't cast charms or change minds. Mr Dover, in a rare show of obvious power, had engendered a tiny rainstorm directly above Dina's head and murmured, "Perhaps it is merely useful to ensure a fine crop for the...*wine*." Dina, abruptly made aware that she was indeed whining, and shocked by Mr Dover's blatancy, had lapsed into silence and had not since spoken of emotional enchantments.

"But *Ruth*," she said now, in a tone of such despair that Elsabeth was inclined to laugh at it.

"We must consider Ruth, and ourselves, very fortunate, Dina. Oakden will stay with us now, and Ruth is happy. You would not be happy with Mr Cox. Better to find a man who will please you than rush into marriage simply to be a Mrs before any of your sisters."

"You will all be married before me," Leopoldina said dismally. "Rosamund is practically engaged and you are fashionably tall and slim and Ruth is to be wed and Tildy..." Her litany died away as she considered Tildy's prospects. Finding them to be no better than her own, she brightened a little, and Elsabeth, laughing, drew her into an embrace.

"We shall all find what makes us happiest, Dina. We shall all be so graced. I believe this," Elsa murmured, and snapped her fingers to call up a dance of flame upon their tips, "because we are all too much like ourselves to accept anything else."

Dina gave a glad gasp of surprise and clapped her hand over Elsabeth's fingertips. "Elsa!"

"Shh. It will be our secret. Now"—Elsabeth stood and pulled Dina to her feet—"let us go and congratulate Ruth, who deserves our happiness."

(27)

In no wise did Leopoldina Dover believe that Ruth, however prim and dull *she* might find her, did not deserve happiness. Indeed, Dina did not think that far at all: despite Elsabeth's ministrations, she saw little other than the incontestable fact that Ruth was to be married and she was not. The only acceptable aspect of Ruth's engagement was that Mr Cox, having settled the matter to his own satisfaction, had departed for his vicarage; as to the rest, something must be done. If Captain Hartnell, the still-desired object of her affections, had had his head turned by an older sister, surely it was Leopoldina herself who had drawn his attention originally. Having done so once, she could certainly do it again and, in so doing, secure her own marriage to the dashing young captain. Elsabeth, she consoled herself, would not be long broken-hearted, for Elsabeth was never long sorrowful over anything for any reason.

These were the thoughts that occupied her as the family Dover bustled about in preparation for Ruth's marriage. To Bodton and back again; to the Enton estate for shared gossip; to dinners and luncheons and walks held with Captain Hartnell, who paid ever-special attention to Elsabeth; to Newsbury, or at least, Rosamund to Newsbury with rarely more than Elsabeth as chaperone; to inevitability, Dina feared: *three* of her sisters would soon be wed, and one of them to the man she fancied for herself. And yet opportunity failed to arise: she dared not fling herself into a river again, and for all that the wind danced at her beckoning, wretched magic stood strong against the casting of glamours and sentimental attachments. Even beasts were insensible to such enchantments: Leopoldina could no more make a cat fond of her than she could Captain Hartnell.

And yet it was impossible to be sullen, with the promise of new gowns for Ruth's wedding and the warm beauty of late summer heating Oakden. If Elsabeth could not long be unhappy, neither, it seemed, could Leopoldina, and, in her flighty way, she had almost forgotten her intentions when at long last opportunity presented itself. They were gone to town—Bodton, of course, not the luxurious dream that was London—to collect the promised gowns, upon which an unquestionable indulgence had been granted: the dressmaker had created them, rather than the fabric being purchased to be sewn at home. Dina's heart lifted each time she thought of her new dress, and the journey from Oakden to Bodton was done in good spirits with much laughter as she and Tildy whispered secrets and dreams to one another.

They were fitted into their dresses first and regarded as successful; Ruth, who had very little pretty to begin with and who was the bride besides, was fussed over to a much greater degree, until Dina could bear it no longer and announced she would go for a walk, and return to admire Ruth's success in a little while. Mrs Dover, beset by daughters, agreed to this proposal at once, and Dina slipped out into the heavy August afternoon.

She had gone very little distance before she regretted her choice: the air was oppressively still, with the sky gone the strange dark blue that promised no break in the weather for some time to come. Sound carried peculiarly in the thick air, slowing and stretching it, until what few voices there were, were distorted and unpleasant.

Walking briskly made some small pretense of wind, but made for considerably more perspiration, and she dared not awaken a breeze to cool herself when the whole of Bodton shimmered with undisturbed waves of heat. Even the river gave little surcease from the warmth; indeed, great swarms of late-summer biting flies buzzed and hung by the water as if lying in wait for anyone foolish enough to pass them by. Dina struck off up the bank to avoid them, wishing very much that she had stayed with her sisters at the dressmaker's. The labors of her own ascent drowned out other sounds for a moment; when she became sensible to them again, it was to hear the prancing clop of hooves. Breathless, she paused beside the bridge to search out the rider, and in admiration saw that a coach-and-four some distance away moved in such unison as to sound like one animal. Glancing the other way, she saw in the town square the entire regiment, amongst whom Captain Hartnell must number, and, in an instant, she was decided.

With a whisper to the wind, she turned her back on the bridge and began to make her way toward the square as if all unknowing of the upcoming coach. The wind, at her bidding, swept up a great swarm of the biting flies and sped them across the river and down the road until they met, and fell to biting, the splendid set of four horses. One of them screamed with outrage, shocking even Leopoldina: she spun, as did each and every other body within hearing, and saw that the four were out of control with rage and pain. They stampeded: this had been Dina's ill-conceived intent, but she had not thought clearly of their speed or strength or, most terribly, of the other denizens of Bodton who were out and about on this still and heavy day. She had thought only of herself, imagining in an instant the drama of a near-disaster, and how Captain Hartnell would emerge out of the regiment to take her in his arms and realise how he could not have lived without her.

But there were others nearby, *children* nearby, little ones curious enough to run toward, and not away, from the shrieking and panicked horses. They ran from shops, their mothers giving frightened chase; Dina herself snatched one up and ran after another, but the street was suddenly full of people, all trying to drag one another out of the way of runaway beasts. The horses' hooves made their first clatter on the bridge: a handful of strides and they would be over it and into the town square, crushing all who were unfortunate enough to stand in their path.

A thunderous voice roared words that carried the faintest hint of familiarity, but could not be placed or repeated. On the tail of these words rode magic, racing past Dina from the town square. Its focus was unlike anything she had ever encountered: even Mr Dover's rare deliberate magics felt lackadaisical and trite beside the onslaught of this spell.

Its destructive power embraced the centre of the Bodton bridge and ripped stone from stone, undoing masonry a century and more in age. The racing, terrified horses bucked and bent, struggling to stop their headlong rush when the road before them no longer existed; one, in its terror, leapt, but its partners did not, and the whole foursome was dragged forward by its weight. It, by pure fortune, caught the far side of the broken bridge with its hooves and heaved itself forward; its nearest brother struggled and surged, trying to stand beside its match, but even as they struggled together, the pair behind them, and the coach, fell into the broad gap at the heart of the bridge.

A second bellow sent more magic surging across the bridge. *Below* the bridge: beneath the fallen carriage, structured power seeking to build a surface on which the weight of the fallen coach could rest. Something in the shouted words spoke of *lifting*, just as the wind might lift a leaf, and Dina saw, quite clearly and quite suddenly, that it would not work. To lift a leaf upward the way this magic wished to lift the coach-and-four, it had to be directly beneath the leaf, and the spellcaster was in the town square.

Calmly, as if thinking it through, Leopoldina placed the child she held in someone else's arms and slid down the bank again to walk steadily into the river. It did not capture her the way it had in the early summer; its waters ran lower now, reaching no higher than her waist, and, in a few resolute surges, she was nearly beneath the struggling coach-and-four.

If only she had clearly heard the words used by the spellcaster! But she had only the idea of them, and a gift of speaking with the wind. She gathered the stillness of the air to her, whispering the memory of motion to it, and, with a great cry, thrust wind upward to shore the struggling spell and hold the coach-and-four safe a little while longer.

Only a little while: that, she knew as truly as she knew her own name. The wind was not a solid thing upon which a beast could stand. It was strong, terribly strong; it could do impossible things with its strength, could lift a man like a bird or drive a straw through a piece of wood, but those were wild actions, gusts and twists. Wind could not be *held*, and its updraft would last only as long as her will.

She was the flighty one, Dina thought, and her magic trembled.

Captain David Hartnell slid into the water beside her and once more shouted the words of his spell, strengthening Dina's magic as she had strengthened his, until the horses and carriage, uplifted as if by the hand of God, were able to scramble forward and gain purchase on the shattered remains of the bridge. Once secure upon the ground, they held stock-still, as if afraid the stones beneath their feet would once more betray them; Dina and Hartnell, assured that the horses would not move, turned to one another, Dina torn between profound guilt and equally deep admiration as she gazed into the Captain's face.

His colour was poor. More than poor: he seemed nearly green with illness, and perspiration rolled down his face as if he had dunked himself wholly in the river water. He wet his lips, perhaps to speak, and instead pitched forward, insensible, into Dina's arms.

(28)

MRS DOVER, NEVER ONE TO LAY BLAME AT HER FAVOURED DAUGHter's feet, stood just within the dressmaker's door, and, fluttering with dread, whispered, "What has she done? Oh, Lord, what has she done!" as Leopoldina, wet to the waist, walked slowly across Bodton's town square with Captain Hartnell, drenched entirely, leaning heavily upon her. Red-clad soldiers paced near to them as if willing but not eager to assist. Beyond them all lay the bridge, its ruined centre a gaping and terrible gash to the eye as a coachman urged four matched horses gently off what remained of it.

What she had done was, of course, self-evident, or at least, the four astonished sisters grouped behind their mother found it to be. The thick summer air reeked of magic, a pungent, bitter scent like burned gunpowder. Elsabeth had never before known magic to smell, but neither had she ever seen such power released. "It could not have been Dina," she said aloud, half in hope and half in confidence.

"How could it not?" cried their mother. "And poor Captain Hartnell caught in it, too! Oh, I am a wretched woman to be mother to such daughters! Thank heavens that Ruth is safely engaged! No gentleman would now consider any of you if he had a choice in the matter, but Mr Cox has none!" She chose quite purposefully to misinterpret the look bestowed upon her by her middle daughter, too overwrought with her own calamity to consider the cruelty of her words. "Do not look at me so, Ruth! A gentleman cannot break an engagement, simply *cannot*, and we are now desperate for your marriage that we may survive as a family!"

"Mamma," Elsabeth said softly, and then more sharply, "Mamma!"

Mrs Dover, taken aback by Elsa's tone, ceased wailing. "How dare you speak to me in that manner? My only concern is for the welfare of my girls, and—"

"Captain Hartnell has a gift for magic."

To observe Mrs Dover absorbing this information was to observe a sea change: she fell from horror to surprise and into relief so swiftly that the last might have been the only expression ever meant to grace her features. "We are saved!"

"Mamma," Rosamund said in genuine concern, "if this *is* Dina's doing, you cannot mean to lay it at Captain Hartnell's feet. It might ruin him."

Mrs Dover sniffed. "Nonsense. He is a soldier and, as such, permitted such vile talents if they are useful to his command. It will ruin us, but it could make him." Her eyes, usually so wide and guileless, narrowed in thought as she examined Elsabeth. "Indeed, as he seems fond of Elsa, it might even make *her*—"

"Mamma," Elsabeth said, exasperated, and left her mother behind to bestow necessary concern upon Dina and Captain Hartnell.

"He fainted," the former said to Elsa as she approached. "I caught him, but—"

"She is my saviour, as I was once hers," Hartnell agreed in a voice much fainter than his usual robust tones. "Indeed, had she not come into the river after me—"

Elsabeth saw the sharpness of Dina's glance toward the captain, and at once surmised the truth that he hid with his phrasing. Grateful for the falsehood he engendered, she did not press him on the point, nor interrupt as he concluded, "I should have drowned without a doubt. I am trained in the art of magical combat, but I have never done two such dramatic castings back to back. I fear I badly misjudged my own strength. Miss Elsabeth, I owe your family everything."

"It seems the people of Bodton owe *you*, Captain Hartnell. I cannot imagine what spooked the horses—" At this comment, Elsa noted the guilt that darkened Leopoldina's eyes, and bit back a curse that surely would have shocked all who heard it. "But I fear lives would have been lost if you had not acted as swiftly as you did."

Hartnell offered a sweet, if pained, smile. "I do not believe the town will thank me for making a ruin of their bridge. I can only hope that my superiors will allow the army to make redress by reconstructing it, else I fear the town will be some time in waiting, for I am not a stonemason, and will not be able to work swiftly on my own."

"Surely, you could use magic." Dina's cheeks flushed as though the very idea thrilled her, but Hartnell's weary smile in response slew what hope had been birthed in her gaze.

"I'm afraid that my skills lie solely in the art of destruction, Miss Dina. We few military men who have magical talent are not often encouraged to build, when there are so many who know the practical arts of such activities. And now that my shame is publicly known, I am certain that your mother will permit you to have no more to do with me." Hartnell heaved himself upright, although he looked as though Dina's support was much missed as he drew a ragged breath. "So, let me take my leave of you as gently as I may. Miss Dina, we are even: a life for a life, so the balance is made. I will be ever grateful for your presence in my life. Miss Elsabeth, thank you for your friendship; I wish that it might have been more."

Elsabeth, moved to sudden tears, stepped forward to clasp Hartnell's hand. "I cannot believe this will be the end of our acquaintance, Captain Hartnell; there is too much left unsaid between us. And," she added on a wryer note, "you have perhaps forgotten what you know of my mother, if you believe a little display of magic might turn her away from you. But come: you are not well, and must be looked after. Surely, there is a physician amongst the regiment who is schooled in how to ease the weariness of a soldier who has fought with magic?"

A strangeness came over Hartnell's expression. He glanced from Elsabeth to Dina with a cunning query in his gaze, though it faded so swiftly that Elsabeth might have imagined it. He spoke with as much gentle humility as he ever had, and if she had thought there was slyness in his eyes before, it was drowned now by fondness. "You are easier with my shame than I might expect, and perhaps I might someday be permitted to know why. But for now, you are right: I find myself somewhat weaker on my feet than a man of my modest years might wish to admit, and the doctor will know best how to revive me. Take Miss Dina home and see her warm and dry again, will you not? I am indebted, and should hate for her to become ill..." As he reached the end of his speech, Hartnell's words grew slower, as though thought was increasingly difficult to marshal. Nearly as one, Elsabeth came forward to take her sister and several men of the regiment stepped forth to collect Hartnell, and the Dovers' last glimpse of him for some time to come was his unsteady step as he was escorted away.

(29)

Captain Hartnell's departure may have been the last the Dovers saw of him for some time, but it was not, by any means, the last he was heard of. The story of his deed—or misdeed, depending on the speaker—flew through the town of Bodton with the unflaggable speed of gossip; by evening, there was not a soul within the town's borders who did not know that Hartnell had worked that most military of activities, *magic*.

With such stories to be spread, it was inevitable that distant memories of other magical workings should come to mind. Many harkened back to the War for the Colonies, where His Majesty's army had faced not only the reprobate French soldiers, who were known for their enthusiastic embrace of magic, but the strange and powerful sorcery of the savage American natives, which came as naturally to them as breathing. Indeed, it was commonly thought that it had been the League of Iroquois who had pressured the colonies into declaring independence, upon pain of their own intimate and exquisite deaths; since the War had been lost, colonists had been allowed to settle only in the numbers and locations permitted by the League in New England, and nowhere at all in the southern territories. Western expansion, never as aggressive as desired, had met an uncrossable barrier at the Ohiyo and Misiziibi rivers; even today, old soldiers remembered bullets and men alike rebounding while birds and beasts roamed freely.

But others recalled tales from closer to home. No self-respecting person, regardless of class, would admit to being plagued with power, not unless it was in service to the Crown and reluctantly sanctioned by necessity. There had been burnings, even so recently as Cromwell, when women were suspected of witchery, and men had been pressed into taking the king's shilling. It was not done, not at all, save by savages, but, in the wake of Hartnell's display, some began to recall the unlikely fine weather that had graced the Dover marriage some twenty-five years earlier. Others spoke of the Dover garden, reputed to go unriddled by rabbits, and of the surprising softness of their staff's hands, as if they had less need of plunging them into boiling water for washing dishes or clothes. After a day or two, those lucky—or luckless—servants began to find themselves crowded at the butcher, as if they might be intimidated into speaking, or cosied up to at the pub, as if they might be liquored into talk. Neither was to succeed, and, within five days, it was agreed that their silence was as condemning as their speech would have been.

Before a week was out, most of Bodton had managed to recall at least one, and perhaps several, incidents that they had personally witnessed: cats coming when called, cows failing to give milk, a spell of sunshine while the Dovers shopped in town when it had rained consistently for days; a laugh on the wind when no one was to be seen, and certainly half the town had seen Leopoldina Dover go into the river and try *something* before Hartnell crashed into the water. Indeed, it was agreed that the horses bolting like that, with no clear cause, was suspicious itself when a Dover was about, although the gentleman whose team had been beleaguered was himself certain it had been only a dreadful cloud of flies, and it was impossible to say whether he was more relieved that his horses had been stopped before trampling anyone, or that the beautiful creatures had been saved from certain destruction as the bridge collapsed. He did not care to pursue it; it had been too uncomfortably close a brush with magic for a man of his stature, and the sooner it was put out of mind, the better.

Bodton's gossips were deeply disappointed in this show of practicality; had the gentleman cared to, his pursuit of the matter might have unearthed certainty in the matter of Dover magic. But where certainty could not be had, gossip would do, and the enthusiasm with which incidents of Dover magic were recalled might have awakened a certain suspicion in the heart of an unbiased observer. Sadly for the Dovers, no such being existed in Bodton in the days following Hartnell's display of power.

It was therefore inevitable that whispers would reach Newsbury Manor, and nestle in the ear of one Fitzgerald Archer.

Hartnell's part in this was, of course, no surprise to him; indeed, had he in some way been able to trace the source of these rumours back to Hartnell himself, Archer would have rested easy, confident that a reprobate was doing nothing more than trying to pass off his own actions as belonging to someone else. But it was widely—wholly—agreed that Hartnell had acted heroically, confessing his embarrassing secret to the world at large because to do otherwise would allow tragedy to strike. He had not, in the days of his recovery, made any attempt to deny his magic; had, in fact, gotten off his sick bed to plead with the town council that he be allowed to help in reconstructing the bridge. The council, charmed, had sent him back to bed, and the people of Bodton turned out to watch the army rebuild the bridge in a good humour; all condemnation for its destruction was filtering squarely down to sit upon the shoulders of the Dover family, and Leopoldina Dover in particular.

Archer himself was not loath to believe that the youngest Dover girl was magic-ridden; magic could go no further in emphasising his disapproval of her than her general nature already had. Similarly with the mother, although, through quiet investigation, he determined that it was Mr Dover who was commonly accepted to be the magician, and that Mrs Dover had married him in spite of it. The two eldest daughters, it was held in both wide belief and in Archer's own, were unlikely to be actual magicians themselves; their behaviour had never suggested it, and it was clear that the spectacled middle daughter who disapproved of everything could not possibly be magically inclined herself. The second youngest was conceded to follow in her younger sister's wake and therefore presumed to have magic herself, but, in truth, none of that mattered. If a single one of them practiced magic—and it appeared unquestionable that Mr Dover himself was suspected of it—then the family as a whole was tainted.

Webber, Archer concluded, had to be saved from himself before he made a dreadful mistake. Rosamund Dover's attractive qualities could in no way make up for the risk of magic-bearing heirs. And yet, he could not quite bring himself to tell Webber the truth about Rosamund. Not for Webber's sake, he found, but for his own: should Julia Webber learn of the Dovers' unfortunate talent, he would be obliged to endure endless sniping regarding Elsabeth Dover, and would be expected to endure with good humour or remorse.

It was not, Archer told himself firmly, that he wished to defend Miss Elsabeth or that he had become infatuated with an entirely unsuitable female; it was merely that he was not a man who endured much of anything in good humour or remorse, and was inclined to save himself the exasperation of trying. Julia already did not approve of any match made with a country family, particularly one of comparatively little means, as the Dovers were; it was easy enough to draw her into a confidence one afternoon, murmuring that he thought it best they return to London before the weather turned poorly. Julia, who did not socialise in Bodton and who had heard none of the rumours, was eager to seize upon any opportunity to leave quickly, but mentioned a certain grim concern that her brother would want to stay on in hopes of encountering Miss Dover once again.

"Allow me to deal with Robert," Archer said, and, that very evening, took it upon himself to note aloud that Miss Dover had refused all invitations to Newsbury for almost two weeks now.

Webber, who had observed this unhappy fact himself, drooped into a chair. "Not since that dreadful incident with the bridge," he agreed. "I should think a gentlewoman like herself must be afraid to leave the house with such brigandly magics going on, but if she will not answer our invitations, it seems impolite to thrust ourselves upon her in her own home. I am at a loss, Archer. What am I to do? She is the fairest and sweetest lady I have ever met."

"Robert," Archer said as gently as he knew how, "has it occurred to you that perhaps the lady's affections are not as intense as your own? That perhaps she has ceased accepting your invitations because she does not wish to encourage you?"

"Poppycock." Webber spoke with the bluster of a man afraid. "Nonsense, Archer, she is the very soul of gentility and I am sure she...I *was* sure she...You cannot be right, Archer. You simply cannot be right."

"She is charming and sweet," Archer agreed, "but has she made any protestations of love, Webber? Can you be sure of her?"

"Love! Are you mad, man? Of course she hasn't! A gentle, reserved woman of her stature would surely never speak of love to a man who has not spoken of it to her! And yet, I believe I had seen it in her eyes, Archer, in the soft and accepting way she looked at me..."

"But she has not answered your invitations," Archer said, and, judging the job done, offered to pour brandy, which Webber glumly accepted.

(30)

It was true Rosamund had not accepted any Newsbury invitations in some time, for after the incident with the bridge, she had taken very ill with worry over Leopoldina and the family as a whole. Mr Cox had, thank heavens, already departed, putting Ruth's marriage and happiness less at risk than had he been in Bodton to hear the rumours regarding the Dover family.

"Rumours," Elsabeth had said tartly, "that he ought to take no heed of anyway, being the same blood, however diluted, as Papa, and therefore as likely to burgeon with magic of his own as any one of us might be," a statement which had done much to revive Rosamund, who could not help but be amused at the idea of pompous Mr Cox wielding magic in any wise. Even so, as her health improved, her worries about what might have been heard at Newsbury Manor increased, until nerves prevented her from accepting the invitations she so dearly wished to. Elsabeth, less tartly this time, had pointed out that the invitations would not continue to come if they considered Rosamund a pariah, but that they might well cease if she did not soon respond positively.

This was a calamity that had not occurred to Rosamund. Armed with its potential, she resolved to joyfully agree to the next invitation, and, having so decided, seemed a little stronger for it. Ruth, who had softened quite considerably since her engagement, agreed to read a novel to Rosamund, so pleased she was at her recovery. For a few days, the family were all most diverted by Ruth's reading, for it proved that when she was not determined to be sour, she commanded an impressive performance skill that made listening to her a delight instead of a chore.

Sophia Enton arrived one afternoon near the end of Ruth's reading, and sat to listen with considerable enjoyment before joining in the applause as Ruth closed the book. Ruth, best pleased, retired to her embroidery with a suspicious degree of modesty whilst Tildy and Dina argued over what would happen next in the book. Sophia took to speaking with the two eldest Dover sisters, beginning with "Ruth is looking very well, isn't she? Engagement suits her."

"It does," Elsabeth replied happily. Her marriage partner ensnared, Ruth Dover had not instantly, as Elsabeth had half imagined she might, return to the dour gowns and unattractive hair she had once worn. Neither did she make a habit of borrowing Tildy's best dresses, nor take any extraordinary effort at curling her hair, but Sophia was eminently correct: Ruth looked very well indeed. "It is as if her determined unhappiness was a manner of making herself different from the rest of us. Rosamund is sweet, and I am stubborn. Dina is silly and Tildy suggestible; what else could be left for Ruth but to be sour? Had Mr Cox not happened to us, she might have been sour into spinsterhood, but, instead, she has caught what she wanted and can perhaps relax into satisfaction. I had not thought of it before, but now I cannot help but wonder if that has always been the case."

"If it is so," Rosamund answered, "and I think that you may be correct, then I fear that we have done our sister a disservice all these years. Perhaps we might have helped her into satisfaction rather than becoming gently vexed with her behaviours."

"Perhaps we might have," Elsabeth agreed, "but without this change, how were we to know?"

"We could not have," Sophia said placidly. "And may I say that you are also looking very well, Rosa? Better than I had expected, if I may be frank, given the circumstances."

Surprise coloured Rosamund's features. "What circumstances might those be?"

Where she had been placid a moment before, Sophia Enton was now horrified. "Have you not heard?"

Rosamund seized Elsabeth's hand, both sisters gazing upon Sophia in anticipation of news so dire, they could not yet imagine it. "We have been quite shut in these past two weeks, Sophia. What is it we are meant to have heard?"

Sophia's hand covered her mouth; above it, her eyes were wide with apology. "I'm sorry. I never imagined you couldn't know. The Webbers are gone back to London, three days since."

Mrs Dover, who had, by all appearances, been entirely involved with her needlework, barked, "*What*?" and, for once, both Tildy and Dina were entirely silenced by shock. Even Mr Dover, who had listened to the whole of Ruth's reading with his eyes so firmly closed, it would not have been remiss to think him asleep, opened his eyes to reveal dismay in them. "Surely, that cannot be right. They are surely only on a brief visit, and will return?"

"No," Sophia replied, grim with being the bearer of unwelcome news, "I am afraid that Newsbury Manor has been put up to let. They will not be returning this season and perhaps not ever again."

"But—but *Rosa*!" cried Mrs Dover with such force that it might have been she whose romantic ambitions had been thwarted. "Mr Webber cannot leave without marrying *Rosa*!"

Rosamund, most faintly, said, "It seems that he can, Mamma. Do not worry yourself about me. I am sure...I am sure that it is all for the best."

"Nonsense! There is some deviltry at work here—"

This phrase, spoken in a rage by Mrs Dover, caused Elsabeth and Rosamund to look at one another with a sudden terrible understanding. Mrs Dover carried on in a fine fettle, supported by Leopoldina and Matilda. The specific words used to express their collective dismay were unnecessary to hear; their sentiment was clear enough, and did not in any way touch upon the fear shared by Rosamund and Elsabeth Dover. Shared, too, by Sophia Enton, whose knowledge of Dover magic was more accurate than most, and who, in genuine sorrow, reached out to take the sisters' hands. "I'm so terribly sorry, Rosamund," she said beneath Mrs Dover's venting. "Had I realised you didn't know, I would have at least broached the awful subject more gently."

"No, no," Rosamund said with false brightness, and squeezed Sophia's hand. "Perhaps it's better to have heard it bluntly: the shock is sharp and hard that way, but it will fade all the more quickly for it. There...there was no letter sent." This she spoke as if asking a question, though Sophia could not have an answer; after a moment she repeated it, no longer questioning: "There was no letter sent. It is my own fault," she said with greater clarity. "I was remiss in responding to his invitations; he must have concluded that I did not care, and, indeed, why should he not?"

"Rosamund," replied Elsa in tones of despair. "You cannot think—I will not allow you to imagine—that it is *your* fault that they have left Newsbury. You know that it is not. You know it!"

Rosa turned a smile so brittle it looked in danger of shattering toward Elsabeth. "Of course it is, my sweet sister. What other possible answer could society accept?"

Elsabeth could not help but turn a black look on Dina, at this question. The youngest Dover girl intercepted it with unfeigned surprise, crying, "I know; is it not dreadful, Elsa? The regiment has quite closed ranks, doing nothing but rebuild the silly bridge, and now the Webbers have gone! What are we to do for entertainment now? Why, now that I think of it, I cannot remember a single invitation to visit having arrived in the past week! We are most bereft of company, and winter will be here soon! Mamma!" Dina turned to Mrs Dover, alight with the arrival of an idea. "Mamma, we must go to London. We must have a Season. There is nothing else to be done."

Mrs Dover, who could be led if the draw was slow enough, seemed most struck by a single one of Dina's many statements. "You are right," she replied after a moment's terrible silence.

"There have been no invitations for a week or more, Leopoldina. Not even from my dear friend Mrs Enton, your own dear mother, Sophia. There have been no invitations at all."

"How peculiar that is! I should have imagined us very busy, and with this news that the Newsbury contingent have gone, I should have imagined us even busier than that! Why, surely there must be curiosity in Bodton about poor Rosa's state, now that she has been jilt—"

"*Dina*," said her father, sharply, and Leopoldina lapsed into hurt and bewildered silence.

Rosa, who could do almost nothing less than beautifully, blushed unattractively and swiftly bent her head over a piece of embroidery that had, moments earlier, been regarded as perfectly finished by any who might lay eyes upon it. Sophia Enton gazed in agony at a wall, the better not to meet any Dover eyes, although the remaining whole of the Dover family, as one, regarded the youngest of themselves with horror. She alone among them seemed incapable of grasping the most likely reason for the Webbers' departure; she alone seemed entirely innocent to her own culpability in their retreat. Neither did the weight of her family's gaze in any way enlighten her: after bearing it for some long moments, she muttered, resentfully, "Well, is it not true?"

"It is true," Mrs Dover said with great strain. "It is true, and I am loath to admit that, had such an unfortunate occurrence happened to another family, we might have been first on the doorstep to learn all the details of the calamity, whilst secretly enjoying every misfortune laid at another's feet."

This was insightful enough to Mrs Dover's own periodically cruel character that Elsabeth was obliged to disengage her attention from Leopoldina and briefly examine her mother. Shame was not an expression familiar to Mrs Dover's face, but the lines of it were there now. Beyond Mrs Dover, Mr Dover's own countenance showed his years by way of a weary sympathy: he loved his wife, Elsabeth thought, but was not blind to her faults. Nor, it seemed, was she; not entirely, and not when it might be most pleasant to be so.

"There will be no Season in London," Mrs Dover said quietly. "We shall see Ruth married and retire quietly back to Oakden, where we will pass the winter without incident, and hope that the spring brings new diversions to Bodton so that this all may be forgotten."

"What? No! I will not be able to bear it, Mamma, even Rosa's undesirability as a wife cannot possibly keep me contained for the entire winter! We—"

"Leopoldina," said Mr Dover with such implacable gentleness as to stem her flow of words, "I am reluctant to play the part of the Gothic father and lock my daughter in the cellar, but simply because I am reluctant does not mean that I lack the capability or the will. You will do as your mother says."

Faced with this unexpected severity in her genial Papa, tears filled Leopoldina's eyes as she stood. "You need not show such heartlessness! I know Rosa's hopes are dashed, but must all of ours be as well? I cannot bear it! I cannot bear you!"

With this cry, she threw her embroidery to the floor and dashed from the sitting room.

Almost at once, Sophia Enton rose. "I think I had best be going."

"We are so sorry to have exposed you to this display," Rosamund whispered. Elsabeth sprang to her feet and said, at the same time, "I shall escort you to the door." A flurry of farewells and apologies followed as they left the sitting room, whereupon Elsabeth said, "I am so sorry, Sophia. This has been unspeakable."

The faintest line of humour etched itself at the corner of Sophia's mouth. "On the contrary, Elsabeth, I believe I have rarely seen quite so much revealing speech. Oh, do not worry," she added, embracing Elsabeth. "I shall say nothing of it; of course I will not. But Leopoldina is...extraordinarily myopic, is she not? I do not think she realises herself blameworthy at all."

"No, and if it is explained to her, as I think it must be, she will only regard it as another injustice against her. She will feel it should not be such a crime, to have magic, and that Society is in the wrong."

"A sentiment which I believe you share," Sophia said gently. "I shall visit as often as possible, Elsabeth, to try to lighten the length of the winter days."

"You are very kind. I shall, in between times, endeavour not to do bodily harm to my youngest sibling. I believe my soon-to-be brother-in-law would have quite a long lecture on the sins of sororicide." Elsabeth shuddered theatrically and Sophia obliged with a laugh and another embrace.

"There, I knew you could not long be melancholy. Go," Sophia urged. "Care for Rosa, and forgive me again for my dreadful tidings."

"There is nothing to forgive," Elsa promised, and did as she was bidden.

(31)

So it went: in the early winter, after more quiet weeks than Elsabeth could comfortably recall, the Dovers went forth to see their middle daughter and sister married, and if Leopoldina and Mrs Dover put on a performance with too many tears, it could not be said that Ruth herself showed any great sorrow at parting from her family. Only once, unexpectedly, as she gathered herself to enter Lady Beatrice Derrington's carriage, which had been sent for the newlyweds, did she present any indication of hesitation. Elsabeth, standing nearby and watching the commotion with a smile, suddenly felt Ruth's hand in hers and found her sister gazing at her with wide and serious eyes. "You will come visit me, won't you, Elsa? You and Rosamund, at least, from time to time. I am certain I will be very busy with my own life, but...but it will be a long way from home, and quite solitary after so many sisters. You will come visit?"

Startled, Elsabeth embraced Ruth and whispered a promise in her ear. So it was that Mr and Mrs Cox drove away into the afternoon sun with a great sense of happiness and accomplishment on all sides, and Mrs Dover turned to Rosamund with a determined set to her jaw. "Well, we had all imagined it would be you who would save us, Rosamund, with your marriage to Mr Webber assuring the family's future, but it seems Ruth is our most dutiful daughter of all."

"Mamma!" Rosa protested, truly hurt. "I have not been remiss in my duty!"

"Of course not, my sweet, but Mr Webber had five thousand a year, and we must now wait for Ruth to have a son or two before we can breathe easily." Mrs Dover tucked her arm into Leopoldina and Matilda's to sail triumphantly into the house. "We shall visit Mrs Enton, of course, and tell her of the wedding. We shall not mention that poor Sophia is twenty-eight now, with no more prospects than she had; we will only be happy for our Ruth, whom I always knew would do well." Her words were lost as Oakden enveloped them, and the two eldest sisters, left outside with Mr Dover, gazed speechlessly after them.

Elsabeth, mindful of Rosa's heartache and yet unable to leave Mrs Dover's blitheness untouched, said, "I thought it was three thousand a year he had," to Mr Dover, whose smile sharpened momentarily.

"In another six months, it shall be ten thousand, and Leopoldina's part in it all will be forgotten entirely. Not by me, Elsa," he assured her. "I meant it quite seriously when I spoke of restraining her within the house for the winter; Bodton must be allowed to find itself a few other scandals, that ours might be forgotten."

"At least our Aunt and Uncle Penney have come for the wedding, and will be staying on a while," Rosamund said with false brightness. Much of what she said now was under the guise of forced gaiety; Elsabeth thought that their mother did not even recognise it as such, and knew that the two youngest of the Dover sisters did not. She was more sensible to Rosamund's true state, and believed that their father was as well. Indeed, Mr Dover offered Rosamund a fond arm, and encouraged her to lean heavily upon him as she concluded, "Surely, our winter cannot be so dull, when Mrs Penney is here."

As if summoned by her name, that worthy appeared. By some measure younger than her brother, Mrs Penney looked younger still than that; the provenance, Elsabeth thought, of having neither children nor financial worries. She was at the moment bedecked modestly well in pale green muslin that suited her without making it overly clear that her gown was considerably finer than the bride's had been. It was a generous gesture on her part, and the measure of the woman that Elsabeth would expect nothing else from her aunt. Mrs Dover's sister, Mrs Moore, on the other hand, had worn her very finest gown for the wedding, and had gleamed with pearls throughout the afternoon. It could not be regarded as inappropriate, but neither was it kind, and Elsabeth found she valued Mrs Penney's kindness above almost all else.

"You will not have a dull winter at all." Mrs Penney linked arms with Rosa and offered her other elbow to Elsabeth, so that a chain was made of Dovers-who-were and Dovers-who-had-been. "You have provided me with a great deal of intelligence regarding the untenable situation created here this summer; now that I am here, I shall learn the rest of it and set about restoring you to rights, my dear girls. We are all too aware of the legacy that plagues my brother and his family, but I intend to go about Bodton being so tremendously ordinary as to disprove any possible complaint of magic that might linger. Do not forget that I, too, grew up here, and having married nicely, might be considered a success despite the inconvenient question of our family gift. With Ruth married and therefore unquestionably safe by Society's rather narrow-minded standards, we only have to show that you dear girls are equally untouched. I will, in the end, prove my thesis by bringing Rosamund to Town for several weeks, for surely no one would dare bring a sorceress into her own home. Forgive me, Elsabeth, that I cannot bring you as well, but if I am to do well by Rosamund—"

"Then you cannot be crowded by a second unmarried woman," Elsabeth conceded gracefully. "I have no objections, Aunt Felicity; I am quite content here in Bodton."

"I am not sure," Rosamund protested, but neither could she deny the note of hope that graced her face and voice.

"Nonsense," proclaimed Mrs Penney. "A month or so of remedial activity in Bodton and then the Season in London will do you a world of good, Rosamund. I am sure that if you do not wish to, you will not encounter anyone in Town who might offer you heartache; we live quite away from certain circles, and socialise with another set entirely. Now, it is possible," she conceded, "that we may have to do as my brother has threatened, and keep Leopoldina in rein for the weeks I am here. She is impetuous."

"She is impossible," opined her father, and, upon this observation, detached himself from the ladies and retreated once again to the safety of his library.

With no other choice given to them, the ladies in question joined Mrs Dover in the sitting room, where she recounted with great enthusiasm the details of the wedding they had all just attended. Mrs Moore abided this as long as she could, only to finally interrupt with news that had no doubt been lying eager upon her tongue since the Moore family had arrived earlier that day. "My dear sister, it cannot wait any longer! I must tell you that the bridge is complete, and the regiment is once more expected to be seen regularly in Bodton!"

Leopoldina shrieked with delight and clapped her hands with Matilda's. "Oh! We are saved, then! Our winter shall not be as hopeless as we had feared!"

Elsabeth cast a concerned glance toward Mrs Penney, whose well-formed jaw set into a line of unusual determination, although there was nothing but solicitude in her tone as she spoke. "It is most splendid that there will be some small opportunity for diversion this winter, Dina, but of course with Ruth's marriage just past, I know that you will not be eager to incur greater expenses upon your mamma and papa's pocketbook. There will be no especial parties, I am certain, and the winter shall proceed quietly, as previously intended."

"Oh, no," Dina protested. "No, we have new gowns now, and the newest fashions yet, brought to us by you yourself, Aunt Felicity! There is no more expense—"

"Save the cost of entertaining, which is considerable," Rosamund said with greater forthrightness than was her wont. "I for one am eager to spend a quiet winter."

This bordered so closely on falsehood that Elsabeth looked with admiration upon the eldest Dover girl, whose head was bent so assiduously over her needlework that she could not be imagined to have any thought in the world save for it. Dina's eyebrows drew down in consternation, but before she spoke, Tildy, at her side, pled, "But we might have a few guests ourselves, might we not? Even if we do not go out a great deal, we might invite a select few to visit? Captain Hartnell, perhaps?"

The prospect of having her saviour once more come to Oakden silenced all of Dina's objections, and Matilda, who had no significant ulterior motives, preened beneath the general praise she received for her suggestion. Mrs Dover herself could not have been more pleased by the idea if she had put it forth herself, and it was shortly arranged that Mr Dover should invite the Captain for dinner that very Saturday.

Mrs Penney, who lacked nothing in observational skills, drew Elsabeth apart some little time later and, in asking after this young captain, noted a blush of fondness colouring Elsabeth's cheeks. In no time at all, Elsabeth related the whole of Hartnell's tragic story, and Leopoldina's foolishness—none of which she had dared commit to paper in the form of a letter—to her aunt, whose understanding of the situation betwixt Robert Webber and Rosamund Dover was much improved by the whole of the tale.

"You know that we are somewhat acquainted with Streyfield, visiting, as we do, Mr Penney's holdings in that area," Mrs Penney put forth thoughtfully when Elsabeth's tale was done. "Indeed, I am certain I met the old Mr Archer, though it would have been many years ago; we have not been to the country much these past five years, with Mr Penney's business in Town demanding so much of his time. But I recall that he was known as a good landlord and a man concerned with his community. I am awe-struck that his son could become such a poor example of a gentleman."

"Even if we were to wholly dismiss Captain Hartnell's plaint," Elsabeth replied, "I believe it would be widely agreed upon here in Bodton that Mr Archer is lacking in social graces. He is proud, Aunt Felicity, and does not care to deny it. Perhaps the old Mr Archer was too fond of his son, and too gentle with him."

Mrs Penney cast a glance toward where Leopoldina sat nestled very near to Mrs Dover. "Such fondness has been known to lead a parent astray from time to time." This gentle admonishment, directed at Elsabeth and not Mrs Dover, was as close to an opinion on the task of mothering as Elsa had ever heard her childless aunt proclaim. But she put even that mild sentiment aside to conclude, "I am a little sorry that I shall not meet Mr Archer. Instead, I will look forward to meeting your Captain Hartnell, and rendering an opinion thereof."

Elsabeth smiled. "He is not *my* Captain Hartnell, Aunt Felicity, but I am eager to learn your assessment of him. I believe you will find him as charming and amiable as any of us do."

(32)

The day came to host Captain Hartnell and some few of his closest companions. It was with glad hearts that the Dovers found Hartnell to be much recovered from the incident at the bridge, of which he could not be beguiled into speaking. It was enough, he demurred, that no one had been injured; the doctors had been well able to tend to him, and, indeed, he now felt more robust than he had before the incident. No more would be said on the matter, and Mrs Penney allowed as how his modesty became him.

It was on the occasion of his third visit inside the week that Captain Hartnell asked Miss Elsabeth if she might walk with him a while in the garden, an invitation that sent Mrs Dover's heart into palpitations. Elsabeth herself was pleased to acquiesce, if not so breathless with potential as her mother, and Mrs Penney, observing these disparate reactions, made note to discuss the handsome young captain with Elsabeth as her earliest leisure.

"Miss Elsabeth," Captain Hartnell began no sooner than they were far enough from the house to speak privately, "there is something I should like to ask you, although I fear it may be a delicate subject."

With the advent of these words, Elsa did entertain the possibility that the Captain meant to ask for her hand; by the end of them, she was quite certain he did not, for although a proposal was certainly a subject for delicacy, Captain Hartnell did not seem to her the sort of man who would approach it in such a way. "You may ask," she replied cautiously. "I cannot, of course, promise that I will tender the response you wish to hear."

"No man should ever expect that he will be given the answer he most wants." Hartnell smiled gallantly, then took it upon himself to walk several steps before gathering himself to speak. "I have been loath to discuss it with an audience, but I should like to mention the matter at the bridge to you, Miss Elsabeth."

"Ah." There were curved stone benches scattered throughout the garden; Elsabeth found and sank down upon one, disregarding its dampness and the damage it might cause her gown. "I believe there may be a great deal to discuss there, Captain Hartnell."

Hartnell, looking troubled, settled himself only a little distance from Elsabeth on the bench. "I wish that there was not. Or perhaps I am glad that there is! I find myself at a loss, Miss Elsabeth. I have never before encountered quite such a scenario. Please, before you speak: let me put forth what I have surmised, that you need not confess what might be unpalatable to you.

"My first suspicion ought to have come when you were so vehemently relieved that my dreadful secret was merely a talent for magic. I did not then think anything of it save that you were an uncommonly kind-hearted lady, and that you had little use for Society's strictures. And that was already no secret: you are known to be fond of exercise and unafraid to speak your opinions, Miss Elsabeth, neither of which is deemed entirely suitable by Society. No, do not protest; it is what sets you apart, and I would no more undo it than I might over-paint a Rembrandt.

"But, in looking back, your acceptance of my gift is only a step along a path I now see clearly. The first step, indeed, may well be the day I met you, when Miss Dina had her unfortunate encounter with the river. It was a very still day," Hartnell said more softly than he had been speaking before. "A very still day, and the river ran low, and yet between wind and water, it snatched poor Miss Dina up and nearly drowned her. Again, by itself, I thought nothing of the circumstance. But when it is drawn along with your response to my talent, and then drawn further to the incident with the bridge...Miss Elsabeth, please know that I am disinclined to listen to town gossip, as it is largely one and the same from one town to the next, but here in Bodton, there has lately been a different tale being told. Miss Leopoldina is a sorceress, is she not? And, if rumour is true, your father is a magician too."

A cry broke from Elsabeth's lips. It was answer enough for Hartnell, who clasped her hands to offer comfort, and in no wise understood that Elsa's surprise was born from his belief that *only* Leopoldina among them made use of magic.

Nor did she have time to explain, as Hartnell went on without hesitation. "Please understand that I would never betray Miss Dina's secret—or your father's—as certain knowledge. I think you must know that, as I think you must know I had my suspicions at the bridge that day. Surely, if I could retain my wits enough then to protect your sister, I may do so now as well, when I am in full command of my faculties. I only wish you to know that, touched by magic as I am myself, I could never in any way condemn your family for its talent, nor could it in any wise alter my affections for—for your family."

Stricken, Elsabeth gazed at Captain Hartnell. She *ought*—she could barely abide *not* to!—tell him the whole truth, that of the Dovers, only Mrs Dover herself had no talent for magic. And yet, to do so would curse poor Rosamund, whose prospects had been so bright. Elsabeth had herself heard the rumours; she knew full well that she and Rosamund were largely excused from the poisonous assumption of magic. It bothered her not a whit whether she was or was not known to be a sorceress, but to confirm that her darling Rosa carried the power as well seemed an untenable decision. It was then that she knew she held out some slender thread of hope for her sister's reunion with Robert Webber, unlikely as it seemed. He was good-hearted and kind; he might easily overlook the Dover family affliction, if he did not know with certainty that Rosamund herself was affected by it.

"I have shocked you. Perhaps even horrified you. I promise,

Miss Elsabeth, that my purpose was entirely other. I hoped that by confessing my suspicions—my knowledge!—that you might find some comfort in being able to speak freely to at least one soul on this earth. I can see that I have failed; I will leave you, and you will perhaps inform me if you can forgive me such intimate family knowledge with the delivery of a note or, if your heart is generous enough to allow it, an invitation to return to Oakden. Oh, Lord, let that not sound as though I am blackmailing you for such a note or invitation; that is not my meaning at all. I am making this worse. Forgive me, Miss Elsabeth. I shall take my own leave, and I will wait for some sign from you that I have not fallen entirely from your good graces." Upon this heart-felt delivery, Hartnell rose and departed, leaving Elsabeth Dover to sit, enveloped by a stunned silence, for quite some time.

It was Mrs Penney's observation that Elsabeth looked uncommonly pensive upon her return from the excursion with Captain Hartnell. While not given to Mrs Dover's gossiping tendencies, she found she could not allow their time together to go unremarked, and, when the moment was convenient, undertook it to speak to Elsabeth about the handsome young captain. "He is, to be sure, charming and as pleasant a man to look upon as I have ever seen, but, Elsabeth, let me caution you about falling in love too deeply. Charm and pleasantry are excellent companions for a man with even a modest fortune, but Captain Hartnell has no prospects beyond the military, and, my dear, I do not think you would enjoy being a soldier's wife."

"Were it not for Mr Archer," Elsabeth replied sharply, "Captain Hartnell might have all the prospects any modest young woman might require in a husband, when charm and pleasantry are added to the mix."

Elsabeth, Mrs Penney reminded herself, was the stubborn one of her brother's daughters, and the slightest wrong touch in guidance could all too well drive her into the arms of an entirely unsuitable paramour. It was therefore the most delicate hint of rue and curiosity, as if her own uncertainty was hardly worthy of note, that she said, "I can hardly doubt your stories of Mr

Archer's arrogance, when they are so fully supported by all of those who have met the gentleman. But neither can I wholly doubt myself, having known the old Mr Archer even a little! He may have gone wrong in the raising of his son, but it troubles me to think that the fault lay entirely with Mr Archer in the matter of Captain Hartnell's dismissal from Streyfield."

"You," Elsabeth said, her sharpness turning at once to wry amusement, "are much like Rosamund, my dear Aunt. She also cannot bear to think poorly of anyone, even Mr Archer. But I am sensible to your concerns, and because I love you, would like to reassure you that you need not fear, Aunt Felicity. I do not believe myself in love with Captain Hartnell. It is true I find him more appealing than any other man of my acquaintance, but I am insensible to romance; you must know that by now. Look what it has wrought in poor Rosa; I cannot desire that for myself. If you require assurances, know that the Captain and I had a pleasant walk with no talk of infatuation or fondness at all, save his general fondness for our family. Indeed, I should be surprised to learn that he has any romantic inclinations toward me; we are merely the closest of friends."

"He visits very often for a friend, Elsabeth."

Elsabeth laughed. "He visits so often because you are here, Auntie, and we are in the height of our social activity with your presence. We will return to our quieter ways when you are gone and have taken Rosamund with you. She is not well, Aunt Penney," Elsa concluded in concern. "She behaves as though she is, but I see a fever-brightness in her eyes and fear the blush in her cheeks is from illness, not health. I think it would be better to take her to London sooner, even if it should mean cutting away at our own time with you. And I promise that I will not in the meantime become engaged to anyone at all without your previous approval."

Mrs Penney laughed as well and embraced her niece. "I would not ask you to make such rash promises, Elsabeth. Only step cautiously in matters of love; marriages cannot easily be undone."

(33)

The news that Mrs Penney—and, by necessity, Mr Penney, who was less involved in the arrangements, if no less fond of his nieces than his wife was—would be departing immediately rather than staying on for some weeks was met by dismay by all parties save Rosamund, who bloomed again at the thought of Town.

"Not," she told Elsa privately, "that I have any hopes regarding Mr Webber; of course not. But it will be pleasant to meet as friends, and, to that end, I have written to his sister Julia, to tell her I will be in London."

"I would that you had written Mr Webber himself," Elsabeth replied, shocking Rosa with the very idea. "Well, I do. I know you are surpassingly fond of Miss Webber, but you are fond of everyone, Rosa."

"Sophia Enton likes Miss Webber as well," Rosamund said mischievously, and Elsa, happy to see her able to tease, allowed that this was true and that perhaps Miss Webber did, after all, have some hidden qualities of greatness.

When it was learned that Rosamund would be accompanying the Penneys to London, Leopoldina put up a great fuss that was only quieted by Mr Dover proceeding sedately to her room, selecting the best dress Mrs Penney had brought for her and holding it threateningly near the burning hearth. "I should have no difficulty in destroying each and every gown you own," he announced in his genial fashion. "I should be quite entertained, I am sure, by the pleasant talk of my wife and daughters as you sat through the winter, sewing new clothes that would be serviceable enough to allow you to be seen in public. They would not be fashionable, of course; with the expense of Rosamund in London, we will have no extra money for frivolities such as fashionable clothing."

"But Aunt Felicity will be absorbing those expenses!" Leopoldina cried, before being obliged to cover her mouth with both hands as her gown drifted ever nearer the flames. Tears welled in her dark eyes and she flung herself face-down onto her bed, but no more complaints about who would stay and who would go were to be heard. Mr Dover, satisfied, retreated to his library, where, later, Mrs Dover would be heard to demand if he had *truly* intended to burn Dina's gown, and how could he show so little consideration for her nerves, and what did he think he would accomplish by presenting his daughters in rags, when there were still four of them to be wed?

"Perhaps I could make arrangements for you after all," Mrs Penney murmured to Elsabeth, who smiled and shook her head.

"No; without me here, Papa might give in to Dina's excesses, and it would be better for all of us to pass a quiet winter. I will miss Rosa terribly, but she will write to me often, as I hope you will."

"Of course," promised Mrs Penney, and, within three days, they were off to the distant promise of Town.

Only then did Elsabeth feel prepared to ask Mr Dover to issue another invitation to Captain Hartnell, whose delight upon returning to Oakden lifted the melancholy that had settled with Rosamund's departure. "Oh, she will do well in London," he said warmly. "She is both fashionably fair and so kind; she will have more suitors than she can imagine within a week or two."

"I wish *I* had more suitors than I knew what to do with," Dina responded petulantly, but Hartnell only laughed.

"Miss Dina, I cannot imagine how many suitors that would

be. I should think you would have every man lucky enough to catch your eye running errands, reading novels and stitching your embroidery for you, and you would sit above them like a queen. It would be a magnificent sight."

"Then you may begin by reading for us," Leopoldina declared, and, when Elsabeth closed her eyes in resignation, demanded, "What? Does Captain Hartnell not read well? He does; he has read for us before, and since Ruth is gone, no one else cares to!"

"I should be happy to read for you," Hartnell replied, and so he did, not only that day but several others. His company was much welcomed by the Dovers, who were otherwise very quiet at home indeed; only Rosa's letters from Town, and Sophia Enton's visits, broke the tedium of the cold and short winter days.

Julia Webber had not responded to Rosamund's letter; perhaps, Rosa wrote to Elsa, it had been lost in the post. It did not matter, Rosamund wrote; it was easier, perhaps, to not see Miss Webber, and therefore not see Mr Webber, although she confessed that she would like to once, just to move past the unpleasant shock of it. Elsa privately believed there was little chance the letter had been lost, or that Miss Webber would make any effort to seek Rosamund out, but was gladdened to hear that Rosamund had been well received in the social circles Mrs Penney moved in, and had it from Mrs Penney herself that there were several young men most keenly interested in visiting the Penney household now that Rosamund was a part of it. Happy for her sister's good fortune, Elsabeth put special effort into crafting a pretty shawl, and sent the delicate gift to Rosamund at Christmas. In return, she received not only a cunning hat but a long letter full of the delights of London at Christmas, and the exhausting duties of parties, afternoon visits and walks in the Park. Robert Webber was mentioned no more, and Elsabeth began to hope that Rosamund's fondness for him had been no more than a passing fancy.

At the Twelfth Night, Sophia Enton arrived upon the Dover doorstep with a heightened flush in her cheeks and an excitement she could barely contain. In this state of unlikely agitation, she hurried Elsabeth into boots and a warm coat and led her on a brisk walk through the fields, until no other soul save for a cow could possibly be thought to hear them. "Elsabeth, I have been invited to London!"

"Good heavens, by whom?"

"By Julia Webber, of all people!"

Such news could be not come as more of a shock than a bucket of cold water being up-ended over her. Indeed, Elsabeth felt that perhaps such a thing had happened, and that it had then frozen, holding her quite in place. "Julia Webber has invited *you* to London? Oh, Sophia, that sounded dreadfully mean, and I did not intend it that way. But—she has invited you to London?"

"No, you have no meanness in your soul."

Elsabeth could not allow such a comment to go unremarked, and gave her response voice by the lifting of an eyebrow, which caused Sophia to laugh. "Very well, it is Rosamund who has no meanness in her soul, but you are never mean to me, Elsabeth, and I do not take your words as being so. I have been in contact with Miss Webber," she confessed more shyly. "We have been writing to one another all autumn, and now she has invited me to visit."

"How splendid for you." Elsabeth could not quite hide her astonishment, nor stop herself from enquiring, "Sophia, have you mentioned to Miss Webber that Rosamund is in London?"

Sophia replied, "No," with some surprise. "Had Rosa not written her before she left? I am sure they have seen one another!"

"They have not. Perhaps Rosamund is right after all, and her letter went astray. And she has been so busy since—well!" There could be, Elsabeth felt, no other answer, for she thought little enough of Miss Webber to believe that she would not invite Sophia to London if doing so meant risking her brother and Rosamund encountering one another. A certain sly delight awoke within Elsabeth's breast: how delicious, if all of Miss Webber's plottings should come to naught thanks to her friendship with another Bodton girl! Wickedly pleased, Elsa concluded, "You will have to see her for me, and tell her how much I miss her! London, Sophia! Is your mother happy?" Elsabeth slipped her arm into Sophia's, and together they walked across the fields, laughing and chatting. Mrs Enton was beyond delighted; she intended on sending Sophia to Town in their best coach, and had already conceded some significant portion of a budget for new gowns. Miss Webber's exquisite taste would see Sophia bedecked in the most magnificent of London finery, and Mrs Enton was already imagining herself at her daughter's wedding to a tall, intelligent politician of distinctive means.

"I only wish that you could come, too," Sophia said as they finally made their way back toward Oakden. "I know you are not fond of Julia—of Miss Webber—but what fun we should all have in London together, Elsabeth! What a gay time it would be!"

"I shall be happier to hear it in letters," Elsabeth promised. "Then I will have all the fun of admiring with none of the bother of being polite. Imagine if you should encounter Mr Archer! I might have to dance with him again!"

In truth, Elsabeth felt a little bereft, although it was not in her to resent either Rosamund or Sophia's good fortunes. But she had depended on Sophia for the months Rosa had been gone, and had expected to continue in such a vein; to find herself without close female friends brought her as near to heartache as Elsabeth Dover could come. She entertained Captain Hartnell less, and waited for the post more, though one of the most striking missives came the very day Sophia left for London.

"I have encountered Miss Webber!" Rosamund wrote happily. "Only this very morning, which will be some two or three days since, when you receive this letter. I was correct: my letter to her did not arrive, and she was most agitated to learn I had been in London all this while without her knowledge. She will come to Aunt Felicity's in three days' time—perhaps on the very day you are reading this!—and we shall finally have a little visit. She has already fallen upon me with apologies for their departure from Newsbury; they had believed, she says, that they would be gone only a week or so, but circumstances in Town demanded that they stay on. There! Now we know, and I can confess that my heart is greatly relieved. I am eager to write you again, Elsa, with all the news of the Webbers and even, perhaps, a certain Mr Archer..."

Do not task yourself with learning about Mr Archer on my behalf, Elsa wrote in response. *I am sure I need know no more of him than I already do. But it is my pleasure to share glad tidings! Sophia Enton has been invited to London to stay with Miss Webber, and so, I am sure you will all see a great deal more of one another than might have been expected.* Entirely satisfied with the situation, she posted the letter immediately, knowing that it would arrive in Rosamund's hands no more than a day or two after Sophia settled in London.

(34)

Indeed, no gladder tidings could have reached Rosamund Dover, whose fondness for Sophia Enton was exceeded only by Elsabeth's. She wondered that Miss Webber had not mentioned Sophia's impending arrival during their visit at Mrs Penney's home, but concluded that it was only natural for Miss Webber to want Sophia for herself for a few days and, of course, to allow Sophia time to become settled in London. Rosa was not above admitting to herself that she would have been inclined to visit her Bodton companion at the earliest possible moment, perhaps well before propriety allowed; by those lights, Miss Webber had done her quite a favour! Content with this explanation, Rosamund waited an appropriate number of days before sending a note to Sophia and proclaiming her fervent desire to see her.

It might have come as some surprise to Rosamund to learn that Sophia had been agitating to visit Rosamund for some days already by the time that note was delivered. It was not that Sophia lacked things to do; rather, she had been so busy with dress fittings, dinner parties and social engagements that she could hardly be said to have settled. All of this had been arranged by Julia Webber, who took unparalleled pleasure in Sophia's popularity. Julia was never far from Sophia's side, attending her so assiduously that Julia's elder sister, Mrs Gibbs, observed that it seemed Sophia was Julia's star, and Julia but a satellite in Sophia's orbit.

Sophia blushed heartily at this remark and protested it could not be true, that she was only a small and uninteresting country girl, which caused great gaiety on Julia's part. "You could never be small," Miss Webber assured Sophia, "and that you are from the country only gives you a genuineness often unseen in Town. Now, tomorrow, my dear Sophia—"

"Tomorrow, I should like to visit Rosamund," Sophia said with as much firmness as she could muster. The words proved fateful, for, at that very moment, Mr Webber, who had been in the country to shoot since before Sophia's arrival, appeared in the doorway with a genial smile.

"Miss Enton! I had not known you were already come to London! How splendid it is to see you!" This greeting was delivered with the expected polite enthusiasm, and a less sensible woman than Miss Enton might have imagined it to be wholly genuine. But Mr Webber's smile began to show strain around the edges, and, though his voice remained light, it would be impossible for any but the very least sensitive of creatures to recognise the urgency of his next query. "I could not have heard that correctly, could I? That Miss Dover is in Town as well? Surely, we would have learned this intelligence..."

Julia Webber's own smile was strained as well. "I have only just learned it myself, whilst you were away, dear brother. It seems Miss Dover has been in London since well before Christmas, and her letter to me went astray. I am sure we are all eager to see one another again, but pray tell, Robby, where is Mr Archer? You have not left him at Streyfield, have you?"

"No, he will be here momentarily. He is...We must have her to supper, Julia. Good God, she must feel entirely neglected. I cannot have it!"

"How she can feel neglected when we were not even aware of her presence—"

"Who has been neglected?" Mr Archer, stripping gloves from his hands, entered the drawing room with the air of a man about his business, only to stop in pure startlement upon seeing Sophia. "Miss Enton? I had no idea we were to be so graced. You are looking tremendously well: London seems to agree with you. Surely, you cannot feel neglected, even if Webber and I are only lately come to Town and no doubt bothersomely inattentive."

He was, Sophia thought at this rush of words, an entirely different man in London. Perhaps it was the comfort of being surrounded by those of his own class, which he had made manifestly clear he was not in Bodton; certainly, her own small presence could not be sufficient as to disturb a man otherwise in his element. "I have been in London a week yesterday, Mr Archer, at Miss Webber's invitation, and I hasten to assure you I have been in no way neglected, although I shall consider myself all the more fortunate to have such elegant companionship as yourself and Mr Webber now that you are returned. I hope you have been well."

"Entirely," Archer agreed, "and up until this moment, I might have said Webber had been as well. Webber, you are pale. Does London's thick air disagree with you now, after the freshness of the country? Sit down; Peters, get the man a brandy."

The Webbers' butler, as inconspicuous a man as Sophia had ever seen, presented Mr Webber with a brandy so swiftly that she could only imagine he had been attending that very pursuit before Archer ever spoke. Webber both sat and drank as commanded, then tended to the question Archer had asked first upon entering the room: "It is Miss Dover who must feel neglected, Archer; I have only just this moment learned she is in London."

Webber could not have forced a more dramatic change onto Archer if he had spoken with full malice and aforethought. The Streyfield man's posture became rigid and his colour blue ash. "Miss Rosamund Dover is in London?"

Astonished at the change in him, Sophia entertained the notion that *he*, and not Webber, was the man in love with Rosamund, though the lie was put to that thought as his next words burst forth: "Does Miss Elsabeth attend as well?"

A short silence followed this question, broken after a moment by Sophia herself: "I do not believe so, Mr Archer. That is to say, no; Elsabeth remains in Bodton." A spark of mischief awakened in her and she continued, guilelessly, "I shall tell her you have asked after her when next I write."

"That is not necessary." Archer sipped from the brandy that Peters had discreetly pressed into his hand before looking at the drink as though it had appeared unsummoned. "Webber, I have no doubt that Miss Dover is well indulged and in no way neglected. It would no doubt be superior for us to not impose ourselves upon her time; I am sure she is busy with social calls and new friendships."

Surely, a more crestfallen expression had never graced a gentleman's face. "Perhaps you are right, Archer, although it strikes me as unseemly to not pay our respects now that we know she is in Town."

Although it was clear even to the most unobservant of persons that both Mr Archer and Miss Webber did not wish for Mr Webber to once again encounter Rosamund Dover, Sophia was herself possessed of two things: one, a genuine and long-standing friendship with Miss Dover, and two, a kind, if not romantic, heart hidden within her bosom. With a gaiety verging on false, because she knew her next words would distress both her hostess and Mr Archer, Sophia cried, "Oh, but *I*, certainly, cannot go without seeing Miss Dover; that would be the height of rudeness, and my visits could not be considered an imposition on her time, for we have been friends since childhood. And she is such an amiable creature: I cannot imagine that she would not welcome one or two additional visitors when I attend her."

Mr Webber's misery reversed itself as swiftly as clouds cleared from the skies. "Yes, of course you must visit with her, Miss Enton, and you will ask, will you not, if I might join you the next time? I mean, that Miss Webber and I might join you. I am confident that, if you ask in person, she will not be able to refuse you, as she might very sensibly refuse a letter; she must think me a cad for our abrupt departure to London, without so much as a word of explanation. Oh, I ought not have allowed you to sway me so, Archer; after her sister's disastrous encounter with the river, it is no surprise that she was slow in responding to our invitations."

"I fear her sister is precisely the reason Miss Dover did not respond." Archer fastened a gimlet eye on Sophia as he spoke. "I should think Miss Leopoldina's antics were sufficiently appalling as to make Miss Dover understand that her small affection for you could not possibly be enough to overlook her family's deficiencies. I would consider it cruel to impose myself on her in your position, Robert, and we are all well aware that you are not a cruel man."

None of this was spoken for Mr Webber's benefit: Sophia recognised that as clearly as she might recognise her own name. No: it was entirely meant for her own ears, and said—to her, who knew the Dover family secret—that Archer knew it as well, and that he would not be above exposing their sorcerous heritage if needs must. She met his hard expression and, by degrees, felt her own grow as unforgiving in return.

There was, Sophia Enton discovered in that moment, a certain freedom to being the sole disappointing child of her parents: without marriage prospects to consider, she could speak without fear of condemning her future comfort, and, without siblings, she had no one to protect through her own flawless behaviour save herself. The Dover girls were as sisters to her, and it seemed, there in the Webbers' very civilised sitting room, that, if she had no expectations of her own happiness to fight for, it cost her nothing at all to fight for Rosamund's.

She rose with slow grace, until her preposterous height, always a source of embarrassment, allowed her to gaze directly into Fitzgerald Archer's startled eyes. "I am confident that your presence would be a cruelty to Miss Dover, Mr Archer. I am equally confident that Mr Webber's would be a comfort; I know for my own part that she was most distressed when the Newsbury contingent departed so abruptly, for I was the bearer of that unfortunate news. Miss Dover is not excessively demonstrative, a trait I would think a man of your particular reserve would admire, but she is very fond of the Webbers, and Leopoldina, however appalling, has no effect upon that. I dare say that, if you had any respect for your own friend's judgement, you would be most pleased to have him visit Miss Dover to, at the least, tender apologies for his abrupt departure. Polite society would expect nothing less."

Archer was of too black a complexion to blush easily; despite this, Sophia believed she saw colour rise in his cheeks. He had expected her to be cowed; had expected his unspoken threat to expose the Dovers to silence any disagreement that a pliant female might feel. Well, she was not pliant, and, standing to face the gentleman, Sophia concluded she might never be bothered with compliance again. Men had wanted nothing to do with her, and she little enough to do with them, save for the stability that marriage offered; without it as a possibility, she saw no reason to behave as men would have her do, most particularly if to remain silent might hurt the women with whom she had always been closest. Bolstered by her own convictions, she continued to look into Archer's eyes, until he said in a voice much offended, "Perhaps I have been mistaken about the appropriateness of all the Bodton females. Robert, Miss Webber; good night," and departed in a whirl of coattails.

Sophia discovered her hands were shaking; she gazed at them a moment, then settled carefully back into her chair, where their tremble could be hidden by her skirts. "Forgive me," she said after a moment, and sought Julia's gaze with her own. "Forgive me; I did not intend to cause your other guest discomfort."

The very corner of Julia Webber's mouth curled reluctantly upward, as if she struggling against great humour. It made her extraordinarily beautiful, not with Rosamund's soft beauty, but, rather, with a stronger and more compelling attraction. "On the contrary, Sophia, you most certainly did. I should be cross with you, but I believe I have never seen Archer so thoroughly routed, and by a woman, no less. Would that you were a man, Sophia: I should marry you instantly, for the anticipation of watching such tête-à-têtes for the rest of my life."

If Archer had perhaps blushed, Sophia did so in earnest. "I thought your cap was set for Mr Archer."

Julia glanced after the departed gentleman as though Sophia's comment came as an unwelcome reminder. "I had rather have you, Miss Enton. I should not approve, but I cannot dislike the fire that sets you to defend your friend so magnificently."

"I think Mr Archer can," Sophia whispered. "Perhaps I shall become your bosom friend, and argue with him for your entertainment, for I can imagine no other companion I should like better in life than yourself."

"Nor I," Mr Webber proclaimed warmly. "Sophia—Miss Enton—I must thank you for your strong moral compass, and your understanding of the straits poor Miss Dover has been left in. Even if we should only encounter her once, and then distress her no more, I shall be forever grateful for your assistance in offering my apologies to her. Archer will come around to seeing how right you are; he may be prideful, but he is not a fool. Please, I beg of you: write to Miss Dover at this very moment, so we might have hopes of smoothing these unsettled waters between us."

"I shall, Mr Webber," Sophia agreed, but found it was Miss Webber to whom she looked for approval. Upon finding it in the form of a smile both resigned and intrigued, Sophia did as she was bidden, and put pen to paper.

(35)

"I CONFESS THAT IT WAS AWKWARD," ROSAMUND WROTE TO Elsabeth not too many days later. "But it is over now, and should we meet on the street it will be as fond friends, nothing more. My heart is quite healed, Elsabeth; I believe London has been good for me. And it has done very well indeed for Sophia, whom I have surely never seen look so happy! You would hardly know her, Elsa, and, indeed, if you could see the way Miss Webber dotes on her, you could no more doubt Miss Webber's kind heart than you might doubt my own. Miss Webber says, quite possessively, that she intends to keep Sophia in Town until at least the spring, and Aunt Felicity says she does not know how she has done without me and that she cannot bear to let me go. Oh, Elsabeth, are you well there, alone with Mother and the young ones? I miss you so very much, and yet find myself selfishly loath to leave London. Not for hopes of encountering Mr Webber—I am quite shut of those dreams!—but for the elegant company and the diverting entertainment. London is so grand, and I am sure that I am now entirely well."

Do not fear, dear Sister, wrote Elsabeth in return.

Ruth has written and asks me to visit; I shall do that, and see how being a wife suits her, and I will write to you of all I learn in her company. I am glad you are well, and that there were no horrors in meeting with Mr Webber again, though I cannot myself entirely forgive him for absconding in such a fashion. Nor can I be expected to forgive Miss Webber for keeping Sophia away from me for so many months, though I concede that there is far more hope for Sophia's happiness in Town than in Bodton under Mrs Enton's roof. I shall think of all the opportunities you and she shall have, and not at all of my own loneliness, which cannot, of course, be so very great, with our beloved Papa to keep me company. And I would be remiss if I did not confess that Captain Hartnell still visits from time to time, which keeps an air of excitement in our otherwise quiet lives. I fear Mamma is growing impatient with him, though; I believe she feels he has shown enough attention, and should soon make an offer. For my own part, I am quite content that he should not, but there is no telling Mamma this; she will not hear it even if I say it in plain language. I hope Aunt Felicity is more receptive to your own opinions, my dear Rosamund. I shall write again from Ruth's; write to me there, and I will certainly receive it upon my arrival.

With the greatest affection, your sister, Elsabeth.

Elsabeth departed Oakden at the same time her note did, and arrived at Charington Place in good time. She was brought directly to the rectory, which was settled in its own fine garden that, even in the last week of January, showed a remarkable greenery and a promising early harvest of root vegetables. She alighted with some curiosity, in no wise displeased when Ruth alone flew from the house to greet her. "Mr Cox is away at Lady Beatrice's home," Ruth announced. "He shall return before dinner, but he will want to tend his garden, and so we may have a pleasant interlude before he joins us. Elsabeth, you are looking well! Let me show you to your room, and the house—"

"*You* are looking well, Ruth," Elsabeth exclaimed with some surprise. Ruth Dover had attained as much prettiness as her sallow, thin features could allow; Ruth Cox had gained both colour and weight, as well as a healthy sheen to hair now worn in sensibly attractive curls, perfectly suitable for a pastor's wife. Her gown was finer by far than Ruth had previously chosen to wear, and, indeed, could well rival Leopoldina's best dresses in terms of quality, if not frivolity. "Marriage suits you, Ruth. I would hardly know you."

"The Lady Beatrice feels it is our duty as pastor and wife to manage the balance between her ladyship's wealth and patronage and the parish's more modest means. I do not want to look *too* fine; I should not put myself above the parish."

"You are splendidly appropriate," Elsa assured her, and, with more interest and delight than she had expected, allowed herself to be ushered within the house.

It was a pretty nest with an extravagance of bedrooms: four, the second-largest of which was warm and waiting for Elsabeth. Between them, she and Ruth unpacked her belongings with ease and more laughter than Elsabeth could ever remember sharing with her middle sister. "This shall do very well, Ruth," Elsa said in admiration. "Very well indeed. Thank you."

"Thank you for visiting," Ruth said with more shyness than was customary. "Do come and see the rest of the house, Elsa. I should like to know if it is to your liking. I have made some modest changes since arriving, mostly in the paper and paint, which were in want of updating. Mr Cox says he has never seen the house looking so well."

With no former knowledge for comparison, Elsa could do little more than agree that Ruth's home did look very well indeed. A formal sitting room, appointed with very fashionable paper and furniture too stately to be considered outmoded, looked over the drive, where a wealth of flowers bloomed despite February awaiting just around the corner. Behind that room lay a less formal sitting room; that one held embroidery of a pattern easily recognisable to Elsa as one of Ruth's favourites, and warmer colours on the walls. They suited Ruth, Elsabeth realised in surprise: pinks and greens gave her increasingly handsome colour, as had the natural light of the front sitting room. That any of this was within Ruth's purview astonished Elsa: her sister's former rigidity had hid a wealth of graces. A cook and maid were to be found in the kitchen and dining room, although, Ruth hastened to say, they were the only servants; it would not do for her to be above housework, when so many in the parish had no help at all.

"Sure and she's an easy enough Missus," opined the maid, whose accent betrayed her as Irish. "I've never seen a house with so few cobwebs, and the windows are like to clean themselves when it rains."

"Is that so?" Elsabeth cast Ruth an amused glance that was returned with such innocence as to betray guilt, though all she said was "So Colleen says. Come and see the garden, Elsabeth; I think you will admire it. Mr Cox spends a great deal of his time in the garden, which I encourage. It is an excellent place for him to practise his sermons, as well as offering him healthful exercise in the fresh air. I listen to his sermons and comment upon them, and do a little garden work myself, but Mr Cox is most pleased to discover he has something of a green thumb." She threw open a large door, revealing the back gardens: closest to the house lay sandy earth replete with chickens and ducks; beyond them, soft mounds of vigourously growing vegetables within a fenced area that stretched to both sides of the house; they were among what Elsabeth had seen upon her arrival. Beyond that lay a scattering of fruit and nut trees on low hills before a cultured forest rose to hide the distance.

Elsabeth, gazing at slender, strong pea stalks and burgeoning heads of lettuce, enquired, "*When* precisely did Mr Cox discover his green thumb, Ruth?"

"Almost immediately upon our retirement here from Oakden. He confesses to having been little more than a dilettante in the matter of gardening before our marriage, but supposes that his new status as husband has lent him a certain fecundity."

"How perfectly astonishing."

"Indeed," Ruth agreed. "And how fortunate, as it seems we shall have fresh greens for supper tonight, which is rare enough in January."

At this, Elsabeth could not help but laugh, nor could she prevent herself from laughing again when Ruth subjected her to a second glance of incomparable innocence. "It is a lovely garden, Ruth, and a lovely house. You have landed on your feet, I think, and I shall write both Rosamund and Papa to tell them so." Gay, she caught her sister's hands and held them. "You are happy, are you not?"

Ruth's answering smile was a wholly new expression to Elsabeth: never before had she been so easy with joyful emotion. "I am."

"Then *I* am happy," Elsabeth replied. "Come, show me the rest of the gardens, Ruth, and then perhaps as the parson's sister-in-law, I may make myself useful about the house as well. I dare say I can peel a potato with as deft a hand as any."

"I may even allow you to." Together they explored the gardens, until Elsabeth exclaimed, "That all of this is nestled into a corner of the estate, and yet so finely appointed—! I have grown eager to see the main house, which must be splendid indeed."

"We are invited to dinner two nights hence," Ruth announced with satisfaction. "You will see it in all its splendour."

"I look forward to it," Elsabeth said in all sincerity. She could muster no equal enthusiasm for seeing Mr Cox, though for Ruth's sake she had determined to be pleasant. He arrived home only after supper, which, had he been a more bearable man, Elsa might have felt rude; as it was, she was merely glad to have been without his company for a little more time than she might have expected.

He was, to her surprise, less than the man he had been upon marrying Ruth; less by a quarter of his own weight, she guessed at a glance. To him, she said, "Gardening suits you," and to Ruth she bestowed a surprised glance that begot another satisfied smile.

"I find it very healthful," Mr Cox assured her, and continued on at length about the benefits of fresh air and hard work; clearly, his trimmer figure had done nothing to improve his ability to gauge a listener's interest in his speech. Ruth responded when and as appropriate, thus encouraging him to speak even as she and Elsabeth carried on a quieter discussion of their own. In only a little while, Elsabeth knew that Ruth's little phrases of encouragement and agreement were wholly intended to keep Mr Cox in his own company, that she might spend hers with Elsa. It was a far more skillful management than Mr Dover had ever managed with Mrs, and Elsabeth once more found herself admiring Ruth for talents that had gone unnoticed in the Dover household. A full day and a half of such pleasantries were spent, until it seemed to Elsabeth that she had never before been properly acquainted with Ruth. *She is become quite my second-favourite sister,* Elsabeth wrote to Rosamund before supper on the second day. *You must visit her, Rosamund: you would not know her from before.*

A knock on the door interrupted her before she could go on; Ruth appeared there, an expression of nervous apology writ across her features. "You are too tall to borrow my gowns, else I should lend you one for supper with Lady Beatrice. Never mind: your best will do. At least you are sensible," she said with sudden passion. "Lady Beatrice has asked twice about my younger sisters, and I can hardly bear to speak of them. I cannot imagine allowing them to visit, Elsa: however should I control them?"

"If Mamma and Papa cannot, you would surely not be expected to." Elsabeth rose to embrace her middle sister. "If Lady Beatrice asks again, only tell her that Dina and Tildy are too young to visit a woman of her class, and that they would be stricken silly by her grandness. It would not even be an untruth."

"They will eventually be old enough," Ruth said miserably, and Elsabeth laughed.

"Perhaps by then, they will have learned some sense, but more likely they will be wed and with children of their own and too busy to visit. You have never been one to borrow trouble, Ruth: do not start now. This is my best dress; will it do?" She took from the wardrobe a simple and pretty ivory gown with lace at the bosom and sleeves.

Ruth's eyes brightened with pleasure as she touched the lace.

"Rosamund made this; I remember. Yes, it will do beautifully. Thank you, Elsa, for bringing it. For thinking to."

"I am not entirely hopeless," Elsabeth assured her, and in no little time, they were adorned for the evening, and obliged by necessity to accept Mr Cox's escort.

He, rather than admire Elsabeth's choice of gown as Ruth had done, allowed his mouth to retreat into a pinch. "Well, you are a country cousin," he said with all the magnanimity of a generous man. "My patroness, Lady Beatrice, will not expect too much of you, after all, so long as your manners are good."

In due course, when Elsabeth had recovered her powers of speech, she had also recovered the wit to not respond, and the humour to be glad that the walk to Charington Place was dry and smooth. Had there been a speck of mud to take advantage of, she was quite afraid Mr Cox would have taken a terrible spill, worse than Mr Archer's ignominious fall at the Bodton dance.

Almost as satisfied with the imagining of such a calamity as she would have been with the actuality of it, Elsabeth was entirely able to enjoy the majority of the walk, which wended through parklands and magnificent old trees still leafless with winter. Wispy clouds scattered blue skies and were caught from time to time in the thin black branches that reached for the sun, until the trio of walkers came upon an avenue that approached a manor house of no small magnitude.

It was of a very modern style, and surrounded by hedge gardens that bloomed with early wildflowers. Mr Cox seemed prepared to partake in a jig of excitement. "Is it not grand?" he demanded. "Is it not everything I've told you?"

"And more," Elsabeth agreed obligingly. "I am most eager to see the hearth of which I have heard so much."

Mr Cox could not be said to have enough self-awareness to guess that he might be being teased; Ruth, who did, gave Elsabeth a sharp look that was returned with a smile of genuine honesty. It was, in Elsabeth's opinion, nearly impossible to *not* wish to see such a lauded hearth, if perhaps for no other reason than to wish Mr Cox had remained within it.

They were greeted at the door by a butler with an accent more refined than any Elsabeth had ever encountered, and escorted to a sitting room into which the whole of Oakden might have tidily fit. It was immaculately appointed and dominated by the redoubted hearth, which was indeed broader than Mr Cox's arm-span, and beside which a frail-looking young woman sat. A rather becoming hat, obviously intended for warmth, covered a considerable amount of her black hair, and an ermine shawl sported a collar that brushed her jaw.

She rose with grace, smiling gently as Mr Cox sprang forward to say, "Allow me to introduce Miss Annabel Derrington, daughter of Lady Beatrice. Miss Annabel, my sister, Miss Elsabeth Dover."

"Miss Elsabeth." Miss Annabel's voice was as reedy as the fingers she extended to take Elsabeth's hand with. Her fingers were cold despite the furs and the fire she sat beside, and she withdrew them into a muff the very moment they had shaken hands. "Do forgive me. I have never yet grown accustomed to the dreadful English climate. Please, sit. My mother will be here soon."

Elsabeth sat, gazing curiously into the furs and blankets that ensconced Miss Derrington. The woman herself was hardly to be seen amongst them, save a glint of brown eyes and a full mouth. "You are not England-born, then, Miss Annabel?"

"Oh, no." Miss Annabel settled into her chair, which was so velvet-covered it looked as though it must be a source of warmth on its own. "I was born in Oyo, a kingdom of Africa. Do you know it?"

Elsabeth shook her head, and Miss Annabel extended one-hand from the depths of her wraps to create a fist that she tilted until her thumb was parallel with the floor. "Imagine my hand is the northern, broader part of the continent, and my wrist the tapering horn. Oyo is here," she said, and her other hand emerged from the wrap to touch her wrist where it bent at the most inward point of the "continent's" curving western coast. "I lived there the first twelve years of my life. I have not been warm since leaving." She tucked her hands back inside her furs and shivered gently to punctuate her story.

"How dreadful," Elsabeth said with utter sincerity. "I suppose having never known any weather other than our own, I cannot think of it as cold as you must, although the damp is sometimes hard to bear. Miss Annabel, if it is not too impertinent—and I confess that it probably is—do you suppose you will ever be able to return to Africa, and be warm?"

"That will, I suppose, depend upon my husband. My grandfather was cousin to the *oba*—the king—and a part of the *Oyo Mesi*, who are counselors to the *oba*. It is a position of prestige, and my family have not lost that prestige although we no longer serve on the *Oyo Mesi*. We are—dukes, you might say, or perhaps earls, and owe our land and our loyalty to the *oba*. It is a generous position in our society, and if I should marry a man without property of his own, certainly it might behoove him to consider Oyo over England."

"And if you are to marry a landed gentleman?"

Annabel Derrington smiled. "Then I had best be certain he is very fond of me, Miss Elsabeth, and that he is also fond of travel. Now, here is my mother: let us make introductions."

(36)

Already entirely taken with Miss Annabel, Elsabeth rose and turned to the door, eager to lay eyes upon Lady Beatrice. Mr Cox lurched forward to provide introductions, and in so doing briefly obscured his patroness from Elsabeth's view, but when it was cleared, Elsabeth did not find herself disappointed. They were introduced, and then for some time, Lady Beatrice showed no interest in Elsabeth, choosing instead to engage with Ruth. Elsabeth was more than content with this scenario, seizing the opportunity to study the woman of whom Mr Cox had spoken so highly.

A broad, hawkish nose would have, on almost any other woman, defined her entire being, and, given the arrogance of her stare, perhaps it did. It could equally, however, been simple beauty that both defined her and offered her such arrogant confidence. Her eyes were black, her cheekbones magnificent, and her jaw had softened very little with age. Indeed, although her hair was snowy white, the face beneath it might have been anywhere from fifty to seventy, and no one could be the wiser in knowing which age she lay closer to.

Her gown, while impeccably tailored to a woman of age whose taste for fashion had been settled in the previous century, was also vibrant orange, and patterned with squares of black centered by splashes of yellow. It highlighted the earthy undertones of her umber skin, giving her a warmth of presence that Elsabeth gazed at with admiration until Lady Beatrice spoke. "You are obviously Mrs Cox's sister, although, at first glance, you show none of her social graces. You are staring, Miss Elsabeth."

Elsabeth inhaled, caught on an edge between guilt and willing admission. "I am, Lady Beatrice."

Before she could continue with an apology, Lady Beatrice demanded, "Why? Is age so astonishing to you, or is it the colour of my skin?"

"The colour of your gown, rather, Lady Beatrice," Elsa replied stiffly. "I have never seen such a richly dyed orange, nor such bold patterning, nor, if I may say so, anyone upon whom it could possibly be so well suited. I am afraid I *was* staring, but I did so from admiration. I should imagine anyone would wish to reach an age of wisdom with such beauty and confidence as you possess."

"Anyone would. Few shall accomplish it. Your sister is too opinionated for an unmarried woman," said Lady Beatrice to Ruth. "You must lead by example, or surely she will never earn a husband."

Ruth, with humour so repressed as to make her sanctimonious, answered, "I have often said so, Lady Beatrice," and, with some effort, refrained from looking at Elsabeth.

Mr Cox, however, showed no such discretion, and began a sermon on the value of the wedded state and how a suitable husband might elevate the females in his life to a station, whether emotional, intellectual or social, that otherwise lay beyond their reach or indeed, he concluded, their capability of desiring. There were, of course, certain females to whom this did not apply, he said with an ingratiating bow toward his patroness, who, it seemed to Elsabeth, was not immune to flattery, however badly presented: rather than express her disgust at his belittling of the female half of the race, she gracefully allowed as how she was of superior breeding, and thus of more ambitious and clever mettle than most. This last was spoken with a sharp glance at Elsabeth and a far softer one for Annabel, for whom she had the kind words of "but there are those, of course, whose physical frailty cannot withstand the fire of their ambition; that is why we must marry well even if we *are* of unusual quality."

"And what of those whose breeding is less superior but whose hearts burn as brightly with desires?" Elsabeth, thinking of Hartnell, asked. "Are they to be condemned to a lower class forever due to the unfortunate circumstance of their birth?"

"A person of truly superior make would never permit himself to be born into a family that could not support his ambitions."

"Surely," came a startling and familiar voice, "that cannot be entirely true, Aunt Beatrice."

"It is," Lady Beatrice proclaimed. "Ambition in the lower ranks leads only to trouble. Come here, Gerry, and give me a kiss." She presented her cheek for this display of affection, then, without much changing her petulant tone, continued, "And now I suppose I must introduce you to this opinionated young lady."

Mr Fitzgerald Archer, with a flash of pain in his gaze at the diminutive used by his aunt, obediently kissed her cheek before saying, "Not at all, Aunt. I am already quite acquainted with Miss Elsabeth and her opinions. Miss Elsabeth."

Elsabeth had, without knowing it, stood; now, when Archer offered a precisely proper bow of greeting, she returned it with a properly downcast gaze and curtsey of her own. Her laughter at Archer being his aunt's *Gerry* was well smothered by the time she lifted her eyes. "Mr Archer. What a surprise to see you again."

"Indeed, I had no notion you were at Charington. I have only lately seen your sister; had I known I would be seeing you, I am sure I would have offered to carry a letter or a greeting from her."

"Oh! How is she?"

Archer had not, in fact, imagined to encounter Elsabeth Dover in his aunt's sitting room; had, indeed, fled London in order to avoid the eldest Dover sister, although he would have claimed familial duty, not discomfort or alarm, had sent him from his friends' bosom to his aunt's estate. Given by nature to an honesty he felt was only appropriate for a gentleman and surprised by Elsabeth's presence, he responded, "Unfashionably thin," without considering the effect such an assessment might have on the second Dover sister.

On *both* Dover sisters: Mr Cox's new wife looked up sharply to reveal a vaguely familiar countenance: the third Dover sister, although looking far more handsome than Archer's faint memories of her could conjure. "*How* thin, Mr Archer?" Ruth Dover—Ruth Cox, now!—rose in clear concern and took Elsabeth's hand, the two of them gaining strength from one another as Archer looked between them in consternation.

"Mrs Cox. Forgive me, I had not realised—I had not recognised—she is highly coloured and quite slim; I am sure she is entirely well. I meant to cause no alarm."

"Where did you see her, Mr Archer?" asked Elsabeth.

"At—with—with Miss Enton, at the Webbers' Town residence. They were visiting."

He did not imagine that he saw a spark of triumph in Elsabeth Dover's eyes, although her tone was perfectly demure. "How lovely for them all. I am surprised, Mr Archer, that you did not stay on in London, if my sister is visiting with the Webbers."

"I have no especial interest in Miss Dover."

"Of course not." Elsabeth glanced toward Annabel Derrington, whose lovely face was turned toward the fire as if she had no interest whatsoever in the conversation betwixt Archers and Dovers. "I am given to understand that your interests lie here," Elsabeth went on, sounding blithe now, "although I am sure you are greatly missed by the Webbers. How very pleasant it is for all of us, to find such a wide range of amiable acquaintances in so many places."

"Pleasant indeed," Archer said in a voice that allowed no pleasure at all. His cousin Annabel looked toward him then, a finely sculpted eyebrow lifted in silent commentary, but if she intended to speak, her intentions were quashed by Lady Beatrice.

"I am sure I do not understand you," that lady put forth forcefully. "What nonsense young people speak. But there is the dinner bell: we need no longer dwell upon these absurd topics."

"Surely our sister's health cannot be regarded as absurd," Elsabeth murmured, and, for her troubles, earned a glance of horror from Ruth.

Lady Beatrice sniffed. "If she is so fragile as to be worthy of comment, then she is sure to die soon and will be of no further use to the conversation. Gerry, you may escort me." The great lady arose with no visible concern for her appalling statement, though even Archer found himself hesitating in shock. Lady Beatrice delivered him a blistering glare and he stepped forward, offering his arm, but could not help casting a look at the Dover females.

Neither had moved; indeed, neither looked as though she *could* move, and Archer thought it was not his imagination that saw Elsabeth's pulse fluttering irregularly in her throat. But his chance had passed: he could not possibly disengage from his aunt to offer Elsabeth support, and Lady Beatrice showed no intention of waiting on the others. She sailed forward, Archer both at her side and in her wake as Mr Cox lumberingly arose to offer Mrs Cox his escort.

Annabel stood as well, putting forth a hand to Miss Elsabeth, who, provided with the impetus to move, did so; Archer, seating his aunt in the dining room a moment later, saw how they supported one another, as if neither quite had the strength to move on her own. A footman held their chairs for them before Archer had time to do it himself, and he sat at Lady Beatrice's right with a feeling of discontent. There were not enough men to balance the table; Mrs Cox sat at his right with Annabel beside her, and Mr Cox sat across from him with Elsabeth at his left. Archer could think of no arrangement that would please him less, save that Cox should be beside him, but that would never be permitted at his aunt's table. Mr Cox addressed his wife only to be silenced by Lady Beatrice's opinion that a man should never speak to his wife while dining; there were many other opportunities for them to converse. Mr Cox rightfully concluded his duty was to speak to, and about, Lady Beatrice in sufficiently admirable terms that their mutual pleasure carried the conversation for some time. Archer made a few polite comments to Ruth, who responded in kind, and Elsabeth, despite the awkwardness of speaking across the table, seemed to enjoy her talk with Annabel until Lady Beatrice, quite suddenly, said, "Mrs Cox is quite old enough to be well married, but I am given to understand she is the third in your family, Miss Elsabeth. Am I to believe you are her elder?"

Elsabeth appeared to consider that comment a moment before giving in to speech. "You may believe what you wish, Lady Beatrice. It is fact that I am Ruth's second-oldest sister."

"I do not understand," Lady Beatrice proclaimed. "How came Mrs Cox to be married first, then? She could not possibly be out, not with two unmarried older sisters."

"Ah." Elsabeth cast a glance toward Mrs Cox, whose gaze was quite fixed on her dinner plate. "Well, you see, Lady Beatrice, with five daughters, my mother did not feel it was kind to bring us out one at a time."

"You cannot mean to say you are *all* out."

"That is precisely what I mean to say."

"No wonder you are unmarried, with so much competition. Are you the plainest of the lot?"

Elsabeth cleared her throat. "Our older sister Rosamund is much considered to be the fairest of us, Lady Beatrice. Beyond that, I could have no opinion toward ranking our beauty, save to say we are all satisfied when we look in the mirror."

"What utter vanity you possess," Lady Beatrice said incredulously. "To sit here before me and say without shame that you are fond of your own face? How dare you; it is not that remarkable of a face."

A look that sent a frisson down Archer's spine came into Elsabeth Dover's eyes. Rather than fill his gaze on that look, he turned his attention to his aunt, the better to see her expression as Elsabeth's rejoinder settled in, and he was not disappointed. In a tone of sweetest supplication, Miss Elsabeth replied, "Perhaps you might teach me the art of looking into the mirror and being distasteful of what one sees there, Lady Beatrice, for it seems to me that even remarkable beauty might be difficult to look upon with admiration when venom lies beneath the surface."

Lady Beatrice turned quite sallow and she stared, unspeaking, at Elsabeth for a full half-minute, during which time Elsabeth retained an expression innocent of guile. "You are rude," Lady Beatrice finally proclaimed.

Elsabeth allowed herself the smallest smile possible in response, and her gaze darted to Archer so briefly he could hardly be certain she had looked at him until she spoke. "But not without pride, Lady Beatrice."

Archer locked his own gaze on his plate, much as Ruth Cox was doing, and held his expression tightly in school. When he dared lift his gaze, Lady Beatrice had set aside her napkin. "I believe my appetite has gone. Gerry, you may escort me to my rooms. I require a rest."

"Of course, Aunt Beatrice," Archer murmured, and, squiring Lady Beatrice, departed.

(37)

A pall might have settled in the wake of Lady Beatrice's departure, had not Mr Cox had something to say regarding Elsabeth's manners. Elsabeth, who felt no shame in defending herself to Lady Beatrice, took a kinder stance with Mr Cox, not for his sake, but for Ruth's, and sat unprotesting beneath the wash of Mr Cox's words. She could not, it seemed, be expected to know better; she was of too country a family, of which only Mrs Cox had elevated herself through solemnity and education. She would, of course, tender apologies to Lady Beatrice as soon as the great lady was enough recovered, an opinion which caused Elsabeth to lift her eyebrows if not her voice, and, in so doing, she caught an ill-concealed trace of amusement on Miss Derrington's face.

That amusement held a familiar note, though it was some moments before Elsabeth recognised that it brought a likeness to Mr Archer into Annabel's features. Once seen, though, the likeness could not be unseen: they were both stamped with Lady Beatrice's mark, or, Elsabeth supposed, the mark of the grandfather they both shared. Archer had more of Beatrice's nose, but Annabel had her cheekbones and jawline, and their mouths, while not like Lady Beatrice's at all, were like one another's, particularly when quirked with humour. How must other people see her and Ruth, Elsabeth wondered: they were sisters, not cousins, but surely an outsider might take their features apart and put them back together again to find the likenesses and dissimilarities. This thought kept her occupied until Annabel announced, with no evident sign of fatigue, that she felt faint and ought to retire to the sitting room at once.

Mr Cox's lecture instantly flowed into a solicitous parade of words that saw Miss Derrington out of the dining room and into a chair by the sitting room fire. He showed every evidence of intending to continue to scold Elsabeth once Annabel was properly settled, only to be thwarted by the arrival of Mr Archer, whose countenance was immoderately cheery for a gentleman who had just observed his aunt come out on the losing end of a tête-à-tête. "Lady Beatrice is certain she cannot rejoin us this evening. I think, though, that if we might commence to enjoy ourselves, the sounds of gaiety might bring her from her rooms even yet. Miss Elsabeth, perhaps you would play the pianoforte for us."

"Have I not told you, Mr Archer, that my talents at the pianoforte are limited?"

"You have, but, surely, you know me well enough to realise I should like to judge that for myself."

"Surely, you know me well enough to trust that I am an accurate judge of my own skills," Elsabeth said shortly, "and that I do not require a gentleman's opinion to verify my own. Indeed, Mr Archer, any woman of confidence should say the same, and any true gentleman would never think to contradict her on the topic of her own strengths."

"Perhaps there are many women who lack confidence" was Mr Archer's rejoinder, "for there are innumerable ladies who wish nothing more than to decry their own skills and then be pressed into showcasing them under a guise of false modesty."

"And why would they not, when they are met with the supposition that they cannot themselves judge their own talents and must have a man speak for them? How should women be able to trust themselves, when they are constantly undermined by the men around them? I do not play well, I say; nonsense, you say, let me be the judge. And then, heaven forbid, Mr Archer, that I should actually play as poorly as I say I do: then will you not be disappointed in my qualities as a lady? Yes, as we have already heard your thoughts on what an accomplished young woman must be able to achieve. But will you voice that disappointment, or will you insist that I play beautifully after all, thus confusing my original belief and perhaps ultimately causing me to believe I am far more skilled than I know myself to be? No, Mr Archer, I will not play that game with you. I will instead be confident and comfortable in my judgement of my own talents, and you will be obliged to accept my assessment without rendering your own."

Long before the end of Elsabeth's speech, Archer sat, as if with stunned admiration, and only smiled as she went on. "I ought to have known that,if you would not back down to my aunt this evening, I should be no more than a leaf in the wind of your opinions. Forgive me, Miss Elsabeth. I ought not have pressed you."

Elsabeth was about to fully agree with this statement when Ruth put forth, "It is true that while Elsabeth doesn't practise nearly as much as she ought, she has a much lighter hand at the pianoforte than I do. I practise but admit to playing somewhat didactically, so perhaps you might grace us with your limited talents tonight regardless, Elsa."

Elsabeth bestowed a look of rueful betrayal upon her middle sister, although any true exasperation could only be mitigated by the surprise of hearing Ruth acknowledge that her playing was stiff. "You are not helping, Ruth. And now you have put me in an ungainly position, for the only other person we might ask to play is Miss Derrington, and it would be impolite to presume upon our hostess. Unless you play, Mr Archer," she added pointedly. "That would be a treat indeed."

"If you will play us a song," Archer replied, "I shall follow valiant suit."

Astonishment pulled laughter from Elsabeth's throat and she rose to attend the pianoforte. "I have been defeated," she announced as she sat there, "but I believe in defeat I have achieved victory."

"Indeed you have." Archer and the others, even Miss Derrington, gathered around the pianoforte, whence Elsabeth commenced to play with as much skill, and no more, than she had claimed was her own. She had, as Ruth observed, a light touch, but little smoothness to the flow of notes, and, after a full half hour of playing, lifted her hands from the keys to announce, "I have emptied my repertoire. You, Mr Archer, may take my place and astound us with your skills."

A brief smile bent Archer's lips. He settled into place, casting what could only be considered furtive glances at each of the gathered listeners, and then, somewhat to Elsabeth's astonishment, began to play with as light and flowing a touch as could be desired from any musician. A spate of surprised laughter and applause rose from the audience, and Archer, too, played undisturbed for a full half an hour before letting his hands fall from the keys.

"I have been had, Mr Archer," Elsabeth reported with delight. "You play extraordinarily well. How came you by it?"

"And you," Archer replied ruefully, "play passingly well, but no more. I shall endeavour not to question you again, Miss Elsabeth. My own skill comes from my sister Persephone, whose talents at the keyboard are unparalleled and who could not bear for me to play badly, much less not at all. She has spent innumerable hours at practise, and at least that many again as my own fierce taskmistress."

"She is to be commended if she can persuade one such as you to the practise of anything until you have mastered it. Perhaps she ought to next teach you the art of dancing, Mr Archer. Your cousin," Elsabeth said to Miss Derrington, "is most difficult to engage in dancing. I have watched him stand aloof in the midst of a ballroom full of ladies in need of partners, and refuse any more than four dances, all of those with those with whom he is already closely acquainted."

"That *is* a pity," Miss Derrington conceded, "especially as I know Gerry to be as accomplished a dancer as he is a pianist."

"Oh, but he is not," Elsabeth disagreed. "For to be an accomplished dancer, one must converse, and he will not; I know this from experience."

"I am not good at holding conversations with those with whom I am not well acquainted," protested Archer.

"And yet you will not practise and therefore gain more acquaintances," Elsabeth responded, by now enjoying herself thoroughly and not even loath to admit it. Archer was a fine partner in wordplay when he cared to be; such quick wit coupled with excellent features made it possible to think well of him, when she had been so long determined not to. "It is not, after all, as though it is impossible to meet people at a ball."

With a sigh more theatrical than sincere, Archer enquired, "Are all my flaws to be laid out before us this evening?"

Elsabeth offered him a fulsome smile. "I am sure we could not possibly touch on all of them in the course of a single evening, Mr Archer. Now: be so good as to play for us again, as I think we can safely agree that you are by far the most talented musician in the room, and I shall escort Miss Derrington back to the fire, as she is trying hard not to shiver." With an arm looped through the other lady's, Elsabeth did just as she intended, and together they spent some cosy little while listening to Archer play.

As they sat enraptured, Miss Derrington, whose observational skills were well honed from so many years of sitting aside and watching rather than participating, saw with delight how soft Miss Elsabeth's gaze was upon Archer as he played, and what delight she took in being surprised by the gentleman's skill. "He is rather handsome, is he not?" she asked quietly, so as not to break the spell, and was rewarded with Elsabeth's murmur of amusement.

"More than rather, Miss Derrington; you need not tread lightly in admiration of your own cousin. Indeed, his handsomeness was much admired the first time Mr Archer was introduced in Bodton, although I fear his manners were rather less so. I confess, though, that when he chooses to be finely behaved, he is much more appealing than I had previously imagined. One could grow to quite like him."

"One could," Annabel agreed, and judging a little guidance better than a strong push, subsided into silence again. Elsabeth, who was not so innocent as to be unaware of Miss Derrington's thrust, smiled more readily at Archer even so. It was a pity he *had* been so badly mannered, and perhaps even a pity she had been so prideful as to insist broadly that the man held no appeal. Even if he had not been handsome, or rich, his wit spoke to her, and that he *was* handsome *and* rich—she laughed softly, and put the thought away.

A game of whist was commanded after Archer's musical interlude was concluded, with Miss Derrington happy to observe rather than participate, and then Archer, mindful of his cousin's happiness, insisted that she read for them a little while. Annabel, who read well, recalled Elsabeth's passion on the topic of not belittling her own skills, accepted the charge, but after half an hour put the novel in Archer's hands and commanded he entertain them all a while himself. "Will we each read?" he asked pleasantly as he finished, and Elsabeth, finding herself willing, accepted the book still warm from Archer's grip. She fitted her fingers against that warmth and, smiling, read a few chapters before Ruth declaimed any right on the part of the Coxes to carry on, thus saving them all from Mr Cox's rendition of a racy stretch of fiction, or worse, a lecture on whether fiction was appropriate for young women at all.

The sounds of merriment did not, as Archer had predicted they might, draw Lady Beatrice from her rooms, but as the evening came to an end, Annabel Derrington squeezed Elsabeth's arm and asked if she might come to the house often during her visit with Ruth. "My mother treats me as though I am quite fragile," she confessed, "and perhaps I am. But I have never seen anyone stand up to her quite so boldly as you have tonight, and I am now obliged to wonder if some measure of my delicacy is of her making."

"I believe Ruth and Mr Cox come here almost daily," Elsabeth said warmly. "I should be delighted to come with them often myself, and spend more time in your company. Until to-morrow, then, Miss Derrington!"

The anticipated pleasure of improving the acquaintance with Miss Derrington allowed Mr Cox's lecture about manners, which Elsabeth might have thought she had escaped during the post-dinner activities, to go almost unheard by Elsabeth as they returned to the vicarage. The weather had turned: it was colder by far than it had been when they arrived, and in the morning no one was surprised to see snow on the ground.

Elsabeth, emboldened by a warm coat and good boots, took it upon herself to walk that morning, and found great happiness in the leaden grey skies meeting the virgin white earth. Even the black trees spiking the clouds were things of beauty, and the silence of the land under snow made her invigourated breathing sound more alive than ever. Birds cut across the sky in flurries or alone, with the occasional bright-breasted robin standing out against a world made colourless by winter.

Her steps became strides and those strides turned to running through bursts of mist made by her breath. She dashed up hills gasping and down them again laughing, until she thought her chest might burst with the joy of being alive. She could not, here, as she might have in Oakden, allow herself to erupt with some wild dance of magic, though she could imagine the easy brilliance of flame spinning against the sky. But if she could not risk the magic, she could certainly allow herself to dance, and so she did, atop a hill with a view for miles. She spun, laughing, until she could spin no more, and then fell to her back on the snow, where she swept an angel and lay in its arms, gasping and smiling at the featureless sky.

The labour of her breath was too great to hear footsteps, and Fitzgerald Archer's concerned appearance in her line of vision came as a great startlement. Elsabeth sat up with a cry, then as swiftly concluded he could be no more appalled by her activities than he surely was already, and fell back into the snow without concern. Knowing how greatly at odds it would be with her activities, she was careful to apply the most formal tone she had at her disposal when she spoke. "Mr Archer."

"Miss Elsabeth," Archer replied with equal formality. "Forgive me. I saw you fall, and imagined you might be in some distress. Instead, I see you have been producing a work of art. I fear I have marred your wing." He moved his foot and Elsabeth turned her head to see the impression of his shoe upon her angel's wing.

"My medium is a forgiving one." She swept her arm upward again, wiping the footprint away, then folded her hands over her stomach while retaining her solemnity. Archer remained at the corner of her vision, looking down at her. Concern had fled his expression, though she could not say what had replaced it: curiosity, perhaps. "I did not see you at all, Mr Archer."

"I thought not. I was some distance behind you, and on a different trajectory until I saw your...dance. Miss Elsabeth, I find myself at something of a loss. I am not entirely certain how a gentleman is to behave when he finds a young lady encased in the arms of a snow angel. Ought I offer a hand, that you might rise?"

"I believe it would be more suitable for you to lower yourself into the snow and create an angel of your own."

"That is absurd."

Elsabeth turned her head to smile directly at him. "It is, isn't it? That is why it seems most suitable. Otherwise, I suppose you might go on your way, leaving angels behind."

"I suppose I might," Archer replied slowly. "I suppose I must. Good morning, Miss Elsabeth."

"Good morning, Mr Archer."

(38)

TO SAY THAT ARCHER LEFT THE ENCOUNTER WITH MISS ELSABETH disturbed did not do sufficient credit to his state of mind. There were certain expectations of ladies and gentlemen in Society; lying serenely at the bosom of a snow angel fit none of them. More distressing by far, however, was Miss Elsabeth's utter lack of embarrassment at being found in such an unusual position. Her only moment of discomfiture had been upon Archer's arrival, and it was clear she had been surprised, not humiliated. A woman who was ashamed by her activities would have leapt to her feet, all blushes and downcast eyes; she would have been unable to express herself without stammering, nor able to explain herself at all. Instead, Elsabeth Dover had spoken easily, as if they were in the very heart of a ballroom or parlour, and with such blissful serenity as to cause Archer to feel as though *he* was in the wrong for not joining her in the making of snow angels.

He could not possibly have done so, he admonished himself, and wondered that somehow he thought himself a coward and a fool for his propriety. Webber, he thought in a mix of horror and regret, might well have flung himself into the snow; but Webber had the knack of making himself liked, which Miss Elsabeth herself had emphasised that Archer did not. But Webber would not have found himself in a position of wondering whether he ought: even if his affections had once lain with Rosamund

Dover, Miss Dover was not herself one who would be discovered in a country field sweeping snow about like a child.

That thought lay perilously close to a conclusion he did not wish to reach. Archer shook his head ferociously, as if to put thoughts of Elsabeth Dover out of his mind, and, when that did not succeed, strove instead to think of the impropriety of her behaviour rather than its charms. With that idea fixed firmly in place, he strode toward Charington Place and refused to look back.

For her own part, Elsabeth could not be mortified: she had had no notion of Archer's presence, and was only glad that she had quelled the urge to dance with fire beneath the winter sky. Making snow angels was quite outrageous enough, though, for an intriguing moment, she had imagined Archer was considering the idea of joining her in the preposterous activity. It was a shame that he had not: she could have warmed to him quite considerably, had he stepped down from his manners to play a little while. But no: never Mr Archer, whose dignity could be stretched to fill two or three gentlemen with the usual amount, and leave him with enough to be regarded as stiff, even if he did play the pianoforte surpassingly well. And that was her last thought of Archer for some time: the cold seeped through her coat and dress and boots, and Elsabeth sprang to her feet again, shaking snow loose as she began a vigourous walk back to the vicarage.

There she was greeted with tea by Ruth, and for some little while, they cosied together before the kitchen fire before Ruth spoke of an obligation to visit Mr Cox's parishioners. Warm, dry and happy, Elsabeth joined her, and saw as they walked that there were innumerable homes with small gardens pressed up against the house walls. Many were covered with a linen propped on sticks, to keep the snow off, and all were more vigourous than might be expected so early in the year. At each of those houses, Ruth went out with one or more of the children to help tend the garden, and returned with fingers reddened by cold and black beneath the nails with dirt.

"The linens are clever," Elsabeth said as they went from the dozenth house. "How foresightful to prepare them; I had no notion of the oncoming snow."

"Nor I," Ruth replied serenely, "but it *is* only January. One might expect snow, Elsabeth, and Mr Cox and I may have brought some old linens around the parish to make protective coverings. It would be a shame to see such an early harvest go to rot."

"But I noticed that your own garden is unprotected."

"I am sure it will recover."

Elsabeth laughed and caught Ruth's arm, quite stopping her in their travels. "Oh, yes, so am I. Just as Papa's has always recovered. Ruth Dover, you have hidden your light under a bushel!"

Ruth smoothed her skirts and met Elsabeth's eye with no hint of guilt at all. "I am Ruth Cox now, sister, and I have a duty to Mr Cox's parishioners. Lady Beatrice is an excellent patroness, but there are very few families who could not do with more. If digging in the soil with them for a little while, and helping to build linen houses for their gardens, is of some small use to them, then of course I can do nothing less than lend my God-given strength to their health and happiness."

"God-given, is it, Ruth?"

"We are made in His image, and He does not make mistakes, nor burden us with gifts or faults we cannot bear."

Tears sprang unexpected to Elsabeth's eyes and she embraced her middle sister with more passion than she could ever remember before doing. "I am proud of you, Ruth."

To Elsabeth's surprise, Ruth, always the most stoic of the sisters, had tears in her eyes as well when Elsabeth released her. Tears, and a smile that shone more brightly than Ruth's ever had as a Dover. "Thank you, Elsabeth." For the space of a heartbeat, it seemed she would say no more, but then the words rushed from her breathlessly: "You won't tell anyone, will you? Especially not Dina and Tildy. I should never hear the end of it."

"My dear sister, I believe you could parade a winter garden in full bloom before them and they would never suspect anything was amiss, but of course: your secret is safe with me. Although—I do think Papa and Rosa would be so pleased to hear it!"

"I can depend on their discretion as well as yours," Ruth said, solemn once more. "You may tell them, if you wish. But not by post, Elsabeth! It cannot be trusted to the post."

"Of course not. Now, come. Have we more gardens to tend? And then I will visit Miss Derrington, and be home before supper."

"We might be all day tending gardens, Elsa. Go to Miss Derrington, and return when you can. I'm pleased you've made a friend of her; I have had less success there."

"I suppose Mr Cox holds her in too high esteem to regard her as material for something so common as friendship," Elsa guessed. "Perhaps I shall endeavour to acquire an invitation for you to visit alone, if you should like to make such a friend."

"I have done well enough among the parishioners, and am not lonely. That is your concern, is it not? But if you wish to meddle, neither would I object."

Elsa laughed again, and embraced Ruth a second time, and with a happy heart traipsed to Charington Place, where she was greeted warmly by Miss Derrington and invited to sit by the fire. "I cannot imagine your fortitude," Miss Derrington proclaimed. "Taking yourself out in such weather deliberately, and on foot! I should insist upon a carriage to bring you home."

"And I should insist that you not bother. Surely, it is far more unfair to rouse a horse or two, not to mention a coachman, out of their own warm roosts, than to trouble myself to walk a trifling distance. I enjoy the winter, Miss Derrington. I could no more deny myself the pleasure of walking than you might deny yourself the pleasure of sitting by the fire."

"I should find myself an icicle if I denied myself that pleasure. It is pleasant, though, to watch the snow fall and see how it quiets the world. Now, Miss Elsabeth, I was surprised to learn you knew my cousin. It seemed to me you and he shared an uncommon camaraderie."

"Oh, uncommon indeed. I suppose he has told you of my unconventional behaviour this morning."

"Not at all! But you must: I am so admiring of unconventional behaviour, perhaps because it is so far beyond me."

"I believe it would be beyond me, too, if I found the entirety of my surrounds to be unforgivingly chilly at all times. I have told you of my fondness for constitutionals; I am afraid Mr Archer found me indulging in another fondness. He happened upon me making a snow angel in an otherwise lonely field."

Annabel Derrington's laughter rang like sunshine through the parlour before she clasped her fingers before her lips. "Oh, dear. I fear Gerry could not approve. He is most concerned with propriety."

"I fear he did not approve. He seemed in quite a state when he left me, but as he neither damaged my angel's wings nor, it seems, betrayed my silliness to another, I suppose it was not such a state as to do himself any harm."

"Nor you any," Miss Derrington agreed, "for I am certain that although I might find it delightful, others might look upon such a tale with more concern. But my cousin is very sensible of what might adversely affect others: indeed, I have it from him that only last summer, he prevented a match that could have been most unsuitable for one of his close friends."

Elsabeth Dover was rarely cold, but her hands became icy at this proclamation. "Is that so?"

"Oh yes. His friend Mr Webber—perhaps you know him as well?—was, to hear Gerry tell it, quite infatuated with a young lady, perhaps even ready to make a proposal to her. But there was something unsuitable about her family, and Gerry encouraged him to leave hastily, before any permanent entanglements were made."

"Something unsuitable about her family. What an extraordinary claim. Surely, we all have unsuitable aspects to our families, whether it is an unfortunate nose or a tendency toward a weak gaze. Was the lady herself objectionable?"

"Oh, no. I gather from Gerry that she was all that could be considered right and proper, so it must have been something far more alarming than an unfortunate nose to consider her family inconceivable."

"I can hardly imagine that I am hearing this correctly," Elsabeth said in a low, slow voice. "Mr Archer took it upon himself to decide whether Mr Webber's fondness was appropriate, and removed Mr Webber—with whom, yes, I am familiar, and who is an amiable and persuadable man—from this lady's presence?"

"Just so," Miss Derrington said with satisfaction. "I gather it was no difficulty to persuade Mr Webber to Town, whereupon I suppose he forgot the lady swiftly enough. I should like to go to Town myself sometime, although I suppose my general health is such that a Season would not do."

With a shudder, Elsabeth allowed herself to be drawn into the new topic, the better to deny the fury that threatened to burst from her. Miss Derrington could have no notion of Elsabeth's closeness to the matter she had so casually discussed, and to clarify it would only mortify her. With an effort, she replied, "A Season? I thought—forgive me for my rudeness in saying so when you have not yourself mentioned it—I thought that you were engaged to Mr Archer."

"Oh, there is no official arrangement. Mother has great hopes of the match, and Streyfield is beautiful, but I confess that my own desires, should they be of any import, would be to marry a man less qualified and retire back to Oyo with him."

"Then you should have a Season," Elsabeth said, somewhat distantly; she felt as though the conversation happened by rote, rather than through any determination on her part. "The ballroom crush in London would certainly keep you warm enough, Miss Derrington, and I am sure you would meet many pleasant gentlemen."

"Mother would be enraged!"

"Ah." Elsabeth smiled, though it felt cold. "But you would be engaged, and therein lies your purpose, does it not? We shall only have to hope that Mr Archer does not find *your* choice unsuitable and move to sway you where you might not wish to be swayed."

"Oh, you cannot think Gerry was wrong! We know nothing of the circumstances!"

The smile remained forced upon Elsa's lips. "You are right, of course. We know nothing of the circumstances. We do know yours, though, Miss Derrington, and it is certain that if you are not interested in marrying Mr Archer, then you will remain unmarried so long as you reside at Charington Place. I think you must ask your mother to take you to Town."

"I cannot imagine that she would agree to such a scheme."

Elsabeth's smile sharpened as a plot occurred to her. "Then I shall ask my aunt, with whom my sister Rosamund is currently staying, to have you visit. I shall suggest to her that she put on a performance of dismay that a young woman as lovely as yourself, with such excellent connections, has not yet been brought out, and she shall propose to Lady Beatrice that if *she* cannot manage to bring you out, then perhaps *my* aunt could be of some small service to her Ladyship and bear the expense of bringing you out herself."

Miss Derrington's lips parted in astonishment. "Mother could never allow that. The very idea would be an insult!"

"I imagine so. And so you will achieve what you wish: a Season in London, and I dare say the freedom to choose your own husband, if you pursue it with conviction."

"Miss Elsabeth, are you always so cunning?"

"No." All the sharpness left Elsa's tone and she knew that what remained of her smile was sorrowful. "Not always." Were she always, she might have laid the blame for Mr Webber's departure at Archer's feet directly; instead, she had supposed it was Miss Webber who had persuaded Mr Webber away from Bodton. She spoke a little while longer with Miss Derrington, and left her determined to speak to Lady Beatrice about a Season; that seemed both monumental and minimal, in the face of what she had learned about Archer's behaviour. And to think that, only that morning, she had thought of softening toward him! No: she had not been wrong from the start, to think him arrogant and cruel, concerned only with his own position and superiority.

Her sedate walk home became a blind run when she passed out of sight of Charington Place, and did not resume a more casual pace until she was very near the vicarage. There she smiled and did supper duties with Ruth, then, pleading weariness after a day of refreshing exercise, retired to her room to weep for Rosamund's loss, and the mercilessness of the very wealthy.

(39)

A knock came on Elsabeth's door early the next morning: Ruth, pleasantly awake and prepared for the day, invited her to visit other parish houses. Elsa pleaded a headache that nearly had Ruth staying home, but Elsabeth promised that she would be much restored by a cup of tea and a quiet morning alone. Ruth assured her Mr Cox would be busy out of the house until at least the middle afternoon, and departed with a concerned glance over her shoulder. Elsabeth waved her away and returned to bed for a little while, until the temptation of tea was too great to ignore, and, in a morning dress with a dressing gown over it, made her way to the kitchen.

Even the cook was out, perhaps searching for the evening meal. Elsabeth, relieved by the solitude, sat by the fire with her tea and thought bleakly of Rosamund's dashed prospects. An unsuitable family: how dare Archer make that determination if Webber himself had not! And even if they were—and they were, Elsa admitted that in the privacy of her own thoughts; they *were* unsuitable by Society's standards, beleaguered by magic as they were—but even if they were, Rosamund herself was the most suitable creature to have ever lived, even touched by a little gift of sorcery! Even Ruth, primmest of the sisters, proved to find a sensible use for her talent, and if Ruth could embrace such skill, then Mr Webber, by far a mellower soul than Ruth, could overlook it, had he not been misled by the odious Mr Archer.

A knock came on the door in the midst of her raging thoughts; Elsabeth threw off her dressing gown and stormed through the house to answer it in a fury that lent magnificent height to her colour and snapping vividness to her dark eyes. Anyone who stood beyond the threshold might have been stunned by it, but it was Archer who stood there, and he was in the moment of her arrival thunderstruck. To him, it was as if a living goddess had struck open the door that he might gaze upon her glory; this, with the memories of her laughter and her dancing in the distance, with the recollection of her arch conversation and uninhibited delight of playing in the snow, moved him to speak freely and without caution to the astonishing creature before him.

"I had thought myself twice or more in danger at Newsbury, but knew myself to be beyond danger only yesterday. Miss Elsabeth, I cannot repress my feelings; I cannot look upon you and not speak those feelings you have awakened in my breast. You must allow me to tell you how much I love and admire you, and upon the strength of these emotions I must ask you to marry me."

Not even Elsabeth could retain her outrage in the face of such an astonishing speech delivered upon the vicarage doorstep. Nor could she command voice of her own, and only gazed at Archer in wordless amazement. He took this as encouragement and stepped forward, seizing her hands in his own; his, Elsabeth noted, were warm, and though she would have said a moment earlier that her own burned with fire, they were now cold and small in his. She regarded them briefly, then, still unable to speak, felt obliged to look up again as Archer spoke on.

"I am not insensible to the difficulties offered by not only your social status but your family's peculiarities, and yet I find I cannot allow them to dictate my feelings, much as I know they should. There is nothing to be done: my heart is yours and I must rise above the inferiority of your status in order to have you as mine. I am even willing to risk having children with you: that is the depth of the love and desire that have come to command me."

"Oh," Elsabeth said in a voice hardly recognisable as her own. Her hands were warm again, not from borrowed heat but of their own fast-flowing blood. She disengaged them from Archer's and took several steps down the hall; a bit of reflection showed her how Archer took a step after her, as if surprised that she had left. She turned then, voice quite in control, if honed to a cutting edge. "How very generous of you, sir. How generous of you to overlook the circumstances of my birth, which were not as fortunate as yours, and to overlook my family's *peculiarities*, which I assure you I am myself in full possession of."

"Yes." Archer smiled as if suddenly relieved. "Yes, it is generous, and I am gladdened to hear that you understand that, for it is not easy for a man of my station to—"

"Be rejected in a proposal of marriage?"

Archer flinched and stepped back as though she had struck a blow: it had not, she saw, occurred to him that she might deny him. Nor was she unaware of the import of his asking: he *was* of more elite breeding, and to propose marriage to a lady of her class, whose family was rumoured to be magic-ridden, was indeed a great stride for such a man.

True love, Elsabeth felt, would not feel the need to dwell on those topics as Archer had. "I should offer an apology for disappointing you, Mr Archer, and I would, save that I feel that an offer of marriage should not come hand in hand with a litany of insults; it is no delight to be proposed to by a man with a list of reasons as to why he must act against his better judgement to make the proposal. Moreover, even if you had foregone such charming footnotes, even if you had been a gentleman worthy of the title since the hour I met you, how could you ever imagine I should agree to marry the man who has been the architect of a beloved sister's unhappiness?"

For the second time, Archer startled. Elsabeth pressed forward, fingers snapping with outrage. "And yet you now dare lower yourself to propose to me, when you would not permit Webber, a far more amiable soul, to marry Rosamund, and instead left him looking like a creature of caprice and my poor sister looking a fool for disappointed hopes? That is an unforgivable offence, Mr Archer, and were Webber a whit less kind-hearted, he, too, might have rejected you as I do!"

By this time, Archer's control had returned, as had a measure of icy calm in his voice. "I make no apologies for separating them; I believed then and believe now that it was the only appropriate action to take. I thought it wiser to allow him Miss Dover's memory than the unpleasant discovery of—"

"Of what, Mr Archer? Do finish so that I might fully understand why you have destroyed Rosamund's future."

"Of her family's magic," Archer replied in deadly tones and after only the briefest of hesitations. "It is known in Bodton that your youngest sisters and father, at the least, are inclined toward sorcery, and I have made discreet enquiries in London. Old rumour tells tales of *all* your family being afflicted with magic, although I confess I have seen no indication of it in you or Miss Dover, and cannot imagine it of Mrs Cox."

"No wonder you were able to lower yourself to propose to me. Let me set your mind at ease on the topic, Mr Archer. I am most thoroughly *afflicted*, as you call it! Let me show you the power I am invested with, that you can be quite certain of your folly!" It was no difficulty to call her natural flame to hand, balls of it in her palms and flickers dancing from her fingertips. "There! Is this what you wish to have proven?" Elsabeth flung a palmful of fire the length of the hall, casting shadows where none had been before, and threw sprites of flame about Archer himself. Not *at* him; even in her fury, she could never threaten a living creature with the pain of fire, but *about* him, so that it spun and darted an arm's-length halo. Archer, to his credit, did not look in the least afraid or even astonished, although his attention was fully taken by the fire. It burnished his skin, bringing out its warmth, and reflected in his eyes as he turned his gaze from it to Elsabeth.

"I wonder that any of your family has gone unremarked-upon, if this is the display you are prone to when in a temper. The floor-boards at the ball: that was not my clumsiness, then. I only wonder if it was your own insulted heart that laid me out, or if another of your clan rose to defend you."

"I take no shame in admitting that it was I, nor any more shame in being born to magic than Captain Hartnell does! Oh, do not imagine I know nothing of your treatment of him! Rather than allow him the best years of his life in independence, you have reduced him to the comparative poverty of a soldier, all for what you consider a *taint*!"

Elsabeth's fires winked out with a clench of her fist, leaving Archer quite inscrutable in the comparative darkness, and it was with remarkable calm that he replied, "You are too concerned with Captain Hartnell's misfortunes."

"And why should I not be, when that which has driven them is that which you have condemned my own sister for, and that which you are willing to *risk* your own status and heirs upon!"

"Do you think I should take joy in your misfortunes?" demanded Archer. "Do you feel I should make light of those scruples that I have mentioned? I cannot, nor would I have dreamt that a female such as yourself might not appreciate the honesty I have shown in admitting to them! That I am prideful I will not deny, but neither can I bear deception, which I might have believed you had yourself realised and even admired! No: I will not rejoice in the inferiority of your connexions nor the magic that afflicts your family, but I am surprised that you list my honesty amongst your reasons for refusing me."

"You fail to understand, Mr Archer. All your honesty has done is removed any sense of compassion or concern that I might have felt in refusing you, had you behaved in a more gentlemanly manner."

For the third time, Archer looked startled, but did not speak; Elsabeth took advantage to press her point: "I assure you, Mr Archer, that I should have refused you regardless; there are no circumstances that might have persuaded me to accept your offer. You hold in disdain the feelings of others, whilst impressing with arrogance and conceit the superiority of your own position and manners. I give you the great credit of doubt to say I had known you a full month before I was certain you were the last man in the world that I could ever wish to marry."

"You have made yourself perfectly clear, madam. I beg your forgiveness for taking up so much of your time." Archer snapped his heels together and turned for the door; only when he reached it did he pause and say, "Please accept my best wishes for your health and happiness; Miss Elsabeth. Good day."

With these words, he departed, leaving Elsabeth to fall against the wall in tremulous shock. But the wall was not support enough: she slipped down it to sit on the cut stone floor, and gazed, shaking, at the door through which Archer had left. That he *loved* her! That he should ask for her hand in marriage! These were not possible things, and a great trembling sob caught her chest. For some time, she sat against the wall, surprised at the strength of her tears, which were born of high anger, not regret, and which faded only when the sudden thought of her cold tea came to mind. She rose from the hall and returned to the kitchen to boil a second kettle, and sat staring over her teacup's rim for immeasurable time, until she heard the sounds of someone returning home and, unable to face the prospect of conversation, fled to her room.

40

When she was obliged to finally leave her room and meet with others, Elsabeth felt the day passed as a performance: she behaved as though nothing untoward had happened, and Ruth, knowing no better, accepted this performance as entirely natural. Elsabeth slept poorly and rose early to take breakfast and a walk, the latter of which was first begun along familiar paths, and then, when she realised how close it might bring her to Charington Place, struck out among the trees in search of solitude. She could not leave behind the astonishment of the previous day's encounter no matter how she strove, nor the varied degrees of offence that had been given and taken alike. She longed to visit Miss Derrington, or better still, Rosamund, but she was meant as Ruth's companion for weeks yet; there could be no swift departure on her part, and she could only hope that Mr Archer might find reason to leave Charington soon on his own. Surely, every meal taken at the manor house would be a misery otherwise, and there could be no satisfactory explanation as to why without revealing at least some of Mr Archer's ill-conceived emotions—or worse yet, perhaps, some mention of her own display of fiery temper.

That was an action upon which she had not permitted herself to dwell. Elsabeth sank to a snow-covered branch with a moan, and sat silent in the wood for some time, thinking once and again on her foolish confirmation of the Dover magic. Rosamund would never have stooped to such absurd behaviour, nor Ruth. Leopoldina and Matilda, perhaps, but that was a brush with which Elsabeth did not want to paint herself; a brush with which even Mr Archer had avoided painting her up until then. Nor was there any taking it back; the damage was done, and, for all of Elsabeth's admonishments to the younger sisters, it was she who had in the end perhaps condemned them all to spinsterhood. Although Mr Archer had shown no fear, he could not be expected to hold his tongue on the matter Elsabeth had made so clear to him, though—bright and happy thought!—perhaps he would not wish to explain what extraordinary circumstances had caused Elsabeth to display her talents in such a spectacular manner.

And then as quickly into woe again: they were not, as a family, known for being circumspect; few would question it if Archer presumed to speak and simply imply Elsabeth had been taken by a fit of boldness. So consumed was she with these thoughts, she did not hear Archer approach until he cleared his throat; then she came to her feet in a startle, and without thinking, accepted a letter that he offered to her.

"Forgive me," he said. "I have been obliged to follow your footprints in the snow to find you, when I could not find you at home. Do not be afraid: I have not come to pursue the topic that you found so distasteful yesterday. Indeed, all I wish to say is written within that letter, and yet, having put it in your hands, I fear I am embracing a kind of cowardice, and that I should instead speak what I have struggled to write. Will you allow me?"

Startlement impelled a candid response: "Could I prevent you?"

"With a word."

Elsabeth gazed a moment at the gentleman before her. "I believe you mean that." In that moment, she was decided, and sat again on her branch in a posture of acceptance.

Almost instantly, Archer turned his back, as he could not both look upon her and speak. "There are two matters I would discuss with you. I only ask that you try to put aside your disgust for me and listen without prejudice, as I am putting aside my own pride to speak."

No lady could admit to the sound of derision that passed Elsabeth's lips upon hearing those words, but neither could any merely mortal creature fail to listen on, now that curiosity had been awakened. Archer turned his head at her sound, and she covered it with a cough. The corner of his mouth turned upward, though she could not say that humour propelled the expression. "The first is the matter of your sister and Mr Webber. Let me address this first: I am guilty, as you say, of parting them. I believe all of my reasons were good ones, but there is one, beyond the matter of your family's...talent...that has not been addressed, and which, in the end, I felt was stronger even than the question of suitability. Webber is, as you say, an extraordinarily amiable soul, and I have seen him fall in love a dozen times. I should have thought his attachment to your sister no more than that, save as the days progressed, his demeanour toward her seemed ever softer, until I believed him truly in love. Upon my realisation that it was generally thought in Bodton that he would propose, I felt obliged to consider Miss Dover's presentation of affection, and that was what I found so lacking as to be the final push to move me as I did."

Archer paused and gathered himself. "From your consternation over her grief, of the wrong done to her, and of her disappointed hopes, I am forced to consider that I have been wrong in this matter. I should not think a young lady who had formed no attachment could be disappointed in hopes save for frivolously, nor—and I am uncomfortable thinking of this in regards to my own actions—seem as unwell as I believed her to look in London."

This statement by itself was enough to drive Elsabeth to her feet as if she would set off for London at that very moment; Mr Archer, sensing her intentions, lifted a hand. "You cannot be there more swiftly than if I was to drive you there myself; knowing this, will you not hold a little longer, and listen?"

"I could listen well enough in a carriage," Elsabeth replied, and could not bring herself to sit again, nor hold her tongue upon the topic of Rosamund: "My sister is vanishing shy, Mr Archer. To confess to me, beneath the covers at night, that Mr Webber was the most amiable man she had ever met, is the height of indiscretion for her; how much more could you expect a lady of gentle breeding to represent to the gentleman she cared for? She was never seen to dance twice with any *other* gentleman, nor to accept a dance when she could otherwise stand at Mr Webber's side in light conversation. Because *my* emotions are baldly read does not mean Rosamund's must be, and you have done her ill indeed."

"And for that I am sorry," Archer replied simply. "Were it in my powers to set it right—and I do not flatter myself to think it might be—I would. But this is the smaller matter, madam, and I am loath to discuss the larger in the confines of a carriage for fear of my eyebrows being singed."

"You find this humourous, Mr Archer?"

"I believe that, with all the intent and searching in the world, you would not find a note of humour within the letter I have written."

"And yet standing here before me?"

"I have made it plain that I find it difficult to retain my composure in your presence, Miss Elsabeth. I shall endeavour to quell any show of unwanted emotion, a task which should be made easier by the subject of my second topic. I cannot know what it is precisely that Mr Hartnell—Captain, we shall say, Hartnell—has said to you, and so, if you will be so good as to hear me out, I shall present to you the story as I know it, and leave it to yourself to determine where the truth may lie."

"I will hear you out—I will even do so without comment—if you will do something for me."

"Anything," Archer said so swiftly as to send a shiver of uncertainty through Elsabeth's breast.

"Persuade your aunt that I must go to London immediately, and that I could not do so more safely than with the use of her carriage. And, as it would be unseemly for a young lady to travel alone, persuade her also that your cousin, Miss Derrington, must travel with me." The last Elsabeth suggested in a fit of inspiration that caused Archer's eyebrows to rise.

"Annabel? Travel by carriage in January? I believe she would be frozen through before you arrived."

"Then she shall thaw at my aunt's fire. These are my conditions, Mr Archer; will you agree to them?"

"I will. Whether Aunt Beatrice agrees is another matter, but if she refuses, it will not be for my lack of effort."

"Then speak your piece, Mr Archer. I will listen." Elsabeth sat again, somewhat regretting that they were obliged to have this conversation in the midst of a snowy wood rather than by a parlour fire, but equally comprehending that it would not be had at all should there be any chance of interruption.

"Captain Hartnell is given to all those graces that you accuse me of lacking: he charms, he smiles easily, he converses at length on any topic, from the frivolous to the profound. It was always thus; I have known him since infancy, as his father was the vicar at Streyfield, and we were born within weeks of one another. My father was very fond of the old Mr Hartnell and equally fond of the son, to whom he was eager to provide the best education and living available. It was my father's intent that David—Captain Hartnell—should inherit the vicarage on the estate."

All of this was so in keeping with what the Captain had told Elsabeth that her curiosity was piqued; surely, the tale must diverge, and she had no notion how Archer might paint himself the hero of the story, which surely he must.

"As we grew, being young men of an age together, I came to believe that those very graces I have enumerated might lend Mr Hartnell a disinclination for the clergy: he was, to put it indelicately, too fond of the company of ladies, and they of him. Nor did he seem to have any serious measure of concern for the well-being of the estate's parishioners; he appeared to see himself as above them—ah, you smile, madam. You see in my words a reflection of myself, and I cannot deny the reflection is there.

Nonetheless, David did not seem concerned with their worldly needs, much less their spiritual health, for they were peasantry and he, while born of that rank, was well-enough educated to regard himself as above it. I spoke once or twice of this to my father, who believed the best of Mr Hartnell and could not accept that any sensible young man would reject an inheritance of a thousand pounds and a living offered to him in the best of intentions. And perhaps, if my father had long outlived his, David might have found himself settled into the vicarage despite himself, but both of those good men died within two months of one another, and when the dust was settled, David came to me and confessed he did not believe himself well suited for the Church.

"He was my friend; I could not in conscience persuade him where I agreed he did not belong. He was of a mind to pursue law, and I, knowing both his quick mind and his charm, thought him well suited for such a pursuit. Nor was I insensible to the fact that—and please forgive me for speaking so crassly of money, Miss Elsabeth; this seemed a less direct thing to admit to in the pages of a letter, but, when spoken aloud, sounds shocking—the fact that a thousand pounds would not see him through law school. He did not even have to ask for the sum of four thousand additional pounds that I provided to see him through."

Elsabeth Dover, whose father had a thousand pounds a year and six females to share it among, swallowed and cast her gaze downward. A lump sum of five thousand pounds, offered out of friendship, lay near to incomprehensible. There, then: this was how Archer made himself to be the hero of the story, by a tale of unstinting generosity. But she could not quite bring herself to disbelieve him. Five *hundred* pounds; that would have been unbelievable for its insignificance, but five thousand, by its very outrageousness, begged credibility.

Archer, determined to have the story out now that it had begun, carried on as Elsabeth discovered she had crumpled his letter, and smoothed it against her knee while he spoke. "We parted friends, with, I confess, little expectation on my part of seeing him again: he would be in trade, and I a gentleman, and our paths were unlikely to meet. Nor did they for some four or five years, whereupon he came to me again a dissipated stranger. Law school had not been for him, if he had pursued it at all, and he now claimed a deep calling for the Church.

"I could not offer him the parish at Streyfield: a new vicar had long since been established there. Neither had I any other answer for him; I could not be responsible for the decisions that had wasted what capital he had, and, at the last, I offered the best that I could do: the purchase of an officer's commission in the Army.

"He rejected this offer forcefully, and disappeared again. I was certain, this time, that we would see no more of one another."

Here, Archer hesitated and turned fully to Elsabeth, waiting until she lifted her eyes to speak again. "This part of the tale is one I have held close, Miss Elsabeth, not for my own sake but for the sake of the other party affected by it. I believe that, despite your distaste for me, I can rely upon your discretion, but I also ask your patience if I struggle to speak what I have not before discussed."

"Perhaps you would prefer I read it in your letter," Elsabeth replied softly. "Assuming it is detailed there?"

"It is, but, having begun, I wish to carry on. You will perhaps recall that I have a sister, much younger than myself?"

Elsabeth grimaced. "Miss Persephone, yes. I also recall my rudeness over the matter of her name, as well, and once again must ask forgiveness."

"It is forgotten. Miss Archer is, as I have said, much my younger and has, I am not ashamed to say, led a very protected life. It is natural, I think, to want to protect younger sisters, and even more so when she is wholly without a mother. She has had much of what she desired without question, and, for the moment, her riding lessons were chief amongst those desires. She was not more than nine or ten when Mr Hartnell left Streyfield, and only fourteen when he returned; I had not imagined they would meet at all, but he proved cunning enough. With some little effort, and after enough time as to assuage any suspicion I might have, he learnt from the village that Persephone was known for her riding skills, and made some effort to acquaint himself with her—reacquaint himself, he claimed, thus allowing him to avoid introductions made by myself—without my knowledge."

"Mr Archer," Elsabeth said softly, and with a cold dread clutching her belly. It was impossible to think poorly of Captain Hartnell, but very easy to think of harm that could befall an unworldly young woman, and Archer's brief smile did little to reassure Elsabeth on the topic.

"They were on the verge of elopement when I discovered them. Only Persephone's dismay at keeping their romance a secret from me betrayed them, in the end, and even then, she believed entirely that Hartnell was in love with her. It was only when I was forced to tell her that he had freely asked for thirty thousand pounds—the full sum of her inheritance—to leave her that she was willing to believe that it was money and not love that drove him. I refused him the sum, of course, but—once again, and this time in mind of my sister's reputation—offered a military commission, which he accepted. You are surprised. I do not mind telling you that I impressed upon him the likelihood that he would otherwise awaken from a night of revelry on a ship bound for Australia, whence there would be no reasonable expectation of return."

Archer fell silent a moment, then concluded with "I had neither heard from nor seen Mr Hartnell again until Miss Enton mentioned his name in Bodton, and that was too soon a reunion for me; any reunion at all would have been too soon. This is the story as I know it, Miss Elsabeth. I thank you for listening, and I will leave you now to make arrangements with my aunt for you to travel to London."

(41)

RUTH, UPON HEARING OF MR ARCHER'S SECOND, EQUALLY DIRE assessment of Rosamund's health, was eager to let Elsabeth go. Elsabeth, thus blessed, wrote a swift letter to Mrs Penney, announcing her arrival with a guest on the very heels of the letter, and hurried it to the post that it might have half a day to travel ahead of them. "I will visit again as soon as I can, Ruth; the week I have been here is hardly a visit at all."

"Only see Rosa well again first," Ruth insisted. "I am quite sturdy, for my own part."

"I will bring her with me," Elsabeth promised, and the very next morning saw the sisters separating. Lady Beatrice's carriage came first for Elsabeth and her belongings, then returned to Charington Place to collect Miss Derrington, who proved surprisingly able to pack for an indefinite stay in London. Good sense would have had Miss Derrington in the carriage first, but Lady Beatrice, whose disapproval of the entire affair permeated Charington Place, would not have her delicate daughter in the carriage one moment longer than necessary.

"No matter," Elsabeth said to Miss Derrington as the door was closed behind them. "In short order, my aunt will write your mother, and then Lady Beatrice will come to London and bring you out. It will be a splendid affair, and worth all the sudden fuss."

"I believe it is your sister who is worth the suddenness of the fuss," Miss Derrington challenged with a smile, though before Elsabeth could form a rejoinder, the carriage tilted with the weight of a man on its step, and Mr Archer entered its warmth.

"Forgive me," he said abruptly. "Aunt Beatrice has concluded that two footmen and a coachman are insufficient escort for two young ladies on such a journey, and insists that I join you."

"But how lovely!" cried Miss Derrington. "With three of us, the coach will certainly stay cosy, and with Mr Archer's presence, we can have no fear of highwaymen!"

"I have every confidence that Miss Elsabeth could rout any highwaymen we are likely to encounter without my assistance, but I am flattered to be regarded as a manifestation of safety." Archer thumped the door and the coach set off, masking the curiosity of his next question. "Cousin, what *are* you planning? I have never known you to have any interest in London, or anything more than ten feet away from a fire, and this sudden departure seems unlike you."

"It is Miss Elsabeth's scheme," Miss Derrington announced with some pleasure. Elsa considered hiding behind her hands, but the flickered glance of amusement Archer sent her way caused her to straighten her spine instead and meet his gaze without embarrassment. "You have Streyfield, cousin," Miss Derrington went on, a fawn-coloured gloved hand laid on Archer's arm, "and you must know that, while I admire it, I have no earthly desire to remove myself to it for all time. Miss Elsabeth has convinced me of the wisdom of a Season, where I might select some intelligent, attractive and penniless gentleman as a husband, and take him back to Oyo with me."

"So, my suit is rejected before I have made it," Archer replied in an odd voice, and this time did not look toward Elsabeth at all. Elsabeth, mortified, fixed her own gaze firmly on the window, wishing that it was not covered in the name of warmth.

Miss Derrington only laughed. "If you had intended to make it, Gerry, you would have done so long ago. Do not pretend that I have not been convenient for you, and that it is easier to be agreeably silent in face of Mother's intentions than to confess to her that you don't wish to marry me. Indeed, although certainly Miss Webber has set her cap for you, I wonder at times if you intend to marry at all. You are twenty-eight, Gerry! You are growing shockingly old! But do not look so. I am quite set on this plan, and I think that once I am in a marrying mind, we all must be. Miss Elsabeth—oh, may I call you Elsabeth, please? I think we are friends, are we not? And we shall be greater friends before this journey is through. I shall be Annabel and you Elsabeth, and Gerry—"

"—shall remain Mr Archer to me," Elsabeth said, looking away from the window in swift horror. "I am sure I could never presume upon the familiarity of his first name."

"Nonsense," said Annabel, but did not press the matter. She remained merry the entirety of the journey, sharing stories of her childhood and once or twice drawing Archer into recounting his own visits to their ancestral homeland of Oyo; Elsabeth, who had never travelled beyond England's shores, knew a sting of envy at their tales, and was both relieved and disappointed to arrive, in due time, at Mrs Penney's home in London.

Archer's opinion of the address was clear upon his face; later, Elsa, recounting to Rosamund all that had come to pass in the eventful days she had visited Ruth, confessed that she imagined Miss Derrington would be removed to a more fashionable address even before Lady Beatrice could be prevailed upon to bring her out. It was, nevertheless, an enjoyable journey, marred only by the accuracy of Archer's assessment of Rosa, who was more beautiful and more frail than ever before. She could not be said to look unwell by Society's standards: she was as perfectly pale and fragile as the most elegant of ladies were expected to be. Her cheeks were aflame with unpainted colour, her lips rosy, and her gowns, becomingly thin, clung to her so revealingly that Elsa, alarmed, said, "You are not dampening your muslin, are you, Rosa? You know it is an unhealthy habit."

"Of course not, Elsa." Rosamund's smile was fever-bright. "I should never be so bold, though I do confess that I seem to perspire more than I should. Perhaps it is that which gives me the look of dampening. Does it suit me, the dampened look?"

"You are beautiful," Elsa replied with honesty that—she hoped—hid her concern. "The gentlemen must be very taken with you."

"No more than is seemly," Rosamund hastened to assure her. "I find my dance card is often full, and I am asked to dance twice by several of the gentlemen, but I cannot always oblige, when so many other young men have already spoken of their hopes for a dance."

"And Mr Webber?" Elsa asked cautiously. "Does he dance with you twice?"

"Oh! Mr Webber and I rarely see one another, Elsabeth. No more than thrice in the past month, and, when we meet, I am sure it is only as the best of friends. And how lucky I am, to have such excellent friends. I do see Sophia often. You must see her, Elsa. She has blossomed, and I believe her card could be as full as my own if she wished it to be."

"Does she not?"

"She attends to Miss Webber most assiduously. Indeed, even Miss Webber has been seen to refuse dances that she might have stood up during, the better to keep Sophia's company. I do believe that they both have an unspoken desire to be back in Bodton, where there are often so few gentlemen that the ladies must dance together in order to have any pleasure in a ball!"

At this, Elsabeth could not help but laugh. "I cannot believe there are any circumstances under which Miss Webber would prefer Bodton to London, but I suppose I must be pleased that she and Miss Webber have become such famous friends."

"You suppose," Rosamund teased. "How generous of you, Elsa. I should think Sophia will be married at last, and finally be secure in her future. We should want nothing more for our dear companion. But I am talking endlessly, Elsabeth, and you have not yet told me anything of Charington Place, or Ruth."

"Ruth is extraordinarily well. I have a secret from her, Rosa, one that is to be shared only with you. You will recall how well

Papa's gardens have always grown? It seems Mr Cox's parish is blessed with the same winter greenery."

For a moment, Rosamund did not comprehend; then she did, and her lovely eyes grew wider. "No! *Ruth*? *Our* Ruth?"

"I am no less surprised than you," Elsa assured her. "She thrives in it, Rosamund: you and I must go to visit her soon. You will be astonished at the change in her. Mr Cox is, I fear, much the same, but Ruth is very well indeed."

"And Charington Place, and Lady Beatrice? You have made great friends with Miss Derrington, I think; she has come with you, after all! She is a great beauty, is she not? And engaged to Mr Archer? Tell me all!"

"Not engaged to Mr Archer; it is her intention to find a husband this Season, and return to Oyo. She finds England too cold. Lady Beatrice is quite overwhelming, both in beauty and opinion, and I fear I was unable to stay mute in her presence. I suspect she did not care for me to begin with, and now I have stolen her beloved daughter away to London. I could do little more harm, save—"

All at once, the import of what had passed between Elsabeth and Archer overwhelmed her, and with a cry, Elsabeth thrust Archer's letter into Rosamund's hands. She had read it a dozen times: a hundred times, in the night before she left Charington, and what it imparted was in no significant way different from what Archer himself had said to her on the day she had received it. "Read it. Say nothing until it is read, and then tell me what to think, Rosa. I am at loose ends, and you are the star to my wandering bark."

Rosamund, distraught, took the missive and began to read; her attention had only been on the paper a few seconds when she gasped Elsabeth's name in question. Elsa shook her head in desperation. "Do not ask. Not yet. Just read it, Rosa, and tell me what to think."

To her credit, Rosamund read it twice, and parts thrice, before lowering the tightly written pages. "I cannot know what to think of Captain Hartnell, Elsabeth, nor of—of Mr Archer's confession to his—his interference in the matter betwixt Mr Webber and myself. I am perhaps relieved there, to know that there *was* interference, although I cannot fault Mr Webber entirely, as I did *not* return his calls, and could easily be seen as uncaring."

"Never!"

"But that is not the matter of most importance to me here, Elsabeth," Rosamund went on gently. "What is this matter Mr Archer speaks of in his first sentences? Surely, I cannot be reading it correctly. Has Mr Archer made you an offer? One which you have rejected?"

Elsabeth, unable to speak, only nodded. Rosamund, flushed with more than fever-brightness now, sat quietly a moment, examining her closest sister before a rueful smile curved her lips. "Well. We must certainly never allow Mamma to hear of this. She would begin with palpitations and continue with endless lectures about thankless daughters who lacked the sense to marry ten thousand pounds a year when it came asking. You would be harried into your grave by it."

"Oh, Rosamund!" Elsabeth fell forward into her sister's arms with a sob. "You do not think me a fool?"

"I never could. Your heart is for you to decide, and though I care to see only the very best in people, even I must concede he has a somewhat arrogant air and an unpleasant inclination to insult those around him. I should never think you could marry him, no matter how prettily he asked."

"And he did not ask prettily at all." Elsabeth wiped her eyes, and in a little while could tell Rosamund about Archer's appalling proposal.

"I am surprised he left with as much of his dignity intact as he did," Rosamund said peacefully at the conclusion of the tale, and smiled when Elsabeth laughed. "You have no need to see him again, Elsabeth; this unpleasant chapter of our lives is concluded."

"Is it?" Elsabeth asked. "What of Captain Hartnell? Surely, until that matter is resolved, this cannot all be said to be behind us."

"You must speak to him," Rosamund replied. "There is nothing else to be done, Elsa. You must speak to him and draw your conclusions from the two stories you have been told, and then—I know you are fond of him, Elsa, but have you—had you—any thought of marrying him?"

"None."

A little relief swept Rosamund's pretty features. "Then bring him what you have learned from Mr Archer and learn what he says in response, and from there decide whether his friendship is one to retain, or to allow to slip away into pleasant memory, as I have done with Mr Webber."

"I thought London was meant to fill your mind and hours with frivolous entertainment. Instead, it has honed wisdom in you, Rosamund." With this observation, Elsabeth set all troublesome thoughts aside, and slept contentedly at Rosa's side.

(42)

The morning saw Elsabeth much restored, if still burgeoning with concern for Rosamund's well-being. Careful observation proved that Rosa ate well, slept well, and was as charming in company as anyone might hope for, but no matter how well she ate or how deeply she slept, the fever-brightness did not leave her eyes. She was all the more in demand for it: it heightened her already-considerable beauty until not a soul could approach her who did not wish to stay at her side, even at the expense of other acquaintances. At the end of each day, she seemed a little more fatigued, although she only laughed when Elsa noted this aloud. "Why should I not be fatigued, when we are so splendidly diverted? Truly, you are too worried, Elsabeth; I am sure I have rarely felt better. And did you see that Miss Derrington has a letter from Lady Beatrice, who will be in Town before the month's end? There is to be a ball of astonishing proportion upon her arrival, and I am sure it will be Miss Derrington's debut."

"I did see," Elsabeth confessed, and could press Rosa no more on the status of her health. Annabel Derrington invited them both to the dressmaker's with her, and a delightful two days were spent in the midst of organzas and muslins and silks. Sophia, accompanied by Miss Webber, joined them for an afternoon, and they went away with new gowns of their own on order. Elsabeth watched them leave with a note of longing in her breast: once she might have happily confided the tale of Archer's proposal in Sophia's ear, but there was no opportunity with Miss Webber in attendance, and, more, there lay a thread of fear that a tale told might wend its way back to Miss Webber, and through her, to Archer. To have been badly proposed to was awful enough; to have it become gossip and the offending gentleman aware of it was worse by far, and so, Elsabeth, regretfully, did not speak of such matters to her one-time closest friend.

To her surprise, Miss Derrington insisted that both the Dover ladies and Mrs Penney should have an entirely new gown in the very latest fashion for the purposes of Lady Beatrice's ball, and to Mrs Penney's surprise, Miss Derrington would hear nothing of the Penneys footing the bill. "There is hardly any point in having money of one's own if one cannot spend a little of it on friends," Miss Derrington insisted, and then more shyly confessed, "and I have had few friends indeed, since coming to England. Please, allow me to be generous; it is only a small way to thank Elsabeth and her family for their kindness."

And so, they were bedecked nearly royally on the fateful night at the end of February; so well bedecked that even Lady Beatrice, whose arrival had been accompanied by a thunderstorm so ferocious, it appeared to echo her temper, forgave Elsabeth for conniving to take Annabel to London. Her Ladyship was once again adorned in the strong colours and bold patterns that honoured her Oyoan heritage; beside her, Mrs Penney, who was pretty, looked quite ordinary in plum, and the three young ladies were eye-catching in orange, which suited Miss Derrington every bit as well as it did Lady Beatrice, blue, which turned Rosamund into a beauty meant to be captured in oils for eternity, and, somewhat to Elsabeth's discomfort, red that was so striking and appealing that she found herself shyly looking for shining spots in which to glimpse her own reflection.

The ballroom into which they arrived was already a sad crush, and yet, as Mrs Penney and the Dover ladies were introduced, it began to fall silent and attentive; by the time Lady Beatrice was put forward with her daughter, Miss Annabel Derrington, the entire party was attuned to them. Whispers of admiration rushed through the room and beyond, and before they had reached the bottom of the ballroom stairs, innumerable young men were jostling for position in hopes of an introduction and a dance.

Rosamund's time in Town became suddenly invaluable: she, who had kind words for everyone, knew now who was likely and who was not; her sweet voice warmed when she spoke of those she genuinely admired. Those she only liked because she liked everyone were dismissed by one chaperone or the other, and, within the half-hour, Miss Derrington's dance card was as full as she wished it to be.

So, too, were Rosamund's and Elsa's, though Elsa's was no more than half-full. "No, do not mind me, Aunt," she replied to that lady's concerns. "I do love to dance, but I would like more to observe Annabel and Rosamund, to see if the one seems to find a gentleman particularly to her liking and to ensure the other does not exhaust herself too quickly."

"She seems very well, Elsabeth," Mrs Penney replied with newly born concern. "Or do you feel she is otherwise? I thought London had been good for her."

"I am sure it is only a sister's excessive worry," Elsabeth promised, but did not accept any further invitations to dance.

In some little time, she began to believe perhaps it *was* merely excessive concern: Rosamund, always so shy, blossomed now, able to laugh and flirt gently with gentlemen who were clearly besotted. She danced gracefully, never with the same gentleman twice, and when she asked for a strengthening drink, three handsome young men raced to be the first to acquire it for her. Elsabeth, between her own dances, scolded herself for unnecessary alarm, and turned her attention to Miss Derrington.

Elsabeth found Miss Derrington warm and kind, and was bemused to see that, on the dance floor, the lady shared something of Mr Archer's stiff formality. But, she reminded herself, Miss Derrington had had very little chance to dance and socialise in her life at Charington Place, and could well find Lady Beatrice's ball overwhelming. She danced with a handsome youth now, a gentleman Rosamund had described as a fourth son to a family whose fortunes were in question. Entirely unsuitable in Lady Beatrice's opinion, but precisely what Annabel might be looking for. His polite formality on the ballroom floor had a soft edge to it: he clearly could not take his eyes from Annabel, and as they danced and spoke, her smile became slowly less strained, until it brightened into fulsomeness near the set's end.

It was too much to imagine Miss Derrington might find the very gentleman she sought on the first night of her Season, and yet the thought pleased. Elsabeth turned away with a smile, seeking Rosamund again, and instead, to her delight, encountered Sophia Enton, who fell upon her with an embrace. "Elsabeth! You have been in London a month and we have barely seen one another! Your gown is magnificent: I would hardly know you."

"Nor I you," Elsabeth replied with a laugh, and returned the embrace. "London suits you, Sophia. I cannot imagine you returning to Bodton now. Have you a beau?"

"There are gentlemen who call upon me," Sophia said carelessly. "More than enough to please my mother, although not one of them has turned my head."

"Must they now turn your head?" Elsa asked in amusement. "You *have* changed!"

"Perhaps, when I thought I must marry for security, I could not afford to love, but that was before I had even one admirer, and now I have several. Oh, do come with me; we are all huddled against a wall, avoiding the crush as we indulge in Lady Beatrice's table. I believe it is the finest table of the Season so far, and there are innumerable dishes I have never before encountered. Mr Archer tells me they are of African origin, and their depth of flavour is astonishing. Do come with me! I must know how you have been!"

Until the announcement that Mr Archer was with Sophia's party, Elsabeth was most inclined to join her; upon it, she was already engaged in walking that way with Sophia, and unable to refuse without giving offence. “I am well,” she promised. “I have visited a little with Ruth, who is happy, and have come to London to look after Rosamund, who seems—”

“Well, too,” Sophia inserted with pleasure. “We have seen her—not so often since your arrival, which is curious!—but we have seen her, and I have never seen her looking so fine.”

“Nor have I,” Elsabeth said after a moment’s silence. Sophia had once been the most likely after Elsabeth herself to show concern over Rosamund’s health; to hear her accept it as presented now was disconcerting. “I must only stay a few minutes with you, Sophia: I am to keep Miss Derrington company a little while after her next dance. Will you not dance yourself?”

“I have stood up with Mr Archer and Mr Webber, whose attendance on me makes the line of eligible gentlemen grow ever longer. I had never thought I might find it tiresome, Elsabeth, but there are times when I wonder if I must marry at all. I should rather remain with Miss Webber, though I suppose someday she will marry Archer and we will be parted. Here! Look who I have found, Julia, Mr Webber.”

“Miss Elsabeth!” cried the latter, and bowed with delight. “How long it has been since we have seen one another! How splendid you look!”

“Too long.” Elsabeth smiled and curtsied about, murmuring greetings to each of Sophia’s party. “I understand you have been keeping Sophia in excellent style, Miss Webber. Allow me to commend you on your unparalleled choice in friends.”

“Oh, do not be jealous, Miss Elsabeth; I am only fortunate that Sophia is so willing to share her time with me.”

“You misunderstand,” Elsabeth replied instantly. “I truly meant to commend you. I could never resent that which has brought Sophia so much happiness as you have. I only wish that we might have seen more of each other these past weeks, and I do not mean to exclude you when I say *we*.”

“But you have been very busy with Miss Derrington, have you not? It is an extensive piece of work, settling a young lady into Society.”

"And we have been of virtually no assistance at all," Mr Webber proclaimed with obvious dismay. "It is one thing to allow someone time to settle in Town, I have argued, but it is another to be entirely removed, as we seem to have been. And Miss Derrington your own cousin, Archer! I believe we have been badly neglectful."

"You have happened into the heart of an argument that has been going on for several days now," Sophia whispered to Elsabeth. "We cannot agree on whether it is more proper to have given her the opportunity to settle herself or if we ought to have been more attentive."

Elsabeth, who was for her own part grateful that she and Mr Archer had not crossed paths, could only reply, "It is in the past now, and, as of tonight, Miss Derrington is out; surely, it would now be wholly appropriate for you to see her as often as you might like."

"There," Mr Webber said in delight. "Archer, you must approach your cousin and inform her of our intentions to visit tomorrow. You will, of course, be there, will you not, Miss Elsabeth?"

"Oh, no, Mr Webber. Although Miss Derrington has been visiting with my aunt these past weeks, with Lady Beatrice now in residence, she has of course joined her there. It is a more fashionable address," she added, the better to take a moment in which to gauge each expression at the delivery of this news.

Nothing less than relief could be said to have settled on Miss Webber and Mr Archer's features; nothing less than disappointment lay heavily upon Mr Webber's. Of the three, the first two were precisely as Elsabeth had expected, and the third, as she had hoped. She did not think it her imagination that Miss Webber still preferred to keep Mr Webber from Rosamund's presence, nor did she in any measure doubt that Mr Archer wanted nothing more than to avoid any location where Elsabeth herself might likely be found. But unless she mis-read him badly, Mr Webber had hoped to visit the unfashionable Penney address and encounter Rosamund; Miss Derrington was a pretext, from a man for whom deception was an unfamiliar tool.

"I could never ask you to break tomorrow's engagement with Miss Derrington," Elsabeth continued lightly, "but perhaps, if the opportunity is available on the following day, you might be so good as to escort Sophia to my aunt's home? She and I have had so little opportunity to catch up since we have been in London, and I should very much like to hear about your own adventures over the past months as well."

"A capital idea!" burst Mr Webber before Miss Webber could rally. "And I should think we will all be at our best two days hence, whereas tomorrow, we may still be suffering the effects of a ball of this magnitude." This clearly struck a thought in him, and he turned to Archer with some concern. "Perhaps we ought not impose upon your aunt so soon as tomorrow, at that, or would it be unspeakably rude to not call on her as soon as possible? Oh, Julia, I leave it to you: you have an excellent head for social engagements."

"I shall arrange something," Julia Webber said in the voice of one thwarted, but nothing more beyond that was said, as a commotion shifted the crowd behind them and Mr Penney, who had been so little involved in the ball as to have been forgotten, stepped through, his face pale with concern.

"Elsabeth, you must come quickly. Rosamund has fainted."

(43)

It was not uncommon, of course, for ladies to faint at balls, especially ones so crushed with attendees, but it was commonly acknowledged that many of those swoons were dramatic in nature. Not so with Rosamund Dover: by the time Elsabeth and Mr Penney arrived at her side, much assisted by the bulk and barking deep voices of Misters Webber and Archer, Rosamund had not yet wholly recovered, despite the aroma of ammonia in the air.

Her colour, which had been so fever-pitched and flattering to the blue of her gown, was now so pale as to be reflective of her gown's hue, and the curling tendrils at her temple and nape were wet and cold with sweat. She lay trembling in Mrs Penney's lap, at the centre of a circle opened in the crowd to give her air, and when Elsabeth fell to her knees beside her, she offered Elsa an uncertain smile and whispered, "Oh, do not look so concerned, Elsabeth, I am quite well," before shivering so hard her eyes closed again.

"She is not well at all," Mr Webber said in a terrible voice. "Miss Elsabeth, our home is only a few streets away. I must insist that Miss Dover be brought there rather than risk the cold night across the distance to your uncle's premises."

Elsabeth cast a look at her aunt and uncle, whose grim nods

were all she needed to seize upon Webber's offer. "We would be grateful, sir."

"Archer, send for my carriage and have a doctor sent to the house. Now, man!"

Mr Archer, as unlikely a man to act on another's command as could be imagined, spun and pressed through a crowd that fell away before him. Without further permission, Webber scooped Rosamund into his arms. "My God, she weighs nothing at all. Miss Elsabeth, implore Miss Derrington for her furs: I am sure that whatever coverings Miss Dover wore here will not be sufficient against the cold."

"I'll go," Sophia said, and, with a brief smile at Elsabeth's grateful acknowledgement, disappeared through the crowd with as much ease as Archer had.

"No," said Webber as Mr Penney moved as if to take Rosamund from his arms. "I have her safely, sir, and I think she should be as little disturbed as possible. Only clear a path that I may carry her to the door." This he did with such tenderness that Elsabeth was touched by it, and obliged to fight away tears when Rosamund opened her eyes once and smiled in bewildered astonishment to see her dear Mr Webber so close at hand.

"There will not be room enough in the carriage for the entire party." Archer strode to meet them as they approached the door. "Julia, I must ask you and Miss Enton to remain here with me a little while so that Miss Dover can ride as comfortably as possible. Miss Elsabeth, you will join Webber and your sister. Mr and Mrs Penney—"

"We will call our own carriage," Mr Penney replied with dignity. "I hope it would not be too much for us to come to your home, Mr Webber. Rosamund is as dear to us as a daughter."

"Of course you must. I would have nothing else. Ah, Miss Enton—"

Sophia arrived burdened by furs and followed by Miss Derrington, whose agitation at Rosamund's state was nearly as great as Elsabeth's own. In her wake came Lady Beatrice, and in hers, the young gentleman Annabel had danced with earlier. He put himself forward with a confident diffidence, saying, "My uncle is Dr Swift, of whom you may have heard; he is considered a premier physician in London. Let me send him to you, if it might be of any assistance."

Archer's face lit with approval. "I have commanded the services of another, but we would be grateful for your uncle's expertise. If there is any extraordinary cost, Webber, I shall undertake it myself."

"Do not be absurd." Webber spoke in more clipped tones than Elsabeth had known were at his disposal. "Miss Elsabeth, if you will help me with the furs—"

Within moments, they had bundled Rosamund so well that there was no part of her save her nose exposed to the air; even so, Webber remarked on her lightness, and carried her swiftly to the carriage. Elsabeth ran behind him, forgetting her own wraps in her haste, and was astonished to feel Archer's hand on her arm before she climbed into the carriage.

First, he settled a cloak around her shoulders, then, as he fastened it beneath her chin when her trembling hands could not, he said, "You can warm the inside of that carriage more quickly and efficiently than any other mortal might in this moment. Do not fear exposure, nor Robert's opinions. I will speak to him if I must, although," he said, with a glance into the carriage, where Webber held Rosamund as if she was both fragile and precious, "I think it will not be necessary. Do what you must for your sister's health."

He boosted her into the carriage, closed the door, and, with a thump on its side, they were away, leaving Elsabeth staring through the window at him in numb astonishment.

"She is so cold," Webber reported grimly. "Even through the furs, I can feel her tremble. I am not enough to warm her."

"Mr Webber," Elsabeth whispered. "Mr Webber, I can warm her. I—I only ask that you do not cry out, do not condemn me or my sister for what I must reveal to do so." Twice she fumbled the window-shade before successfully drawing it down, whilst

Webber protested he could never condemn anyone who might drive the cold from Rosamund's bones.

"It will not harm you," Elsabeth said, still in a whisper, and called the fire that had always come so naturally to her.

The carriage lit with warmth and beauty as flame wreathed her hands. Elsabeth remained very still for a few long seconds, cowering with anticipation of Webber's disgust, but he was beyond such emotion: he flinched back at first, then registered amazement before surging forward a few inches to hold Rosamund out to Elsabeth's fire. "The furs—"

"Nothing will burn that I do not wish it to." Elsabeth knelt in the middle of the carriage, holding her hands as close to Rosamund's breast as she dared. Flame, even flame that would only burn what Elsa wanted it to, was insufficient: it could not wrap around Rosamund's skin and press warmth in, could not heat her core that her extremities might know warmth again. For the thousandth time in her life, Elsabeth cursed the limitations of her magic: surely, there must be some way to shape it in more useful ways, but all she could do was hold fire to her sister's skin and hope for the best.

"She is warmer," Webber whispered in awe as the carriage drew to a halt at the doors of his town house. "She trembles less. Miss Elsabeth, you have wrought a miracle."

"It is not a miracle unless she heals. Quickly, into the house. The warmest room, no matter which it might be, because I do not dare call such power where others might see."

"But you *should* be able to," Webber replied with sudden ferocity. "You may have saved Rosamund's life, and there can never be any shame in any power that could offer such hope! Now open the door, and I will be as swift as I can be."

The door opened without Elsabeth's assistance, a footman standing beyond with an expression of such worry that tears sprang to Elsabeth's eyes again. She followed Webber at a run, grateful that the magnificent front door swung open without hesitation. It closed as quickly, too, and the butler—Peters,

Elsabeth was surprised to see; she knew him from Newsbury, but had not known he travelled with Webber—sprang ahead of them to open a parlour door.

Heat swept out in a wave that flushed Elsabeth's cheeks in an instant. Webber never stopped, rushing Rosamund to the fire's side, but Elsabeth turned to gaze at the butler in grateful astonishment. "How did you know?"

Real concern shone in the butler's eyes. "Nothing travels faster than gossip, Miss. Word came from below-stairs at Lady Derrington's ball that Miss Dover had taken ill, and I knew Mr Webber would bring her here if he could. There's tea ready, if you think it may be of help."

"Please," Elsabeth whispered. "And soup, perhaps, or eggs mashed with cracker. Something simple and fortifying. She has been strangely unwell, and I know not what else to offer. But the doctor will be here soon."

"I'll show him in when he arrives," Peters promised. "Go to your sister now, Miss. I'll take care of the rest."

There could be no possibility of sufficiently expressing her gratitude. Elsabeth smiled, hoping to convey some aspect of it, then followed Mr Webber into the heat-infused parlour.

He knelt beside Rosamund, whom he had laid on a chaise that had been pulled directly in front of the fire. She had awakened, and smiled in soft bemusement at him, then brightened in confusion as Elsabeth hurried in. "Elsabeth, I had the most peculiar dream. I dreamed I was floating on a bed of fire, but it did not burn, only warmed me. And now I have awakened and it seems to be rather true, although I cannot imagine how that can be. Were we not just at the ball?"

Weakness collapsed Elsabeth's knees and she caught herself on the chaise's back with a shaking laugh. "You fainted, my dear sister, and Mr Webber has quite come to your rescue. Are you cold?"

"No," Rosamund responded dreamily. "Nor am I too warm, although I can see that you and Mr Webber are both shining with perspiration and imagine I should be as well. Elsabeth, I feel quite detached. Am I flying?"

Webber exchanged a concerned glance with Elsabeth, who knelt and took Rosamund's hand beneath the heaps of fur that swathed her. "No, but you are not well. Peters is fetching egg mash and tea; that will help you to feel more at one with yourself."

"Oh, that sounds lovely. How kind he is. How kind everyone is! Mr Webber, I am terribly sorry for having caused so much trouble. I had no notion I felt so poorly. Although I am not certain that I feel poorly at all. I feel quite as though I could fly." Rosamund unwound herself from the furs, her wrist turning gracefully and leading her arm upward like a feather caught in the wind, and rose with it until she sat upright and reached toward the ceiling. "It is the most delightful feeling, Elsabeth. You must try it. I should like to fly, I think. I should fly up to the cornices and inspect them for dust! Not that I would ever find dust in such a fine house as Mr Webber's, or report upon it if I did. That would surely be the height of rudeness. Am I talking nonsense, Elsabeth? I feel as though I may be talking nonsense."

"I think you are feverish," Elsabeth replied uncertainly. "Do not worry. The doctor will be here soon."

Rosamund allowed her hand to drop and turned to Elsabeth with eyes enlarged by surprise. "The doctor? But I thought you said Peters would be here with egg mash! Elsabeth, is Peters a doctor? Mr Webber, I did not know you kept a doctor as your butler! How extraordinary! How could a man of such learning come to be one of the serving class? Where is Peters? I should like to ask him directly."

Webber's concern turned to alarm, a sentiment Elsabeth shared vigourously. "Peters is not the doctor, Rosamund. Peters will be here soon. So, too, will the doctor. They are separate, do you see?"

"Oh, of course! What a relief, Elsabeth. How silly of me to imagine Peters could be the doctor. I have become as silly as Leopoldina. Oh, *dear.* Do not tell her I said such a dreadful thing, Elsa: promise me you will not."

"Of course I won't. Here is Peters," Elsabeth added with relief. "A few bites of egg mash will see you sorted, Rosa. Oh, and he has put butter in it; thank you, Peters, this will be splendid. Rosamund, here, let me feed you a bite."

Rosamund obediently parted her lips for a spoonful of egg mash, then swallowed it with an expression of uncertainty. "No. No, I do not believe this is right. This is heavy and I am quite light, Elsa. This will sit in my belly like a lump, and I do not wish to be a lump. Perhaps later I will try it, but now I prefer to fly."

"Give us a moment," Webber instructed Peters. The butler departed, promising again to bring the doctor as soon as he arrived. Elsa, feeling close to tears, pled with Rosamund to eat a little more, but Rosamund refused to even speak, instead pressing her lips together and shaking her head like a child afraid someone would slip a bite into her mouth if she did not stand fast against it.

The doctor arrived before she could be convinced to try another bite, and shooed both Elsabeth and Webber to the far side of the room. Elsa refused to go farther, and Webber could not in conscience leave her, so together they huddled, watching the doctor check Rosa's pulse, her eyes, her tongue after assuring her he had no interest in forcing her to eat, and straining to hear as he carried on a long and quiet conversation with her. In the end, she accepted a small phial of drink from him, and almost at once sank into a boneless sleep.

Only then did the doctor approach Elsabeth and Webber with the practical air of a man confident in his abilities. "You are the patient's sister? I must ask you a question that you won't like to answer."

"If it concerns my sister's health, there is nothing I will not tell you."

"You may prefer for this gentleman to not participate in the conversation."

"I am the lady's affianced," Webber said with such determination that Elsabeth looked at him and he blushed.

"Then it most certainly affects you as well. Miss—"

"Elsabeth Dover."

"Miss Elsabeth, let me be plain. Is your sister afflicted with magical ability?"

Elsabeth's lips parted, then sealed again as she looked a second time at Webber. She had made *her* secret known, and it was accepted that a family touched by magic was tainted with it through and through. Still, to confess it aloud before the man who had just claimed himself affianced to Rosamund—

"It will make no difference to me," Webber said softly. "Surely, I already know the answer."

"As do I," the doctor said as bluntly as before. "I was a battlefield doctor for many years, and I certainly know when magic has been stoppered up. She must use it, Miss Elsabeth, or it will kill her."

For the second time, Elsabeth's knees weakened, and this time, without Webber's intervention, she would have fallen. He helped her to a nearby chair, where Elsa sat a moment before breathing deeply and nodding her preparedness. "Go on."

The doctor showed the kind of matter-of-fact sympathy that might be expected from a man who had seen battle, but did not soften his approach in any way. "Judging from her condition, I would say she has never been much accustomed to exerting her power and that she has not used it at all in the past six-month or more. Magic is an unforgiving gift, Miss Elsabeth. If it is not released, it builds, and then it begins to sicken the blood. She will have seemed feverish these past two months, although eating and sleeping well, yes? That is the first sign of poisoning. The next is what she is undergoing now, a physical collapse and outlandish impulses. It takes each magician differently—has she a natural talent?"

"Ice," Elsabeth whispered, thinking of the incident that had driven the Dovers from London in her youngest years. "She could make ice, even as a child, although...I cannot recall the last time she indulged in it."

"Had she, this feverish desire for flight would never have materialised. It is not uncommon; it seems that we earth-bound creatures are endlessly captivated with the thought of flight, and when sorcery goes unused, it very often unconsciously manifests itself as the power to fly. Miss Elsabeth, you need to understand me: if she doesn't use her magic, she will one day soon find herself in flight, and will be in paroxsyms of delight until the moment that the power she has neglected burns itself out and she falls to her death."

"This is *common*?" Webber asked in horror. "How can it not be generally known?"

The doctor's affectation of sympathy slid toward disdain. "Because magic isn't accepted in the upper classes, sir. The more appalling families would prefer their afflicted children to die rather than face the embarrassment of having a magician in the family. The less appalling find some way to keep their talents quiet—perhaps by retiring to the country, or emigrating to America—but they have no resources to tell them of the danger repressing their magic can put them in. You seem robust, Miss Elsabeth; either you're not talented or you're more inclined to use your magic. Whichever it is, if anyone else in your family shares the power, you must inform them of what I've told you, for their own sakes."

"But Rosamund," Elsa whispered. "Will she recover?"

"If I were you, the moment she awakens—and she will in a few hours; I've given her a dose of laudanum to keep her from flying away—I would put her to work making ice sculptures. She has a great deal of magic that needs to be burned up before she's out of danger, but if she'll embrace her talent instead of denying it, then yes, she ought to recover."

"Then I will set the drapes on fire to force her to it, if necessary."

The doctor laughed. "An unusual display of sororal affection. Please call on me again if you require my services, but for now,

I'll show myself out. Good night." He departed with the same brisk efficiency he had shown throughout his visit, leaving Webber to fall into a chair and exchange a long and weary look with Elsabeth.

"What shall we tell people?" he asked after some time. "It cannot be consumption, or she would not be expected to recover; it cannot be magic until after we are married, or my sisters will never allow the union."

"A fever," Elsabeth said slowly. "Nothing more or less. Mr Webber, your intentions...?"

"I intend to marry her," Webber replied with soft ferocity. "I was a fool and allowed myself to be swayed on the topic once before, and now I have come dreadfully close to losing her forever. If your sister will have me, Miss Elsabeth, I will marry her, and damn the consequences."

(44)

Some little while later, Elsabeth, smiling with both relief and anticipated joy on Rosamund's behalf, left the parlour to find an agitated gathering all but pressed to its door. Archers, Derrington, Penneys, Webbers, and Entons alike had not taken themselves to the sensible location of another sitting room, but instead milled in concern around the hallway, partaking in brandy and pies as they waited for news. Almost as one, they descended upon Elsabeth, their questions clamouring against the ceiling and walls, until she was forced to raise her hands and bring the sound down.

"Rosamund will recover," she announced happily. "It has been a very bad fever, and she will need time with little interference in which to heal, but she will recover. She's sleeping now, and will, I think, until morning, at which time she will begin the regime set out by the doctor. I must thank you all, *all*, for your assistance tonight; I do not know what I would have done without you. And I am very sorry for the disruption to your evening."

"Where is my brother?" enquired Miss Webber.

Elsabeth glanced behind herself at the parlour. "We did not think Rosamund should be left alone; he is within, and Peters has joined them. I will take his place and send him out at once. I only wanted to express my gratitude before returning to Rosa's side."

"Is she well enough that I may sit with you?" Sophia asked. "I cannot bear to leave you alone if you might have company. Rosamund is as much a sister to me as you, Elsa, and I wish to do *something*."

"I would be so glad of your company," Elsabeth confessed, and in a little time, Webber was without and Sophia, Elsabeth and the sleeping Rosamund within. Under the crackle of the fire, Elsabeth confessed what had truly transpired to the one soul whom she could, and was met with genuine distress on Sophia's part.

"But, Ruth!" was her first concern, and then, with usual insight, "No wonder you and Dina are the strongest of the sisters. You are discreet but inclined to dabble, and Dina..."

"Is Dina," Elsabeth agreed ruefully. "Do not worry about Ruth; she is proving more than able to care for herself in all ways necessary. Oh, Sophia, I am weary, and yet I dare not leave Rosamund."

"I will have the fires in my own room stoked, and you and she can sleep there."

"I cannot put you out!" Elsabeth said, shocked, but Sophia shook her head with a smile.

"I am certain Julia will allow me to share her bed tonight and as many nights as need be, whilst Rosamund regains her strength."

Elsabeth embraced her. "You are the most generous of souls, Sophia. I only hope Miss Webber is as amenable as you imagine."

Miss Webber proved to be an enthusiastic proponent of the plan, and, with the smallest fuss possible, Rosamund was installed in Sophia's room, with Elsabeth attending her. Behind the safety of locked doors, Elsa felt no compunction against fanning the fire to unlikely heights, and slept very little until near dawn, when Rosamund sighed suddenly and fell into a sleep that seemed more natural than the laudanum-induced torpor.

A knock awakened Elsabeth at what seemed to be no more

than moments after she succumbed to sleep, although from the light at the window she saw it had been a few hours. Rosamund stirred without wakening, and Elsa pressed a kiss to her still-warm brow before hurrying to the door.

A maid bearing a tray of toast, egg mash, sausages and tea stood on its threshold, smiling hopefully. "We thought nothing too strong of scent, though I'm happy to bring you something of more substance if you wish, Miss."

"This will be perfect," Elsabeth assured her. "Thank you. I shall send word of Rosamund's health in a little while."

The maid bobbed a curtsey and hurried off as Elsabeth brought the tray into the room. Rosamund sat up, angelic with confusion. "Wherever are we, Elsa?"

Elsa gave a glad cry and ran to embrace her sister. "You are awake! And we are at Sophia's room at the Webbers' town house. Rosamund, you must listen to me now, and take what I say to heart. You have been—you *are*—very ill. It is the doctor's order that you must make use of your magic."

Astonishment pulled a gentle laugh from Rosa's throat. "That cannot be true."

"But it is," Elsa replied softly.

"How can he even know I *have* magic, much less that I must use it? Why must I? Am I to condemn myself in Society?"

"It was Doctor Swift, the noted battlefield doctor, who tended to you. He has seen the effects of magic denied before, so knew before we even spoke what you suffered. Rosamund, I do not wish to frighten you—"

"I am already frightened!"

"Then begin with this: the tea is too hot to drink. Make me an ice-drop for my cup, and one for your own. You must, Rosa. We will be cautious, but you *must* use your magic."

Rosamund cast a furtive glance toward the door, then extended a finger as if to drip ice into the teacups. "I shall cool your tea, but—oh!" Ice cascaded from her fingertip, filling Elsa's cup to the brim and spilling over in glacial ripples. Rosamund clenched her fingers shut, then pressed her fist against her mouth to gaze in horror at what she had wrought. "That has never happened before!"

"Perhaps it is that there is so much magic pent up in your blood that controlling it is difficult," Elsabeth hazarded. "The doctor said it has begun to poison you, Rosa; that is why it must be spent. If trying such a small task achieves such results, you may need to try something larger, to expend as much at once as possible. I wonder; could you conjure a storm?"

Rosamund wrenched her gaze from the ice-filled teacup to look in astonishment at Elsabeth. "I cannot unleash a storm in London, Elsabeth, even if it were within my power to do so. First and least importantly, I should no doubt be discovered as the heart of it, but far more importantly, think of all the poor souls who can barely heat their homes to begin with! I might kill hundreds! Even thousands!"

"Then we must return to Bodton, where there are fewer lives to risk and far more countryside to spread a storm across. I am sure Mr Webber will lend us a carriage. We will leave today."

"This is madness! You cannot be serious!"

"This is your life, Rosamund. I have never been more serious."

"My life?"

"So the doctor said." Elsa took Rosa's hands, which were cold in her own. "It happens more to ladies of gentle birth than anyone else, he says. We are so forbidden to have magic that we deny it, and, in time, we die of it. Mamma and Papa did us more kindness by moving us to the forgiving countryside than they knew. You are very ill, Rosamund; please, let me take you home to heal, in whatever manner is necessary."

"And what will we tell the Webbers?" Rosamund whispered. "That I am weak with fevers, as I was at Newsbury? What a useless creature they will see me as."

"But you are not," Elsabeth rejoindered gently. "You are ill only because you have fought so hard against the magic in your veins; release it and you will regain more strength than I dare say you ever knew yourself to have. The Webbers—Mr Webber, at least—will think none the less of you for it; that I can promise.

Now, Rosa: eat, while I arrange a carriage, and inform Aunt Felicity that we must leave at once."

Rosa, more petulantly than Elsa had ever before heard her, said, "I don't *want* to eat."

"You must. It will help you to keep from flying away from me, Rosa. I shall send Mr Webber in to make certain you have a few bites, at least; I know you cannot resist his pleas, even if you might resist mine."

"That is not fair."

Elsabeth smiled. "I know."

Emotion akin to anger flushed Rosamund's face. "Then at least allow me to dress in something more suitable to having Mr Webber nursemaid me. Sophia will not mind if I borrow one of her morning dresses."

"And you will look very fashionable indeed," Elsa agreed a moment later from within Sophia's wardrobe; even her morning dresses were of a certain elevated degree now that she was so familiar with Town. In a few minutes, Rosamund was dressed in the warmest of Sophia's outfits and looking very well as Elsabeth went in search of Mr Webber.

She did not have far to go: he paced the hall beyond, and fell upon Elsabeth with thanks when she invited him to oversee Rosamund's breakfast. He hurried within, leaving the door open for propriety, and Rosamund, who was of a mind to deny even Mr Webber, found herself blushing suddenly at the look of raw relief and love that flooded his face as he stepped into the room.

"Mr Webber," Rosamund said, steeling herself, and then fell silent in astonishment as he dropped to his knees before her, words rushing from him.

"I am here to make certain you eat breakfast."

A touch of laughter filled Rosamund's voice, and, with that laughter, she could not deny the fondness she felt for the gentleman. "This is a somewhat dramatic pose from which to implore me to eat, Mr Webber."

"But it is the very best possible pose to ask that—once you are done with breakfast—you marry me, Miss Dover."

Joy and sorrow both rose in Rosamund Dover's breast, until her eyes brightened with tears. "At the very moment I am finished? Is that when this wedding should take place? But I cannot, Mr Webber." The answer broke, and she made to turn away, but Webber caught her hand and turned her gently back again.

"Because you are ill?" he asked softly. "Because of the source of that illness? I know all, Rosamund. I was with Miss Elsabeth last night when the doctor came, and even if I had not been, she employed her own personal and remarkable talent to warm you in the carriage from the ball to this house. I know that you are gifted with magic, and I know that, to live, you must use it. Do not deny me on that front. Deny me, if you must, because you do not love me; deny me because I have been a coward and allowed myself to be led into believing that you did not care, but do not deny me because you fear or loathe your own sorcery: it is a part of you, and I could not but love it for so being."

Tears were fresh upon Rosamund's cheeks long before he finished speaking, and her hands trembled in his. For the first time, nervousness came into Webber's voice. "You do love me, do you not, Miss Dover?"

"I do!" cried Rosamund. "Oh, Mr Webber, I do! Oh, there is nothing in the world that could make me happier than to be your wife, and if I must eat breakfast and conjure storms to prove it, then I shall! Oh, I shall!"

Webber came to his feet and caught Rosamund in an embrace that crushed the breath from her, then, smiling so broadly that it was nearly a laugh, he drew her toward the breakfast that had been set aside. "Then eat, and we shall be wed. Well, after I have asked your father's permission. And after the bans have been published. And—"

"And after I am well," Rosamund whispered, and sat down to eat.

(45)

The storm that saw the Dover daughters back into Bodton was spoken of for more than a century, as children caught in its wonder aged and spoke of it to their own children, who in later years told their children and grandchildren of it as well. Snow flew for three days, burying all of Bodton in a blanket four feet deep; the new bridge strained under its weight, and Rosamund Dover lost the unhealthy flush that had haunted her for so long.

If the thaw that followed came on more swiftly than might be expected, and found hay and homes drier in its aftermath than anyone had predicted, then no one felt any urge to complain, and one or two more generous souls may have even tipped their hats in the direction of Oakden, when they imagined no one else could see.

Mr Webber installed himself once more at Newsbury, and showed no signs of dismay that his sisters seemed disinclined to join him there. Indeed, he was rarely to be found there himself: having gained the sought-after permission from Mr Dover to wed Miss Dover, the young lovers were not often parted. Mrs Dover's delight could not be contained.

Nor could Leopoldina's dismay. She did not resent that Rosa was to be married; she resented that she was *not*, and would not understand when the strictures set against her socialising extended out of winter and into the spring. "I have barely been out, Mamma," she was heard to complain more than once. "You certainly cannot bring me back in!"

"We shall see what is to be done after Rosa is married," Mrs Dover oft replied, and, to no one's astonishment more than Dina's, appeared to mean it: Rosamund's exceedingly fortunate marriage, so nearly thwarted, was not now to be threatened by anything, even Mrs Dover's favourite daughter.

"It is made worse," Matilda confided to Elsabeth one afternoon, "because Captain Hartnell stopped calling so often when you were gone, and then the regiment was sent away for exercises. For six weeks, we had almost no social activity at all, Elsa, and none with young men. I pretended I was you, and read books and walked with Papa in the gardens to discuss them."

"Did you!" Elsa cried in astonishment. "Very good, Tildy! And was Papa pleased?"

"Delighted, I think," Matilda confessed shyly. "He said perhaps I was not so silly as Dina after all, and gave me more books to read. So, I passed our quiet winter with more enjoyment than I had expected, but Leopoldina has been almost unable to bear it. Elsa, when Captain Hartnell comes calling again...will you marry him?"

"I will not." Although she did not consider herself faint of heart, Elsabeth was not saddened that the regiment was away. A frank conversation with Captain Hartnell was inevitable, but should he not return until after Rosamund's wedding, Elsabeth would not be troubled by it. She had read Archer's letter so many times now, she knew its words by heart, and she could not comfortably reconcile the tale he told with Hartnell's own. They were too alike, save Archer's contained unsavory details that any man, wishing to present himself in a favourable light, might be inclined to edit them from his own history. But presuming they were true—and Elsabeth's disinclination to believe Archer was in this instance mitigated by the uncomfortable fact that he had chosen to include his own sister as part of the narrative, a choice she could not imagine him making if it was not in pursuit of the truth—then a man who chose to elide those details from his own history was by his very nature untrustworthy.

Elsabeth sighed, aware that she had fallen into silence and that Tildy had allowed it for some long moments, although she now looked at Elsabeth with curiosity. "No, I will not marry Captain Hartnell," Elsabeth repeated. "And neither should Dina, although I cannot imagine a way to tell her so without sending her directly into his arms."

"Find her another beau," Tildy said with such alarming pragmatism that Elsabeth laughed.

"And then one for you, Tildy, and then all of my sisters will be happily wed. I could ask for nothing more."

"Not even a husband for yourself?"

"I have yet to meet the man I would want to marry," Elsabeth replied cheerfully. "Should I, then I will be happily wed. Should I not, then I will read books with Papa and be Mamma's despair until I am old and grey with them."

"But we will not allow that to happen," Mr Webber said, opening the parlour door to enter with Rosamund. "Surely, between us all, we might find *some* fellow suitable to you, Miss Elsabeth."

"You may try. So long as he is intelligent, well-mannered, inclined to walking and ideally wealthy, I will be satisfied."

"Should he not be young and handsome as well?" asked Rosamund, smiling.

"Oh, young. Youth would do me very well. I should not mind if he was as handsome as Mr Webber, either, but I think a lively mind and humour make a man handsome even if his features are imperfect. Have you any candidates in mind, then, Mr Webber?"

"I shall draw up a list," Webber replied solemnly, and Leopoldina came running at their laughter to discover what diversion she was missing. The afternoon was passed in pleasantry, as many before and after passed, until May, and Rosamund's wedding, were upon them.

Hers was a grander affair than Ruth's, with innumerable visitors from London and the whole of Newsbury Manor bustling with activity. Sophia Enton finally returned to Bodton, but announced she would stay at Newsbury with Miss Webber. Mrs Enton descended upon Mrs Dover to proclaim her distress over the whole matter, for what kind of daughter would refuse her own mother's house, and Sophia not even engaged after an entire Season in London—a Season held at the Webbers' expense, of course, and therefore not of *such* import to Mrs Enton that Sophia had not been successful—and what would Sophia do when Miss Webber married and no longer required a female companion: she surely could not then be expected to return to Mrs Enton's house, which was, Mrs Dover shrewdly concluded, the crux of the matter. Mrs Enton saw herself as finally ridded of her unmarriageable daughter, and did not wish to re-enter that state of maternal uncertainty.

"It will all work out," Mrs Dover promised Mrs Enton with a confidence borne from having had, a year earlier, five unmarried daughters with no confident prospects, and now having one married with a child on the way—for Ruth had arrived for Rosa's wedding in a most decidedly gravid state, and Mr Cox, his weight reduced considerably again, had spoken pompously of the inevitable son spending a great deal of time at Oakden, which would, after all, be his inheritance—and another about to marry a rich man.

"Perhaps," Mrs Enton responded with a note of determined despair, for she intended fully on leaving for the continent in the summer and not returning, possibly for years: Sophia's fate would be her own, and Mrs Enton was more than content with that, if also sensible to the fact she could not be seen to be so little concerned.

For Elsa's part, she was only delighted to have Sophia in Bodton again, if only for a little while: she could not fool herself into imagining that Sophia would not return to London with Miss Webber, nor could she wish, except briefly and selfishly, for Sophia to choose otherwise. London suited her far better than Bodton, and with Mr Webber safely on the verge of marrying Rosamund, Elsa's dislike for Miss Webber, of whom Sophia was clearly so fond, receded. It could not fade entirely, though in moments when she found Miss Webber vexing, Elsabeth reminded herself that Mr Archer had, however unwelcomed, proposed to *her*, and had clearly not made the same offer to Miss Webber. This thought was prone to bringing a smile to her lips, and though Miss Webber did not care for that smile, neither could she object to the appearance of friendly overtures from Miss Elsabeth, and a sort of peace was established between them.

It was generally received with surprise in Bodton that Mr Archer attended the wedding, although Elsabeth would have regarded it as the height of bad manners for him to avoid it. He and Webber were too close of friends, and despite Mr Webber's sudden confidence in his suit upon Rosamund's illness, Elsa could not believe that he would not still have sought Archer's approval. That he would have carried through with it regardless she *did* believe, but his was a gentle soul, and his happiness would come as much from his friend's blessing as his love for Rosamund. Archer could not refuse to attend without breaking Mr Webber's heart, and they were of too equal a social standing for Archer to find that acceptable.

So Elsabeth and Archer stood among the bride and groom's attendees, distantly polite to one another, and, when obliged to dance, did so with grace and little conversation beyond Mr Archer's enquiry of "Have you spoken with Captain Hartnell?" and Elsabeth's response of "He has been away."

Another topic lay upon her tongue but could not be voiced: she had not spoken with him in any measure since the night Rosamund had fainted and he had encouraged her to reveal her own magic in order to help save Rosa's life. That had been a concession far beyond any expectation she had of him, and it was difficult not to soften a little in its face, even to regret her harsh—if just!—words to him on the day he had proposed. But discussion of neither magic nor marriage could be broached in public, or indeed at all; one was impolite for Society and the other an embarrassment for all parties. They parted civilly at the end of their dance and did not speak to one another again.

Mrs Penney, Elsa's beloved aunt, came to embrace her at the end of the day, as Rosamund and Webber, both shining with joy, drove away in a carriage pulled by four extravagantly white horses and under a cascade of petals that scented the air magnificently. "Are you very sad to see her go, my dear?"

"Oh," Elsa burst, and could not decide if she would prefer to laugh or cry. "Yes, but also no, Aunt Felicity. She will be very happy, and I want nothing more. But I will miss her terribly, and, without Sophia, I shall find myself quite bereft. It will not last," she added for her own benefit as well as Mrs Penney's. "I am not suited to being long sorrowful. But I will miss her. Thank heavens for Peters," she concluded quite suddenly. "He is a good man and will keep the rest of the servants from taking *too* much advantage of them. They are both so kind."

"They are, and they shall live generously and gently. I think you will see her often, Elsabeth. She is too fond of you to be long parted from you, and then you will see Sophia as well."

"Miss Webber will not be forever under her brother's roof, and Sophia must marry as well, sometime, else how is she to survive?"

A gentle smile curved Mrs Penney's mouth. "Miss Webber's inheritance is not inconsiderable, and Mr Webber would never keep it from her if she chooses not to marry. I do not believe she intends to."

"But she is quite attached to Mr Archer."

"She is quite attached to Miss Enton," Mrs Penney replied. "Mr Archer is no more to her than the means to a socially acceptable end. If she marries, it will not be him."

Elsabeth's eyebrows furrowed, then cleared as she smiled. "Then perhaps Sophia can have him after all. He was greatly admiring of her once."

Mrs Penney laughed. "Yes, Elsabeth. Perhaps so. Now, shall we retire to the—Elsabeth? What is it?" For her niece had gone quite rigid at her side, and now stood blushing as she gazed into the distance. Mrs Penney peered through the afternoon light to catch a glimpse of sunshine falling against red-clad shoulders, and at once understood. "Very well, then: go, and if you need a listening ear later, you will find me at Oakden."

"Thank you, Aunt Felicity." Elsabeth smiled briefly, then set off through the gardens to the distant figure of Captain Hartnell, whose own smile was bright as she approached. He was handsome still, as genuine and without artifice a man as she could imagine, and looking splendid in his uniform. Yet, for the first time, he seemed a peacock to Elsabeth, unsuitably brilliant in comparison to the reserved intelligence of certain other gentlemen. She curtseyed when she reached him, and murmured, "Captain Hartnell. We did not know the regiment had returned."

"Miss Elsabeth," the Captain replied with a bow. "Or is it now Miss Dover? It is! Miss Dover, It has been far too long."

"Perhaps. Captain Hartnell, I am possessed of some intelligence that we must discuss."

Surprised concern flinched over Hartnell's face. "That sounds as though it cannot bode well, Miss Dover."

"That may depend on what you have to say about it."

Hartnell's concern deepened into utmost seriousness. "I see. Let us have it, then, Miss Dover. What troubles you?"

Faced with the moment, Elsabeth could find no kind way to lay Archer's charges at Hartnell's feet. "Is it true that you attempted to elope with Miss Persephone Archer?"

Hartnell took this question as he might have taken a blow, with a backward roll onto his heels that swayed him before he regained his equilibrium. "I see. Troublesome intelligence indeed. Is there an answer I can give that will satisfy you, Miss Dover?"

"Only the truth, which may not please me but will see me satisfied."

"Very well." Hartnell took it upon himself to walk some little way, as if to compose himself, before returning to Elsabeth with his response. "Archer will have told you of all my transgressions, perceived or otherwise. Let me emphasise that the bulk of what I have told you was true: he did refuse me the parish—"

Elsabeth inhaled at this, but did not speak; Hartnell, observing this, continued more swiftly. "—albeit not at the time I implied. It is true that I intended to study law, and found it not to my liking. And it is true that Miss Archer...formed an attachment to me. She was—is—a sheltered child, Miss Dover, and I was a man of whom her brother did not approve. I do not like to think I encouraged her, but neither was I foolish enough to deny the opportunity to marry so well, should it afford itself to me. Archer would consider me the villain of the piece, and I am willing to accept that in order not to risk sullying Miss Archer's reputation."

"How generous of you," Elsabeth replied slowly when it appeared Hartnell had nothing further to say. Every word that passed her lips grew colder. "If I am not mistaken, Captain Hartnell, Miss Archer is ten years and more Mr Archer's junior, and you are of an age with Mr Archer."

"Ten years is not an extraordinary difference in age."

"No. No, it is not, when both parties are grown. But Miss Archer is even now only fifteen or sixteen, and could not have been more than a child when you concluded you would gladly avail yourself of the chance to marry well. Your story does not do you credit." Elsabeth's voice shook, and she could not say whether it was anger with Hartnell or with herself, for having ever found him charming. "I think I need not ask about the following matter of inheritance or Australia."

Hartnell blanched again, offering all the answer Elsabeth could possibly require. "I believe our conversation is concluded, Captain. I do not expect to see you again soon."

To Mrs Penney, watching from the steps of Newsbury Manor, there seemed a finality in the scarlet-clad soldier's bow, and Elsabeth did not curtsey at all before she turned and left him to stand alone on the distant hillside.

(46)

THE GAIETY SURROUNDING ROSAMUND'S WEDDING WAS TO LAST several weeks, as much to while away the sorrow of Rosamund's departure as for the pleasure of gathered family. Mrs Dover considered herself to have been much slighted by Mrs Penney the previous autumn in the matter of the visit surrounding Ruth's marriage, although she was obliged to admit it had all turned out quite admirably: had Mrs Penney not insisted upon bringing Rosa to London when she did—but she had, Mrs Dover concluded, and all offence was entirely forgotten at the wedding's conclusion. The Penneys remained under Oakden's roof, so the place of one lost daughter was taken by a beloved aunt and uncle.

To no one's dismay, Mr Cox returned to his parish the very day after the wedding, but Ruth stayed on as well. Mrs Dover exclaimed often how well marriage suited her while meaning how well gravidity suited her, and in no way considered that perhaps the long pleasant hours Ruth spent in the garden or the remarkable early harvest might have more to do with Mrs Cox's glow of health than marriage or motherhood. Indeed, Mrs Dover, long since accustomed to an unusually generous garden, failed to notice that, with Ruth's helping hand, the garden gave half again its normal yield.

Mr Dover did not fail to notice this, and warmed to his middle daughter in marriage as he never had when she lived beneath his roof. As spring days grew warmer and longer, they were often heard to be laughing over their work, and partaking of such earnest discussions that Matilda could not bear it, and was obliged to go forth and participate.

Leopoldina could not be troubled to join in such effort, and instead moped about the house, bemoaning the lack of attention from Captain Hartnell or indeed any other officer. Her mouth pulled into a sour pinch of pleasure, though, as she observed that Captain Hartnell did not visit Elsabeth, either, and she concluded that he had lost interest in her. Elsabeth, she thought, should show more dismay over losing the attention of the only man likely to want to marry her, but she did not share this thought for fear Elsabeth should realise her error and move to rectify it.

For her own part, Elsa moved happily enough betwixt family and friends, never imagining that Dina had relegated her to inevitable spinsterhood, nor that Mrs Penney watched her with soft concern. She thought little of Hartnell, and—to her own surprise—more often of Archer, whom it seemed she had misjudged; it became strangely easier to recall that he was handsome and clever with words, and more difficult to remember his infuriating superiority. But even Mr Archer did not prey too heavily on her thoughts; Sophia was installed at Newsbury Manor for the summer, at least, as Miss Webber had—curiously, in Elsabeth's opinion, but it was a curiosity she was happy had been indulged—opted to keep her brother's house whilst the new Mr and Mrs Webber toured Europe.

Sophia often joined Elsabeth on the vigourous excursions Elsa was known for; Miss Webber never did, and Elsa was grateful to feel some of her old closeness with Sophia returning. "I know you will return to London in the autumn for another Season," she said one morning as they struck across fields still wet with dew, "but I am glad to have you here for a little while, Sophia. The house is much changed, without Ruth or Rosamund."

"I dare say it seems sillier," Sophia guessed, and smiled at Elsabeth's rueful nod of response.

"Tildy is perhaps growing a little less silly. A quiet winter did her good; without any of the elder sisters about, she earned a little more of Papa's eye, and Dina could not lead her astray when she was hardly permitted out of the house. And now, with her under Ruth's tutelage, the garden is growing remarkably."

"If you have apples ripening in June, people will talk, you know."

"Let them talk as they may. In the end, it did Rosamund no harm."

Sophia stopped in wide-eyed astonishment. "You cannot mean to say Robert *knew*?"

"Oh, Sophia." Elsabeth turned to her friend and extended her hands. "We have had so little chance to talk. I told you in London what the doctor said, the night Rosamund fainted, but I did not confess that Mr Webber did, indeed, learn all." Together they settled into the grass after Elsabeth chased the dew away with a flicker of warmth from her fingers. "He proposed the very next morning, and he has assiduously and gently encouraged Rosa to do small but constant magics, that her health might remain strong. I am so very glad that Ruth has found a green thumb, and that she is inspiring Tildy in the garden, but I have not yet dared tell Dina any of this, for fear of what excesses she should indulge in, in the name of retaining her health. She will never accept that the magic she uses already is quite sufficient. *I* have certainly never gone to such lengths as she has, and I am fit and hale."

"You cannot tell her," Sophia agreed instantly. "To do so would be to send her wild. Ruth should be told," she decided after a moment's thought, "and Matilda, although not until she is considerably older and can be trusted not to whisper it in Dina's ear. Have you told Mr Dover?"

"Papa is in no danger of becoming ill," Elsa replied, but Sophia shook her head.

"Not for his own health, but for the dissemination of knowledge. Would it not be safer for all to have this information in as many hands as it could be trusted in? And I do not mean just for your family, but for anyone with sorcerous talents. We British are repressed, Elsa, and we English women moreso than the men. Think of what we are told of the French, or the colonies, or Africa, all places where sorcery is more accepted than it is here. I should think in a society where they are permitted their talent without censure, there must be far less fear of a fit of consumptive flight ruining lives! How many other differences within one another do we overlook or deny, so that the majority might carry on in its placid pursuit of all those things it has deemed right and proper! Certainly, it can be said that I stand among those who are ill suited to society's expectations of marriage to a man, and yet, without Miss Webber's intervention, I should have been condemned to such a life—had I been lucky enough to *command* such a life—without ever knowing the source of my misery! And I dare say you, Elsabeth, are strong enough of spirit that you should successfully determine never to marry except where it suits you, and what has Society to say about that, save that you are unmarriageable, which is not the same thing at all! Even poor Leopoldina, who is dreadfully untoward, would be praised and winked at and encouraged in her lusts if she had been born a man, so how can it be right that she is condemned for it as a woman? We are not unfeeling creatures who lack passion or thought of our own. Why must we be treated as we are, whether we are sorcerous or meant for women's company or happy to stand on our own? We are repressed!" Sophia cried again, and fell back, gasping and aghast at her outburst.

Elsabeth brought her hands together in staccato applause, calling, "Brava, brava!" over its sound. "Sophia, what has happened to you in London? I have always known you to be kind and intelligent, but you are now afire! Oh, should such a presentation be given in Parliament, then surely the world could not help but be changed by your ardor!"

"But it will not be," Sophia said, suddenly affecting weariness. "Such pleas will not be heard in the Parliament until they strike so closely to home that the Lord Chief Justice himself must rule with his heart to see the right side of the law, as happened half a century since with the Case of the Slaves. Oh, I have changed," she admitted. "I do not know myself from who I was, Elsabeth, and I am torn between wishing I had remained unawakened and clinging to my new awareness with tooth and nail. I had never dreamt of anything beyond marriage; now I dream of changing the very world in which we live. Do not laugh at me, Elsabeth; I could not bear it."

"Never." Elsabeth leaned forward to take Sophia's hands again. "Never, my dearest Sophia. I shall instead take up your banner and act where I can. I will tell Papa, and I will tell my Aunt Penney, of what the doctor said, and we will spread that grain of knowledge in hopes of sparing even one life. Even one life, Sophia: that is something, is it not? And we have changed one already, for Mr Webber has married Rosamund knowing that she is a magician. Is it not a beginning?"

"It is." Sophia squeezed Elsa's hands in gratitude. "It is. And you do not think me mad, which is even more than a beginning."

"I could never think you mad. I *may* think it necessary to find an unwed member of Parliament to marry you to, that his fire should be lit by yours, but I could not think you mad."

"I should rather stand for Parliament myself," Sophia said, and blushed at her own audacity.

"And I should like to vote for you!" Elsabeth cried, and then, laughing, embraced her friend. "But until then, let me speak to Papa and tell him what we know. Will you come with me, or must you return to Newsbury?"

"We are meant to meet Mamma for lunch. She and Papa are leaving for a tour of Europe, you know, and Mamma feels that she must, for form's sake, tell Julia that I have impinged on the Webbers' good natures long enough and that I am to join them in their tour. I can hardly imagine her dismay if Julia were to agree," Sophia said candidly. "I can hardly imagine my own. But there is no danger of that; Julia intends to insist that she cannot manage Newsbury Manor without me, and everyone will then be satisfied and able to go their separate ways. I would not think less of Mamma if she concludes herself shut of me, and forgets to write."

"I would think far less of her," Elsabeth said strongly, but forbore to speak on; Mrs Penney thought Sophia was in no danger of being dismissed by Miss Webber, and though Elsabeth held less confidence in such a belief, she could not easily wonder aloud to Sophia what she would do if neither the Webbers nor the Entons wished to maintain her. In due time, of course, she would inherit the Enton estate, but until then was not Elsabeth's concern. In truth, she knew that she herself would never allow Sophia to fall upon difficulties. Nor would Rosamund; nor, upon consideration, did Elsabeth believe Ruth would, and so, if Sophia should fall from Miss Webber's favour, or—inevitably, as it seemed to Elsabeth—be replaced by a husband, then she would never be left wanting so long as a daughter of the Dover blood breathed.

Satisfied with her own conclusion, she embraced Sophia once more, entreated her to remember each detail of luncheon with Mrs Enton the better to discuss it later, and went her way home to knock lightly upon Mr Dover's library door.

"Enter," called Mr Dover, upon which Elsabeth did, and discovered to her pleasure that Mrs Penney was within as well, the brother and sister thoroughly enjoying tea and scones laden with jam. Elsabeth acquired some of each for herself and at once sat to partake of both good company and good food.

"Papa," she began when a scone was half-devoured, "I have something to discuss with you. It affects you as well, Aunt Felicity; do stay. It has to do with Rosamund's illness, and what I have learned of it." In some little time, she had explained the doctor's orders, causing many exchanged glances betwixt Mr Dover and Mrs Penney in the explaining. "Did you know?" she asked, faltering, at the end.

"No! Oh, my dear, good heavens, no," said her father. "I should have never permitted Rosa's frailty to go on, had I known. But while I did not know, I am not surprised. I—we—had a brother," he said after a moment. "I suppose you know this, although we have rarely spoken of him."

"My Uncle William," Elsabeth replied slowly. "He was between you in age, was he not? And he died quite young; I had always supposed it hurt too much to speak of him."

"All of those things are true," Mrs Penney answered. "But the manner of his death was...curious, and not easy to discuss. It was always clear, my dear Elsabeth, that John," for that was Mr Dover's rarely used given name, "was a magician. He was—not quite as bold as Leopoldina; perhaps more like you. Not *brazen*, but neither shy to use his talent when discreet opportunity arose. It appeared from an early age that both William and myself were unlike him; William was never seen to use magic, and I, try as I might, could not. Oh, yes," she said with a smile at Elsabeth's posture of surprise. "I have never quite given up on the hope that some day I might make flowers bloom with a touch, but I have no innate talent for sorcery."

Her smile faded, and Mr Dover continued where she had ended. "It seems that William did. Perhaps an extraordinary talent, given what you have just told us, or perhaps it is merely that he quenched it so firmly that this sorcerous sickness took hold much earlier than it did in Rosamund. He was twelve and I sixteen when the frailty and fevers began to come upon him. He had always been of a more delicate bent than I—indeed, he was very like Rosamund, was he not, Felicity? Now that I think on it, she looks very like him. How strange, that I should never have seen it before."

"William died a long time before Rosa was born," Mrs Penney said gently. "It must be difficult even for you to conjure his face after so long; for me, it is nearly impossible. I was only six when he died. But I recall the...the circumstances."

"He fell from an apple tree," Mr Dover said. "Which would not have been strange in any other boy, but he had a sensitivity to apples; they made him very ill, and he was always cautious around them. He was also deathly afraid of heights, so to think he had climbed an apple tree high enough to fall and kill himself...."

"You never believed he had," Mrs Penney said, gently still. "I remember your anger and disbelief so clearly, John."

"I have never told you the last of it." Mr Dover sat heavily a long while in the anticipatory silence of his sister and daughter. Finally, he turned his head, gaze going to the window, though Elsabeth believed he saw not the gardens beyond but his younger brother, all those many years ago. "It was put out that his neck was broken, Felicity, but I found him. It was not. He had not a mark on him, only a faint look of surprise, as though he had seen something unexpected at the last. Mother and Father believed he had killed himself, Felicity. The apple tree, the unmarked body; they believed it to be suicide, and put it out that he had fallen from the tree so he might have a consecrated burial."

"*John*!"

"I know." Mr Dover passed a hand over his eyes, then reached blindly for his cup of tea. Steam rose from it as his fingers brushed the porcelain, and he cradled the hot drink against his chest without sipping from it. "I did not object, because although I did not believe he had fallen from the tree, nor did I believe he had killed himself, and thought an unconsecrated grave was a condemnation he did not deserve. Nor did he," he added softly, "for it seems I was right on both counts. It seems unburnt magic slew him, and that my own daughters have avoided such a fate only through luck and my own careless encouragement of their talent. I cannot imagine how Ruth survived long enough to marry."

"Perhaps she practiced her magic in secret from time to time." Elsabeth returned Mr Dover's skepticism with a faint smile. "Perhaps not. Perhaps she has less inherent magic than your brother did, then."

"For which we must be grateful. Elsabeth, she is soon to bear a child. You must tell her what you know."

"Should you not tell her, Papa?"

"I believe you are closer to her than I am," Mr Dover replied, then looked again to the gardens, seeing them this time. "Although we have grown closer this past week or ten-day than I had ever imagined we might. Do you suppose she would want to hear it from me?"

"I think she would like it very much, Papa. Tell her you are proud of her, and tell her what you know, and I think she would like it very much."

"I shall do so forthwith." Mr Dover rose and left with sudden energy, leaving Elsabeth surprised and Mrs Penney with a sorrowful gaze.

"He has always taken William's death very hard," she said when he was gone. "I believe he felt responsible, and I think that this will not ease that sense of responsibility. I fear he may wonder if his own willingness to use sorcery quashed William's, either for fear of competing with someone more skilled or for Society's censure."

"There is no way to know." Elsabeth caught her lip in her teeth. "I had not known you wished for magic of your own, Aunt Felicity. I had always supposed..."

A brief, sad smile curved Mrs Penney's mouth. "That Mr Penney and I had chosen not to have children, for fear of them being inflicted with sorcery? No. Very early in our marriage, I had a bad pregnancy, and I nearly died of it. Mr Penney hanged the risk and called a midwife reputed to be a witch, who could save me but not the child, or my ability to bear children. I knew early that it was not right; there was too much pain. I have often wondered, myself, if I had had magic of my own, could I have kept it from setting, and...changed everything."

Anger and loss heated Elsabeth's face and brought tears to her eyes. "Oh, Aunt Felicity, I am so sorry. I didn't know. Oh, what *use* is magic!" she cried. "What use, when it is only wild and cannot be tamed for such things as knowing our own bodies! It is all well and good to hurry the crops along or warm myself with a touch of heat, but it is the talent of a dilettante! There is no scope, no improvement; I can do nothing more extraordinary now than I could as a child! What *use* is it, Aunt Felicity, if only the lowest of the low have the means to save or slaughter with their skill, and the rest of us cannot even do that much?"

"It is magic, Elsabeth. I am not certain it is meant to be of much use."

"I cannot believe that. I cannot believe we are given talents only to be squandered on the ripening of fruit and the heating of tea. I cannot believe it." Elsabeth fell back into her chair, her own gaze now despondent on the gardens. "I cannot believe it, and yet I must."

(47)

To Mrs Penney's practiced eye, the news Elsabeth had shared had an immediate and marked effect. Mr Dover walked in the gardens more often than ever before, and was often found standing bleakly beneath an apple tree, as if its weight had drawn him there and then could not release him. Mrs Dover, indulged and self-centred as she was, could not miss the change in him, and took herself from the comfort of her sitting room with greater frequency to draw Mr Dover out from beneath the apple trees and back into the world. She was not by nature a gentle woman, Mrs Penney thought; she was too inclined to busy-bodiness and prattle, but she did not ask Mr Dover what troubled him, only stood by his side in unexpectedly silent support, save when she judged a little gossip would bring him out of himself and into laughter. As spring days slipped into summer weeks, Mrs Dover grew a little slimmer and a little browner from her walks in the sun, until one day Mr Dover was heard to laugh and call her nut-brown, and Mrs Penney, walking in the gardens herself toward that happy sound, was obliged to find another direction to amble in order to provide them their privacy.

Ruth, always solemn, became increasingly considering in expression, as if judging the world, rather than its denizens, for worthiness. She could not be said to encourage them, but she was easier on Leopoldina and Matilda than she had ever been, until the former began to believe Mrs Cox was an entirely different person from Ruth Dover. To her utter astonishment, Dina was dismayed when, just after Dina's sixteenth birthday, Mrs Cox was obliged to return to Mr Cox, and wept through several nights while Tildy stroked her hair and promised they would soon visit Ruth at home. "Papa will never allow it!" Dina cried, and Matilda, considering the firmness with which they had been kept in hand for much of the past year, could not argue, which only made Dina's sobs more wretched.

Elsabeth could not forgive Society, or magic, its caprices; the news of her uncle's long-ago death and Mrs Penney's own troubles burdened her light heart, and not even visits from Sophia or letters from Rosamund could wholly lift it again. She was sedate in their visits to Bodton, and did not look admiringly at the officers, but avoided their gazes entirely and instead frowned at the new bridge, which to her represented the usefulness of lower-class magic and the uselessness of her own. Mrs Penney's heart ached to see such despondence in her oldest unmarried niece, and, determined to return Elsabeth's countenance to its usual joy, proposed a plot first to Mr Penney, then to Mr Dover, and finally to Mrs Dover, who had been entirely too taken with her husband's sorrows to notice any in her second-eldest daughter, and who was perfectly content that someone else should tend to it.

It was thus that at breakfast one day near the end of June, Mrs Penney said, "Mr Penney and I will be taking a tour of the lakelands for the rest of the summer. We hope Elsabeth might join us, if it would not be too much trouble to you, Mrs Dover."

"*Elsabeth!*" cried Leopoldina before Mrs Dover could draw breath. "Oh, why must it be *Elsabeth*, when she is content to mope at Oakden and write dreary letters to Rosamund while I am *forced* to remain at home, ensuring that I shall forever be a spinster!"

"You are just sixteen," Mr Dover said more sharply than was his custom, "and rude. Your age cannot yet permit you to consider the possibility of spinsterhood, but your ill-considered commentary and your preoccupation with your own happiness above that of everyone else's may well. You have Matilda, Dina; Elsabeth has always been closest with Rosamund, and she is within her rights to feel some loss with Rosamund's marriage. Objecting to an opportunity for her diversion is small-minded and unkind. I expect you will wish to tender an apology."

Leopoldina, gazing sullenly from one face to another at the table and finding no support even from her darling Matilda, could not bring herself to apologise, but did, for the moment, subside with the air of one much maligned. Mrs Penney waited a polite moment, then addressed Mrs Dover again: "Do you suppose you could spare Elsabeth for some six weeks, Mrs Dover? We should be so glad of her company, and while the lakelands might not have the gaiety of Brighton—"

"Brighton!" Leopoldina burst. "Oh, that we should go to Brighton! We must, Papa, all of us! I am sure the sea air would do Mamma great good!"

"Brighton would be diverting," Mrs Dover said rather too hopefully, and for a moment, Elsabeth, whose attention had been quite fixed on her plate, lifted her eyes to meet Mrs Penney's in contained amusement.

"We are discussing Elsabeth's tour of the lakelands with Mr and Mrs Penney, not our own holiday to Brighton, which I assure you I have not budgeted for and do not intend to take," Mr Dover said in a tone frightful enough to dismiss all thoughts of Brighton from Mrs Dover's mind. "Felicity, I fear it is my own heart that would be the most broken to see my dear Elsabeth away again for so long, but I think we can have no objections to your enjoying her company for the summer. I might recommend Windermere, which I recall from my own youthful travels as an especially attractive locale."

"It is on our itinerary," Mrs Penney replied, pleased, then turned her smile on Elsabeth. "Do say you'll join us, Elsa. I think you have not previously toured the lakes? It is something every young lady should do, if the opportunity arises."

"I believe you brought Rosamund on such a tour two years

ago, or was it three?" Elsabeth replied. "She wrote so happily of the time she spent with you. I should be very pleased to join you, Aunt Felicity, Uncle Charles. Thank you for inviting me."

If this was not spoken with the spark that Mrs Penney might have hoped, that only served to illustrate the need for Elsabeth to be distracted. "Splendid. We will leave in two days, if you can be packed suitably in such little time."

Elsabeth deigned to laugh. "I could be ready by this afternoon if you wished, Aunt Penney, but I shall endeavour to take two days to pack so that you will not feel rushed."

"Capital of you," Mr Penney said drolly, and everyone's humour, save Dina's, was well restored.

Leopoldina, having had the thought of Brighton put in her head, would not let it go; Mr Dover, the very morning Elsabeth and the Penneys were meant to depart, was heard to mutter, "I shall have to send her to have any peace, and yet I cannot bear to imagine what havoc she might wreak," upon which he retreated to his library and could not be drawn out again until the carriage was ready and Elsabeth was prepared to alight.

"Do not dare to send Dina to Brighton, Papa," Elsabeth said firmly as she kissed his cheek. "If there is the slightest danger of you doing so, I will have to remain at home to shore up your determination."

"That will not do," Mr Dover replied, for he, unlike Mrs Dover, saw the change in Elsabeth and knew its source, and, like Mrs Penney, hoped that diversion would restore her to herself, as he had been restored.

Elsabeth herself was not insensible to her aunt's intentions, and at first made more of her delight than she could be said to truly feel. They travelled in comfort, rarely staying a full day in a carriage; there were too many sights to see, and no rush to be in any particular place at any given time. As summer's full hold turned the countryside lush with life, Elsabeth could no longer resist the pleasures of a holiday, and often awakened early to walk through hitherto-unknown fields before the Penneys were prepared to depart for the day.

Mr Penney had let a house in Hawkshead, and, for two lazy weeks, the amiable trio resided there, ambition thwarted by heavy air and hazy days. Elsabeth saw little society save her own aunt and uncle, and received only as much news from home as to find pleasant; several letters from Mr Dover, touching on the books he had read and the health of the garden, two rather more rambling discourses from Matilda, who spoke glowingly of the regiment officers seen in town, and none at all from either Mrs Dover or Leopoldina, the latter of whom had never in Elsabeth's recollection sat to write a letter.

She should have been much less pleased had either Mr Dover or Tildy's letters clarified certain aspects of the Dovers' improving social lives, but Mr Dover would not think to write it, and Tildy imagined all was made clear by her own gossip-filled missives, although if pressed she might have admitted to a certain consciousness that she had chosen, out of respect for what she supposed Elsabeth's feelings to be, not to mention how often Captain Hartnell came calling once again, now that Elsabeth was no longer in residence at Oakden.

Surely, it was nothing more than innocence to have encountered the handsome Captain in Bodton only a scant handful of days after Elsabeth's departure; surely, the young Misses Dover, released from what Leopoldina could only regard as a positive state of arrest, were certain to see gentlemen and officers they knew in town. Leopoldina had, as was her wont, merrily waved the Captain down, and when he, standing at the side of their carriage, enquired after Miss Dover's health, Dina first laughed and proclaimed her married, then laughed a second time and cried, "Mercy, but you do not mean Rosamund at all! I have forgotten: Elsabeth is Miss Dover now. She is well, I suppose; we have not seen her this five-day, as she has been invited to tour the lakes with our Aunt and Uncle Penney. She will be gone all summer, and we two sisters left at home are wholly bereft without her company. It is very lonely, when one is accustomed to four sisters, to find oneself with only one!"

"I am sorry to hear of your troubles, although certainly if one must be left with a single sister, then Miss Matilda is the closest confidante any young lady could wish for." The Captain's smile left Matilda quite undone, and Dina, fearing to lose an opportunity, spoke before Tildy could recover herself.

"I am surprised you did not know of Elsa's departure; you had once seemed so very close. But then, perhaps Elsabeth did not even know the regiment had returned to Bodton, so quickly upon the heels of Rosa's wedding did she depart."

Well over a month had passed, and Elsabeth, living as she did with Leopoldina, could not possibly have gone such a length of time without being made aware of the regiment's return. Captain Hartnell forbore to say so and instead assumed a look of passing regret. "Perhaps that is the case, although one cannot be expected to keep up with the activities of one's acquaintances, no matter how dear."

"Acquaintances," Leopoldina echoed with interest. "I had thought you and Elsabeth quite fast friends."

"Oh, certainly, but never so intimate as to need to share each detail of our itineraries," Captain Hartnell replied carelessly. "But let us not think of those who are—lucky creatures!—enjoying holidays; let us instead think of yourselves, Miss Dina, Miss Tildy, and on whether or not it is possible to alleviate the loneliness of your—dare I call it? Yes! I shall!—your exile at Oakden!"

"It could not be called *exile*," Matilda began in protest, but was silenced by the sharp pain of Dina's heel meeting her instep.

"Exile is precisely what we have suffered in the regiment's absence and our sisters' departures. You must come to visit, Captain Hartnell, you and perhaps a few other officers, and as often as possible."

"I will visit, but I confess to a reluctance to invite others along with me," Hartnell promised with a wink. "I should hate to have to share your friendship with so many, Miss Dina."

"Oh, think of Tildy," Dina said brashly, and Matilda, injured both in spirit and body, could do nothing but feel slighted without fully appreciating why.

From that day onward, Captain Hartnell was at Oakden as often as his duties would allow, visiting two and three times a week and showing no reluctance to stop a moment in the street should the Misses Dover come upon him in Bodton. Mrs Dover foresaw a third wedding by the autumn, and to think that only a year earlier, she had been convinced of five spinsters living under Oakden's roof until age or the odious Mr Cox threw them out. Matilda could not confess, even in letters, that she wished it might be *her* wedding that Mrs Dover dreamt of, and so, the topic of Captain Hartnell went blissfully unknown by Elsabeth, whose sense of restoration would have been much marred by the intelligence. Away from Oakden's bustle, she had rediscovered a sense of peaceful joy, and was not insensible to its likely sources.

"Perhaps," she said to Aunt Felicity during the course of one long golden evening, "it is that I have been too much in company these past months; since January, and it is now well into July. Perhaps I like a little solitude as much as time spent with friends."

"You are very like your father," Mrs Penney agreed, and laughed to see Elsabeth's surprise. "He does not remain within his library only to avoid the innumerable women who rule his life, Elsa. He finds solitude comforting. I wonder at times if it is something that comes with the sorcery, although then I think of Leopoldina and cannot reconcile it."

"Surely, no one is precisely the same, not even magicians. Perhaps it is a tendency amongst them, but a tendency is not a rule, and even rules bend or break. Think on it: within the family, the tendency does lie that way. Papa has his library, I, my walks. Ruth had, for so long, her uptight ways that may not have required physical solitude but certainly offered a certain isolation of the spirit, and dear Rosamund has always been gently withdrawn. Tildy follows Dina, but even she—Matilda, that is—has shown a recent inclination to join Papa in the gardens and remove herself from most other society from time to time. Dina is the only one to strictly throw herself against the observation! All we need now is a larger sample to study; how shall we convince Society to give up their secret mages to us, or how dare we go amongst the lower classes to learn what their behaviours might be?"

"I think you are much recovered," Mrs Penney said with satisfaction. "The remainder of our travels should be merrier."

"Have I been so very despondent as to spoil your holiday, Aunt? I hope not; I would not ruin your pleasure for the world."

"Not at all, my dear. It is only that when one travels with Miss Elsabeth Dover, one expects to laugh a great deal, and we have had only smiles from you these past weeks. Now: your uncle is quite set on journeying to the north, although I have insisted to him the weather will be better if we should turn south. What say you?"

"That you are right about the weather but that I have visited more of the south, and little of the lakelands at all," Elsabeth replied promptly. "I should like to go north some little ways, and if the weather turns ferocious, I will tender all due apologies to you."

"Your uncle will be delighted," Mrs Penney replied with sufficient contentment that Elsabeth could not think she had chosen poorly. For three days more, they resided at the house in Cumbria, and if, when they resumed their travels, they proceeded at an even more stately pace, it was only because Elsabeth insisted time and again that they should pause that she might alight and inspect a distant hill on foot, or admire some grand manor nestled in the countryside.

It was this latterly habit which caused her uncle to one afternoon call out to the coachman, who obliged by turning down a road narrower than some. "A moment, my dear," Mr Penney said when Elsabeth gave voice to her curiosity, and then some moments later, "Now turn, I think, and you shall be most delighted."

Smiling with interest, Elsabeth did as she was bid, and released a laughing gasp as the carriage crested a small hill and the land dropped away toward a manicured lake that lay before a low garden of such fine keeping that not a leaf appeared out of place in its hedges and bursts of flowery colour. Beyond the garden lay a manor that could not, at a glance, have held fewer than one hundred and sixty rooms.

The carriage stopped and Elsa stood, the better to see the estate. Its facade was made in an extremely fine fashion of the sixteenth century, though the faintest change of colour in the roofing tiles told her that an older dwelling stood at its heart. It was all of lightly coloured ashlar sandstone, and sat comfortably in its surrounds as well as commanding them. "Good God," Elsabeth said with warmth. "Have we stolen by some unknown palace of the Regent's?"

"On the contrary," Mr Penney said in obvious pleasure. "We ourselves are slightly acquainted with, and you are, I believe, well acquainted with, the gentleman whose holdings these are. This, my dear niece, is Streyfield."

"Good God," Elsabeth said a second time, with far less vigour, and, discovering her legs could not hold her, she sat and gazed—gaped, she dared say—at the house that could well have been hers. "That cannot be Streyfield. That cannot be...real. I have never seen..." She turned as if to look back at the manors they had gone by over the past several days; all of them, and Lady Beatrice's manor besides, could have fit within Streyfield and gone unnoticed. As if drawn by a great weight, her gaze returned to Archer's demesne, and finally she laughed, if highly and uncertainly. "Well. No wonder he is so inclined to pride. Had I awakened every morning of my life within those walls, I too might have become prideful."

"It is, I believe, open to visitors," Mr Penney announced with sufficient delight as to imply to Elsabeth that this had all been quite part of his plan. "We must go; we are sometimes in the area for my business, and yet I have never visited the grand manor itself. I should like very much to see Streyfield, and if the gentleman himself is home, I am certain he would be pleased to see you."

"Oh, no, Uncle, surely we cannot. I could never wish to impose upon Mr Archer."

"Nonsense; if he is not home, it will be no imposition at all, and if he is, I cannot see how he would fail to be pleased to renew your acquaintance. Drive on," he instructed the coachman, and Elsabeth, unable to protest further without providing her reasons as to why, fell back into the cushions and could do no more than watch in ever-increasing awe as they approached the manor.

In the distance, it had been impressive; in nearness, it imposed, with windows rising higher than Oakden stood, and with a courtyard of steps that led eventually to a doorway broad enough to allow a carriage through. Those great doors stood open, and beside them, a trim older man of impeccable garb whose dress and manner indicated he was the butler of Streyfield Manor.

"Forgive us," Mr Penney called genially as they approached. "We had heard that Streyfield was open to visitors, and should like to pay our respects to the gentleman of the house, if he is at home!"

"Mr Archer is not," the butler replied with a bow, "but you are welcome to be shown the house. Mrs Wells will show you about."

A housekeeper of later years and a kindly face appeared at his side to curtsey and smile. "Sir, Madame, Miss. Please, I should be pleased to give you a tour. Will you come this way?"

Mr Penney glanced to Elsabeth, who, assured that Mr Archer was not at home, felt a sudden excitement at the prospect of investigating Streyfield. She nodded, and with a smile, they were escorted into the grand manor.

(48)

There was nothing wanting at Streyfield; indeed, there could not be one room shown that did not then look beggared by its sister, save that none could be said to be beggarly at all. It was only that each was so well appointed that the last could not, upon reflection, be measured up to it, and yet returning to a previous room was to discover that it outshone those seen more lately. Mrs Wells spoke warmly of each room, remembering some momentary grace or laughter that brought a spark of life to that which might otherwise have been overwhelmingly austere, and made no objection to the guests pausing to gaze in wonder through windows or at the elegant cornicing of high ceilings.

To Elsabeth's eye, so long accustomed to judging a land for its walking appeal, Streyfield's view could not be more lovely. It was not overly kept, but neither was it wild: beyond the tasteful gardens lay tangles well worth exploring, and the hearty lake proved to be fed by a stream of some consequence; both were in view of the house, and bridle paths lay nestled between the bank and the land of each. Meadows were no more cleared than was suitable for hunting, and sat comfortably before the dark green of old woods; Mr Penney, observing, could say no more than "My word, my word."

Mrs Penney chatted more easily with Mrs Wells, drawing from her more stories as the house unfolded before them; it was she whose breath caught when in a hall of portraits a youthful Captain Hartnell was seen, and Mrs Wells who said, "That would be David Hartnell, who was raised here with the young master. He's run very wild, I'm afraid, but he were a handsome lad, and I hear that he wears the scarlet well. But let me show you Mr Archer, ma'am."

This phrasing threw some alarm into Elsabeth's heart, though it settled again swiftly enough as they were led to another portrait, this of Mr Archer and recently enough painted as well. Mrs Wells, with a fondness Elsabeth could never expect, said, "This is the young master, Mr Archer. Ah, I wish he was here for you to meet, madam. A kinder soul I have never known."

Mrs Penney was not quite able to keep astonishment from her voice as she responded, "Mr Penney and I have met Mr Archer once, and I should say the likeness is striking. Elsabeth, you are better acquainted with him; do you not think it is like him?"

"Does the young lady know the master?" Mrs Wells asked in delight, and Elsabeth, gazing at the portrait, replied, "Perhaps less well than I thought; indeed, perhaps only a very little at all."

Archer was not in repose in the portrait; she could not imagine him in repose. But neither was he so stiff and formal as she had known him; he stood with his hand gentle upon a horse's nose, and though his gaze was turned to the viewer, it seemed his attention was still on the beast, for the hint of a smile curved his mouth and he appeared in all ways attuned to its needs and thoughts. In such a posture Elsabeth could easily see all those she knew to be associated with him, within him: a little of Lady Beatrice's nose, a hint of Miss Derrington's gentility; even, she fancied, a touch of Hartnell's ease, if not quite Webber's disarming openness. Even so, he looked altogether approachable, and this, contrasted with her first memory of his black-clad shoulders turning away from her at a country dance, was nearly enough to make Elsabeth laugh. Or perhaps cry: she felt suddenly overwhelmed with emotion, and could not put a name to that which moved her most strongly.

"Is he not handsome?" Mrs Wells asked. "Is it not a fine likeness?"

"It is a very fine likeness. The artist has captured all that is ideal in him."

"There's little else to capture, Miss, if I may be so bold as to say so. I've been here at Streyfield since before the old master married, and the young master is very like his father. A finer man I'd never met, God rest his soul. Had I any complaints to make about the young master, they would be only that we do not see him enough; he is kept in London on business far too often, and we miss him as much as Miss Archer does."

"What he needs is a wife," Mrs Penney predicted cheerfully. "A wife should keep him at home, and a man as handsome as this cannot be wanting in finding one."

"I think there is no woman who has of yet captured his eye. It is a difficulty for these very wealthy gentlemen, I think; I think they find it hard to know if they are wanted for their estates or their persons. He has spoken lately of a friend's good fortune in finding a lady whose heart was steadier than expected, and I think that is what he most wishes for himself. You surely never heard me say so," Mrs Wells added hastily, and laughing assurances met her concerns.

"Did his friend's fortunes go awry?" Mrs Penney wondered then. "That is a sure way to know a woman's heart, certainly, but how sad for them if their lives should be plagued with poverty when fortune had once been had!"

"Oh, mercy, no. They are recently wed and away on a tour of Europe now." Mrs Wells replied cheerfully. "You must think me very above myself, but it's all what I heard from Miss Persephone, to whom Mr Archer gives all the news. Miss Persephone couldn't speak to the details, only said that his friend had once parted badly with the lady—upon, I fear, advice from Mr Archer himself!—and that, when Mr Webber came to his senses, the lady's heart had not changed."

Such an assortment of coughs and wheezes arose from Mrs Wells' guests at this comment that she came alight with concern. "Can there be dust? Let me call for a maid; we will have water or lemonade. Mr Archer would scold me for being remiss, taking you on such an endless tour without refreshment!"

"No, no," Elsabeth protested when it became clear the Penneys were rendered speechless. "No, forgive us, Mrs Wells. It is only that—it is only that you have told a tale quite familiar to my aunt and uncle and me, as it is my own sister, Rosamund, who has lately married Mr Webber!"

No sooner had she confessed this than she wished she had not, for poor Mrs Wells went ashen and pressed a hand to her heart. "Oh, forgive me, Miss! I did not mean to gossip, surely! It is only that Mr Archer was so pleased for his friend's fortune—!"

"No, no, not at all!" Elsabeth seized the dear woman's free hand, clasping it in both of her own. "It is more delight than I can tell you to know that Mr Archer is glad for Mr and Mrs Webber, and surely, there could be almost no chance of finding oneself relating a tale to those whom it most closely affected! Please, think nothing more of it! We shall say no more ourselves!"

"But you...but you must then be a Miss Dover," Mrs Wells said in slow realisation. "Would you be Miss *Elsabeth* Dover?"

"Good heavens, you cannot know my name?" Elsabeth cast a startled glance to her aunt and uncle, who looked no less stupefied than she felt. "I am, yes, Miss Elsabeth Dover, but I cannot imagine how you might be possessed of that intelligence!"

Mrs Wells, at once thoroughly embarrassed and wholly pleased, cried, "Oh, but we here have all heard so much of you, Miss Dover! You have done yourself a disservice; you claim to only know Mr Archer a little, but surely, from his tales, you must be the closest of friends! Oh, do come this way, Miss Dover; there is more that you must see." She left with such haste that the three relations were obliged to scurry behind her or risk being lost in the labyrinthine manor, and such was their pace that the Penneys could do no more than widen their eyes in curiosity at Elsabeth rather than plague her with questions.

Elsa could do little more than widen her own eyes in return, and could not have done more had they had the leisure of sitting to talk. It was beyond imagination that Mr Archer could have spoken so highly of her, and within hearing—or to!—his staff, and yet she was otherwise entirely unknown in these parts; there could be no other way Mrs Wells might know her name. Surely, though, Mr Archer could have had very little favourable to say on her behalf since January at least, and it was more than half a year on from that month now. Mind aflutter, Elsabeth did not realise they were approaching the sound of a pianoforte until they were in the very room in which it was being played, upon which the music ceased and a tall, slender young woman of perhaps sixteen years rose from behind the keyboard to look curiously at the quartet who had descended upon her.

That this was Miss Archer could not be doubted: she had a look very like Lady Beatrice about her, though her hair was brown instead of black, and had an entirely different texture to it from her aunt's, and she wore a gown far more conventional in colour than Lady Beatrice was inclined to. But she had every bit of that lady's beauty, and indeed, by comparison, Mr Archer was the considerably less handsome of the siblings. Her gaze was light with interest, darting from the three unknowns to Mrs Wells and back again. "Mrs Wells?"

"Miss Archer," Mrs Wells pronounced with an air of triumph, "Taylor will have told you there were visitors to the house, but I have discovered their identities and cannot resist introducing you. Miss Archer, this is Miss Elsabeth Dover! Miss Dover, may I present to you my mistress, Miss Persephone Archer."

"Miss Dover!" Miss Archer extracted herself from behind the pianoforte and came forward with her hands extended in delight. "What a pleasure! I should never have thought to meet you, and yet here you are, all unasked-for! And who are these?"

"My aunt and uncle, Mr and Mrs Penney," Elsabeth replied faintly. "Aunt Felicity, Uncle Charles, Miss Persephone Archer. Miss Archer, had we known anyone of the estate was home, we should certainly not have intruded...."

"And then I would never have met you, which would have been a terrible shame. Mrs Wells, would you be so good as to call for refreshment? It is warm," Miss Archer said to Elsabeth with a certain enthusiasm, and then, as if recalling herself, echoed herself with a very different inflexion: "It is warm? Is it not? You must want tea or lemonade—lemonade!—and scones or—perhaps you have not yet taken lunch. Is it too early? Surely, it is not too late. Might we have lunch, Mrs Wells? And if it is too late for lunch, we will have something else, and then you will stay for supper. You must stay for supper. Won't you stay for supper?"

"We could not impose," Elsabeth began, but Miss Archer released her hands to spread her own wide, as if to encompass the entirety of Streyfield.

"You cannot possibly impose upon a single young lady who has all of this to command. Indeed, you and a party of forty others would be no imposition at all, but rather a little bit of glad sound in these lovely halls. Mr Penney, I implore you; surely you are the leader of this expedition and will insist that, because I have asked, you must stay for lunch. Unless it is not lunch, in which case you will stay for supper. Do you reside nearby? Surely, you must not stay at an inn when Streyfield is here and so longing for company! Mrs Wells! Oh, she is gone to get lunch. Taylor! He cannot hear me. Well, when Mrs Wells is returned, we will have her send a carriage to the inn for your belongings, will we not? Am I too bold in my demands? It is only that I am so glad to meet you, Miss Dover! I should never have expected the opportunity! How *did* you come to Streyfield?"

"We have been on a tour of the lakelands," Mrs Penney interjected gently, much to Elsabeth's relief. Miss Archer reminded her of all the best parts of Leopoldina, and, casting her mind now to Captain Hartnell's version of how the relationship with Miss Archer had begun, worried that perhaps there were some of the more distressing aspects of Dina within Miss Archer as well. "We had heard of Streyfield's magnificence, of course, and, finding ourselves nearby, were eager to view it. Miss Dover is correct, of course; had we any notion that the family was at home, we should never have imposed."

"It is only I who am at home," Miss Archer reported mournfully. "Gerry is meant to return in a day or two, and he will be entirely vexed that he has missed you. Unless you can be persuaded to stay!" Her aspect reversed itself at once, lighting her face with a smile. "I shall endeavour to persuade you. Please, will you not come with me to the breakfast room? I know it is definitely not breakfast we shall be partaking of, but the room is so pleasant and with such a tremendous view that even in early afternoon, I am inclined to take my meals there. And the worst of the light has passed it now, so it is cosy, not hot, and I am sure you will find it much to your liking." She led them away from her drawing room as she spoke, and in very little time introduced them to what was indeed a lovely small breakfast room with windows on three sides, that a vast stretch of Streyfield's estate might be admired while breaking fast.

"Capital," Mr Penney was heard to murmur more than once. "Absolutely capital. I suppose the fishing is unparalleled."

"So my brother tells me," Miss Archer replied. "I have proven a very poor fisherman myself, showing an inclination to shriek and throw the wretched wiggling creatures back into the water. I did that once with a very fine perch Gerry had caught. He has never entirely forgiven me, I think. The creature's size grows with every telling; if I should persuade you to stay on until his return, I am sure he will share the tale with you. Miss Dover, *do* tell me what you think of Gerry; I know you have seen him in every social sphere!"

"I am far too astonished to hear he has spoken of me at all to be able to think of how I might describe him, Miss Archer—"

"You must call me Persephone. But not Persy; please, not Persy."

Elsabeth laughed. "I would never think to. Persephone, then; thank you, and you may call me Elsabeth, if you would like."

"Miss Elsabeth, I think," Persephone replied hopefully. "It is how Gerry most often refers to you, and I cannot help but think of you that way myself. You were telling me what you thought of my brother."

"I think it is very strange to hear him called Gerry," Elsabeth replied with a smile, "although this is not the first time I have heard that name applied to him. He has seemed too mannered to me to allow for nicknames, even bestowed by those he loves the most. He cannot be the one who calls you Persy?"

"No; to him, I am Perry. Perry and Gerry, because it makes me laugh. You might call me Perry, if you wished."

"I should never presume to impinge on Mr Archer's name for you, especially when I think Persephone itself is such a lovely name."

"People think it mad. It is not proper; Mary or Rose would have been proper. Persephone is too wild. Oh, Mrs Wells, you have outdone yourself!"

"Say instead that Cook has outdone herself," Mrs Wells corrected as she allowed a brace of servants with arms loaded by plates and food to step past her into the breakfast room. "She could do no less in welcoming Miss Dover to Streyfield."

Elsabeth could not help but catch her aunt's glance at this comment, and schooled her features into incomprehension. Mrs Penney was not satisfied, but neither could she query Elsabeth upon the topic in such company, and so, the luncheon was shared by all with no difficult questions to answer.

(49)

During the course of the meal a lively discussion ensued regarding whether the little party should remain at the inn or come to Streyfield; Miss Archer ended it by declaring flatly that she should be injured beyond comprehension if she was refused, and, in the face of such pressure, Mr Penney acquiesced. He would not, however, permit Taylor to send Streyfield footmen to fetch their belongings; he went himself, and Mrs Penney—reluctantly, as her burgeoning curiosity regarding the general knowledge at Streyfield of Miss Elsabeth Dover made her wish to stay—joined him.

Elsabeth, arm in arm with Persephone, saw them off before finding herself positively seized by Miss Archer and drawn into as small and intimate a corner as could be found in a manor of Streyfield's magnificence. "Miss Elsabeth," Persephone began, "I am about to be terribly bold, and beg your forgiveness for it before I even speak."

"I can hardly imagine what you should require forgiveness for, given your great generosity towards us, but it is of course given, Mis—Persephone."

Miss Archer emitted a sound small enough to be regarded as a squeak and brought her head closer to Elsabeth's. "Miss Elsabeth, I have guessed at something and I must know, but cannot ask my brother. He has made you an offer, has he not? And you have turned him down."

Elsa blanched so swiftly, she felt the sensation of her own hands going cold in Persephone's, then coloured so violently as to bring tears to her eyes. It was on the tip of her tongue to say she had been wrong, that there *were* questions that required—and should not receive!—forgiveness for asking, but the forgiveness had been sought and applied already, leaving Elsabeth unable to speak for a span of heartbeats that stretched toward forever.

"Oh, dear," Persephone whispered. "That was even more dreadful than I thought it would be. Forgive me, oh, Miss Elsabeth, forgive me, and you must not answer. I ought not even have asked!"

Accustomed to Leopoldina's outbursts, Elsa could not entirely censure Miss Archer, but neither could she avoid agreeing, "No, you ought not have," before beginning to recover herself. "You ought not have, but I have promised my forgiveness, which is—granted, Miss Archer. Why...do you suppose Mr Archer has asked, or that I have...refused him?"

"I have never before seen him besotted," Persephone replied with grave frankness. "He could not feel so passionately and not ask, and as you have not been announced as engaged, I surmise that you must have refused. Why, Miss Elsabeth? Do you not find him suitable?"

"Suitable." Elsabeth glanced upward, allowing a laugh to travel toward the elegant cornicing. "Miss Archer, there may be no man more *suitable* in England, but his manner of asking was not suitable at all."

"Oh, dear. Gerry does not always know when to hold his tongue instead of laying a foundation bare. I am given to understand that your younger sisters are...enthusiastic? It is a folly I myself have sympathy for, although I fear my own enthusiasm may have set Gerry against it more strongly than is necessary."

"Enthusiastic. Yes. That is a word that could be used to describe them, my youngest particularly, and indeed, he was perhaps unnecessarily...blunt in the matter of my family's situation. I may also have held certain prejudices against him that I have since learned were...not entirely founded, or have been rectified, but they do not dismiss the matter he was most condescendingly willing to overlook in order to marry me."

A certain intriguing steeliness came into Miss Persephone's eyes. "What matter might that be? I am inclined to like you, Miss Elsabeth, because my brother has spoken so highly of you, and I can hardly imagine what should be so insurmountable that he would have to overlook it in order to be your husband. If you can only explain it to me, I should rather like to discuss it with *him*, for I would so like to have a sister of my own."

"I would rather you did not," Elsabeth replied softly, "but I find I am increasingly desirous of performing that which I am forbidden. I would not ask you to keep a secret, Miss Archer, but if you could be discreet?"

"I am the very soul of discretion," Persephone promised with, Elsabeth thought, perhaps as much veracity as Leopoldina might claim, but her mind was already made up: Persephone had barely finished speaking before Elsabeth lifted her hands and wreathed them in fire that cast pale gold light in the warmth of the summer sun.

"Magic is in my blood," she said beneath Persephone's astonished cry. "My family is thick with it, and it is the gift that Mr Archer was obliged to risk in order to consider me as a wife and the mother of his heirs." She extinguished the flames and, at once, Persephone seized her hands, turning them this way and that as if she might find some trick to the power Elsabeth had displayed.

"I have never seen anything so magnificent! Gerry knows? Then he has told you of the library! And still you deny him? Miss Elsabeth, you are of sterner stuff than any other woman I have ever known! I envy you, that you should know yourself so well; I fear I am more easily led, or that I was as a child, at least. Oh, will you show me again? What else can you do? What spells, what charms, what potions do you know?"

Under this rush of questions, Elsabeth could not but laugh, and cast again to make dancing creatures in the sunlight. "I am afraid he does know, and I know no spells or charms, Miss Archer. Persephone. All I have is my native talent, which is most inclined to show itself in flames, although I have some small skill in ripening an apple before its time, that it might be feasted on during the course of a hearty walk. Would that I could do more; it is a bane upon me that this gift, so disdained, should be of so little use."

"But he has told you of the library," Persephone said again, this time with a query in the words.

"I am told that Streyfield's library is awe-inspiring, but that is knowledge I have from Mr Webber, not from Mr Archer himself."

A breath escaped Miss Archer. "Then I can only conclude he kept the knowledge from you in order to not influence what he believed to be your most honest and deeply felt answer to his proposal. You must come with me, Miss Elsabeth. I must show you the library at once."

Elsabeth allowed herself to be drawn to her feet and led through the house, though she could not do so without the amused protest that she had been in libraries before; that, indeed, Mr Dover's own library, while by necessity inevitably smaller than Streyfield's, was of no small regard, and that she herself was very well read from it.

All of these protests were silenced by the magnitude of the room Persephone brought her into: half of Oakden might have fit comfortably within it, and all of Oakden could have been stacked inside without reaching the ceiling. Polished marble floors reflected mahogany shelves that stretched three stories high; wheeled ladders leaned against them, and a circular stair spun upward and radiated narrow walkways leading to balconies encircling the second and third stories, that the books there might be reached on the ladders that were placed on those levels as well.

There were, at a glance, more books within than Elsabeth

had ever seen in one place before; more books than she had fully appreciated existed, much less in a private library. Even with marble floors and stone walls behind the shelves, the scent of books hung in the air, and the sunlight filtering in through tall windows caught on motes of dust that did not appear willing to settle on any gleaming surface.

"Forgive me," Elsabeth said in a small voice. "Mr Dover's library is as nothing, after all."

"I doubt that," Persephone replied pertly. "It is more that Streyfield's is as Alexandria, or so I fondly imagine. Please, this way; I hope you have a head for heights." She mounted the curling stairway, climbing to the third story and traipsing lightly to the railed balcony, where she led Elsabeth, who carefully did not look down, to a corner of books that, while dusted, had the look of being long undisturbed about them. Persephone gestured to them; Elsabeth stepped forward, then frowned uncertainly at Miss Archer, who nodded encouragement. "Take one. Any of them. See what it says to you."

Her frown deepening, Elsabeth crouched and extended a hand to glide it over the books, barely touching them; barely daring to. A strange piercing made her palm ache as she passed by one, and she returned to it, removing it from the shelf. Its weight surprised her; it was thick, but hardly taller than her hand, and imprinted with beautiful, nonsensical gilded lettering, as if someone had pressed living flame into the leather. Eyebrows drawn down, Elsabeth opened it to find more of the same meaningless letters, which suddenly shifted and resolved as she gazed at them, becoming words. Elsabeth startled and glanced at Persephone, whose face was alight.

"A gift for magic is required to even read them. Go on, Miss Elsabeth. Tell me what it says. I have always wished to know."

"Firepower," Elsa replied slowly. "Or perhaps, Fire Power, or...perhaps Fire Spirit, as the title, and beneath it...beneath it, it reads *she who naturally calls this book to hand shall be known to herself as a Promethean; she is charged to read these words and defy the very gods for the good of all mankind.* Miss Archer, what is this?"

"One of the oldest collections in the Streyfield library," Miss Archer responded. "These books were old when my father was a child; he could not recall which grandfather, nor to how many greats, had sought out so many books of magic, or why, when the Archer blood was as mundane as any. That ancestor only thought they should be protected, and so, our grandfathers kept them even when Her Majesty Queen Elizabeth commanded that all such books should be delivered to her army, that they might have the knowledge necessary to defeat the Armada. They are a secret; I suppose they might even be considered treasonous to hold. Father spent many hours with Gerry and myself, making certain we knew the library's contents before he died; it was important to him that we should never lose sight of the knowledge we are privileged to protect here. He made no more fuss over these books than any other, but even a flighty girl of seven could see that they were unusual. I could not read them, nor even recognise the letters as any knowable language. But for you—!"

Elsabeth set aside the book of fire, then sat to draw another, then another, book from the shelves. Several were like the one she had first selected, only entitled Wind and Water and other elements; perhaps they were the most basic building blocks of magic, aspects which a gifted individual might have affinity for. Others were more massive tomes, and upon the opening of one, it became clear that the components of spells lay within: they called for ingredients and gestures both, and went on for pages. Another, entitled Æther or Spirit, was written in a crabbed but precise hand that became clearer as Elsabeth read aloud. "...my friend Marco, with whom I have maintained a long and pleasant correspondence, has travelled the world over and observes that we Europeans who consider ourselves so civilised have all but lost the gift that runs strongly throughout other more natural nations. Today, it is perhaps little loss, but I fear that someday it will be the ruin of our continent. It is to this end I write what history of magic I have been able to learn, as one who cannot practise it herself. When I am done, the spell will be cast over these pages so that only one who is herself a magician will be able to read it; when I am done, this story will be mine no longer. Even in these early pages, I feel some loss in that, although what I have studied can never be stolen from my mind. Here is what I do know: without the written word, magic and its history will certainly be lost in Europe, and even as lacking in talent as I am, I cannot bear that thought.

"Fortunately, there is no magic that cannot be learnt by one with the natural talent, although some workings may come more easily than others. I will write only of the history of how it has been studied and developed, but my friend M—," and this name Elsabeth could not read; no matter how often her eyes returned to it, the word twisted and shied, as if it did not wish to be known. After tripping through it a time or two, she went on, reading with greater urgency. "M— puts pen to parchment as well, and records all of the spells and charms, the castings and incantations, that he has learned in his long life; between us, we may have some hope of saving a working knowledge of magic for generations yet undreamt-of."

Elsabeth clutched Æther to her breast and gazed wide-eyed at Miss Archer, feeling a mad urge to abscond with the book and all its brethren. "Any magic can be learnt...!"

"I will leave you," Miss Archer said with a strange gentleness far beyond her years. "I'll have tea sent, and scones and meats and cheeses, and I will leave you to your studies."

"Miss Archer—Persephone—!"

"No," Persephone said again, still with the strangeness. "You must stay, Miss Elsabeth; you must study what no other here can. There can be no other reason for your coming to Streyfield, if it is not my brother who draws you here. I will entertain your aunt and uncle, of whom I am sure I will soon be very fond, and when you are ready, perhaps you will show me a trick or two." Her eyes shone with shy hope. "I should like very much to see what you can learn from our library."

"I should like nothing more than to show you," Elsabeth whispered in return. "I—thank you, Persephone. All my life, and more this past year, I have tasted bitter dregs that there should be so little to be done with magic; these books are riches unimagined."

Miss Archer smiled and curtseyed, and before she had reached the library floor, she was forgotten, so engrossed did Elsabeth become. She sat with three books about her: Æther and Fire and a book entitled simply Incantations, and she could not read a few pages of one without being drawn to the pages of another, for the author of Æther and the sorcerer she called M— had worked together indeed, and the history often referenced a spell or explanation detailed in another book.

In due time, three books became six, then ten, until Elsabeth sat in a nest of increasing knowledge. Fire spoke of creating a consistent warmth without the need for fiery hands; Elsabeth, warm enough in the library on a summer afternoon, wished she had known that spell during Rosamund's illness, and committed it to heart against needing it again. More immediately useful was a calling of light; as the sun sank and the library dimmed, she pinned flames in the air around her, like floating candles that burned air instead of wicks, and laughed in delight as they hung there obediently. They did not, despite appearances, burn air, according to Æther; they burned æther, or spirit; they burned the magical will of the sorcerer who set them alight, and would burn until the sorcerer lost strength or doused them. It was no more difficult than using her fingertip as a candle; knowing the fingertip flame could be pinched off and placed in the air, believing that it would not fade, was all the difference. So it went with easily the first half of Fire; nothing in its pages was beyond Elsabeth's skill, only her imagination, and upon introduction to it, the ability evolved naturally.

A latterly spell, though, caught both her attention and her imagination; it was not as simple as the others, but its applications were gloriously obvious. To Scry, read the twisted lettering at the top of the page, and below detailed how an element might be used to find another like it, and give speech through it.

It could be done most naturally by two users of the same sorcery: had she another Promethean to call upon, their æther-born flame would lend itself comfortably toward communication. Next most easily came scrying with two fires burning from the same wood; the more in common they had, the stronger the link would be, but even a single stick would suffice so long as the common wood lasted. Third came fires lit from disparate sources, and finally æther fire to natural flame, which was conceded as nearly impossible for all save the most strongly talented Prometheans.

Elsabeth, smiling, glanced at the mighty hearth in the library below. It was summer and she the only occupant of the library, so of course the fire was not lit. She thought that a pity: it would certainly burn the same wood, or very similar, to that which might be lit elsewhere in the manor. She turned a few pages back, reading a second time the manner of stretching her senses to discover whether other fires burned nearby, and felt the real heat of the kitchen fires almost overwhelming a smaller point of comfortable flame in a sitting room. Miss Archer and the Penneys would be there, perhaps; Elsa herself should give up her studies and go to see them, as she was unconscionably rude to have remained with the books for so long.

Instead, she allowed her eyes to close, and, imagining her relatives in the comfort of the Streyfield sitting room, thought she could indeed see them, cast in golden light from the fire. Mrs Penney sat beside Miss Archer, their hands entwined and Miss Archer alight with laughter over something; Mr Penney sat across from them with the benevolent expression of a fond father. Elsabeth felt a pang that they had no children of their own, but held on to the sweet image a moment longer. Miss Archer, laughter ending, glanced toward the fire, and all her pleasure turned to perfect surprise as a footstep fell on the library balcony.

Elsabeth, surrounded by rings of floating flames, shook off her reverie to look up into Mr Archer's astonished face.

(50)

Elsabeth cried out in surprise and released the magic holding the light; in an instant, the library was impossibly dark, with the starlit windows only gradually achieving a grey relief against the blackness. Mr Archer was not so much as a shadow, the books which surrounded Elsabeth less even than that, and infinitely more precious. She dared not move for fear of knocking one aside and damaging it, and could not think what to say.

Mr Archer, so often unable to converse, proved quite able to in this instance; he spoke in a precisely controlled voice that seemed quite doom-ridden in the darkness. "There will be a moon tonight, but it has not yet risen, and I should hate for either of us to plunge from this balcony onto the marble three floors below. Miss Elsabeth, if you could restore the light...?"

"Yes, of course." Elsabeth's own voice, and her returning flame, both trembled, and she rose from her seat with a mixture of embarrassment and guilt. "Forgive me. I was startled, and I am not accustomed to maintaining such a magic in company. I...had no notion you were here, Mr Archer. I would not have stayed and risked offering you such discomfort if I had."

"I have only just returned. Just this moment, in fact; I saw the lights in the library when I rode up, and came here straightaway, imagining I might find Persephone here." Indeed, Elsabeth now saw that he wore riding clothes, and that his usually polished demeanour was somewhat dishevelled. Nor was her own much better, wrinkled and dirty-fingered as she was from settling in a corner and perusing ancient tomes. She saw Mr Archer observe her own status and imagined the corner of his mouth turned up in amusement as he continued: "Perhaps you will forgive me for my tone a moment earlier. I must confess to a...particular dislike...of heights; I have never been especially comfortable on this level of the library, and to find myself both at a height and in the dark..."

Elsabeth said, "Oh," faintly, and then her amusement caught up to Archer's. "Oh. I had rather assumed it was my blatant display of magic that had earned your censure. It is one thing, perhaps, to encourage its use to save a life, and another to find your library alight with it."

Archer allowed himself the slow exhalation of a breath before speaking, and when he did, it was as a man engaged in idle and interesting conversation, rather than one at an ungainly height discussing a topic widely considered beyond the pale. "Indeed, those two purposes are very unalike, but its use for the one purpose has perhaps softened me to its possibilities in other areas. One disapproves of magic because that is what one does, and I confess my personal reasons for doing so may be twofold. Firstly, it is easy to disdain when one's only experience with the art is through one such as David Hartnell. He did little enough with the gift that I knew him to have," Archer said dismissively, "but knowing what manner of man he is, it was easy to imagine that all persons who commanded magic were equally reprobates; that is certainly the common view. But I have come to realise that magicians must be like any other men, or any other women: some must be good, and some bad. Certainly, Mrs Webber cannot be thought of as anything other than good, and you may be vexing, but there is no evil in you. So, I fear that, in the end, I find your lighting of the library intriguing rather than censorious."

Could she douse the airborne flames without alarming her host, Elsabeth would have done so instantly to hide her astonishment. To hear Archer speak cautious approval of using magic lay beyond the bounds of expectation, and she struggled to enquire, "And the second reason, Mr Archer?"

The corner of Archer's mouth twisted, almost enough to be imagined a smile. "My English heritage is quite beyond reproach, but I am of a quarter African blood. No one can doubt that magic is practiced in all reaches of Africa, as it is in the Americas and India and, I suppose, even in the Orient. My ancestors were not practitioners of any arcane arts, so far as I know, but my bloodlines are exotic enough to some that I should come under suspicion if I appeared in any way to condone that which is widely condemned. I have no wish to be pressed into service, and that is the most amiable end that a man of magic might reach."

To this, Elsabeth could make no response; it was only the practise of manners that kept her from gaping at Archer's confession. She was too accustomed to magic being mistrusted for its own sake; it had not occurred to her that Archer might have such deeply personal reasons for avoiding those who practiced it. Her silence drew out until Archer, convinced she would not speak, continued, "You have met my sister, then, I must assume? Or have you in some secret way learnt of our sorcerous library and slipped into Streyfield all unseen to study? What are you doing here, Miss Elsabeth? Forgive me," he said again almost instantly. "It is Miss Dover now."

"It is of no consequence," Elsabeth replied faintly. "I am long accustomed to being Miss Elsabeth. I am touring with my aunt and uncle, and we happened upon Streyfield, and then your sister, and...I am afraid we have been pressed into staying overnight, sir. I assure you that we will vacate the premises at the earliest possible hour tomorrow; we do not mean to intrude. But," Elsabeth could not help but add, despite fearing she sounded as petulant as Leopoldina could, "you were not expected back for a day or two yet."

"My business concluded early, and I had the thought of surprising Persephone. I might have been wiser to stay over in a town when darkness fell, but the night was fine and I was not so very far from Streyfield; I could not resist riding home, although I left my coachman in comfortable surrounds for the night, and will expect him around mid-morning. My untimely and unwelcome arrival could not possibly force you to return to a common house for the sin of accepting Persephone's invitation, nor put you to the trouble of going back and forth. You must stay, Miss... Dover. I should like to meet your aunt and uncle, and perhaps hear a little of what you are doing here." This last word was accompanied by a gesture that indicated Elsabeth's being in the library and the books she had removed for study, rather than her general presence at Streyfield. "Perhaps I might offer you assistance in carrying them to the tables below, so they will be convenient for you in the morning?"

This could not, Elsabeth concluded, be the same gentleman she was acquainted with. Her Mr Archer would regard the imposition of her family—her family, of all people!—to be an impossible burden; he could not sound so genuinely glad at the prospect of meeting them. Nothing in her experience of him suggested a willingness to be of use, much less of use in a scenario that would inconvenience him, and given his confession regarding heights, carrying awkwardly large books from the third floor of a library down a winding staircase could be nothing but an inconvenience. Nor could she imagine that he might willingly have her stay on to study; there was nothing for it than to think him a changeling, and Elsabeth glanced at the books around her with a wry curiosity as to whether one of them might have a spell to accomplish such a change of personality. Her grasp of magic did not allow for glamours or swaying of men's minds, but she knew now her grasp of magic was so limited as to be nonexistent, and there were depths to be plumbed in the Streyfield library

Without knowing it, she had made up her mind, and spoke without guile: "I will allow you to help me, Mr Archer, if you would not object to me providing a certain fullness of light; those stairs are, I believe, tricky enough even if one has a head for heights and lacks an armful of books. As for staying on, perhaps that is a topic that should be broached later, with my Uncle Penney."

"I cannot imagine that he does not bow to your rule," Archer replied, but nodded acquiescence. "I would be grateful for the light, Miss Dover." He did not crouch to collect books, though, until Elsabeth, lip caught between her teeth in concentration, extended her hands to send the fiery glow surrounding them into the æther. Flickers of flame lined the walkways and followed the curve of the stair banister down, until it seemed the whole of the library was lit by a central column of flame. Its light was both generous and soft, and Archer, curious beyond caution, cupped his palms beneath the nearest dart of fire. "There is no smoke. Miss Dover, I believe if Society properly understood certain aspects of magic, you should be eternally in demand at balls. Imagine enough light to see one another clearly in all corners of the room, without the heaviness of candle smoke or the threat of wax drippings."

"I assure you I am not studying in order to become the lighting fixture at a soirée, Mr Archer."

Archer chuckled and released the flame he held. "Of course not. It was a preposterous thought, and not worthy of you." He crouched then and collected more books than Elsabeth could have carried in two journeys, leaving her able to collect a few extras that had thus far remained on the shelves.

Within a few minutes, they were arranged on several of the tables, and Archer held a look of satisfaction that turned to fresh amusement when he noticed a serving tray with cold tea and untouched scones. "Miss Dover, do not tell me you have denied Cook the opportunity to feed you. You will break the woman's heart, and she will in turn break our teeth on hardtack in the morning."

"I had a very fine luncheon with your sister," Elsabeth protested, although, upon the reminder, she could not help but recall that the luncheon had been many, many hours earlier, and that she had partaken of nothing since. Indeed, a headache awakened at the realisation, and, without consideration, she stepped forward to warm the teapot in both hands and pour herself a cup. "Would you like some?"

Mr Archer, with an air of caution, accepted, sipped, and expressed surprise. "I would not have thought it would be so good reheated."

"There is rarely a cold teapot at Oakden," Elsabeth admitted. "One becomes accustomed to strongly brewed tea, as it is often left to sit rather than made anew."

"I cannot help but think that yours is a more extraordinary family than I was once inclined to give them credit for," Mr Archer began, but before he could go further, a familiar voice cried out, "No, I am certain I saw her; it is not a fit of madness, but magic, I am sure of it!" and Miss Persephone Archer burst into the library with Mrs and Mr Penney in her wake. "Miss Elsabeth!" cried Persephone, "did I not just see you within the fi—Gerry!"

In an instant, Persephone had flown across the room to be caught in Mr Archer's arms; the Penneys, entering at a more subdued pace, stopped just within the door to gaze in astonishment from the Archers to the staircase-column of flame to Elsabeth, and then between each of those three things with no especial ability to fixate on any one of them. "Gerry," cried Miss Archer again, merrily this time, "what are you doing here? You are early! And you have found Miss Elsabeth! I have shown her the books, Gerry; was that right of me? Say it was right of me. It was right of me! Look what she has done; would it not be splendid to see every room so lit? And did I not see you in the sitting-room fireplace, Elsabeth? I know that I did!"

Elsabeth, thinking of the gold-cast realism that she had envisioned the sitting room with, replied, "I did not mean for you to, but I think it possible that you did. But no, you could not have: to scry with æther fire to ordinary fire is of the utmost difficulty, and only the rarest of Prometheans might do so."

"You cannot think you are other than the rarest and best of all possible creatures!" Persephone said warmly. "I have no doubt that you are a Promethean of first order, and I will not be told that I did not see you. Oh, Gerry, these are the Penneys, Miss Elsabeth's dear aunt and uncle. I have insisted they stay; you must not cast them out."

"Even if I was of a mind to, and I am not, I could never go against your express wishes," Archer assured his sister, whose skin was not so dark that she could not blush prettily even in the fire-light, and who declared herself satisfied as the Penneys were re-introduced to Archer, who assured them that he did, of course, recall their first meeting the night Rosamund had fallen ill.

"Your library has taught Elsabeth this trick?" Mrs Penney wondered to Mr Archer, who could no more contain an expression of satisfaction than could Persephone. He conceded that it had, and spoke briefly of the library's varying collections, the jewel of which could be considered the very volumes Elsabeth had taken from the shelves.

"Jewel," Elsabeth could not help but echo. "You have said you are only just becoming acquainted with the idea that magic might be less distasteful than you thought, Mr Archer; how might this collection be the jewel, then?"

"It was in my grandfather Archer's eyes," Archer replied, "and there are many who regard the rare or exotic in their collections as jewels, even if they themselves are not inherently taken with those things."

As they spoke, Mrs Penney, admiringly, opened the nearest book to examine its pages, and, after a moment, laughed. "How to transform grain to bread without grinding; how to take the taint from spoilt meat. Have I happened upon a grimoire or a cookery book, Mr Archer? Though I must say if these are matters which magic might address, surely we might be better off pursuing them rather than the making of war."

She concluded this observation into a perfect silence, and looked up with some surprise. Mr Penney smiled fondly at her, as he often did, but astonishment was writ large upon the faces of the other three, and none more so than on Elsabeth's, who asked, "You can read that, Aunt Felicity?"

Taken somewhat aback, Mrs Penney glanced from each of the startled trio back to the book before fixating on Elsabeth again. "Of course. Should I be unable to?"

"Neither Persephone nor myself can," Archer replied. "Forgive me, Mrs Penney, but were you once Miss Dover?"

"I was," began Mrs Penney, and Elsabeth could not help crying out, "You do have the gift, Aunt Felicity! These books are ensorcelled, only to be read by those who might use them! Perhaps your natural talent is subtle, but it can be quickened through study! Aunt Felicity, you shall have your wish at last!"

Mrs Penney folded her hands before her stomach and smiled briefly at Elsabeth. "I fear it is far too late for that, Elsabeth, but...could she be right, Mr Archer? Might I have the ability to learn magic?" No sooner than the words passed her lips did she move her hands to cover her mouth, though more confusion than guilt crossed her features. "To speak so openly and easily of such a thing...forgive me; it is beyond my experience or imagination, even if..."

As one, they looked to Elsabeth's column of flame, still gently lighting and warming the library. "It is beyond all of us," Archer said thoughtfully, "but we may verge on extraordinary times. Do not look to me to verify what your niece has said, Mrs Penney; I think we all know that she does not require a man to confirm her certainty in her knowledge, and if she had not the knowledge before arriving at Streyfield, she has gained it from my sister, not myself."

"What Mr Archer means to say," Elsabeth said with dry amusement, "is that I am right, and if you can read those words, Aunt, you can learn to harness your natural talent. Uncle Robert, if you would open a book and try to read...?"

Mr Penney paused with his fingertips above the nearest book. "I should like to see your face, Elsabeth, if it proves I can read the words within. I wonder which of us it would surprise more, or if it would merely disprove your thesis."

"I believe I would feel very left out," Persephone announced.

"To be so surrounded by sorcery and unable to read, much less work, a lick of it myself; that should be quite sad."

"Society would disagree," Mr Penney replied, and opened the book at hand. He turned a page, then several, and finally to the end of the book before chuckling. "Spider-crawls, nothing more. Twisting shapes that look no more like written language to me than a child's scribbles might. And yet you can read them, Elsabeth? And you, Mrs Penney? How curious." He closed that book and investigated another, chuckling again as he drew Mrs Penney closer and requested that she tease words out of the tangled web he saw.

She read a few words, then paused. "This is a spell, Mr Penney, and it requires no components save the voice and will of the caster. I think perhaps I should not continue."

"Why? What will it do?"

"Cause every hen within a mile to produce an egg by morning." Mrs Penney closed the book firmly, though interest lit a fire in Elsabeth's breast.

"What a useful spell that could be for Ruth! Think of how helpful it might be for her parishioners, particularly in winter months when food grows thin! I must have that spell, Aunt Felicity!"

"You shall have them all," Mr Archer said with grave solemnity. "But, Miss Dover, I might suggest that you have been here—all day?" This was asked to the others, who nodded, and his attention returned to Elsabeth. "All day. And while I do not pretend to understand the source of your magic, I am certain it cannot go unfed, and thus neither should its practitioner. Mr Penney," he said, now addressing that worthy, "I know my sister has pressed you to stay overnight and that Miss Dover would have you leave in the morning, the better to not disturb the unexpectedly returned master of the house. But, as that master, I should like very much for you to stay; the grounds are excellent for both hunting and fishing, so we might entertain ourselves while these remarkable ladies are given over to studies that I think not a ball could divert them from. Will you stay on a day or two, to satisfy myself, my sister and your female relations?"

Mr Penney was a sensible man, wholly aware of the disparate stations held by himself and Mr Archer; he recognised without difficulty that a man of Archer's position might be expected to make such an offer, and that a man of his own certainly ought to refuse it as to not look too hungry for great associates. Nor could he doubt that Elsabeth felt they should go, that Miss Archer felt they should stay and that Mrs Penney would be content with any decision he himself made. Thus caught between propriety, clashing female desires and his own interests, Mr Penney concluded that *he* knew he had no intention or interest in presuming upon his acquaintance with Mr Archer in the future, and that it was therefore most proper that he should accept Mr Archer's proposal, and stay on. That it aligned nicely with his own love of fishing was happy circumstance, but not to be belittled. "We will, Mr Archer, and we thank you for your generosity."

(51)

Elsabeth could not pretend, even to herself, that she was displeased by this turn of events; she was too aware that she would have married Mr Archer on the spot, if necessary, to retain access to his library of enchantments. Indeed, all through supper, he continued so politely and with something so close to charm that she was often reminded of the moment he had come upon her making snow angels, and wondered if perhaps, had circumstances proceeded differently, she might have come to welcome the sentiment, if not the actuality, of the offer he had made. She could not see how events might have transpired so differently, though; all the intelligence she had learned that weighed the balance in his favour had come well after that unfortunate proposal, and she had not permitted herself to much linger on what had then become impossible. Even so, she was obliged to wonder time and again at the change in him; it surely had not been brought on by her own comments to him at Charington Place, not when both Miss Archer and the household staff spoke so highly of him as a kind and thoughtful gentleman. Perhaps it was only that he was at home and comfortable there, although, if that proved to be the case, Elsabeth believed he ought to never again leave Streyfield.

With the late supper concluded, she was given a room of her

own that lay alongside her aunt and uncle's, and was nearly prepared for bed when a knock sounded at the door. Amused, and anticipating the irrepressible Miss Archer, Elsabeth answered with a smile, only to find Mrs Penney standing there in a positive flurry of high colour and emotion. Without waiting for an invitation, she swept in, closed the door, and turned to Elsa with curiosity brightening her features. "What on earth is the situation between you and Mr Archer, Elsabeth? He is not at all the gentleman I heard described at Oakden; he is well-mannered, he is thoughtful, he is handsome—although not so handsome, perhaps, as Captain Hartnell—he has spoken of you with such fervour that all of his household knows your name, and now he has opened his extraordinary library to you! What has passed between you?"

"He is more handsome than Hartnell," Elsabeth opined, much to her aunt's interest, "and greatly changed from Oakden." This was at first all she could say, and then, in a flood, the story came out: his proposal, her accusations toward his treatment of Captain Hartnell and interference with Rosamund and Webber; her enraged actions in chasing him from Ruth's home with fireballs; his subsequent letter, which Elsabeth carried with her still; his relenting in the matter of Rosamund, culminating in his advice to use her magic to keep Rosa warm the night she had collapsed, and finally the confrontation with Hartnell that had confirmed him, and not Archer, as the villain, and now Archer's unlooked-for generosity with the Streyfield library; all of this Elsabeth poured out to her aunt, whose countenance darted between astonishment and dismay, delight and horror, and finally settled into a gentle fondness as the story concluded.

"I think he must still hold you in some esteem, Elsabeth. What a pity that he did not show these nicer manners earlier."

"But he did not," Elsa replied almost helplessly, "and so I can have no regrets over refusing him. I was right to do so, Aunt Felicity, and if he is now more nicely mannered, then it is still too late for any change on my part. No; I cannot think it is because he still has any affection for me, but rather because he is within his own home now and able to be magnanimous within those walls."

"But surely, his support of your sorcery, Elsa—"

"Rosamund nearly died from Society's opinions of sorcery, Aunt. For all his arrogance, I do not imagine Mr Archer to be a murderer, or even to wish harm on those who are his inferiors. His support was a life-saving measure when she collapsed, and if it was of use then, I should think his intelligence sufficient as to allow and even encourage a subtle study of magic that could be of further use to others. He was never foolish," Elsa murmured, the heat gone out of her. "Only insufferably rude, and if he is not any longer—even if I am to concede some error of judgement regarding him—then I am quite certain my emphatic rejection of his offer will have put all thoughts of admiring me out of his mind. I am surprised and grateful that he has opened his library to us; that is more than anyone could expect."

Mrs Penney, seeing that her niece was determined on this matter, let it fall in favour of clasping Elsabeth's hands. "I will hope, then, that we will both learn to be of use to others; I confess, Elsabeth, that I came to speak with you tonight as much because I could not sleep from excitement as to gain an understanding of your acquaintance with Mr Archer. Am I to be a sorcerer after all? Can it be possible?"

"You can read the books," Elsabeth said with assurance. "You will be able to work some measure of magic."

Her prophecy was proven true before dinner the next day: a book proclaiming itself to be Of Minor Magicks came to hand, and within its pages lay the casting of spells for candle-lighting, for dusting, for setting a moonlight low upon one's feet to light the way on dark nights, and a dozen more small and practical magics that, once memorised, Mrs Penney found herself quite able to command at any time. She could not hang fire in the air as Elsabeth could, nor cause every hen inside a mile to lay an egg, but neither, she claimed, did she need to: it was quite enough to drive an infection from an inflamed cut, or to cast a pretense of sunlight into a dim room.

Each of these magics, she reported, created a surge within her. "It is as if I am actually...pushing," she said thoughtfully. "As if that little physical effort necessary to light a candle is still expended within me, save that I do not need to rise and find a spark to do so. The sensation is greater when I set the moonlight upon my feet, as if—as if that is a less natural act and requires more of my spirit to achieve."

"We must find a way to gather more æther," Elsabeth concluded. "It must be possible, so that you can work larger magics."

"Or perhaps we are given as much æther as we can safely burn," Mrs Penney replied, "and ought not press beyond our limits."

"So, we should neither repress nor indulge our magic? Perhaps." Elsabeth frowned with recollection. "Captain Hartnell used more than he ought to have, in the matter of the bridge, and was convalescent for some weeks after. But Dina, who certainly used as much magic that day as Captain Hartnell, was merely drenched, not exhausted, with her working."

"Perhaps she has more natural æther; you, after all, seem to be well supplied with it." For, by now, Mrs Penney had read the rules of scrying, and knew Elsabeth had succeeded in the most difficult manner of it without so much as intending to. More, as Mrs Penney had mastered the book of small magics, Elsabeth had investigated more dramatic castings: she could, and, in the aftermath, somewhat sheepishly, had, caused every hen within a mile to lay an egg; Persephone had gone running to the coops to see if it was true, and returned triumphantly, bearing an armload of eggs and intending a quiche for supper. After that, a pinch of salt seeded the air, and from it, Elsabeth conjured a raincloud that poured water incessantly onto the library's marble floor until the three ladies could throw open a window and chase the tiny storm outside with a frantically read spell that caused gusts of winds. "If only Dina was here!" Elsabeth wailed in the midst of that minor disaster, and Mrs Penney, unaccustomed to hearing Dina wished for, laughed aloud.

Innumerable spells required components; Elsabeth, reading

them, felt certain she could cast them, and as often felt she would not wish to. Too many were for war-efforts, guarantees to damage or destroy flesh and walls; all the best parts of magic turned to delivering ruin. She put those books away with a heaviness in her heart, and sought their counterparts: surely, if magic could harm, it could help as well.

"Ah," said Mrs Penney finally, late in the afternoon. They had lunched in the library, well away from where they might stain the precious books but near enough that they felt they were not abandoning their studies. Miss Archer had joined them after lunch, reading in a corner as Elsabeth and Mrs Penney's studies became more guided by investigation than experimentation. Mrs Penney's quiet exclamation was the first that had been heard for some time, and she rose with the weariness of many long hours at study, to bring a small, beautiful and very old book to Elsabeth's table. "I found this inside another. Look at it, Elsabeth. Tell me if it says what I think it does."

"Æthers of Health," Elsabeth read from the cover, and opened the book to see a now-familiar handwriting in its early pages. "Spells of midwives, of hedge-witches, of wise-women and bone-setters. Once, there was hardly a village in England that did not have an old woman or man who could be turned to for easing of pain and the healing of injuries, but those who can work such magics have been banned; they follow the Crusades and the armies who have more need for them than fear of them. M— says there will be more plagues now, and that perhaps those who die deserve to for their distrust of magic. I cannot agree, and so, I hope that one day, these pages will be found and embraced for the good they can do."

The pages were fragile beneath Elsa's fingertips. She paused after the introduction, looking to some of the larger books of war-magic, which were sturdier and more recently bound. "These smallest books, the ones with this handwriting and the mention of M—, they are the oldest of this collection. They are the ones that have how to cure meat and how to cast light on the darkest roads. These are the precious ones, Aunt Felicity. The larger ones are newer, and given over to warfare; they are all that we have left of magic in the wider world. But here: here are spells to cast to ease the pain of childbirth, or to set a shattered bone, or to cool a fever that will not break. It isn't that only the camp followers and fallen women can cast them; it's that they are the only ones who still remember this magic at all, and men will not learn what a woman can teach. Persephone, your ancestor may have saved all that is good in English magic here. He may have laid the foundation upon which we can build and change this world."

"Change," echoed Persephone wonderingly from her corner. "What would you do, Miss Dover?"

"Elect my friend Sophia to Parliament," Elsabeth replied with a laugh. "I cannot yet say, Persephone. I do not yet know. But I feel that we cannot allow this knowledge to lie fallow now that it is discovered, any more than we could allow Rosamund to go on suppressing her magic when we learned it was the source of her illness. Even if we should do no more than make that common knowledge, we should have changed something; should we copy these books of magic and distribute them, allow them to find those who can make use of them—I do not know what would change, Miss Archer, save everything."

"I do not believe that would be...well looked-upon by the crown," Mrs Penney put forth into the silence following Elsabeth's proclamation. "Miss Archer has said it herself: it is long since the army has come to collect all the known books of magic, and sheer fortune that Streyfield's grimoires went unscathed. There must be some reason the government prefers to have what magic there is in their own hands."

"Do we not only have to look to the Colonies to answer that, Aunt Felicity? To Africa, and to India? Is not a population littered with magery and the knowledge of how to use it less compliant, more demanding, more egalitarian? I have read that the Civilised Nations in America are ruled by men and women alike, in council, not by circumstance of fortunate birth that deems an individual as the ruler of a whole nation."

Mrs Penney spoke with concern indistinguishable from dismay. "You have become a revolutionary overnight, Elsabeth."

"How could I not? How could you not, Aunt Felicity? You, who have longed to share your brothers' power since girlhood, to discover now that you have been kept from it only because someone long ago decided that magic is a barbarous secret, to be stamped out of wealthy families and barely tolerated in lowly ones! I am not ashamed of my gift, Aunt Felicity, and nor should you be! How can I do anything but revolt against the system that has placed us in this position? A system which nearly cost Rosamund her life, and—if you must see it in empirical terms—a system which has cost us the Colonies, for we have so thoroughly rejected our sorcerous heritage that we could not stand against a continent of practitioners! The European presence is tolerated in America, when we had imagined ourselves its conquerors! Oh, that I could fly there myself, and learn a thousand magics no longer dreamt of on England's spiritless shores!"

"Elsa," Mrs Penney responded, faint with shock, but Miss Archer could not restrain herself from rousing applause.

"Well said, well said, Miss Elsabeth! How I wish my brother had been here to hear you orate! I feel as though we are at the start of something, something dangerous and exciting and important, and that I myself am unbearably fortunate to be a part of it. Would that I could read these pages, but if I cannot, let me at least offer sanctuary to those who can! What use is wealth if I cannot do some good with it?"

Smiling, Elsabeth clasped Persephone's hands and drew her into an embrace. "Surely, you must require Mr Archer's approval before throwing open your doors as a refuge for those who would study magic in peace, but I am grateful for your generous heart and the kindness which prompts the offer. It is enough—more than enough—that your family has kept these books of magic safe for so long; our next duty, I think, must be to copy them, even before we make their presence known to the world, so that they are not endangered by being the solitary window we have left into the past, and the skills they had then."

"There are so many," Persephone replied, suddenly daunted. "How will we copy them all, when sorcerers hide themselves?"

"We are seven ourselves, we Dovers," Elsabeth answered. "Or five, perhaps, for the nonce; I am not sure my very youngest sisters have the discipline to sit and copy so many pages with accuracy, but five is a beginning."

"Surely, Ruth would not," Mrs Penney began hesitatingly, but Elsabeth disagreed.

"Once I would have agreed, but now? And if she should not be comfortable in doing the work in her own home, I am sure Miss Derrington would invite her often to Charington Place to copy in peace."

"She would," Persephone interjected eagerly, "save that she is engaged and due to be married before the end of the month, that she and her husband might return to Oyo before the winter storms come on."

Elsabeth cried, "What!" with great delight. "What, Miss Archer? I had not heard this news! Pray tell, who will her husband be?"

"A gentleman named Swift. He is Irish-born and nephew to some renowned physician of whom I have never heard. His uncle's connexions are not so appealing to him as the pull of the African sun, or perhaps it is only that he is the fourth son and his uncle cannot do much for one of so little influence himself. But Annabel is so wholly happy that she has been seen to go walking without a wrap, so I must think her heart entirely taken up with such regard as to warm her through and through."

Elsabeth's hands had gone to her lips as Persephone spoke; now she removed them, trembling, and was not ashamed that tears stood in her eyes as she reported, "I have met the gentleman a little; a very little. It was his uncle who warned us to the severity of Rosamund's condition; without Mr Swift, Persephone, I should have lost a sister. And now, because of him, another lady I came to care for quite sincerely in the little time I knew her shall return to the place that she is happiest; oh, I could not ask for better news than this. Before the end of the month! I must write to her and offer my congratulations." Merrily, Elsabeth enquired, "Is your aunt entirely enraged?"

"Very nearly," Persephone said with a smile. "She is very fond of directing other people's lives, and is never pleased to discover that her players have free will and direction of their own. But she cannot be wholly infuriated, as Annabel will be quite the superior in their marriage, and it is the custom of the Oyo to take a husband into the wife's family; Annabel's children will carry the Derrington name, of which Aunt Beatrice is very proud, and so, in the end, she gains a certain satisfaction that she could not have had if Anna had done as she had wished."

Mrs Penney murmured, "How complicated," but it was said with a smile that gave way to a sigh. "Well, I cannot say that I am alight with the fire of revolution, but I agree that the books must be copied. I hope we might come to some arrangement with Mr Archer, Miss Archer, that will allow us to do so without inconveniencing him."

"We will discuss it over supper," Persephone said, and upon this pronouncement, their studies were done for the day.

(52)

THE TOPIC WAS NOT BROACHED AT SUPPER AFTER ALL; MR PENNEY was too full of praise for Mr Archer's pond and grounds, and whilst it was agreed that the ladies had found remarkable success, it was not until the meal was done and the party had retired to an opulent sitting room that Persephone could no longer contain her hopes and plans for the books of magic.

Elsabeth found she could hardly look at Mr Archer as Persephone waxed enthusiastic; it felt too much an imposition to ask that they might copy the books, knowing as she did that they might easily have been hers. But Archer, self-confessed to be more comfortable with the practise of magic now that he had been introduced to those who used it, was the soul of generosity, solemnly agreeing that they must be preserved and copied, even conceding that the Dover family as a whole was well suited—by dint of being a known commodity, if nothing else—for the task. Every gracious word from him sank anchors more deeply into Elsabeth's soul, until she felt entirely weighed down with mortification.

A maid appeared in the doorway with a most apologetic expression and, upon gaining Archer's attention, bobbed a curtsey. "Forgive me, sir, but a letter has come for Miss Dover. It was sent to the inn, and yer man there took a fast horse to Streyfield;

it was marked that urgent, it was. I thought it best to bring it in, though I hope I haven't spoilt your evening, Miss."

This last was addressed to Elsabeth, who had risen at her name and now extended a hand for the letter whilst smiling at the maid. "Not at all. Thank you." Indeed, nothing could be more welcome than urgent news from home; perhaps Ruth's child had arrived, and Mrs Dover couldn't bear to wait an extra night for Elsabeth to know it. "Forgive me," Elsabeth said to the room in general, and was forgiven to open the missive and read without interruption.

She knew, in time, that she sat; she did not realise she had sunk to the floor until Mr Archer himself, concerned, appeared beside—above!—her, to say, "Miss Dover?" in a tone of genuine worry. Elsabeth gazed up at him without seeing, then returned her attention to the letter, written in her father's business-like hand. The words there remained unchanged; she wet her lips, trying to speak, and could not. Mr Archer, with quite infinite gentleness, knelt and lifted her; Elsabeth could not even protest as he carried her to a chair by the fire and settled her there before backing away to give Mr and Mrs Penney the access to her that relatives must be afforded.

He had seen Elsabeth Dover in nearly every imaginable fit of passion, from joy to rage; they had all brought colour to her cheeks and liveliness to her countenance, but whatever intelligence the letter carried had drained all that life from her. He had not imagined she could be so pale and retain consciousness; her dark hair now seemed a deathly cloud, so white was she, and her eyes were hollowed. She tried again to speak, and Mr Penney passed her a glass of brandy to sip before she could. It brought fire to her cheeks, but not healthy fire: two burning bright spots that reminded Archer too much of Rosamund Dover's face the night she had fainted.

A death; it had to be a death, to wrack her with such terrible emotion. Not her father, he hoped, knowing Elsabeth to be unsurpassingly fond of Mr Dover, and yet there was no one else he might hope for it to be, either; no one whose passing could affect her so dramatically could be better suited for death than the father, who had at least seen a full component of years.

Fortified by the brandy, Elsabeth whispered, "We are ruined," and then could once more say nothing else; instead, she thrust the letter into Mr Penney's hands, and, as a whole, the gathering could only watch as he, too, paled, though his expression crushed with more anger than loss.

"Elsabeth," whispered Mrs Penney, urgently. "Elsabeth, what is it? You are frightening me."

"Leopoldina." Elsabeth forced the words out even as Mr Penney closed the letter and lowered his forehead into one hand. "She has eloped. No. She has run away. She has run away with Captain Hartnell—"

At this name, Persephone cried out, and, for an instant, regret sparked in Elsabeth's eyes: she would not have said so much in front of Persephone, Archer believed, had she been in full command of her faculties. But she was not: the flicker of regret died as she turned her gaze toward the fire and spoke in a voice devoid of hope. "Mama has had a letter from Dina, who says she will one day be Mrs Hartnell. One day; that means there is no chance they are married. She is ruined. *We* are ruined. Thank God Rosamund is married; thank God Ruth is wed. They have done well and will not be tarnished by this, but oh, Matilda. My sweet Tildy. There will be no hope for her."

"You are generous to think of your sister at such a time," Archer replied with a degree of surprise. "Surely, your own fate must be of some concern?"

Elsabeth turned a look so bleak that it might be considered tinged with disgust upon him. "I have every confidence in my ability to secure my own future in a manner both suitable to the world and acceptable to me. Matilda is much younger, and easily led; of course my worries are for her, Mr Archer. I am not so selfish as that."

Shame touched him, though before he could offer an apology, Mrs Penney, struggling to comprehend the dread news that

Elsabeth had so tonelessly imparted, finally spoke. "Surely...no. Surely she cannot have been so...so foolish. Surely...."

"Of course she could have. She has fancied him since the day they met, and I—more fool I—I did not warn her away from him after I found him unsuitable for my own regard. I thought—I believed—I *knew* that to do so would only drive her toward him, but I never imagined—" Her agitation could not be contained; Elsabeth Dover rose, paced and sat again in despair before being driven to her feet again. "Mr Archer, Miss Archer, please forgive me for bringing this dread news into your home. Had I any notion, I should certainly have—" What, she could not say; it was preposterous to imagine she might have returned to the inn and taken a room for the purposes of reading a letter, and this Archer dared to say.

"You have no need to ask forgiveness, Miss Dover; indeed, if any fault is to be laid, it might be at my own feet, for not speaking to your father of what I knew about Captain Hartnell."

This begot him a hint of Elsabeth's usual disdain and a muttered "I am quite capable of speaking for myself on such matters, Mr Archer, and my father would be more predisposed to listen to me than a gentleman of your...stature."

"I believe you may mean 'nature'," Archer replied almost as softly, and was not gladdened to see a flash of weary pain cross Elsabeth's features.

"Your nature as presented at Newsbury, sir; I should not like to abuse you now for the goodness and kindness you have shown me and my family." Elsabeth turned to her uncle, who had not lifted his head from his hands. "Uncle, what will we do? We must prevail upon Hartnell to marry Dina, and yet, should we throw the whole of Papa's fortune his way, I cannot think that it will be enough to satisfy him."

"Perhaps there is some magic that might be done," Persephone suggested in a voice so thin that it could hardly be known for her own. "Some trick of gold, or sentiment...."

"Even if we might conjure coin, surely it would fade, and,

without money, there would be no chance of him staying with her, and in all of our studies today, we have yet to find any hint that magic might be used to sway the heart. Indeed, our reading implies that the æther that is in each of us—the spirit—whether so abundant as to make a magician or merely that which sustains us, is incorruptible in such a fashion; it is what makes us entities of free will and individualism rather than simpler, sheep-like creatures. Emotion is born from within; it might be awakened by art or oration or beauty, but it cannot be forced upon us from without. I could no more make Captain Hartnell love Leopoldina than—" A flush came over Elsabeth and she looked away from both Archers, leaving them to imagine where her thoughts had flown. For Persephone, Elsabeth's speech reflected on Hartnell's lack of fondness for Persephone herself and her ill-treatment there, treatment which she only now appreciated the potential horrors of, and could only now begin to truly be thankful for her brother's interference.

Elsabeth's sudden cessation of words cut Fitzgerald Archer as deeply, for he imagined that, had she continued, she would have spoken of the impossibility of making herself love him. As she looked away, so too did he, with a regret and sorrow as deep as any he had ever known. Elsabeth saw this from the corner of her eye, and thought he turned away for all the reasons that he ought to: she, like Matilda, would never be considered eligible again; the words that had nearly flown from her lips were to equate Hartnell's loving Leopoldina with the likelihood of Elsabeth herself winning back Archer's affections, a whimsy she had not even fully acknowledged harbouring.

Before the silence betwixt the three of them, Archers and Dover alike, became too obvious, Mr Penney rose heavily and spoke. "Your father writes that they have gone to Brighton, of all the cursed places; it is half a country away from us. But I see no other choice: I will go there myself, and apply a pressure that we will hope this Hartnell creature cannot deny. Mr Archer, I must thank you for your hospitality, but I think it best if I myself leave at once, and the ladies depart for Oakden in the morning."

"I must agree. I also must insist, Mr Penney, that you take my own carriage and horses; they will be faster than any hack you can hire. I will join you, in fact, at least until we are near to London, where I am afraid I have had urgent business arise. I know, Persephone," he said to his sister as she once more cried out with dismay. "I had intended to wait until morning to tell you, as to not spoil the evening, but if Mr Penney is to leave at once, it is only sensible for me to accompany him."

"But you are only just back! Your business had concluded!"

"And yet I cannot stay."

"You must not let us keep you, no, Mr Archer. I am certain it is only suitable for us to remove ourselves from under your roof at once; we will call our carriage and return to the inn for the night."

"That is not necessary, Miss Dover. The morning will be soon enough. Mr Penney, we will leave within the half-hour. Ladies, good night." Archer bowed to each of them, then left, Mr Penney in his wake, to call for the carriage and his belongings to be packed once more for travel.

"It is a wonder he can bear the thought of a long carriage-ride with Mr Penney," Elsabeth said bitterly, if quietly, to her aunt, "though perhaps Uncle is less stained with our dishonour than the rest of us, being only related through marriage."

"You cannot blame him, Elsabeth. This is...this is unspeakable business."

"I blame Leopoldina, and that wretched man Hartnell," Elsabeth replied with heat. "I truly do not know what to do, Aunt. Even if he can somehow be prevailed upon to marry her, there is nothing preventing him from carrying on with his seduction and gambling. He will leave her, or even worse, he will not, and she will be dragged further and further down whilst the rest of us are forced to either be tarred with her or cut ourselves off from her entirely. She has ruined the family. Damn the girl!" she cried with sudden fury. "Why could she have not waited just a little longer? We are so close here to so much she wanted, and now she has thrown it all away!"

"Not all of it." Miss Archer spoke tremulously, but with increasing certainty. "Miss Elsabeth, Mrs Penney, you must choose some of our books to bring with you on your journey to Oakden. We are already agreed that the books must be copied, and if you cannot stay—and you cannot, not for my reputation's sake but for your family's support—then you must take some of them with you to copy when you have arrived home. In the meantime, you will have days of study; not comfortable days, perhaps, but days nonetheless, and in those days, you will surely be able to find something that will help to rectify this situation. Spells of forgetfulness, or of eliding; you may not be able to cast glamours, but we are already creatures in the habit of allowing unpleasantries to pass us by unnoticed. Perhaps there is something to emphasise that; you will take the books, and study and find an answer.

"You must," Miss Archer concluded more softly. "You must, for your sister Matilda's sake; you must for my own, for I was all too close to being lost as they both now seem to be. You have said we might take these books and with them change the world, Miss Elsabeth. Let us begin here. Find a way to make it fade, or find a way to throw it so boldly in Society's faces that they will be unable to do anything but accept it."

(53)

To study within the confines of a carriage was no easy feat, but Mrs Penney and Elsabeth both found it to be easier than dwelling on the horror that awaited them at Oakden. Mrs Dover had, by Mr Dover's account, taken to her bed; Elsabeth did not expect her to have risen from it by the time they arrived. Nor could Ruth, the sole bastion of uncorrupted sense birthed in the Dover household, be expected to have arrived to take matters in hand; she was far too near her time, and, indeed, Elsabeth had every expectation of hearing upon their arrival at Oakden that there was a son or daughter Cox now in the world. Rosamund toured Europe; Elsabeth did not even know with certainty where she was, nor did she have any expectation of the dire news reaching Mrs Webber until—Elsabeth hoped with all diligence—after the matter was settled. And Matilda would be heart-broken; there was no chance of calm or reason from her. Had there been two other sisters still left at home, or even Sophia Enton to call upon for support, Mr Dover might well have travelled to London or Brighton in search of the eloped pair, but he could not leave a household so shaken. These were the thoughts that gnawed Elsabeth's mind when she left off her studies; these, and disquieting recollections of Mr Archer, of his generosity and geniality. Had he only shown more of that nature at Newsbury; but those were fruitless dreams, and so Elsabeth studied until she could keep her eyes open no longer, thence to dream of magic.

A week of hard travel saw them to Oakden, where Elsabeth's departure from the carriage was met by the sobbing embrace of a younger sister and a grim kiss on the brow from a father who had aged years in the weeks she had been gone. An arm around each of them, and Mrs Penney at Mr Dover's other side, they retired to the sitting room, where Mr Dover reported once more all that had passed, and carried on by saying, "It seems that there is some question whether they have gone to Brighton after all; there are no reports from the regiment there that anyone has seen Hartnell, and we have not asked about Leopoldina. We hold some thread of hope that they might yet be married, and that the untowardness of it all might be overlooked."

"Is it possible, Papa?" Elsabeth asked. "He would not marry—another—without the considerable fortune at her disposal; surely he cannot be made to marry Dina, who has nothing."

"I have done badly by all of you" was Mr Dover's response to this. "I ought to have laid aside some portion of my income each year, my dear, that we all might have some greater means of support. We are fortunate beyond measure that Rosamund and Ruth have done so well—and do not look at me so, Elsabeth; I hear what it is I say when I think of Mr Cox as having done well. But there is no denying that she *has* done well, exceptionally well given our expectations, and Mr Cox, magnanimous soul that he is, had no care for any portion of the inheritance due to her upon marrying. He has a living already; why should a portion of Oakden matter now, when it will all be his later?"

"It will be his son's!" Matilda interjected then. "Elsabeth, you cannot yet know, for we have only received the letter today! Ruth has had a boy, whom they have named Jonathan, after Papa. Oakden will be *his*!"

A great gasp escaped through Elsabeth's lips, and, for some little while, she was overcome with glad tidings made even gladder in the face of calamity. News that there was a son at last to inherit Oakden, that it should not likely pass directly into Mr Cox's hands, and that surely any boy expected to inherit a dear old manor house should also be expected to spend many long and happy days there as he grew up, could not have fallen on ears happier to hear it than Elsabeth's that day. Mrs Penney shared her delight, and Matilda, greatly daring, intruded upon Mr Dover's library only to return with a bottle of sherry, which was shared around in celebration. For a little time, there was talk of nothing more than the wonder of a grandson, nephew and heir, and when conversation returned—as it inevitably must—to the troublesome Leopoldina, the rich wine eased that discussion, too.

"Rosamund has no need for her inheritance either," Mr Dover went on. "Mr Webber would not hear of it, in fact, not with four other daughters for us to tend to. So, there are two parts, and Leopoldina's own, that might be settled on Hartnell to make him marry her, but I do not like to think of how unfair that is to you, my dear Elsabeth, or you, my good Tildy."

"Do not think of me for a moment," Elsabeth replied. "If I marry, it will be to a man who does not care if I have money; if I do not, then I will be content here in Oakden, and will not cost you the earth with my fanciful desires for lovely things. Think of Matilda, Papa; take what inheritance is left and apply it to her if need be, but we must all be aware that unless Hartnell is made to marry Dina, there will be no other marriages at all. We would be fools to begrudge Dina that inheritance, when it is all that stands between her and ruin."

"Mr Penney has gone to find them," Mrs Penney said. "You must join him, brother; together, the two of you must be able to press sense into the Captain."

"I have only been waiting for your arrival before I left," confessed Mr Dover. "I will leave in the morning. Elsa, I am sorry to ask, but your mother will need attending to. She is apoplectic with the sorrow of never seeing her youngest again, whilst I am equally so over the poor management I have had of this family.

It is, I know, too late now to correct my errors, but know that I will forever regret my carelessness, and the toll it has taken on all of you."

"Papa, it is..." Elsabeth was too honest to wholly exonerate him and, in the end, could only sigh. "It is done, if not yet over. We will somehow carry on, and, in time, it will be resolved. You have not written to Rosamund, have you? She does not know? It would only distress her, and there is no reason to ruin her wedding tour."

"No; it seemed a waste of her joy to pull her into such a sordid mess when there is nothing at all she can do for it. I do not like to think what will come of all this, Elsabeth; I do not like to wonder what I will end up owing as the price of my own follies and indiscretions."

"It is too late to worry about that, John. You might have thought of it twenty years ago, but you did not, and as we have no magic for time-turning—" Mrs Penney fell into silence at Elsabeth's thoughtful, warning look, but Mr Dover, unaware of the books they had brought, could only allow himself a broken laugh.

"Had I such magic, I would work such changes as to make our lives unrecognisable."

"Would you?" Mrs Penney glanced at the two daughters present before returning her attention to her brother. "Would you, and risk all that you now know and love?"

"Perhaps not," Mr Dover said, softening. "But it is as well that no such magics are known, for their abuse would be irresistible. Elsabeth, to your mother now, and myself to my packing, and you will stay on, Felicity, will you not? Until I return and can send you back to your husband, or, better yet, until I bring him here to you."

"Of course, brother. Matilda, am I wrong in guessing that you have had the run of the household in Mrs Dover's convalescence? Very good; show me what you have done, and, until Mrs Dover's recovery, I will do no more than offer guidance should you require it." Mrs Penney rose and, with Matilda eager to show her ability in running the household, departed; Elsabeth, making to follow them, was stopped by the sound of her father's voice.

"Do you condemn me entirely, my dear Elsabeth?"

Surprised, Elsa turned to see him gazing pensively aside, unwilling to meet her eyes. Her natural urge was to run to him, to kneel at his side as a child would and to answer with adoring comfort, but, after a single step toward him, she found she could go no farther. Her answer came slowly, with more consideration than salve behind it. "No, Papa, I do not. Not entirely. Had you been more lenient last summer in the aftermath of the bridge, I might have held you in considerable censure indeed. But you were not: Leopoldina was made then to pay the consequences of her actions, and to spend a quiet winter that ought to have shaken some of the romance out of disobedience and selfish behaviours. She has been spoilt, it is true; she is Mamma's favourite, and encouraged in silliness because of it, but even Mamma was obliged to recognise, however briefly, that Dina was quite in the wrong last summer, and even Mamma did not object on any material level to the penance of a quiet winter. Look at the good those quiet months did Matilda: that was the right and proper course of action for you to pursue then, and that it has failed so utterly reflects, I think, almost wholly on Dina."

"And if I had done differently in all the years of your childhood, would we have still ended in this terrible place?"

"There is no knowing, Papa. I will allow you some of the blame, and Mamma an equal part. I will even take a part myself, as I knew better than anyone how wretched a creature Captain Hartnell could be. I thought he was gone from this household when I broke with him, and so did not think it necessary to warn you; now, knowing I was wrong, I wish dearly that I had spoken. Hartnell must also be assigned a portion of the blame, for no officer or gentleman should behave in such an unseemly manner, but in the end, Papa, I cannot release Leopoldina from responsibility for her own actions, nor the foolishness that prevents her from seeing or being concerned by how those actions reflect upon and affect her family. There is guilt enough to go around. I do not condemn you any more than any of the rest of us."

Before she had finished this measured speech, Mr Dover's gaze had returned to her in sorrowful appreciation. "When you went away with Mrs Penney, Elsabeth, I was sorry for the loss of my dear girl. I see now that she has left me entirely, and that a woman of sense and compassion has returned in her place. Thank you, my dear, for doing me the honour of treating me as your equal, and speaking to me as another adult, rather than as my fond daughter. I think I will sit here a while longer and reflect on what you have said, and whether I am worthy of the forgiveness you imply."

"We do not forgive people because they are worthy, Papa. We forgive them because we love them, and because it gives us peace within ourselves to do so." Elsabeth crossed to Mr Dover and kissed his forehead, and only then, finally, went to tend Mrs Dover and her nerves.

(54)

"My Elsabeth! My dearest, darling girl! My rock; however have I carried on without you these past dreadful days! Do not abandon me, my sweetest Elsa; I am surely never to recover and, in my frailty, must have the strength of one daughter whose heart is true, as my darling Leopoldina's could not be! Oh, Elsabeth, what is to become of us? Mr Cox will turn us out; we have had a letter from him condemning us all roundly and your father most of all—"

"Mr Cox cannot turn us out so long as Papa lives, and while he is as shaken as any of us are in this regard, I do not believe him in any immediate danger," Elsabeth replied placidly. "As for what will become of us, that remains to be seen, Mamma, and as this is the third time this morning that I have said all of this to you, I shall not stir myself to say it again. I believe your nerves are in a state because you have put yourself to some effort to keep them there; instead, you should drink your tea and take some exercise, which will do you far more good than lying in bed, grasping at vapors."

"Heartless child!" gasped Mrs Dover, and sank once more into a shivering, tear-ridden shape beneath the covers, where she would almost certainly remain until she judged Elsabeth had suffered long enough for her sharpness. Then she would rouse herself to accept an apology Elsabeth had not previously, and would not now, offer, and the whole of the performance would begin again.

Elsa had been subjected to this behaviour for the entirety of the afternoon before and some two or three hours that morning since rising and seeing Mr Dover off to London. In that time, she had gained a new appreciation for Tildy's patience, for she, poor child, had been her mother's primary nursemaid for the full fortnight since Dina's elopement. She was to be commended and, if at all possible, relieved for an equal length of time from her duties. The prospect of remaining at Mrs Dover's side for that length of time was more than dismaying but mitigated somewhat by the presence of the books of magic, for Mrs Dover did not care in the least what her nurses attended to when she herself was not demanding their full regard.

She was well into a new examination of one of those books when a tentative knock sounded at Mrs Dover's door. Elsabeth, curious, rose to open it, and found the housemaid, Margaret, burdened with a curious combination of apology and sympathy. "Miss Enton is here to see you, Miss Elsabeth. I told her you might not be able to go from Mrs Dover's side—"

"Go!" shrieked Mrs Dover from beneath the bedclothes. "Go, wretched child! Show me how not one of my daughters cares for my nerves; I am sure that I will carry on quite well here on my own, abandoned by those who ought to love me the most. A child's passionate heart will carry her into the arms of friendship and—and—and *lovers*," she wailed, "while an old and lonely mother waits at home in desperation, but think nothing of me! Go! I will surely be no worse than I am now when—*if!*—you deign to return—!"

Beneath this caterwauling, Margaret's expression of sympathy deepened. "I will stay with her a while, Miss."

"Left with the help!" Mrs Dover howled, and Elsabeth, perfectly balanced between gratitude toward Margaret and rueful amusement at Mrs Dover, embraced the former and hurried downstairs to greet Sophia.

Miss Enton stood at the foot of the stairs, looking up with a pull to her mouth that Elsabeth thought echoed her own. "I hear Mrs Dover is in fine form," Sophia murmured as Elsabeth ran into her arms, and, for a few breathless moments, they shared the laughter of two who had been friends since childhood, and knew every wart and wrinkle of the other's family. "I came the moment I heard you had come home, as I have missed you greatly, but what on earth has happened, Elsabeth? What has Mrs Dover in such a state?"

"You must promise not to breathe a word to anyone, not even Miss Webber," Elsabeth first insisted, and knew she was not wrong to imagine a moment's hesitation on Sophia's part. Her friend looked exceedingly well, just as she had every time Elsabeth had seen her since Christmas, but it could not be pretended that she was happy to think of keeping secrets from Julia Webber. "Please," Elsabeth continued more soberly. "I fear my family's reputation rests on it."

"Good Lord," Sophia said in measured tones, then cut to the thrust of it: "What has Dina done, then? I will say nothing, Elsa; I could not do your family any harm."

"I knew you could not. Come, let us retire to my bedroom, as I do not know if I can as yet relate the story without tears." In very little time, they had done so, and in a little more the story was told.

At its conclusion, Sophia sighed. "Mrs Dover is in finer form than I might have imagined, then; I would not have been surprised if she had been rendered unable to complain, so great is this calamity. Elsabeth, I am so sorry, and sorrier still when I think I had come to share happy news of my own."

"You are engaged?" Elsabeth asked in delight, only to receive a look so peculiar from Sophia that, not knowing why, she blushed. "No, I see that you are not. Forgive me; it seemed the most likely source of happiness, knowing as I do how you are... were...so concerned about being a burden on your parents. Tell me, as I dare not guess again."

"I no longer fear that fate," Sophia replied. "I have grown, Elsabeth; I know myself now, and I dare say that if I must, I shall cut my hair and don a red coat, and join a regiment to pay my own way. Oh, do not look at me so, Elsa! There are less drastic measures to be taken first, although I think I would make a better soldier than governess, and, at any rate, none of those is necessary. Julia has written to Robert and spoken of her intention not to marry. After an exchange and an assurance of her happiness with me, he has gladly released control of her inheritance to her. We are thinking of touring Europe in the autumn, or perhaps even going so far as Egypt and Turkey."

A blush, encouraged by her rapidly beating heart, seemed permanently fixed upon Elsabeth's cheeks, although a cool awkwardness curled through her chest at the same time. "Her happiness with *you*, Sophia? And...and she will not marry, and... nor will you? Not...conventionally? And yet, would I be wrong to imagine that...that your tour of Europe might be, like Rosamund's, a...wedding tour?"

Now a blush leapt to Sophia Enton's cheeks, and, for the first time since she had known Miss Webber, a discomfiture came over her. She glanced away, then with pretended bravery—for Elsa knew her well enough to see that Sophia only pretended at it, though the pretense might be driven by personal determination—replied, "You would not be wrong to imagine such a thing."

"I am a fool," Elsabeth declared then. "A perfectly blind fool, and all the more so because Aunt Penney saw it herself at Rosamund's wedding, and I could not see it even when she called my attention to it. You are in love with Miss Webber, and she with you! How extraordinary!"

"It is not *so* extraordinary," Sophia protested in embarrassment and defiance and laughter, and then with greater defiance at Elsabeth's laugh. "But it is not, Elsa! There are more men and women of Society who prefer romance with their own sex than you would imagine! More than I would have imagined, and perhaps more than I might have ever known had Rosamund not fallen ill that night."

"What on earth has Rosamu—oh, *dear*. I recall now that you

did not return to your own room—oh, *dear*, Sophia! *Sophia!* Sophia, I believe I am shocked! And giddy, perhaps, and—and you *are* happy?"

"I am," Sophia replied with a shyness unlike herself, and Elsabeth instantly embraced her.

"Then, truly, I am happy. I may take some little while to recover from astonishment; I have not previously known—or been aware I knew!—any ladies with Sapphic tendencies. Indeed, I would never have guessed *you*, Sophia—"

"Had I never met Miss Webber, perhaps I would have never guessed it myself. Since my enlightenment, I have wondered a time or two about *you*, Elsabeth; you have never shown any especial preference for any gentleman—"

"Oh," Elsabeth said in surprise. "No, or: I do not think so, at least. If so, I have certainly not encountered my Miss Webber, and I think any curiosity I might have—and I confess to being curious now, Sophia!—is of a textbook nature. *Oh!* Sophia! The texts! I must tell you! Oh, but no, you must want to talk—"

"Most dearly!" cried Sophia, "but now I am alight with curiosity, and so we must exchange our stories a tidbit at a time, that we are both satisfied. What texts?"

For the second time that morning, a story, albeit a happier one, poured from Elsabeth's lips, and for Sophia, nothing would be done that she investigate one of the grimoires herself, in hopes of being able to read it. She could not, and laughed to find she had hoped to be able to. "I would never have considered myself eager to work magic, but if all else has changed, why not that, too?"

"Why not, indeed," Elsabeth replied, then paused as a thought came to her. "Sophia, you have just spoken of a—a society within Society, have you not? Of those you have come to know who pursue discreet love affairs like your own?" At Sophia's nod, she continued. "Do you suppose—might any of them be equally discreet in *other* affairs? I wonder if a trust built upon sharing one secret might allow some few to make their sorcery known, if one seemed open to it? I feel, Sophia, that it will not be so very long before we Dovers are openly known as magicians, and if even one soul should be bold enough to approach you for your friendship with me, we might, bit by bit, find ourselves a—a school, or a society of its own...?"

"Find or found?" asked Sophia, but she was disinclined to quibble over words, and nodded her agreement. "It cannot hurt to try. Although I think it would be wiser to wait until this business with Dina is resolved. There is no sense in adding complications to already complicated lives."

"You are very right. What will Miss Webber think of all this, Sophia? Not of Dina; I can imagine well enough what she would say *there*. But of sorcery and sorcerers."

"I think she will not like it at all," Sophia said candidly, "but Rosamund is already married to Robert, and he has given Julia the freedom to pursue her own desires; she would be petty to condemn him for his own. In time, she will become, if not comfortable with it, at least accustomed to it, and that will be enough for peace."

"I confess that while I might have once thought peace to be dull, I would be grateful for a little of it now."

"I do not foresee it, Elsabeth. I do not think peacefulness is in your stars; I think you are too active a soul. I think for peace, you would need to set aside these tomes, and perhaps your concerns for Dina and Matilda in particular, and perhaps—for true peace—you would even need to allow me to fade from your life, and while it may be fearful vanity speaking, I like to think you would not want that to happen."

"You know I do not. You are as a sister to me, Sophia, and if I cannot cast away Leopoldina even with her wretched decisions, I could hardly turn my back on you, who has at least had the good sense to fall in love with someone wealthy."

Sophia laughed. "How ruthless and pragmatic you've become, Elsa."

"I believe I am only following the line you once drew for me. The purpose of marriage, in your eyes, was financial security;

love was an unlooked-for benefit. Therefore, nothing could be more secure than love *and* wealth, or am I wrong?"

"I can hardly dispute it now, when you throw my own words back at me! No, Elsabeth, you are not wrong, but neither am I: you are not destined for peace, and so, I await the culmination of these tumultuous events that surround you with interest."

(55)

THAT HER ACTIVITIES COULD BE A SOURCE OF CONCERN—EVEN ruin—for her family was not a thought made to enter Leopoldina Dover's pretty head. She was by nature made up of too many other concerns, all of which save her practise of magery had been implanted and fostered by a fond mother: a concern for dressing well, a concern for gentlemanly attention, a concern for gossip and a concern for having her own way were all that had ever mattered to her, and, when thwarted in any one of those concerns, she had not learnt a consideration for others but a petulance best suited to children. To her mind, she had been thwarted in the matter of Captain Hartnell, and so, upon his release from Elsabeth's dubious charms—if they had not all been so certain that sorcery could not produce love spells, Dina might have thought Elsabeth to have used such a thing, in order to play with Captain Hartnell's—*David's,* as she now so affectionately thought of him—affections—upon his release from Elsabeth's charms, it was only natural that he should return his attentions to the one who had most desired them: Leopoldina herself.

In him lay the best of all worlds: handsome, an officer and a magician to boot. He might have been wealthier, Dina conceded, but his gift of magic outweighed all of that, most especially as he was privy to the Dover secret, and so, for the first time in her life, Dina did not need to hide. As spring had turned to summer, she met with the Captain in public as often as Society would allow, and far more often in private than anyone, most of all Mr Dover, suspected. Not even Matilda was aware of these private meetings, as Dina declared a desire to follow in Elsabeth's footsteps in a literal sense, and began to spend her days enjoying long constitutionals. It did not occur to her to wonder how an officer of the army might escape his own duties as easily as Captain Hartnell seemed to; all she had a care for was that she wanted him, and he was there. They often met at a secluded bend in the river, away from the road and the curious gazes of passers-by, and hid beneath a long-branched tree that protected them from wind and rain and sun alike.

Beneath that green fall of leaves, Hartnell found an eager student of magic: Leopoldina Dover thirsted for what he knew, and if she was not so swiftly susceptible to his charms as he might have hoped, it was inevitable that she should succumb. She spoke incessantly of Brighton and its delights, of her dreams of a life beyond Bodton, and her chafing at the boundaries placed upon her by being surrounded by those who had always known her; in all of this, Hartnell saw the lever he required to move the world. A murmur here, a sigh there, a wishful speech about how their time together must end, and soon, Dina settled on the idea of elopement as if it was her own.

They could not, Hartnell demurred; he could not care for her in the style to which she was accustomed. La! she proclaimed: nothing could be worse than being without him; poverty, which they should certainly not be subjected to, would be the greatest joy, so long as she was his. But, oh, he was wiser, and had been poor; but no, do not think of it: in Brighton, nothing will matter. So, to Brighton they went, Leopoldina joyously embracing the sea air and Hartnell alike, and, out of reach of Mr Dover's strictures, making more freely with her magic than she had ever done before. She wanted nothing else; in time, she would of course become Mrs Hartnell, for it never crossed her mind that any man might willingly partake of a gentlewoman he did not intend to marry, and until then, she was free to live, and do magic, as she wished.

Hartnell's magics were all practical or war-like, but she needed nothing more than her natural talent to make sea spray dance in the wind, or to wear droplets of water in her hair like glittering jewels. There were other soldiers and their women in Brighton; Dina's bright spirit made her friends easily, and she could not see the class of those she befriended. Nor did she wish to, when amongst them proved a woman of rough words and gentle hands who taught Leopoldina the binding of a wound with no more than magic, and who supervised the near-painless arrival of another woman's squalling baby girl into the world. It was bloody, messy work, but her talent was to be admired, Dina told her darling Hartnell, and took no notice that his interest seemed to be more for the gambling table than her tale. She leaned over him, blowing on the dice for luck, and saw nothing of Hartnell's twisted mouth as her kisses did nothing to improve his roll.

It was there that Mr Fitzgerald Archer found them, to the dismay of one, the delight of the other, and the equal surprise of both. "Mr Archer!" Dina cried gladly. "I could not have imagined to see you in Brighton; how splendid it is to reacquaint myself with such a fine gentleman! Pray tell me, have you come to enjoy the last of the summer seas? I believe the water is now as warm as it can ever be, and I will tell you that I am very bold and have gone into it more than once."

"You are bold, Miss Leopoldina," Archer agreed gravely, and then, with a hope he did not truly feel, asked, "or is it Mrs Hartnell now?"

Merry laughter was all that met this question. "It shall be someday, Mr Archer; we are in no hurry to wed, though it will certainly come to pass. What a fine couple we are, would you not agree? My Hartnell so handsome and myself a pretty creature, if I do confess it myself!"

"Fine indeed," Archer replied, and to Hartnell, whose sole ambition throughout the whole of this discussion appeared to be nothing more than a wish to escape, Archer said, "A word, David," in such dark tones that no one save Leopoldina could miss their warning. Hartnell, having already been obliged to leave the gambling table, could only accept Archer's invitation, and Dina was left to spend a happy hour or two with the other ladies of her station.

"I cannot long be gone from the table, Archer. I am up a little, and in some dire need of money, so I must not risk what I have taken today," began Hartnell, but that light and easy air faded as Archer turned an expression incredulous with anger upon the Captain.

"I need not even ask *why* you are in need of money, only how much you have already lost."

"Some one thousand pounds," Hartnell replied in as best a careless tone as he could command. "I have been obliged to leave the regiment on those debts, and perhaps one or two of honour, so why should I not come to Brighton, and with such a charming companion as Dina? I should say she quite insisted, Archer; you cannot hold me responsible for that silly creature's follies."

"As I might not have held you responsible for Miss Archer's? Let us pretend even for a moment that I did not, David. Even if I do not, you are wholly responsible for your own. Debts! Why did you not marry the girl and get her inheritance for your debts?"

"God," Hartnell replied with feeling. "Condemn myself to a lifetime of that empty-headed nattering, all for the sake of a few hundred pounds? I could never."

"And yet you shall."

"Or what, Archer? Australia? That is an old threat and carries no weight. You cannot care enough for this foolish girl's fate to buy me off a second time, and even if you should, why would I not come to you again and again, each time I was in need of money, if your sympathies for such a creature run so deep?"

Archer spoke slowly. "Australia is not so old a threat as that, David; I should find no sorrow in watching a ship sail with you reluctantly aboard in the morning. And it is true, perhaps, that Leopoldina Dover is not my especial concern or problem, save that I made no move to protect her or her family from you when I ought to have."

"Did you not? Was Miss Elsabeth Dover not sufficiently informed as to your opinions of my character?"

"She was, but only under duress, and knowing what she does of her sister's nature, she rightfully concluded that to speak ill of you would only send Miss Leopoldina into your arms. I ought to have spoken to Mr Dover; I might have done many things that I did not. That is in the past. I am quite comfortable with Australia being in your future, David, and my only hesitation is on behalf of Miss Leopoldina's reputation. Therefore, I will pay your debts, purchase your commission to the next rank and stand over you to see that you will marry her, upon which time you shall live quietly, within your means, as her husband."

"And if I do not? Will you marry her yourself to save her reputation?" Hartnell's ready laughter proved what he thought of that idea.

"I will find another officer—her sister Matilda will know to whom I ought to speak—who will be willing to overlook Miss Leopoldina's indiscretion and, for the amount I will stand him, declare his tolerant and undying passion for her. He will come to London, where Miss Leopoldina will be found to have been staying with her aunt and uncle, and plead for her hand in marriage, which she will accept while you, David, live the short and harsh life of a criminal in Australia. You are a thousand pounds in debt; I will not even have to trump up charges to see you away from England's shores."

"You would not," Hartnell replied, but his conviction wavered. "*She* would not. She loves me."

"She fancies excellent shoulders in a red coat. I do not imagine it is of great concern to her whose shoulders fill that coat."

"You impugn the lady's honour!"

"The lady," Archer said steadily, "has done that quite well enough on her own."

"I will write to the newspapers! I will destroy her life and her family's!"

"You will be a convict on a long and dangerous journey, and I am sure there will be a hardened soul or two who will take a great dislike to you. It would be of no real worry to me if you were found missing from the ship's roster some stormy morning."

"You *wouldn't*. A gentleman would never!"

"I doubt there will be many gentlemen on your ship. Pack your belongings, David, and choose your destination: wedded bliss or a watery grave. It is of very little concern to me which you prefer."

"We are going to London," Hartnell said to Dina some little while later. "Your aunt and uncle have expressed a desire to see us, and we shall be wed there, with proper family attendance."

"Oh, London! How splendid, my dear Hartnell! I shall miss Brighton tremendously; we will have to return soon, and often! But it will be lovely to see my dear Aunt Penney, and I cannot think but that she will be so pleased to be the first to offer us felicitations upon our marriage! And what fun it will be to return to Bodton a married woman! Oh, Matilda will be so envious! How lucky we are to have found each other, my sweet Hartnell; how sad for those who do not share such a bond as we do."

Mr Archer, subjected to a full day of similar commentary on the journey to London—for he dared not allow them to make their own way there for fear of losing the groom—conceded himself to be astonished that Hartnell had chosen marriage over Australia, even with the possibility of not surviving the voyage made clear to him. He could not, however, find sympathy for the Captain; at best, he felt relief that some other poor soul would not have to be bribed into marrying Leopoldina Dover. Such a fate, Archer felt, was one that should be consigned only to the deserving, and David Hartnell had proven himself most deserving.

The wayward young couple were presented at the Penney house with as much decorum as possible. Archer placed Hartnell in the care of the most likely-looking of the footmen with the promise of a considerable bonus if Hartnell should not manage to leave the house, put Leopoldina in her aunt's capable hands, and took himself to speak to Mr Penney on the topic of the upcoming wedding's costs.

"I believe you are quite successful in trade, and I have no doubt that you are both willing and able—as well as feeling yourself morally obliged—to handle the necessary finances of this affair. Mr Penney, I must ask you to perform a charade, for I intend to be the recipient of all costs in this business, but wish you to be the face of it. No," Archer said, "do not speak; only listen, and, when I am done, you may proceed with all your objections. I have been aware of Hartnell's deficiencies for years and, more, once allowed him to slip through a net that would have saved all of you this trouble. I regret that now but cannot undo it; instead, I will rest easier knowing I have made what recompense I could in this unfortunate situation. You will protest, but I would be no gentleman at all if I did not act now where I ought to have many years ago."

"I cannot allow this, Mr Archer. You have no obligation to us; neither Leopoldina nor Captain Hartnell are your charges, whilst Dina is my family. Moreover, even if I were willing to allow you to ease the financial strain—which I am not!—I could never sit easily with then taking the credit for it myself."

"But you have the right of it," Archer said instantly. "I have no visible obligation, only that which I already know rests upon my soul; to include myself as a visible party in this affair would be a dreadful public curiosity. We might rely on my old friendship with Hartnell to explain how and why I went to fetch them—that, and it is surely more subtle for a gentleman of Hartnell's own age to approach them than a more obviously older relation—but no one must be allowed to imagine that I have any further business to do with it all."

"For your own reputation," Mr Penney hazarded, as a certain suspicion began to form.

Archer allowed himself the briefest of smiles. "I believe my reputation precedes me and I am unlikely to be considered as a party to this folly, but certainly, Mr Penney. The crudest of minds might conclude that it was I who spirited away Miss Leopoldina, and that Captain Hartnell has been acquired to extract me from a situation I no longer wish to pursue. Because I am wealthy, and a man, these follies would be forgiven if not forgotten, but I would indeed prefer not to allow even the suggestion to take root in any small minds. That is an excellent supposition and will do nicely as a reason for your acquiescence, if a reason is required."

"I do not like it," Mr Penney said after a short pause.

"I would not expect you to. But you will agree, and tell no one?"

"I believe there may be one or two who should know, Mr Archer. I believe there may be one or two who might look more fondly upon you if they were to know what you are doing here."

"And that is why they must not know, Mr Penney," Archer replied with an introspection unlike himself. "Fondness ought to be earned, not bought; I have once in my life imagined that being of wealth and stature was enough to earn affection, but I was wrong. Those qualities buy affection from those weak enough or eager to sell it; true fondness is earned through worthy action of one who expects no reward in return."

"Then let it be known that I have grown fond of you, Mr Archer," said Mr Penny after another moment's pause. "It is perhaps bold of me to say so; I am not of your station, nor close enough to you in any way to be allowed a paternal pride, but it is true, and my admiration for you has deepened profoundly. I will participate in your charade, and we will put all of this sad business behind us."

(56)

The wedding was, by necessity, only sparsely attended: indeed, only the Penneys and Mr Archer were expected to witness it, but a favourable wind brought a ship home early, and Mrs Rosamund Webber, arriving at her aunt's home just after nine in the morning the day of the wedding, was informed of the goings-on and with all due haste took herself and Mr Webber to the chapel where the union was to take place at the ten o'clock hour.

It was thus that Leopoldina gave a glad scream and hearty embrace, and that Rosamund stood at her side as the vows were taken. It was thus, also, that the two married couples drove to Bodton together, with Rosamund considering Mr Archer's silent, pained presence at the wedding all the while.

Mr Webber, capitally glad to have encountered his close friend, had sensed nothing untoward regarding the quiet wedding, but Rosamund, reluctant to think the worst of anyone, could not find any measure of satisfaction in it, as no one in the Dover family had written to inform her of Dina's impending nuptials.

Nor were her concerns lessened as Dina exited the coach at Oakden before her: beyond the new Mrs Hartnell were the stoic faces of a distressed family; only Mrs Dover showed any sign of joy as she held first Leopoldina and then Hartnell in an embrace.

"But wait!" Dina cried. "I have brought you not only a husband for myself, but see who else has joined us! Mr Webber, Rosamund, do come forth; you are not meant to stay in the carriage forever!"

All the hope and happiness that might have been present for Dina's arrival now shone on the faces of the remaining Dover family. Mr Dover shook Mr Webber's hand, which he had not done with Captain Hartnell, and both Elsabeth and Matilda fell upon Rosamund with affection. "But how!" said Elsabeth. "You were meant to be gone half a year at least, and it is hardly three months since you left!"

"Mrs Webber has been easily fatigued," replied Mr Webber with an unmistakable pride, and under the implication of this news, Leopoldina was all but forgotten. Rosamund, full of blushes and laughter, was escorted to the sitting room, where she was treated with such solicitude as to render her without words. Mr Webber could and did speak, though, expressing their enjoyment of the travels they had taken, until Dina's growing agony at not being heard burst through his accounting in a flood not to be dammed. *She* was all tales of Brighton and London; *she* was all stories of dear Hartnell's new station, and, under all of it, Rosamund asked Elsabeth, softly, why Mr Archer had been at Dina's wedding, but none of the family had.

Elsabeth lost all colour, then found it again in a rush. "Mr Archer was in attendance?"

"Very much so; he stood at Captain Hartnell's side like a man prepared for a battle. What has happened, Elsabeth? Tell me the truth."

"You will not like the truth," Elsa replied, but, in as few and gentle words as possible, illuminated Leopoldina's folly. "Papa said he would not have them in the house," she concluded, "but your arrival has softened him a little. Oh, Rosamund, I am so glad you are home."

"If I were not already sitting, I would need to," Rosamund whispered. "Oh, Elsa, how could she have been so foolish? And how can she not see it?" As one, they looked to their youngest sister, who spoke endlessly about her dear Hartnell. Hartnell himself sat to the side with a modest smile and a soldier-straight spine, the two postures conflicting with one another.

"It is only ten days until we must leave for my dear Hartnell's post," Leopoldina said.

"Ten days!" echoed Mrs Dover in a dismay felt only by herself. "But my daughter, I cannot be without you so quickly! It is too little time! And you will be so far away!"

"It will be *years* before we see each other again, I suppose," Dina replied with a grandiose degree of tragedy. "You will have to write to me so often, Elsabeth, although I will hardly ever have time to write to you; married ladies are so busy, and there will be so many friends to make among the regiment wives! We must have a dance between now and then; we must, for so few here know of my marriage, and I cannot wait to hear Mrs Enton call me Mrs Hartnell! There are so many I long to hear say that name! Even your own dear sister, Mr Webber! To think that I should be married before her! Why, we must have her to dinner, and I shall sit above her at the table, for I am a married woman now."

"We will not have a dance," said Mr Dover at the very moment Mr Webber proclaimed, "A dance shall be held at Newsbury forthwith." They gazed at one another, Mr Webber stricken with a profound sense of distress that could only be alleviated by Mr Dover's sighed "Very well, at Newsbury, but do not imagine I will attend."

"However could you not, Papa?" exclaimed Dina in surprise that appeared wholly uncontrived. "Surely, you would not begrudge your married daughters a dance, or deny Mamma the pleasure!"

"Now, Mrs Hartnell," murmured the Mr of that pair, "do not pressure your father to do what does not suit him."

"I do not require your defence, Captain Hartnell," rejoined Mr Dover sharply, and, catching Rosamund's look of dismay, sighed a second time. "For your sake, Rosa, I will consider attending. Let it be a dance, though, and not the grand affair of a ball; we do not need such attention now."

"It will be as you wish," promised Mr Webber, who retreated then to Rosamund's side and sat wondering into what drama he had stepped, and how best to tender his apologies to Mr Dover's evident offence. He could not ask, though, for Elsabeth and Rosamund were deep in quiet discussion of Archer's presence at the Hartnell wedding, and this topic brought such pleasure to Mr Webber's heart that he was glad to dwell on it instead of the seeming unpleasantries bubbling beneath the surface of the Dover household.

"His cousin Miss Derrington is to be married soon," Webber offered. "We are not much acquainted with her, but perhaps we might invite her to our dance; the distance from Charington Place is not so very great as to keep her away! She might stay on a week or so; not *too* long, with her marriage pending, but a little while before she is away to Africa forever! I think Julia would like it, now that she herself has determined not to marry and there is no longer conflict betwixt her and Miss Derrington over Archer. Shall I ask?"

"I should like very much to see Miss Derrington again," Elsabeth replied slowly, "but she is a lady of great leisure, and I should hate to put her out, or cause Mr Archer any feeling that he himself might be expected to attend. Moreover, I am disinclined to offer Leopoldina any more glorious Society than we can rouse from Bodton; she does not deserve it, and although I doubt she will ever take note of any censure, neither would I be happy to show her any degree of evident approval."

"I will explain later," Rosamund murmured to Mr Webber, whose growing expression of consternation cleared into instant satisfaction. "In the meantime, we might issue an invitation for her to visit before she leaves for Africa, without including the pressure of the dance in our invitation. Then she and Elsabeth might have an opportunity to say their farewells in person, and yet avoid any unnecessary expectations of performing in public if she is disinclined to do so."

"Perfect. I should never have considered it myself; what ever would I do without you, Mrs Webber?" Mr Webber's smile was one of perfect happiness, and Elsabeth, despite all her own cares, was glad to smile at them both, and to hold Rosamund's hand as she confessed, "It is a relief to me that you have returned, Rosa. I would not burden you for the world, but to know you are nearby steadies me immeasurably. I feel we may all even survive Leopoldina, although I must write to Aunt Felicity and ask her what part Mr Archer has had in all of this, as I should never have imagined him willing to stand for Captain Hartnell."

"You may ask him yourself," Mr Webber said with an air of triumph. "I will invite him to Newsbury for our dance."

Elsabeth's smile became pained. "Please, hear Leopoldina's story from Rosamund first. You will then know why I feel some reluctance at encouraging you in that endeavour; suffice it to say I do not believe Mr Archer's sense of propriety would make it comfortable for him to attend a dance held, however loosely, in Dina's honour."

Mr Webber's questioning gaze lingered on Rosamund, who nodded, and he acquiesced at once. Their little party fell into silence, making Leopoldina's stories all the more the centre of attention; Elsabeth, in only a very little time, could no longer bear it, and rose to make her way out of the sitting room. To her surprise, Matilda followed to ask in a low, unhappy voice, "She is very dreadful, is she not? And I have been very like her."

"You were," Elsabeth replied with more honesty than gentleness. "You were very like her, but I should say this past year has changed you, Tildy. We had all hoped it might change Dina, but if it did, it was only to make her more like herself. And perhaps the same has happened to you: perhaps you have grown out of her shadow and into yourself, and found that you are a steadier soul than she. Indeed, with her less your star, there are things I would like to share with you, Matilda! I have learnt so much of sorcery, and some of it so recently—"

"Did I hear you speak of sorcery?" asked Captain Hartnell, emerging from the sitting room. "What could you have learnt, Elsabeth? I may call you Elsabeth now, may I not, as you are my sister? And where might you have learnt it?"

"From a doctor of war," Elsabeth replied truthfully enough. "Where do Army men learn their magic, Captain Hartnell? On the battlefield, or are you steeped in knowledge through study? I should like to see that: a regiment of scarlet, heads bent over scraps of paper like schoolboys. But it is easier to imagine military magic being tested in fire, although what use saving a falling bridge might be in battle, I do not know."

"Of great use," Hartnell conceded. "A bridge is always a vulnerable point, and its possession or destruction can turn the tide of a battle. What doctor?"

"Oh, a Doctor Thomas, or perhaps Hart; I can no longer recall clearly. I am sure he spoke to other officers at a ball and that I listened unashamedly. He spoke of creating a cannon ball from no more than mud and stones! Surely, that cannot be done, Captain; it is certainly not within my own providence."

"Nor should it be; a woman's magical arts ought to be gentler stuff. But it can be done, sister, and then thrown at such velocity as to have been ejected from a cannon. It is not an explosive; that requires another magic, and an incendiary device, but it is often not the explosion that causes the most damage in war. Doctor Thomas, you say? I do not know him."

"There must be hundreds of doctors in the army, Captain," Elsa replied disingenuously. "You cannot expect to know all of them, can you?"

"There are hundreds," Hartnell agreed, "but only a dozen or two who might know anything of magic, and those I am acquainted with should have more sense than to speak of military secrets in public."

Elsabeth clasped a hand to her heart. "Military secrets! Oh, Captain Hartnell, I should never have thought of it that way! I shall endeavour to say no more; how dreadful to think I may have inadvertently learnt or spoken of something that ought not be widely known! I am a-flutter and must lie down. Matilda, help me to my room."

Matilda, astonished, did as she was bid and, upon arriving in Elsabeth's room, gaped at her in bewilderment. "You became

Leopoldina, Elsa; I have never seen you so lack-witted in your life."

"I would not share my new knowledge of sorcery with him at any cost, Tildy, nor tell him whence it came. He is no more trustworthy than—" Here her imagination failed her and she nearly stomped a foot in exasperation. "He is not trustworthy. You must not reveal any of what I will tell or teach you to him, Matilda, nor to Dina. No: I am sorry, but Dina can no more hold her tongue than Mamma, and in the matter of magic, they cannot be given any greater knowledge than that which is native to them."

"Mamma has no magic," Matilda protested in confusion, and Elsabeth, hardly allowing herself to speak above a breath, said, "Thank heavens. Now, let me acquaint you with what I know, on the pain of your silence to Mr and Mrs Hartnell."

"It should be of little difficulty," Matilda replied in nearly as low a voice. "I have hardly managed a word to her since she has arrived, and none, I think, that she has heard. That is how it always was, is it not? But I did not see it before. How foolish I was."

"It is never foolish to love one's family," Elsabeth assured her. "But, in this instance, we must temper our love with a little sense. Now, first let me confess the details of Rosamund's illness in London...."

(57)

For a full week, two wholly separate families seemed to exist in the Dover household. One, consisting of the Hartnells and Mrs Dover, was endlessly involved in the important social activity of making calls and being visited. Captain Hartnell, who might not have preferred to participate in that business, found himself politely shut out of the other party's existence, with vague apologies indicating a concern for Rosamund's condition and other female matters being the reason for such exclusion. The shape of this excuse necessitated Mr Dover's expulsion from the bulk of activity as well, but he, privy to the actual nature of studies going on, and with his own free access to the books Elsabeth had brought, was content to play the role of an isolated father, and made no effort to bridge Hartnell's own isolation within the household.

Mr Webber, now acquainted with the Hartnells' folly, regretted, but could not renege on, his offer of a dance. With all dignity, he retreated from Oakden to prepare for the party, whilst happily leaving Rosamund amongst her sisters to study books of magic: each day she returned home more robust, her pregnancy less of a strain, and Webber could ask for nothing more. He played glad host to their arriving guests; Miss Derrington had chosen to accept their invitation and arrived just in time for the dance, attended by both her fiancé and her mother, although not, to Elsabeth's relief and chagrin, her cousin. Elsabeth had not written to her Aunt Penney, but, making a certain series of guesses of her own, had written the briefest of missives to Mr Archer himself; the whole of the letter contained only six words and the outer address: *Thank you; in gratitude, Elsabeth Dover.*

Unable to decide if Archer's refusal to attend or his innocence of its happening would be worse, Elsabeth put her letter out of mind and did not ask Mr Webber if Archer had been invited. Instead, she gladly embraced Miss Derrington at the earliest opportunity, and offered her felicitations on Annabel's engagement.

"Thank you," said that pleasantly languid lady. "It should never have come about without your assistance. I must ask you to visit us in Oyo, Elsabeth; I know it is an impossibly far distance to travel, but I should like so much for you to become acquainted with my homeland, as I have come to know yours, and most particularly because you are so much the instrument of my returning to it."

"I believe the very idea would give my mother apoplexy," Elsabeth confessed with a certain cheer. "I will make every attempt to visit you in a year or two, although I suppose, for a journey of such length, I might wish to stay beyond my welcome."

"It is not possible," Miss Derrington assured her, and tucked her arm into Elsabeth's to draw her closer. "I believe my mother has come with me for the express purpose of speaking to you, Elsa. If you wish, I will cause a distraction and allow you to flee."

Elsabeth laughed. "I am nearly tempted for the spectacle of your distraction, but I have faced your mother once before; I believe I can do so again without risking more than a scrap of pride. Is she very angry about your engagement?"

"Entirely. I have been obliged to sit through more lectures in the past three months than in all the previous dozen years combined, but I am much practiced at it and can allow it to wash over me as waves might. Now, if you will introduce me to the newly-weds, I will pay my respects and then retire to the comfort of that very fine chair beside the fire."

"Gladly," Elsabeth replied, but hesitated. "Will you do something for me, Miss Derrington? Ask Mr Swift that he forbear to mention his uncle, the battle surgeon. I made mention of him once and found Captain Hartnell to be unnaturally interested his identity. I should not like to get Doctor Swift into any kind of difficulty after the kindness he has done for us. There is no reason I can imagine that the topic might arise, but, to be certain, would you do this thing?"

"It is no trouble at all," Miss Derrington assured Elsabeth, and, in some little while, each of these things had been accomplished, with the fortunate intrusion of the first dance beginning before Mrs Hartnell had more than a moment or two to speak with Miss Derrington. Dina could not bear to miss even one dance, most particularly her first in public as a married woman, and Miss Derrington was left with the pleasant perception of a light-hearted and charming young woman in Mrs Hartnell, and was not subjected to any behaviours that might change that perception. Elsabeth watched with some trepidation as Mrs Dover was introduced to Lady Beatrice, but their conversation was so brief and agreeable that Elsabeth then wished she had been near enough to overhear what was said.

Only after Miss Derrington deigned to join Mr Swift on a turn around the dance floor did Lady Beatrice approach Elsabeth, and said without preamble, "I expect you know why it is I wish to speak with you."

Elsabeth, glancing toward Miss Derrington, inclined her head. "I suppose that I do, but I cannot say I have any regrets in the matter, madam."

"No regrets?" Lady Beatrice's voice remained at a perfectly civil level whilst simultaneously dropping into such frigidity that Elsabeth wondered there was not suddenly frost in the air. "No," Lady Beatrice went on, "I suppose you would not have regrets over upsetting a long-agreed-upon marriage, when you are the greatest beneficiary of it. How dare you speak so blatantly!"

Elsabeth disengaged her attention from the dancers to gaze at Lady Beatrice in astonishment. "I should think Mr Swift the greatest beneficiary, Lady Beatrice. I cannot imagine what I have gained."

"You cannot be serious. I have it on excellent authority that my nephew has made you an offer of marriage."

A breath expelled itself from between Elsabeth's lips with such force as to be considered a cough. "How astounding. Upon whose authority do you have this news, madam?"

"That is of no consequence. Do you deny it?"

"I should think it of very great consequence. If I am to find myself the subject of such remarkable gossip, I think it very important that I should know who likes to spread it."

"It *is* only gossip, then," Lady Beatrice said with some triumph. "I knew it could not be otherwise. He may have waited too long on marrying Annabel, but he could never align himself with a family so lowly as your own. Your sister is married to a vicar, for Heaven's sake."

"And another sister to a gentleman," Elsabeth said more heatedy, "and a third to an officer. I am the daughter of a gentleman, Lady Beatrice, and Mr Archer a gentleman himself. We differ in circumstance, perhaps, but not in station. And I must assure you that you are not mistaken; he has made me an offer, which I have declined."

Lady Beatrice's rigidity suggested she could not decide between offence that Archer had made the offer or offence that Elsabeth had refused it; the intelligence of both at once struck all blood from her face, leaving her beauty quite sallow for an enjoyably long moment. As she had done at Charington, Elsabeth found herself unable to resist pressing the advantage, and spoke again before Lady Beatrice had recovered herself. "I confess that my acquaintance with Mr Archer until that time had shown his manners to be too poor for me to imagine marrying him; were I not now acquainted with Misses Derrington and Archer, I should think it a broad family fault, but perhaps it is one that only strikes certain unfortunate individuals. Lady Beatrice, I cannot imagine we have anything left to say to one another. Good evening."

"You will not dismiss me!" cried Lady Beatrice in full face of the fact that Elsabeth, in turning away, was doing just that. Still, her curiosity outweighed her offence; she wanted very much to know what else Lady Beatrice might want to say, and so, Elsabeth turned back with an expression she knew to be as cool and aloof as any peer might maintain.

"I wish to have your word that you will not enter into any marriage contract with my nephew. I will not be satisfied until I have it."

A more unexpected demand could not have been made. Elsabeth, wondering what Lady Beatrice knew that she did not, gathered herself before replying. "I would think you have no need for worry on that front, madam. A gentleman, once thoroughly refused, does not often return to seek a second chance. Be that as it may, please be assured that I will accept or refuse a suitor as I choose, and not as demanded by family whose approval is not my concern."

"So, you *will* marry him!"

"I will not promise you that I won't," Elsabeth corrected. "I am in no way beholden to you, Lady Beatrice; you cannot suppose that you have some sway over my decisions, and it already appears you have none over your nephew. I suppose that is your fear, and why you have come to make this preposterous demand of me; if you cannot control him, you hope to intimidate me into the behaviour you prefer. I am not easily frightened, madam, and I am, I think, quite done with this conversation. Good evening." She swept away without looking back, although she did not deny that her path took her directly to the garden doors, where she hoped to pause and gather her breath; one did not have to be easily intimidated to require some measure of repose after facing down a member of the peerage! More, the topic upon which Lady Beatrice had been so focused lay beyond the edge of preposterous; there could be at this juncture no conceivable reason her Ladyship would think Mr Archer might intend to marry Elsabeth. Elsabeth could not fathom from whom Lady Beatrice might have heard such a tale, save from Archer himself; certainly, neither she nor Rosamund nor their Aunt Penney would have carried the supposition to her, and there was, to Elsabeth's knowledge, no one else besides Archer who even knew of his unfortunate proposal.

The name came to her thoughts so suddenly that it escaped her lips at the same moment: "Persephone. Oh, but *no*, she could not have, and even if she had, she is quite assured that there is no chance of the matter being resolved in—"

Her spoken thoughts were interrupted by a sudden, familiar voice crying out in gladness: "Elsabeth!" Matilda emerged from the garden teary-eyed and frightened, and ran to Elsabeth's welcoming arms. "I came out for air," she whispered. "He followed me, Elsa; I did not know what to do!"

"He—?" Before Elsa could speak further, *he* revealed himself: Captain Hartnell, languidly extracting himself from the same section of garden that Tildy had just fled.

"Sister! Thank heavens; I am glad you have found us. I happened on poor Matilda, lost in the gardens, and was attempting to persuade her back to the house when she—"

The rest of his careless explanation was lost beneath Tildy's gasp and the swift shake of her head. "That is not what happened, Elsabeth; that is not it at all! He—he told me—he said that betwixt Dina and myself, I was his much favoured, and that he regretted already that he had married where he had, and he—he tried—he said—"

"Nonsense." Hartnell assumed his most winsome expression as he approached to within a step or two of the sisters. "Hysterical child, misunderstanding a brother's love for passion. Elsabeth, you know me better than this; I should never—"

Elsabeth barked, "Silence!" and, to Hartnell's own apparent astonishment, he acquiesced. "I know you, Captain Hartnell, to be a liar and a gambler who is eager to seduce where he feels he will find profit. *Never* imagine that I would believe your word over my sister's. For Leopoldina's sake, I might keep this quiet, but that would allow you the opportunity to behave in this manner again, either with Matilda or some other unfortunate who might not be rescued by timely intervention. Let me see you, Matilda, poor child; are you hurt?"

"N-no. I d-do not believe so. Only—only frightened, Elsabeth; I did not want to kiss him, or have him make love to me in any way."

"Of course you did not. Inside; and as for you, Mr Hartnell—" Elsabeth reached out with such speed and confidence that he did not think to flinch away until she had his ear firmly in her fingers, and with such a grip as to garner a yelp of pain. She turned and strode swiftly into the Newsbury dance hall, where she flung Hartnell forward with such vigour that he fell full-length upon the floor. Dancers and music alike came to a sudden halt, and, for an instant, Elsabeth felt the weight of Society's reproval upon her: a well-bred young lady did not cause such a scene for *anything*, and what she had to say would heap humiliation upon her family.

In a room full of astonished, hesitant dancers, Elsabeth fixed her gaze on Sophia Enton, who stood with slow deliberation and met Elsabeth's eyes with grave support. Sophia had had the right of it, in her enraged passion over the state of women in Society; it was absurd that the Dovers, that Leopoldina, that *Matilda*, who was innocent of all things, should bear the guilt of the captain's bad behaviour; it was as absurd as Rosamund dying for Society's censure of magic. Sophia could not know what Elsabeth would say, but she nodded once, encouraging her, and, with that single nod, Elsabeth found her voice.

"I have just come upon this devil attempting to seduce Matilda in the gardens. There are certain of us here who cannot doubt Matilda's word"—and, upon this, Elsabeth glanced to her own family, and to Mr Webber, all of whom were too aware of the elopement. Mr Webber looked wretched with embarrassment and Mrs Dover white with horror; for all her determination to pretend only the best of the Hartnells' marriage, she did not disbelieve Elsabeth's accusation.

"What a terrible thing to accuse my dear Hartnell of!" cried Leopoldina. "No, you must not say such things, Elsabeth! Tildy is jealous of my husband, that is all! I am married and she is not, and she cannot bear it!"

"*Dina!*" Matilda cried in anguish. "It is not so, Dina! I love you and want nothing more than your happiness! I could never desire your husband, because he *is* your husband! How can you think such a thing, when I have been your shadow for so long?"

"How can I not, when you *have* been my shadow for so long! There is nothing to you, Tildy, that I have not made! If dear Hartnell is my husband, then you *must* want him, for you have no desires of your own!"

Matilda swayed as though she had been slapped, and Elsabeth, hurrying to her side, was forced to make her way around Hartnell, who picked himself up from the floor to smile with undeniable charm at the Newsbury guests, who looked from one another in pained embarrassment that could not find a suitable method of extricating themselves from the emotional turmoil unfolding before them.

"Forgive us all," he said to them with such gallantry as to beget a nervous laugh from the onlookers. "There has been a terrible misunderstanding, heightened by the delight of a dance and the gathering of family that has been separated for weeks or months."

Matilda, in a lower and steadier voice than Elsabeth had ever previously encountered from her, said, "Once, that was true," to Leopoldina, and although she spoke beneath Hartnell's swift-flowing story, the calmness of her tone slowly overcame his theatrics, until it was she, and not Hartnell, to whom the gathering listened. "Once, I would have desired what you had; once, I would have acted only as you act. I am proud to say I have risen above that now, Dina. I have learned things which you will never know; I have grown closer to Papa and Elsa, and hope to look to Rosamund and Ruth for guidance now, rather than your self-centred silliness. I do not desire Captain Hartnell; indeed, now I fear him, for that which he would have pressed upon me despite my protests."

"I am a married man!" Hartnell protested in such shock that, in other circumstances, Elsabeth might have been inclined to believe his objections. "I will confess that I find each of my sisters fair, but what brother should not? And I find none of them so delightful as my wife—"

"Whom you said to me not five minutes ago that you regretted marrying!" snapped Matilda, and, as one, the gathered members of Bodton Society gasped. Leopoldina began crying, great ugly gulping sobs, and Hartnell's face fell into such dismay as to conjure immaculate credibility.

"I'm afraid Mrs Hartnell is too correct," Hartnell said with sorrow. "I am afraid Miss Matilda is caught in the throes of envy—"

"Do not believe Captain Hartnell."

The soft statement came from such unexpected quarters as to silence the rising gossip in the crowd. Julia Webber, cheeks flushed from calling attention to herself, had risen to stand at Sophia's side; they held hands so tightly that their knuckles were white, but Julia spoke again, no more loudly than before. "I have been loosely acquainted with Mr Hartnell for several years, through my brother's friendship with Mr Archer. I do not like to speak of it, but some three years ago, Mr Hartnell presumed upon our acquaintance, reminding me of his own friendship with Mr Archer and thus assuring me he was, if not a gentleman, at least a man of some pleasantry and propriety. We met several times in the usual manner of friendship; carriage rides and walks in the Park, or at a dance where I was pleased to stand up for a set with him. This carried on some little time, in both public and private, until the afternoon that Mr Hartnell proposed marriage to me. I was taken aback, and when I refused his offer, he threatened my reputation unless I paid him the sum of one thousand pounds to disappear."

"*Julia*!" cried Mr Webber in agony.

"I certainly had no such sum to hand, but, in panic, I gave him several pieces of my jewelry," Miss Webber continued, her blushes now faded into an expression of contained fury. "I have regretted that act of cowardice ever since, and I will not now stand by and be counted a coward again. Do not believe Captain Hartnell; if Miss Matilda Dover has cast this accusation against him, it is not an aspersion. It is the truth."

"I am inclined to believe Miss Webber," Miss Derrington reported from her chair by the fire. "I should not like to be pressed for details, but I am aware of a third situation in which Captain Hartnell's conduct has been less than becoming. Mrs Hartnell, I am so dreadfully sorry to stand with so many others against your husband, but I think you might be wise to heed our words. It is even possible that, under the circumstances, you might be granted a divorce and thought well of for it."

Leopoldina's colour had changed from high to pale: she stood now with her gaze snapping between one well-regarded member of Society and another, forced at last, Elsabeth thought, to face the consequences of her own folly. Mrs and Mr Enton, Lady Beatrice, even Mrs Dover, were reluctant to meet her eye; none of the gentlemen would at all. They did not know whom to believe, or where to lay the accusation; it was those who stood against her—against Captain Hartnell—who could meet her eyes without flinching or embarrassment. Miss Derrington and Miss Webber looked on her with sympathy; Matilda with hurt contempt, and the two elder Dover sisters with a love tempered by too much awareness that her own actions had, to some degree, brought her to where she now was.

Finally, Dina's regard settled on Hartnell himself, whose guileless expression now seemed strained, and grew more so as Dina spoke with a fond phrase that now seemed edged. "My dear Hartnell, is divorce what you want?"

"Of course not!"

"Nor do I," Dina replied slowly, "but neither do I wish to be made a fool of. Oh, laugh," she said bitterly as an uncontained titter ran 'round the ball room; "I know that I am silly, and that I have enjoyed that silliness, but it is one thing to make a fool of oneself, and another to be made a fool of. Do you know what I have wanted since I can remember, Mr Hartnell? To be my own woman. To be a wife, and to not chafe under my mother and father's constraints; to have a husband whom I could adore, and who would allow me my little pleasures without censure. Do you know what has always been chief amongst my denied pleasures? Come, there is no reason to deny it now, when I am embarrassed by my husband and sister, when I am an embarrassment to my family; all of the damage is already done, and to confess to my most-neglected desire can do no more harm. It is, after all, that which brought us together at the start."

She lifted a hand, turning the palm upward, and although wind could not be seen, its effects could certainly be felt: it whisked around the room, freshening the air, and when Dina plucked a feather from her hairpiece, it danced into the magic she made and spun relentlessly above her hand. "Magic," she whispered. "I have wanted more than anything to have the freedom to pursue my magic. Not boldly; that was never necessary to me, despite what my sisters must think. But freely, and without condemnation. Elsabeth told me once my time would come."

Leopoldina closed her palm. The wind died, and with it every other breath of sound in the room. Most eyes were round with horror or disbelief, but a strange pride rose in Elsabeth's breast as her silliest sister took one step toward her husband. "I learnt the magical binding of a wound, my dear Mr Hartnell; did you know that? In our little wedding tour to Brighton, I learnt that bit of magic. How to tourniquet an injury with magic, when there was no cloth to be had; how to loosen it when necessary; and even how to use wind or water to cleanse the injury. But now—just now!—I have begun to wonder, Mr Hartnell. What do you suppose happens if one binds a wound that is not there?" She spun a finger in the air as if tightening a tourniquet and whispered a phrase Elsabeth did not know, but which had an immediate effect on Captain Hartnell.

His face whitened, and, although he did not quite double, his military stance collapsed inward upon itself a little as though it were suddenly difficult to stand. Leopoldina tilted her head, expression hardly so much as curious as she twirled her finger again. Hartnell's breath left him in a rush and he bent further, and, by the third twist, there could be no doubt in anyone's mind what, precisely, Leopoldina Hartnell had chosen to bind. "How long, do you imagine, would it take for an uninjured body to give up its claim to health on what has been bound? How long before it is reduced to decorative, and not much of that?"

"Miss Elsabeth," Hartnell gasped in a high and thin voice. "I beg you. I beg you, stop her."

Elsabeth turned her head and touched a hand to her ear. "I beg your pardon, Captain Hartnell? I did not quite hear you. Perhaps you could—illuminate me as to the details of your request."

It was not necessary: she knew that it was not. But neither, in the end, could she abandon Leopoldina to exposing her magic alone, not if she meant to make any change in the world. With the word illuminate, she called on the spell that she had learnt at Streyfield, and placed innumerable darts of light in the air around Hartnell.

A gasp ran through the assembly as Elsabeth walked to Dina and offered her hand. Dina, eyes filled with tears, grasped it as though Elsabeth had offered an unlooked-for thread of hope, then let those tears fall as Matilda, with more kindness and grace than Dina deserved, came to take her other hand. "Surely. it is not only Captain Hartnell who needs to see more clearly, Elsa," Matilda said, and, with another whisper of wind æther, swept the sparks of light throughout the room, and sent them dancing with a word.

Rosamund, smiling gently, came to put her hand in Elsabeth's. "Let him go now, Dina; he has badly used you, and all of us, but I cannot bear to see him, or anyone, in pain."

"I will release him," Dina whispered, "when I am sure he understands quite clearly the price of any further...breaches of etiquette...on his part."

"I understand," Hartnell whispered harshly. "I entirely understand." He collapsed to the floor as Dina released her hold on the magic, and whimpered without pride when Rosamund, always the gentlest of the sisters, extended her free hand and murmured a few words of healing magic.

Hartnell's sweat broke and his colour returned so swiftly that Elsabeth turned to Rosa in admiration, and found her sister smiling in something like embarrassment. "Perhaps a winter storm is the natural shape of my skill, but my heart has filled with joy in studying the healing æthers, Elsabeth. I could never allow him to suffer."

"You are all witches!" spat Lady Beatrice, and Miss Derrington, who had risen to her feet and reached for the still-swaying points of light in the air, replied, "Yes, and isn't it magnificent? Oh, Miss Dover, had I but known, I could have told you of Oyo magic, and we might have seen what you could learn from it!"

"It is uncivilised!" Lady Beatrice screeched, and Mrs Dover, who had been so stricken by the great lady earlier as to be unable to speak, now retorted, "Do not dare to judge my daughters so, madam!" and silenced Lady Beatrice entirely.

She could not silence the whole of the gathering, though; what had been a convivial social encounter had become something far greater, and no one could determine what was appropriate protocol. There were several, including Mrs Enton, who swept to Lady Beatrice's banner, taking up her outrage where Mrs Dover had silenced it, and others who slowly joined the Dover court. Sophia Enton was among them, of course; more surprisingly to Elsabeth was that Mr Enton drifted their way too, and Julia Webber went directly to Mr Webber and could be heard to demand if he had known when he married her that Rosamund Dover was a sorceress. "You cannot be one to chastise me for untoward choices," Mr Webber replied in as strenuous a tone as Elsabeth had ever heard him use, which was to say, very mildly indeed, but enough to cause Julia to glance Sophia's way and blush.

Mrs Dover arrived in the centre of her daughters' supporters with something like a sigh. "Well, I suppose we are ruined now," she said without evident concern for that truth. "It is a shame that you and Tildy are not married, Elsabeth; I expect you never will be now. I do wish your father had been here; he would be very proud. Dina, will you return to Oakden or keep on with Mr Hartnell?"

"I believe Mr Hartnell and I have come to an understanding," Dina said placidly. "We will leave all of this behind us and go north to his station, where I expect he will be an exemplary husband, and I shall be a wife with as much freedom as I desire. Do not look at me that way, Elsabeth. I can be sensible if I must be."

"Then why were you not before?" Elsabeth asked softly. "Why risk condemning us all with your thoughtless actions regarding Brighton?"

She discerned no comprehension at all in Leopoldina's gaze. "What on earth do you mean? It all ended precisely as it ought, and there could certainly never have been any concern on that front. Now, I believe there is a dance to be finished, is there not? My dear Hartnell, won't you stand up with me? Where is the music? Dear me, where is everyone going? Surely, they cannot imagine the party has ended!"

"It has ended, Dina," Elsabeth said firmly. "It has ended for all of us."

(58)

WITHIN THREE DAYS, ALL PARTIES WERE SCATTERED TO THEIR destinations: the Hartnells to the North, Miss Derrington and Mr Swift back to Charington with Lady Beatrice, the Webbers at Newsbury and the remaining Dovers at home in Oakden. Mrs Enton would not visit; Mr Enton would not be kept away. This became a familiar manner amongst the townspeople; half would turn their backs upon seeing any member of the Dover family, and the other half would approach gladly, some with hopes of enchantments and others simply with shy admiration of the exposure of their secret. A handful came in sickness and in shame, hoping for a word of healing while fearing for their very souls; Rosamund, whose gifts flowered with her pregnancy, offered what she had learned with unstinting generosity, while Matilda, starry-eyed with appreciation for Rosa's talents, studied to emulate her.

Ruth and baby Jonathan visited, much to Mr Cox's chagrin, but it was conceded that he dare not ask if Ruth might have stood with her sisters on the fateful night at Newsbury. She would have, Ruth claimed coolly; she would have been suspect by sharing their blood, and preferred to be damned for what she was than for the suspicion of it. Gossip had reached the Charington parishioners, who now had no doubt where their bounty of winter vegetables came from, and yet none of them were inclined to say a word aloud about it, only smile and embrace Ruth when the opportunity arose. Mr Dover did the same upon her sharing this intelligence; Mr Dover, if still grievously aware of his debt to Mr Penney after Dina's elopement, was much recovered from that shock, and wholly pleased with his daughters for flinging off Society's conventions to support one another. He had made errors in raising them, perhaps, but, in the end, if they were inclined to throw together rather than pull one another down, he could not think he had done entirely badly by them.

Indeed, his greatest regret was one he shared, if perhaps for different reasons, with Mrs Dover; he would have liked to have seen Elsabeth happily wed, for her happiness meant more to him than the world, and it now seemed an unlikely conclusion to her tale. Matilda, too, was expected to remain unwed, and Mr Dover finally began to practise a little frugality, that his remaining daughters would not go entirely wanting in his inevitable absence.

Matilda felt the probable loss more strongly than Elsabeth, who remained comfortable in her own reliance, and content with a quieter existence. She studiously copied pages from the books of æther, incidentally memorising their contents until, given a cabinet of ingredients, she believed there were few magics she could not work on demand, and of those that required nothing more than æther to work, none at all. She favoured the Promethean æthers still, and had sent a box of Oakden kindling with Miss Derrington to take to Africa, so they might occasionally enjoy the intimacy of instant conversation from half the world away. Between bending over paper to commit spells to permanency, she abandoned the work for her beloved long walks, and, as autumn fell away into winter's chill, felt a satisfaction with the world that she had thought beyond her.

A fine afternoon lent the opportunity to both walk and study; she brought with her a book of æther, and found a perch in the lowest branches of a sturdy tree that rose up as the only shade in an expansive field. Cows milled beneath her, offering gentle lows that seemed to Elsa to comment on young ladies who climbed trees, and she rewarded them for their thoughts by the occasional awakening of grass and flower seeds beneath the soil, so that a fresh crop rose up as they nibbled. Half the afternoon had passed in this pleasant pastime when one of the cows voiced a different opinion, more disturbed than was usual, and Elsabeth leaned from her seat to see an unmistakable figure in black striding purposefully across the field.

She sat up again at once, alarmed at the leap of her heart and strangely short of breath, but did not move again until Mr Fitzgerald Archer stood beneath the tree, surrounded by cows and gazing up at her. "Miss Dover," he said after a moment's pause, and Elsabeth, struck by a sense of absurdity, replied, "Mr Archer," with equal formality.

"Are you comfortable, Miss Dover?"

"I was, when I had only cows to converse with. Oh, no," she added in dismay as a shadow crossed Mr Archer's face. "I meant only that it is one thing to talk to cows from above, but it is more awkward to speak to a fellow human being, and I now find myself in something of a situation, as I cannot think of a modest way to disembark from this tree in company."

Another shadow crossed Mr Archer's face, though this one had the shape of a smile. "If I may offer my assistance...?"

"I would be grateful." Elsabeth passed him the book, which he tucked into a pocket before extending his hands upward. Elsa inched forward on the branch until she slipped into Mr Archer's capable hands.

He lowered her to the ground as if she were weightless and did not release her, though by any standard of propriety he ought to have. Elsabeth, her hands resting against his chest, looked up at him and wondered that she had once thought his face so desperately stern; it seemed now to be quite filled with gentleness and even laughter. "Thank you," she said, then, more swiftly, "Thank you," again. "I do not know if you received my letter, Mr Archer—"

"I did, and have worn it thin in the turning of it, wondering what more I might read into it than the simple words on the page. Who betrayed my part in the incident to you?"

Breathless laughter escaped Elsabeth. "You did, sir, in this very moment. Rosamund mentioned your presence at the wedding; I surmised the rest, and you have confirmed it. Mr Archer, I can never thank you enough. You saved Leopoldina; you saved my family, and I know you are not especially fond of them, making your gesture all the greater. I cannot imagine why you put yourself to the effort, but thank you."

"Can you truly not imagine why, Miss Dover?"

He seemed very near, then, his hands warm on her waist, but Elsabeth could neither conclude how to extricate herself nor be certain she wished to. Instead, she said, hesitatingly, "Any reason I might have settled on seemed unlikely in the extreme, Mr Archer. My vanity, which is considerable, is not that great, in the end."

"And yet you wrote to me."

"I had to. I could not allow your kindness to go unmarked, even if you should wish it kept secret and even if I was the last person on this earth from whom you wished to hear."

"I do not think I would have gone to such effort to maintain your sister's reputation if I had no desire at all to communicate with you again, Miss Dover, although I am to understand you undid all the effort only a scant few weeks later," Archer said, smiling now. "My aunt has told me often, and in great detail, of the sorcerous show displayed by all of your family at Newsbury. She now regards Mrs Cox with considerable suspicion, I'm afraid, although Mrs Cox has never offered the slightest untoward act or opinion."

"Poor Ruth," Elsabeth said with a quick laugh. "She is as guilty as the rest of us, Mr Archer, although I am certain you will never reveal that to your aunt."

"Never. I wish now that I had come to Newsbury; Webber invited me, but I felt it would be easier on all parties if I did not attend, and, in my cowardice, I missed Hartnell's comeuppance. I would have given a great deal to see that."

"I am sure you would have been appalled, as most of Society was, by our blatant revelation of our sorcery."

"Would I have pressed those books of magic into your hands if that were true, Miss Dover?"

"No," Elsabeth whispered, "but I do not understand what brought about your change of heart. I am sure my family were once pariahs to you, for our magic among other faults."

"A woman I held in considerable regard impressed upon me that the attitudes I had once considered so appropriate to my station were instead the behaviour of a tyrant, willing to accept only that which I regarded as suitable, rather than treating everyone with respect and thoughtfulness. That this woman chased me from the house with fireballs rather than igniting me with them as I well deserved may also have had some influence on my opinions. I speak lightly," Mr Archer said, more seriously, "but I also speak truthfully. You accused me of pride, Miss Dover, which I own to, but I had come to regard pride as the defining characteristic of a gentleman, when indeed I should think the word itself, gentleman, should impress upon me what aspect I ought to have settled on as the defining one. I treated you abominably, and seek your forgiveness."

"It is granted. I think I could deny you nothing, Mr Archer; that is the size of my debt to you."

"It is not your gratitude I have come here hoping to secure. I have told you already that I have worn thin that note you sent me, wondering without confidence if I might somehow persuade that very word in it, gratitude, to become another; a word that perhaps you, mindful of the sentiments I had laid before you and you had rejected, could not use for fear of seeming cruel."

Elsabeth caught her breath to speak, but Archer lifted his fingers at her waist, not releasing her but asking, with the gesture, that he be permitted to speak on. "Miss Dover, I am here because, two days ago, my aunt let slip a tidbit regarding a conversation she shared with you at Newsbury, a tidbit that she had failed to mention previously, and it has awakened a spark of hope in my breast. Let me say to you now that if I am wrong in my hopes, I will leave this place and you will never again be distressed by my presence, but let me also say that my feelings for you have only deepened, and I have come to ask if...if yours for me perhaps have changed."

"Yes." The word was too much: for long moments after, Elsabeth struggled to say more. Archer forbore to speak, only watched her with burgeoning hope, and when she spoke again, it was in an uncontained rush. "I had quite softened to you before that dreadful offer, Mr Archer; I had come to enjoy our tête-à-têtes, and then to hear you play the pianoforte! And your charming bemusement when you came upon me making snow angels; oh, I thought perhaps I could quite like you after all, but then I learned of the business with Rosamund, and then that awful proposal—" She escaped his grasp then, whirling away in a dervish that disturbed the cows, then spun again to face him as she continued at length. "But then your—your dispensation to use my sorcery to keep Rosamund warm, that was beyond expectation, Mr Archer, and confused me greatly! And I might have thanked you at her wedding, save that you were aloof and I could hardly find fault in that, after the awkwardness at Charington. And then, oh, God! To meet you at Streyfield, where the staff and your sister knew my name; I did not know what to think! You seemed a different man entirely then, and your kindness to my aunt and uncle, never mind the books of magic! I think my affections were quite secured by then, and yet you fled with such alacrity upon the news of Leopoldina's elopement, and knowing already what you thought of my family, what should I think but that you wished to distance yourself from us at once and entirely, for which I could hardly blame you, only to find in the end that you had sped away to save us all—Mr Archer, I had never dreamt to see you again, much less held any hope that you might have remained steadfast in emotion whilst my own was in such turmoil and settling in such an unlikely place. It was not until Lady Beatrice accused me of being engaged to you, and then forbade me to enter into such a contract, that I could consider the possibility you might still have feelings for me, but beyond the letter I had already sent, there seemed no way to indicate—to indicate that I—that I had grown to return those feelings, and every day felt the loss of being unable to say so to you!"

Mr Archer stepped forward and swept Elsabeth into an embrace that trembled with emotion. They stood so, speechless, for a sweet eternity, until one of the cows, impatient with their trampling of tender shoots of grass, pushed Elsabeth with its head, and left the lovers laughing. "I think I had best speak to your father," Mr Archer murmured then, in a voice rich with feeling.

"Oh, Mr Archer, I think I had best speak to him first," Elsabeth replied with a laugh. "He will not be insensible to the honour, but he is well aware of my previous opinion of you, and, regardless of the honour, he will not release me to you unless he is certain it is what I want."

"Miss Dover," Mr Archer replied with all sincerity, "I do not believe it is within any man's purview to release or keep you against your will. I am content for you to speak to him first, so long as I know your heart to be mine; your father and all the stars might stand against it, but I have no doubt that if I am what you desire, I am what you will have."

"Your aunt will be appalled," Elsabeth whispered. "Her darling nephew marrying a sorceress."

"Society will be appalled," Archer agreed. "But they will have a hard time making pariahs of both Webber and myself, or of a vicar's wife, and we will have to marry Matilda to someone of sufficient rank as to begin breaking down these barriers, for I will not have my wife snubbed, and I can think of no better way to ensure it does not happen than to make magic commonplace in our institutions, even Society."

"We are as one in this ambition," Elsabeth said happily, and, winding her fingers through Mr Archer's, drew him back through the fields and toward home, with darts of firelight dancing around them like stars.

the end

／

Acknowledgements

Magic & Manners is what happens when, during a *Pride and Prejudice* watch-and-read spree, I start to wonder what it would be like if the Bennet sisters had a surplus of magic rather than a deficit of money. It's also what happens when I put that question to a hundred or so particularly enthusiastic readers who supported it as a crowdfunding project: this is a book that, without them, literally wouldn't exist.

I am, as usual, particularly indebted to a handful of regulars: the War Room writers, of whom Mikaela Lind deserves a special shout-out; my husband Ted and my son, the latter of whom said to me while I was working on copy edits for this book, "Magic and Manners? I thought you were *done* with that one already!"; Bryant Durrell and Susan Carlson, who know why; Eleri Hamilton, for my charming little MKP logo; Joliene McAnaly, for her generous spirit; and Chysoula Tzavelas, to whom this book is dedicated. (You should read her books too!)

Special thanks to the Magic & Manners Patrons

A B Warwick, Adrianne Middleton, Ailsa Barrett, Alena Franco, Althea Clark, Amanda Samuels, Amy, Andrew and Kate Barton, Andy Merriam, Angela N. Hunt, Anne Walker, Axisor, Barbara Gallant, Bernadette, Beth Rasmussen, Brian Stanley, Bryant Durrell, Carl Rigney, Carol Guess, CathiBea Stevenson, Christine Swendseid, Christopher Buser, Christy Hopkins, Chrysoula Tzavelas, Constance Anderson, D Taft, Denise Moline, Diane DesAutels, Donal Cunningham, Doniki Boderick-Luckey, Earl Miles, Edward Ellis, El Edwards, Emma Bartholomew, Erin Gately, Evil Hat Productions, Gabe Krabbe, Heather Knutsen, Heather Roney, Holly Frantz, Janet Gahagan, Janne Torklep, Jean Diaz, Jennifer Cabbage, Jeri Smith-Ready, Jill Valuet, Joliene McAnly, K Gavenman, Karen Severson, Kari, Kate Larking, Katherine Malloy, Kathleen Hanrahan, Kathleen Tipton, Kathy Rogers, Katrina Lehto, Kenji Ikiryo, Kristine Kearney, Larisa LaBrant, Laura Anne Gilman, Lesley Mitchell, Lianne Burwell, limugurl, Linda Goldstein, Lisa Stewart, Lola McCrary, Lydia Leong, Marnie, Maria Ivanilova, Marjorie Taylor, Mary Anne Walker, Matt Girton, Michael Bernardi, Michael Bowman, Nicolai Buch-Andersen, Pamela Statz, Patricia O'Neill, Paul Birchenough, Rachel & Edie Gollub, Rachel Narow, Rhona, Ruth Stuart, Saifa Rashid, Sandra Jakl, Sarah Brooks, Sarah Foscarini Wilkes,

Sean Collins, Shannon Scollard, Sharon, Sharon Broggi, Sherry Menton, Skye Christakos, Sonia Oldrini, Sue Shelly, Sumi Funayama, Tania Clucas, Tara Lynch, Thida Cornes, Tiana Hanson, Tiffiny Quinn, Tracy McShane, Trip Space-Parasite

About the Author

According to her friends, CE Murphy makes such amazing fudge that it should be mentioned first in any biography. It's true, mind you, that she makes extraordinarily good fudge, but she's somewhat surprised that it features so highly in biographical relevance.

Other people say she began her writing career when she ran away from home at age five to write copy for the circus that had come to town. Others claim she's a crowdsourcing pioneer, which she rather likes the sound of, but nobody actually got around to pointing out she's written a best-selling urban fantasy series (*The Walker Papers*), or that she dabbles in writing comic books (*Take A Chance*) and periodically dips her toes into writing short stories (the *Old Races* collections).

Still, it's clear to her that she should let her friends write all of her biographies, because they're much more interesting that way.

More prosaically, she was born and raised in Alaska, and now lives with her family in her ancestral homeland of Ireland, which is a magical place where it rains a lot but nothing one could seriously regard as winter ever actually arrives.

She can be found online at mizkit.com, @ce_murphy, and (imagine a little Facebook icon here) /cemurphywriter

Made in the USA
Middletown, DE
29 September 2021